SQUADRON SHILLING

Books by Arch Whitehouse

FICTION

Wings of Adventure
Crime on a Convoy Carrier
Adventure in the Sky
Squadron Forty-Four
Bombers in the Sky
The Laughing Falcon

Fighters in the Sky
Scarlet Streamers
Spies with Wings
Combat in the Sky
Action in the Sky
Squadron Shilling

NON-FICTION

The Years of the Sky Kings
Squadrons of the Sea
Legion of the Lafayette
The Fighting Ships
Luke—The Hun Killer
Fighting Wings
The Early Birds
Years of the War Birds
Heroes of the Sunlit Sky
Amphibious Operations
Subs and Submariners

Espionage and Counterespionage
Zeppelin Fighters
Decisive Air Battles of the First World War
TANK—History of Armored Warfare
Heroes and Legends of World War I
Development of the Military Airplane

JUVENILES

The Real Book of Airplanes
Billy Mitchell

John J. Pershing
Heroic Pigeons

AUTOBIOGRAPHY

The Fledgling

◎◎◎◎◎◎◎◎◎◎◎◎◎◎◎◎◎◎◎◎◎◎◎◎◎

SQUADRON
SHILLING

Arch Whitehouse

A. G. J. Whitehouse

DOUBLEDAY & COMPANY, INC., GARDEN CITY, NEW YORK

1968

*All of the characters in this book are purely fictitious,
and any resemblance to actual persons, living or dead,
is purely coincidental.*

Dedicated to

That gallant company of Aerial Gunners
who served so courageously
during World War I

CONTENTS

INTROIT

May 1917

A gloomy night had fallen across the war-torn levels of
Artois, and the ghosts of vanished airmen took turns
sauntering through the indistinct shadows that patterned
the fronts of the hangars. It had rained late that afternoon,
and there were still reflective pools in the depressions of the
tarmac. A light breeze fingered pale engravings of scenes
from some half-forgotten melodrama on the surface of the
puddles. The wings of the theatrical setting were built up
of stacked petrol tins, a two-wheeled dolly, and something
indistinct that may have been a pile of Cooper bombs
covered by a pale green canvas.

The clanks of a wrench and the rasp of a hacksaw could
be heard inside the dimly lit Besseneau. A sooty figure
shuffled about wailing a recent music-hall tune; some jeremiad by Marie Lloyd, explaining why she was late.

What faint light there was took on life and movement,
throwing yellow triangles of gleam, as a Bristol Fighter was
wheeled out and dragged to the cab rank. The flickering
illumination churned out by a power lorry flashed unevenly
off varnished struts, glossy wing panels, or from the bow
and ratchet arms of a Scarff mounting. There was some
brief activity beneath the wing tips as a crouched figure
bolted phosphorus cartridges to a main rib, just ahead of
the ailerons. None of the cast of characters spoke during
these operations, each glumly carried out his duties with

somnolent motions, and when the tasks were finished, they gathered together beneath the jutting engine cowling to renew the break in communications.

"Wot are they doin' tonight?"

Someone touched a glowing lighter wick to a cigarette.

"Who knows? Anything to bugger up somebody's hour or so off."

"I'd like to go on one of these shows—just once. Just to see wot they do do."

"They never say."

"Bloody mysterious to me, it is."

"You say you'd like to go on one of these night jobs?"

"Yes, I would!"

"Bloody funny. No one can get you to go up for an engine test."

"It ain't the same thing. Who knows whether the blasted engine 'as bin fixed? I'd just like to go an' find out wot they get up to over there. They don't take any bombs, an' they don't take too much petrol or ammunition. I'd just like to know wot they *do* get up to over there."

"Why don't yer arsk the flight sergeant to put you in for a flip . . . on one of these night shows?"

"Not me. 'E might manage it, an' there I'd be, a bloody fool, wonderin' 'ow I could get out of it."

"You sound a bit wonky to me."

"You don't understand. I don't really *want* to go. It's just that I'd like to be there . . . some'ow, just to see wot goes on. Just lookin' on, like."

"That'ud be a very nice way to fight the war. Be there, an' see it all—to talk about later—but still be somewhere where you wouldn't get hurt. You'd put all the insurance agents out of work with an idea like that."

"I'd just like to know . . ."

"'Ush! 'Ere comes the major."

"Oh, 'im. 'E'll tell us a lot of nothink, 'e will."

The commander of Number 86-SS Squadron moved into the shadow of the Bristol. He wore heavy brogues, golf stockings, riding breeches, a green sweater, a heavy muffler, and a Welch Fusiliers cap. He was smoking a long-stemmed briar pipe.

"Everything all right here, Nethersole?" the CO mumbled, and kicked a wheel tire.

"Yes, sir. Flares all wired in an' the back seat properly looked at. The dual-control gear is all there. Everything."

"Good! This is a dicey show, and we want everything right —shipshape. Chaps who go on these jobs are entitled to the best, eh?"

"I suppose so, sir. May I arsk wot it is they do?"

"You may ask, Nethersole, but you'd only be wasting your breath."

"Wastin' my breath . . . ?"

"I can't tell you. It's just as simple as that."

"Oh."

"So don't ask."

"No, sir."

"Let's get her warmed up. They'll be out in a minute."

Before the big Rolls-Royce engine had cleared her throat, two muffled figures in tan leather jackets, thigh-length flying boots, and helmets appeared. An armorer followed, cradling a Lewis gun in his arms. The aerial gunner climbed up, dropped down inside the Scarff ring, and leaned over to take the weapon.

"Listen, Chalky. If I get another Number Three stoppage," the aerial gunner promised, "I'm coming back and rough you up with the spare parts bag."

"If you get a Number Three stoppage, you may not come back, chum."

"I'll haunt you."

The pilot and the major were having a few words near the wing tip. "Now remember, you're not to go down unless you get the proper signal. Two whites and a red. You have that clear? Two whites and a red, in that order."

"Two whites and a red . . . right."

"Well, good luck, and don't take too many chances."

"Two whites and a red," the pilot repeated, and went to the fuselage stirrup to climb up. He glanced back at the aerial gunner. "Everything all right with you?"

The gunner peered around his office, felt for the ammo drums, the dual-control lever, and his Very signal pistol. "Seems to be," he concluded.

"Well, it's your problem. You took the shilling, remember."

"I'm not likely to forget."

"I didn't," the pilot retorted after a low guffaw, "and I had a commission before I crossed the Atlantic."

"Let's get on with it."

"Let's get on with it, *sir!* Remember who's in command here."

"Yes, sir," the NCO gunner responded respectfully.

The pilot turned back to his controls. He checked the compass, the clock, and then ran the engine up for a rev test. He throttled down, raised both arms, wigwagged his satisfaction, and watched the mechanics yank the wheel chocks away. The gunner lowered his folding seat and sat facing the broad back of his pilot. He pondered on the string of circumstances that had placed him here, an aerial gunner for this hateful man. "So I took the shilling. I had to win my wing over the enemy lines, not in some English flying school. I should be on my way back to London for a commission and pilot training," he muttered to himself, and returned a cheery wave from one of the mechanics.

The pilot taxied the Bristol Fighter out to the long strip of take-off turf. A three-quarter moon slipped from behind a cottony cloud and bathed the field in a pewter gleam. He hoped there would be as much light on the other side of the line.

The aerial gunner steadied himself for the take-off run and checked his wrist watch for their time. Time was all-important, and he jotted the figures down in a slim, brown-covered notebook.

The Bristol was nosed around into the light breeze. Every

wire, cable, and strut stiffened as the big propeller slashed in broadsword fury. They scraped a skid gash for a few yards, then the tail came up and there was a concerted rumbling below. The big two-seater spewed flame and hot carbon from her nostrils and they were away in less than one hundred yards. The pilot ruddered into a climbing turn to circle the field twice before heading for their rendezvous.

The man in the back seat adjusted his goggles, tightened the wrist straps of his gauntlets, and peered over the side. He studied the field with its slabs of Adrian huts, Nissen shelters, and watched the pimply bell tents assume a distinct pattern. His eyes gradually adjusted for night sight and he then caught the flash of a semaphore lamp. He interpreted the message for a minute, and decided that the letter "M" was being repeated over and over.

He stood up and gripped the pilot's shoulder. He leaned over and spoke distinctly against the ear flap of his helmet.

"We have a 'Return' signal, sir. A letter M. I see it clearly. They are using the Aldis lamp instead of the daytime ground strips. We have a 'Return' signal . . . sir."

The pilot stared out toward the wing tip and then finally caught the intent of the advice. He continued to circle, and looked down at the field. The lamp repeated the letter, over and over, but he glanced at the gunner and waved one hand to indicate a "washout" signal. He cut back on the throttle and yelled: "That's not for us. Must be for the R.E. 8 boys. It's not for us."

"But it's coming from the apron of our 'C' Flight hangar, sir," the gunner protested.

"I tell you it's not for us. Why would we have been sent out, if they want to recall us?"

"It seems clear to me, sir."

"I'll decide whether it is for us. I'm in charge. Sit down and leave matters to me."

"I just want you to remember I advised you . . ."

"All right. Now forget it."

"Yes . . . sir." The gunner was in no position to argue.

This was his first patrol aboard a Bristol Fighter of Number 86-SS Squadron. His previous time had been put in with the F.E. 2b pushers of Number 20 Squadron. He was merely an NCO airman, but his pilot was a commissioned officer. That made all the difference.

Bristol Fighter A7107 climbed to six thousand feet and headed for the Ypres–Courtrai road. A few tatters of fleecy cloud fluttered past the silver of the moon, and when the plane attracted a few desultory anti-aircraft shots, the pilot turned northwest and headed toward the shapeless patch called Roulers. The gunner felt for the cocking handle of his Lewis to make sure it was loaded, and then stood up to carry out a more complete watch over the area.

As they approached Bourlon Wood the pilot took on a more intense attitude, snapping his head from side to side, and then seemingly watching for evidence of opposition from below. With the increase in height the air became colder, and the pilot buttoned the throat flap of his flying coat. The gunner had noted this unusual vigilance, for in previous flights aboard old F.E. 2b pusher fighters, his pilots had shown more interest in what was ahead or slightly above. Still, this could be the mannerisms of an airman who was more familiar with a machine in which the propeller was up front.

Then, suddenly, apparently from nowhere, the gunner caught two fishtails of flame slightly below. They were obviously from the twin exhausts of an aircraft engine. He tapped his pilot on the shoulder, pointed down to the twin glares, and then placed his two forefingers together to form a cross.

"Could be a Hun," he said distinctly against the pilot's ear flap. It paid to be suspicious of everything in the air at night.

The pilot shook his head negatively and reached for a flashlight fastened in a set of prongs screwed to the instrument board. "It's not a Hun!" he bellowed back. "Leave him to me."

The gunner looked down and then remembered that no present-day enemy aircraft carried twin exhaust pipes. He jerked back and explained, "That's an S.E. 5 . . . one of ours. What's he doing up in this area at night?"

"Well! You finally caught on. Of course it's one of ours."

Somewhat chagrined, the gunner studied the machine that was climbing toward them at a good speed. As it approached, he made out some detail from the glare of the exhaust flames. He grabbed his pilot's shoulder and squeezed hard. "Watch out! It has German markings. It's an S.E. 5 all right, but with Jerry crosses!"

"I know," the pilot growled. "I know all about it." He poked his flashlight over the edge of his cockpit.

The gunner was completely puzzled. "Is this part of the patrol . . . the contact?"

The pilot glared in anger at the gunner. "Will you shut up and do your job? I'll do mine!"

The gunner had never encountered such a situation before. It had nothing to do with the instructions they had been given before they left the Recording Office. He divided his attention between the strange behavior of his pilot and the approaching single-seater. It was a puzzle to know what to do. Here was a British plane, well inside the enemy lines, daubed with German markings, and his pilot was behaving as though this was a routine occurrence. As he watched he saw a number of flash signals from the plane below, and with that his own pilot responded with a short message, but it was difficult to transcribe either signal; just a series of letters in standard Morse code. He watched the pilot below give a conclusion signal and actually wave a farewell.

"What's the idea?" the gunner demanded, convinced this exchange of code messages would take some explaining. He was swinging his Scarff mounting around so that his Lewis gun would be convenient to fire down on the intruder.

The pilot caught the move and threw his arm over the back of his seat and grabbed the gunner's left forearm. "Lay off! Don't fire on him. I'll explain later. No shooting! That's an order!"

The aerial gunner lowered the spade grip of the gun and watched the S.E. 5 curl over and drop away. Certainly, strange missions were carried out in Number 86-SS Squadron. No wonder it was dubbed a Special Service unit.

As they continued to head northwest, the gunner decided to make a note of the area in which this puzzling contact had been made. He concluded the plane must have come up from one of the German aerodromes around the Rumilly Forest. He scribbled a notation in his book and continued his rear-seat vigil.

The pilot circled over the Cambrai road, taking in Graincourt and Fontaine. Twice he glared back at his gunner, and then made a keen study of the ground below. He throttled the Rolls-Royce back, almost to idling speed, and the altimeter needle began dropping slowly. He jabbed his elbow into the gunner's shoulder blades. "Keep your eyes open for a ground signal. It will be two whites and a red, remember."

"Two whites and a red," the gunner repeated, and in the next breath cried, "there they are. Flashing from that hedge alongside that field." He pointed to where some faint gleams were winking in the prearranged sequence.

"Good! Plenty of room. They picked a good strip for a change. Get ready to climb down. You remember the passwords?"

"I remember . . . sir."

"Right. Sit tight. I just hope it's as level as it looks."

The Bristol Fighter went into a series of easy S-turns with the engine just ticking over. The gunner studied the surrounding area and marked it as level agricultural country. A few cottages could be noted, but none offered a friendly light. Either they had been abandoned, or the inhabitants were observing wartime blackout rules. While checking the landscape, the roads, and distinctive topography features— for future reference—he sensed that the plane had leveled off and was gliding in for a landing. There was no movement; no sign of life anywhere. It could have been any section of southern New Jersey, as far as the rural pattern was concerned.

Then came the faltering approach as, with stick and rudder, the pilot eased her down for the first touch. There was a low moan of undercarriage and the gasp of depressed tires; slight bounce and a flutter of wing tips, then a long shudder of relief as she finally settled down and dug in her tail skid. The Bristol rolled up to a position almost opposite the section of hedge from where the faint flashes had been noted.

"Right!" the pilot commanded. "Pop out . . . but first help me swing her around for the take-off. Take an outer strut."

The gunner vaulted over the Scarff ring and dropped lightly to his feet. He ran to the wing tip, grabbed the lower portion of an outer strut, and dug his heels in. The pilot held his rudder over, opened the engine, and in that manner fanned the tail around for the getaway. There could be no hoping for an into-the-wind take-off. In these situations one was satisfied to get down safely and have a good engine to take off again.

The gunner took a signal from his pilot, then darted toward the hedge. The flashlight was still snapping its white and red signals. He halted a few feet from the foliage and spoke his line. "Kitchener is dead."

From the shadows came the response, "But Lloyd George lives."

"Righto," the aerial gunner responded, and moved forward and waited for his contact to emerge.

A tall, angular man, wearing a peasant's smock and a crushed felt hat, emerged from the shelter of the hedge. In his hand he held a short cardboard tube at each end of which hung a trigger cord that, when pulled, would ignite a low-combustion powder—just in case.

"You have everything?" the gunner whispered cautiously.

xvii

"Yes. Everything is here." The man spoke with a cultivated British voice.

"Splendid! Best of luck to you, sir. Good night."

"Good night, and the same to you. By the way, if you get back to London, on leave, get in touch with . . ."

Before the man in the smock could complete his suggestion, a spurt of fire screeched past the gunner's head. There was a low, choked scream and a throaty gasp. The British agent fell flat on his face. The gunner threw himself sideways, still clutching the cardboard tube, as another burst slashed through the hedgerow.

"You dirty swine!" the aerial gunner screamed. "You filthy . . ." He now realized that the gunfire had come from the Scarff ring on the aeroplane.

From a low position on his hands and knees he saw the Bristol Fighter spurt flame from its exhaust. The propeller raged and the two-seater hoiked its tail, but the pilot was ready for the bucking and he eased the stick forward. Then, light and free, the biplane roared away, the unmanned Lewis gun pointing to the moonlit sky.

The gunner crawled to the side of the fallen agent. A burst of bullets had crashed into his chest, and he lay vomiting gouts of blood.

The aerial gunner got to his feet, glared at the fleeing Bristol, and snarled, "You filthy swine!"

He slipped out of his flying coat and laid it over the dead agent, and with a final glance around to pick up his bearings, the deserted gunner darted through the hedge and began running.

SQUADRON SHILLING

CHAPTER ONE

May 1916

White Star liner Cymric *torpedoed off the Irish coast. . . . Italian position penetrated by the Austrians. . . . Vimy Ridge attacked by British. . . . German and British navies engage in greatest high seas battle. . . . New type of fighting plane ordered by British Air Committee.*

There was rare style to the girl, and the man who had followed her off the Fifth Avenue bus tried to place her in some distinct column of the American idiom, a language with which he was not completely familiar. No, she wasn't the Gibson Girl type; too svelte and rather boyish. Not that she was angular, but she moved with a smooth, athletic pace. There was grace and rhythm to her every move, and for a few strides he wondered whether she knew she was being followed. He was determined not to be diverted, for he had an important mission to complete. Still, it was difficult to ignore what he took to be a personal invitation, but he reassured himself that she looked to be perfect for the work his superior in Washington, Herr Captain von Reichenau, had selected for her.

But what was it that set her apart—that gave her this undeniable personality? She wore a button-like French sailor's hat and pompon with bewitching verve and style. The stone marten scarf draped across her shoulders in studied carelessness somehow accentuated the swing of the skirt of her

1

Irish linen suit. His eye next picked up her perfectly aligned silk stockings; hosiery that paid glossy tribute to the Coles Phillips illustrations of the day. Those stockings, and the baby Cuban heels that made her walk like a dancer.

Dancer? That was it. That was what she reminded him of. What was that girl's name? The one who danced with that man named Castle? This girl had the same short-clipped hair, same bobbed curls. Now he had it. She looked and walked like Irene Castle, the darling of the social ball-room set.

No wonder Herr Captain von Reichenau had traced her background so determinedly. This girl was perfect—in every respect.

This was the Gotham of clanging streetcars, the polite be-e-ep of taxi horns, the cry of halvah merchants, the glare of sunlight off gleaming store windows. There still were horse-drawn vehicles that played their rhythmic clop-clop-clop with the loose hubs of their wheels; the jangle of myriad bells strung across the box bodies of junk wagons; the high errand-of-mercy tinkle of ambulance gongs, but not too much traffic noise to blank out the challenging bark of dogs. If you persisted you could still raise the tang and perfume of a fruit seller's pushcart.

After glancing at the display in a small shirtwaist shop, the girl twisted neatly and started across Thirty-fourth Street. The man halted as he watched her negotiate her way through the loom of traffic—motorcars, trolleys, and a few comparatively new stinkers, the jitney buses. A motorman clanged his bell, and then with grave dignity tipped his cap as the girl skipped and evaded the maw of the trolley's safety fender.

"I'll get you one of these days, Miss Pollard," he promised as she darted under the nose of a mounted policeman's horse that stood outside the Waldorf-Astoria, and safely made the sidewalk.

"If he don't," the ruddy-cheeked officer added with a

Celtic grin, "I will. You should be in Princeton's backfield. They sure could use you."

"Oh, you be quiet. Listen, O'Doul. When our chauffeur arrives looking for me . . ."

"I know. First, I'll pinch the Frog for loitering, then I'll send him in to drag you out of Peacock Alley. You still drinkin' them Bronx cocktails?"

The girl replied with a taunting smile that set small diamonds in the corners of her eyes.

"By the way, how's yer father? Still makin' guns an' ammunition for them lime-juicers?"

"What do you think? Of course he is. It's in a good cause, isn't it?"

"Does he figure he'll ever get paid?"

"What does that matter, just so long as they beat the Germans? Money isn't everything, you know."

"Yeh, I guess that's how the old boy thinks. He sure came up in the world. I kin remember when he had only a two-bit tool shop down below Canal Street. I should have got a job with him—an' stayed. I might have been a boss by now, eh?"

"Dad's a great man." The honey-haired girl stroked the horse's chest, wrinkled her nose at the mounted officer, and hurried across the sidewalk to the hotel entrance.

The man who had been following Miss Pollard made the crossing with less difficulty, but he was spotted by O'Doul, who rubbed a knuckle under his left nostril and made a mental note of the slim-hipped gentleman.

"Now what would that squarehead be wantin' racing after Ship Pollard's daughter?" he pondered.

The squarehead was only two twirls of the revolving door behind the girl. He picked up a package of Fatimas at the cigar stand and watched his quarry hurry along the potted-palm Peacock Alley until she sat down near the doorway of the Regency Bar. When she had nodded her order to an alert waiter, he lighted a cigarette, inhaled a lungful, and

3

put himself into gear for a leisurely stroll along the golden corridor.

He was fairly tall with bulky shoulders, and tapered down to a pair of custom-made shoes of a revolting saffron blend. He removed his hat with an awkward gesture and showed a mop of Bavarian cream-colored hair that was brushed back with uncompromising severity. His forehead was low and broad, and his eyebrows met over the indented bridge of his porcine nose. There was no doubt of his ancestry, but there was a stolid pattern of attractive masculinity in his general appearance until he slitted his light blue eyes and glanced sideways at a portly dowager. There were no saber scars across his pock-marked cheeks, nor was there any belligerency to his barbered jaw. He was typical of the mid-upper echelon of the German diplomatic service.

The saunter became a hesitation step as the man approached the girl. As if practicing a standard theatrical piece of business, he took the brim of his velours hat in both hands, came to a halt and brought his heels together with a sharp click. Few of the habitués took notice of the move; it was routine along Peacock Alley.

The girl glanced up, flicked at her short crop, and prepared to repel an intruder.

"Please excuse me," the man said as he started his bow, "but you are Miss Pollard? Miss Cynthia Pollard?"

"I am."

"You do not remember me, eh?"

She took him in from stickpin to the crown of his hat held like an ancient stomacher. For an instant her mild tension relaxed.

"Yes. I remember you. We met at the Consulate Ball at the St. Regis a few weeks ago. You are Herr Gustav . . . no, you are Captain Gustav von der Osten, formerly of the Hussars . . . Death's Head Hussars, that is, but now on the German diplomatic staff."

Captain von der Osten rewarded her with raised eyebrows. "Amazing! Most young women would perhaps re-

4

member that I am a captain, but who would remember my regiment?"

"Who could forget a cavalry regiment with a name like that?"

The waiter moved in with the cocktail and put it down on the small taboret beside her.

"Ah, yes, but it takes names like that to develop great regimental tradition. Still, it shows you have a very keen and absorbing mind." He looked about with feigned bewilderment. "I was to meet a colleague here but he seems to be late. May I join you for a few minutes?"

"I see no harm in it. Perhaps you would like to order a drink while the waiter is here," she responded but suddenly felt trapped in an uncertain position. She had no great desire to be seen in a New York hotel with a member of the German diplomatic corps. After all, her father was Shipley Pollard, one of America's important munitions manufacturers.

Captain von der Osten made a vague gesture to the waiter, who bowed and hurried away.

"I have been wanting to see you again," he began once more. "Let me see. You act as private secretary to your father. He is Shipley Pollard, the industrialist, eh?"

"Yes, he is," the girl replied, and sensed what was coming.

"A very important man in his field."

"One your office might be interested in since his plants are supplying important munitions to the British," she added, and after a perceptible hesitation set her dimpled chin and said, "but whatever the aim of this intrusion the answer is 'No!'"

The German placed both clenched fists on his widespread knees, and then sat more erect while the waiter placed a glass of Vichy water on the table. He took a sip, dubbed out his cigarette, and went to work.

"Have you ever heard of a woman named Belle Goddard? She was very prominent . . . let us say notorious, toward the close of the last century. She might have become one

5

of America's great actresses but her morals were, shall we say, not of the highest."

Cynthia Pollard had to restrain a betraying impulse. She tapped her chin thoughtfully. "Belle Goddard? Yes, I believe I remember something of her." She made a trigger-pulling act, pointing an imaginary gun at him. "Didn't she shoot a noted district attorney in his own office—and was acquitted after a trial that was spread across the pages of the yellow press for weeks?"

Von der Osten stared at her quizzically and shook his head slowly. "I believe you know much more than that, Miss Pollard."

"Oh? Why should I? She was at her prime for some years before I was born."

"We'll skip over that. What I want to say is that you could be very useful—to the right people."

"I caught a faint stench of intrigue when we met that evening. You are a trifle heavy-handed, Captain."

"Please hear me out. I may have something of great interest to you." He watched for any telltale throbs at the curve of her throat.

She wagged her head negatively. "I have an idea what you want, but you're ringing the wrong number. Why don't you hang up?"

Von der Osten was puzzled by the phrase, so he took out another cigarette while he revised his approach.

"Do you know who Belle Goddard really was?" he asked quietly.

"I think I answered that question."

"Agreed, but not completely."

"Oh? Perhaps I have her mixed up with Anna Held, the girl who took baths in tubs of milk." Cynthia Pollard grinned.

"No."

"The suspense is terrifying. I hope my chauffeur turns up in the nick of time to rescue me from this ordeal," she said with a smirk.

6

The German put a match to his cigarette, blew out the flame with concentration, and then played his trump. "Belle Goddard was your mother, Miss Pollard."

Cynthia Pollard calmly took up her cocktail and sipped it slowly, but the tendons behind her knees trembled and her Cuban heels began an involuntary tapping sequence. Returning her glass to the table, she said quietly, "I take it this is some sort of cheap joke."

Von der Osten studied the plume of smoke curling up from his Fatima. "I beg your pardon," he said with a sinister grimace. "It doesn't pay to joke in situations of this kind. We have every item of evidence—complete proof."

"How disconcerting. It will come as a terrific shock to my father. I mean to say . . ."

"It wouldn't be news to him. We can't halt the Pollard factories' output even though we made this information public and drove him to social and industrial oblivion. There are stockholders who in no way are concerned with such personal indiscretions."

"I see," Cynthia said with wan submission. "This evidence—it indicates that my father and this woman were intimate?"

"There isn't any question about it. We have traced the association from the Brooklyn Academy of Music where your father first met Belle Goddard in 1893. He wasn't as shrewd a man in those days and she was able to twist him around her little finger, as the saying goes. After all, it seemed important to be seen with a Broadway star at Hammerstein's Roof. Later, when your father became acquainted with a socialite named Adelaide Ponsonby, he immediately saw the more important possibilities in a marriage with a woman of Miss Ponsonby's station. He tried to close out the Goddard entanglement, but by that time Miss Goddard had left the theater to prepare for the confinement couch."

"Just what is it you want?" Cynthia asked in a husky tone, and then looked around the fashionable corridor as

7

if wondering who might see her with this hateful character.

"Let us complete this unfortunate record. You were born in a small nursing home in Sharon, Connecticut. We have copies of all the completed documents, which show that a girl baby was born to Belle Goddard. The father was listed as Shipley Pollard. Miss Goddard was awarded a generous sum of money 'for the inconvenience,' the baby was put in the care of a practical nurse, and later adopted legally by Mr. and Mrs. Pollard. Mrs. Pollard, of course, was the former Adelaide Ponsonby. Your father related his indiscretion, and his wife was wise and understanding."

"I'm beginning to see the light. You think all this gives you access to certain information in the file of the Pollard munitions works."

"We will come to that." He digressed with a wave of his glass of Vichy. "Belle Goddard, who had forsaken the theater prior to her confinement, began to live expensively on what your father had given her, but in a very short time had become a common drunk, and was reduced to what they call the burlesque circuit. She was arrested several times for indecent performances, which accounts for her appearance in the district attorney's office. There was an affair with a pearl-handled revolver, extra editions and banner headlines. You know how these affairs wind up."

Captain von der Osten had prepared his piece with timing and care. He spoke it with calm, biting assurance. He had the girl's undivided attention and made the most of it.

"How did she escape the murder charge? Who knows? But money was provided from somewhere. Perhaps she threatened to bare your father's secret, but we have no evidence of that. What probably happened is that the district attorney's career proved to be no credit to his profession and the court was more than willing to close out the case and get the revelations off the front pages."

"And . . . this Goddard woman?"

8

"Your mother? One year later her body was found floating under an East River pier. No one bothered to learn how that happened, but your father paid for a respectable burial—through his attorney, of course. And that was that. Had it not been for this war we would never have had to bring up this unsavory matter. I'm very sorry, but . . ."

"And to avoid having this made public, you want me to renounce my country, betray my father, and become an agent for your German espionage system. Is that the rest of the story?"

The captain raised both hands in what was meant to be a conciliatory gesture, lowered his eyes, and tried the sympathetic approach. "Let's not use words like 'espionage,' 'spies,' or 'sabotage' at this point. The newspapers are cluttered with such trite, meaningless phrases. Let's consider your personal position, your place in New York society. Let us even consider your position in your own home. What will the servants think when they have to obey your everyday commands once they realize you are nothing more than an adopted waif who had no legal father? What is the term for such a child?"

"Never mind." She spoke over the tips of her gloved fingers. "It could have been worse."

He glanced up, puzzled. "Worse?"

"I could have been born a stinking Hun!"

He recoiled at the taunt, but returned to his original theme of birth out of wedlock.

Cynthia Pollard traced all the probabilities while he outlined Belle Goddard's career, putting it down in 10-20-30-cent melodrama phrases of the Keith-Orpheum circuit. It was beginning to sound like Act II of *Bertha the Sewing Machine Girl*. In fact, the whole dialogue was becoming a comic farce.

Von der Osten droned on in what reminded Cynthia of a Triangle Club delivery. ". . . then you must consider the reaction of this social level. Today, you are Shipley

Pollard's daughter, and everyone treats you like an heiress. Tomorrow, you may have trouble finding a waiter to take your order. Then think of the response to your new status in Princeton—or where you live."

She gave him a wave-off and sought his intent. "All right, Captain. You've raised your stink. What am I supposed to do to regain my birth certificate?"

"It's nothing particularly difficult—or degrading. After all, you are your father's confidential secretary, in certain areas."

"I am when he can find me," Cynthia replied coldly.

"That's good. An unpredictable time program will make this particular task all the easier, and most difficult to trace."

"Come to the point," Cynthia said, anxious to be rid of this repulsive asp. He was not the type who usually squired her at the Waldorf. There were several small groups wandering out from the *thé dansant,* some of whom she had met at important social gatherings and charity functions. There were even two girls who had been at college with her. Captain von der Osten was acceptable in his dress and deportment, but he was well known for his connection with the German diplomatic corps. In these days it was not discreet to be seen with members of any Teutonic organization. Still, she reflected, the idea could have its points.

"We are especially interested in a new—er, weapon your father's firm is known to be developing," von der Osten began again, taking a small slip of paper from a pigskin wallet he carried in his breast pocket. He pondered on the words written there, and with a commanding glance laid the paper before Cynthia.

She looked down and considered the clear Germanic script.

"Oh yes." She looked up at him. Although somewhat obsequious before, he was now assured, even truculent.

"You know of this device?" He took the paper and returned it to his wallet.

"Of course. It should play havoc with your hateful submarine campaign," she said between clenched teeth.

"Exactly. It might prove to be a real threat. A device which . . ."

Cynthia Pollard heard few of his words, though she knew he was explaining some of the details of the weapon. She nodded to indicate she was listening, but her probing mind was putting out sensitive feelers in other directions.

"You must appreciate," he went on, pawing lightly at his lower lip, "that such a device, if successful, would seriously interfere with our war effort, and we are willing to pay well for any personal or social inconvenience, or for any intrusion on your conscience. I do appreciate what this means to a young lady in your position."

"I'm overwhelmed by your thoughtfulness."

"Please. Take what you call the long view. The quicker Germany wins this war the less the chance of your country's being drawn into the conflict. The U-boat campaign can starve out England within a few months."

"How considerate of you to think of us in the matter," she said coldly, "but just how can you repay me for this favor? Money? I have more than enough for my needs."

"Possibly, as long as you are living with your parents, but wouldn't your own personal account—er, regular income from investments come in handy when you decide to marry?"

"Money wouldn't do much good when I am behind bars, no matter how well my investments were going." She managed a wry smile. "I realize I am in a very unenviable situation. If I refuse to work for you I am to be unmasked and shown as the spawn of Belle Goddard. If I accept and become an agent for you I stand a gambler's chance of losing my social standing, being denounced as an ungrateful bitch and probably serving the rest of my life in prison."

11

He shrugged that off. "I don't think you'd come to any such end. After all, you are the daughter of Shipley Pollard. People of your social stature do not go to jail in America. You and your kind are far above such indignities. There might be a few days of discomfiting publicity, but it would soon die down and be forgotten. But you would still be Shipley Pollard's daughter."

"Slightly tainted and soiled, of course," she added, "and Mother would be justified in glaring at Father and saying, 'Well, what could you expect?'"

Captain von der Osten finished his drink with an air of a man who wishes to conclude the discussion. "I fear you are exaggerating all the factors. This little obligation can't possibly give you that much trouble. All we want is a set of blueprints. You could remove a set and carry them away in your handbag."

"You make spy work sound simple. Then what?"

"It is in your case. With some idea of how this mechanism works, it would be the German navy's task to devise a counter weapon that would nullify—"

"They couldn't do that without knowing how the Pollard weapon works?" she asked with disarming simplicity.

He subsided in a labyrinth of conjecture, and then said, "Of course not."

"But since you apparently have some idea of the theory of the device, it should be reasonably simple to counteract."

"I'm afraid not. It would take months of trial and error."

"Then your great scientists are not half as bright as Karl von Weigand of the New York *World* continues to proclaim."

He lost some of his calm and flared up petulantly. "Miss Pollard, you are in no position to make derogatory statements about my people. You have exactly one month to produce a set of those blueprints."

She smiled, and to his amazement said, "I think it

might be fun. I'd like to try it just to prove something to myself. May I have your card?"

He stared in disbelief. He could not account for this apparent switch in her viewpoint and for half a minute he tried to find the answer in her eyes.

"My card?" he almost whimpered. "I have . . . a card, but it would not be wise for you to carry such incriminating material. You know how to use the telephone. I can always be reached in that manner, and I want to hear nothing from you until you advise me that you have the blueprints, or some revealing drawings."

He got to his feet, gripped the brim of his hat with both hands again, and bowed. "Good day, Miss Pollard. I trust we shall meet soon—within a month."

"Good day, Captain," Cynthia replied, and batted her eyelashes. "I shall look forward to seeing you again. I think we can have a very interesting association."

The captain clicked his heels, backed off two strides, and caught a glance of himself in a pillar mirror. A narcissistic gleam wiped some of the unhealthy yellow from his cheeks.

Cynthia Pollard ordered another Bronx and sat contemplating other habitués of Peacock Alley. A short distance away Mrs. Draycourt Harriman held sway over a small committee that was to stage a scholarship festival for Vassar. Eleanora Sears, the Boston heiress and aviation enthusiast, strode past with her Edward Payson Weston stride. Miss Bobby O'Day, Broadway's latest musical comedy star, sat with Harold d'Laing, the society darling who played the piano divinely and was important in the Hasty Pudding Club. Mrs. Devereaux Morton Drax-Drax was sharing some gossip tidbit with Countess La Rochefoucauld, who headed the French Refugee Mission.

Well, this was how it had been up to now, but it was obviously all over. The waiter placed the glass at her elbow, took the dollar bill with a thankful hiss, and backed away. She smiled again and sipped as she reflected. Life

13

could be quite rewarding over the next few months. "What have I got to lose?" she mused with plausible logic, and wondered how a top-flight director would have her play her new role.

CHAPTER TWO

The weather was glorious, but it usually was for the Yale-Harvard-Princeton triangular track and field meet, especially when it was staged at Palmer Stadium. Spring was often laggard at New Haven and Cambridge, but that May she was punctual and at her loveliest in Jersey. The flowers, shrubs, and blooms were in profusion, and there was gaiety on the breeze, for it was the time of proms, dances, romance, bacon buns at Joe's, and knobby-kneed athletes in track shorts. There was a full pattern of sunshine to throw stylistic shadows across green swards, against the tall towers garlanded with gargoyles and buttressed walls that produced echoes of the cries, laughter, and salutations of boys and girls from every corner of the East. Class-cutting maids from Poughkeepsie, Northampton, and Philadelphia were led by rebellious daughters from country parsonages in "tossing their bonnets over the windmills." The rhythm of their talk, chatter, and high-decibel laughter was joined by the clatter of three Curtiss JN biplanes of the Princeton Flying Club as they roared over Nassau Hall, and with that the talk turned to war—the war "over there" in France.

It was said, or rumored, that some of the boys were going just as soon as classes closed. Some were to drive ambulances for the American Field Service, some were going to fly for France, some talked surreptitiously of joining the British . . . the Royal Flying Corps.

As the shadows deepened and the afternoon hours passed, time was sectioned by bombard peals of acclaim

15

from the stands of the magnet-shaped stadium. The dashes had been run, the middle distances completed, and the field events jotted down in the records. Only the classic one-mile relay remained on the program. This four-man event would decide the annual championship. Yale was out of the running, but first place in the relay would decide for Princeton or Harvard. This was a matter of vital importance, a relay race that would complete the tabulations of an intercollegiate championship. At least it was vital to the sports writers.

Had anyone troubled to read the front pages of any metropolitan newspaper he would have noted the latest report to the President from Walter H. Page, United States Ambassador to Great Britain.

> In the meantime, the Allies still holding together as they are, there is no peace yet in British or French minds. They are after the militarism of Prussia—not territory or other gains; and they seem likely to get it, as much by the blockade as by victories on land. . . . By that time, too, it will be clear to the Germans that the President can't bring peace so long as only one side wishes peace.*

But at Princeton the mile relay held thousands in thrall as the three first contestants went off from their crouch with the discharge of a starter's puny gun, a dull plop that would never have been noticed amid the carnage of Vimy Ridge, but here a .22-caliber blank shell aroused the crowded stadium to panic frenzy.

The Harvard man took a five-yard lead in the first quarter. The Yale man made it up in the second 440 with the Crimson and Tiger runners exchanging their batons only half a dozen strides behind. In the third, Princeton's Ralph Macintosh took the baton with a yard or two to spare, but he ran a bad quarter, wasting his initial speed to catch the Harvard runner without waiting to get into his most

* *The Life and Letters of Walter H. Page*, Doubleday, Page & Company.

effective stride. For about seventy yards the three quarter-milers flashed breast to breast as the spectators screamed their tribal encouragement. Macintosh was completely off stride in the final turn and lost yards, but Coach Doc Poultney still held high hopes, for he was positive his anchor man, Bartley Crispin, would easily make up the deficit in the final quarter.

He puffed stoically at his mahogany-toned briar and watched young Crispin marking time coolly, keeping his spikes clean, and calculating the exact second when Macintosh would race up to pass the baton. They had practiced this exchange a hundred times, timing the faltering stride of the oncoming runner to the light-footed departure of the anchor man. Crispin pranced, half turned with his hand held out, his fingers loose and open for the baton exchange. He saw the Yale and Harvard men slashing their way to the tape line while Macintosh was at least four yards behind, and running drunkenly.

Doc Poultney yanked his pipe from his stained teeth. "By God! He's got the baton in the wrong hand!" He gasped and looked around for an agreement from the sideliners. No one else in the Princeton group seemed to notice the mistake. They were aghast at Macintosh's mask of exhaustion and his faltering stride. With one look at Poultney, Crispin backed up a few strides, hoping his teammate would reach him before he collapsed. It was then he noticed that Macintosh was carrying the baton incorrectly. To get it into Crispin's left hand, as they had always done, it meant he would either have to change it to his right hand before he reached Crispin, or Bart would have to take if off stride and lose still another yard or so. A yard, to a man who must do the final quarter in well under fifty seconds, can be a furlong, particularly when he is expected to catch a contestant who already has a three- or four-yard lead.

But the situation did not seem hopeless to Crispin. He was confident he could catch the Yale and Harvard men, with any luck at all. However, he was shocked flat-footed with despair when he saw that Macintosh was completely exhausted. That was bad enough, but Mac's demonic expression, aimed full blast at Crispin, dredged up insults, rebuffs, and snobbish contempt Bart endured, during four years of college life. He instinctively knew that his teammate had no intention of making a helpful exchange. To the spectators in the lower stands, Macintosh seemingly lost his head, floundered again, and then tossed the baton in a fluttery arc toward the outer lime-marked lane. A dull groan of disbelief went up from the crowd.

Bartley moved to retrieve the baton that was flickering end over end toward the feet of the judges, but he also saw that Macintosh was helpless and heading for a painful sprawl across the cinders. He grabbed him before he went to his knees, dropped him lightly, and then scrambled to retrieve the baton. By that time the quest was hopeless. The Harvard anchor man, turning in a 49-second quarter, finished yards ahead of the Yale runner. Crispin could do little more than sprint out the distance to receive warm acclaim from every sportsman in the stands.

This is how it was in the university towns of the United States in May 1916. The mile relay was the event of the day. Gold, silver, and bronze medals were given for such accomplishments, and when it was all over there was the simple matter of academic examinations that some students swore drained them of every ounce of vitality, and left them ready to vomit in dark corners.

Some three thousand miles away a young man named Alistair Poultney, a member of the London Scottish, limping from a wound suffered in the Battle of the Somme, made his way to a red-carpeted dais in Buckingham Palace to receive the Victoria Cross from H.M. King George V. The citation read:

> In an attack against an enemy machine-gun nest,
> Private Alistair Poultney dared a withering fire to get

within thirty yards of the post. Tossing hand grenades from a shell hole, he killed four members of the gun crew and then captured the weapon. He was wounded in the right foot, and while applying his own first aid, he spotted a second machine-gun post which he soon silenced and took over before being relieved.

Coach Doc Poultney did not learn of this honor for six weeks, when his son found time to drop him a line to tell him how things were progressing "over there."

"Well, you did your best, Bartley," Coach Poultney said an hour later in the Princeton locker room. "We should have won that relay by four or five yards." He grinned at the prospect and packed his briar pipe again. Doc had once attended Edinburgh University, and there still was a touch of the Gaelic lilt to his words, but it was only when he became outraged that the idiom of the Scots clipped his speech.

"Mac did his best," the anchor man said as he sorted his gear in front of his locker, "but he ran himself groggy in the first hundred yards." Both men pondered on the theory, and then Crispin added, "I suppose physical exhaustion can play some queer tricks, but when he came floundering up to me he looked like a man with a heart full of hate. Just as though he couldn't bear to hand me that baton."

"I wouldn't put it past him," Doc said, and twisted in his creaky chair. "He'll never convince me he's a Macintosh. There's something queer about that laddie. Do you realize we've never seen either of his parents in the four years he's been here? Who is he? He's not a Scot as far as I am concerned."

"Oh, come on, Doc. What's the difference if he's a Scot or a Hungarian? He's an American, isn't he?" Crispin said with plausible candor.

The old coach stared thoughtfully through the dingy window that offered a restricted view of the green playing field. He snorted, put his feet up on his desk, and turned

19

back to Crispin. He considered the well-knit figure topped with cornflake hair, the neat sloping shoulders, sleek flanks and long leg muscles anchored to slim compact ankles. His track shorts accentuated his boyish waist.

"You never have a harsh word for anyone, do you, Bartley?" Poultney looked for his box of matches. "But you're absolutely right. Macintosh ran his quarter seething with hate."

"He was out on his feet, Coach. Granted, he has never included me in his clique, but he was running for his school, not putting on a university brother act for me."

"He deliberately tossed the bit of stick away. He had no intention of letting you catch that Harvard lad—what's his name?"

"Osgood. Brian Osgood. A fine chap. A real sportsman. Funny thing, he had exactly the same idea. That is, he thought Mac had been 'careless' in the way he handled the baton."

"You shouldn't be so friendly with his girl—what's her name? That Miss Pollard," Doc muttered, and got up to open a window to waft some of the sweat and liniment odor from the area. "By the way, where was she today? She's usually down front screaming her lungs out."

Bartley turned to sort out some clothing he had draped over a chair. He too wondered about Cynthia Pollard. She'd been missing from the college spots for more than a week. "Could be her father is keeping her busy."

"She's always had a smile and a wave for you, Bart," the old man said with a twinkle in his eye.

"Don't get her wrong, Doc. We don't move in the same social circle. The Crispins have always had to work for a living. I like her, but her blood's too blue. We are just a couple of companionable people who met on a college campus. You know how enduring that is."

"The Pollards were nobodies until the old man came up with a new high-speed, rifle-boring gear."

"And a safer method of loading shells," Bart added.

20

"Now they don't know where all the money is coming from."

"There might be a good spot for you, in the Pollard firm," Poultney observed. "Just turf Macintosh out, marry the daughter, and there you are, set up for life."

Bartley was folding an everyday shirt with studied care. "Oh no. The munitions industry is not for me, Doc. It's a hateful business, manufacturing weapons for mass murder. As for the girl, ours is a genial companionship—nothing more." He placed the folded articles in a cheap suitcase. "Besides, have you forgotten? I'm going to Oxford."

Doc removed his pipe with a plop. "Och, yes. I hae forgotten yer Rhodes scholarship. Ye've done well, Bartley boy. Yer mither must be swellin' wi' pride."

Young Crispin smiled reflectively. Doc was just a dreamer. "I'm afraid my mother has little interest in college activities. She thinks I ought to be getting a job and contributing to the household expenses."

Poultney considered that and wondered what his own son was doing at that particular moment.

Bart's parents were dull and anti-social. They had never provided a comfortable or a respectable home. Princeton had offered a brand-new world, and over the past four years Bartley had striven to raise his social thinking to that of many of his university associates.

"But you'll accept?" the coach insisted as Bart drew on his street clothes.

"Yes, of course. It's all set for early fall. I just hope an architectural scholarship will be available. That blasted war might upset my plans. So far, the opening is there, and as far as I know the grants have not been suspended. But you never know, these days."

"Don't think about *not* going. You'll like it over there, Bart. History is being made, and I know you'll like the people . . . and the university life. There is a war on, of course, but you'll get to know what's really going on. Over here, we get what the papers want to tell us."

"Your son is over there, isn't he?"

Doc Poultney beamed with pride. "Ay, Alistair volunteered the first week, and went over on money out of his own pocket. He joined the London Scottish in September 1914."

Crispin walked slowly toward Doc's desk, and then squatted on an upturned water bucket. "Did he *have* to go, Doc? The British government didn't call him up?"

Poultney raised his eyebrows in exaggerated amazement. "*Have* to go? Not at all. He *wanted* to go. That's a wicked man they have in Germany, Bartley. Alistair was born over here. He's as American as you, but he felt he had to go. They say the Old Country roots go deep, an' there's such a thing as a conscience, ye know."

Crispin looked pained. "I'm afraid I'll never understand that kind of reasoning. I like to think our motives and ideals are more peaceful."

"Then perhaps ye'll tell me why we have an army an' a navy."

"But they're for national defense, not for foreign invasion or military conquest."

Doc smiled, and peered out of the window. The shadows were lengthening across the field. "Bartley boy, if you had studied history for information and reasoning instead of providing answers to rubber-stamp questions, you would have learned that since 1775 the United States Army has filched more square miles of this earth by bloody military conquest than any force in the world—except the British army."

"Oh, come on, Doc. What about Julius Caesar?"

"Julius Caesar would have been staggered by the exploits of the U. S. Army," Poultney said thoughtfully. "U.S. sailors and Marines have been sent on dozens of hostile missions into foreign territory. Granted, you probably wouldn't call some of them real wars."

Crispin faintly recalled Memorial Day parades with the crippled ancients riding in open carriages. "But, Doc, you can't compare those skirmishes with what is going on in Europe. Thousands are being killed every day!"

"Well, it depends on how you classify savage Indians. Most of them have been exterminated by now. In 1845 American troops were sent to the Rio Grande *only* to facilitate the transfer of the Republic of Texas to the United States. But what followed? The valuable lands that became California, Nevada, New Mexico, and Arizona were gobbled up. In 1898 we ousted the Spanish from Cuba and eventually the Philippines—and Porto Rico—and we still have a strangle hold on Cuba. I think going over to Oxford will open your eyes."

There was a long period of silence. Doc puffed contentedly; the bushy eaves of his brows twitched and flashed off faint gleams from the window. His pipe drew well. There was a warm flush across his cheekbones, and the dewlaps on each side of his Adam's apple rested on his flannel collar. He tried to recall Alistair as he had last seen him. He was proud of his son who had dared fate and offered himself in the Allied cause of freedom. He missed Alistair, but he hated to lose this lad Crispin.

"Do you think we'll get into this European mess, Doc?" Bartley asked. He was seeing the coach in a new light. The aroma of arnica, sweat, and surgical tape had been swabbed away by this drenching of reality.

"We'll go in," Poultney prophesied. "We'll go in just as soon as Allied credit gives out, which in turn could mean economic collapse in America—then we'll find a reason for going in. It won't be a humane or a patriotic reason. There'll be no 'scraps of paper' for us to fight for, no word of honor to an ally." He waited for the inference to sink in.

Bart took the bait impulsively. "There you are. We have no sound or honorable reason for going in. That's why we'll never become involved."

Doc set his young athlete a problem. "But suppose we did," he prompted. "What would you do, laddie buck?"

"Me?" Crispin was aghast at the suggestion. "I don't think I'd make a good soldier. I wouldn't know what I was fighting for."

Poultney aimed his pipe with open-sights accuracy. "You went pell-mell after those two anchor men when there wasn't a chance in the world of your ever getting within twenty yards of them."

"But this was sport. It was what we had been trained for. It was what I was supposed to do. . . ." Bartley felt like a fool, as he presented his explanation.

Doc lowered the stem of his pipe, satisfied he had made a point, but he went on, "Bartley, you represent the modern American youth at its finest in that you have an abiding faith in your own moral goodness. You just can't understand the self-denial of the French and British. You'll probably never understand war—or its reason—until you and your contemporaries are dying, or risking death together. Then it'll suddenly become an inspired crusade."

Crispin wished he had a sound argument to cope with the logic of this knowledgeable man, but all he could say was, "Doc, I can't believe in war. It's not an American tradition. Basically we are a peaceful nation."

"Teddy Roosevelt's Great White Fleet wasn't a very peaceful display, as I recall."

"Teddy Roosevelt? He's been rattling the rifle bolt ever since he charged up San Juan Hill. He doesn't represent the American people."

"Bully for you!" Doc said, and grinned.

"He'd like to get us into this war so he can prance about in a campaign hat, but he'd be miles behind the battle. He's a professional patriot."

"It's a matter of morality, Bartley boy. The British believe they are fighting to defend France and Belgium."

"It's nothing more than a battle for the balance of power, and you know it."

"Whatever you do, don't give them credit for honoring their word on scraps of paper."

"I speak only for myself. I wouldn't kill a man for a questionable point of honor. That's like fighting a senseless duel."

"Let's leave dueling out. That's a clash of individuals, but perhaps dueling does explain war. Every so often some maniac comes along who is capable of starting a world conflict to satisfy his personal ambitions."

"Yes, I suppose there are such men . . ."

"But suppose we did get in," the coach persisted. "Our history from before the Revolution proves over and over that we cannot rely on volunteers signing up to fight for their country. Look what General Washington had to put up with. Then in 1812, when the city of Washington was threatened, General Winder asked for ninety-five thousand men, hoping he would get at least fifteen thousand. Do you know how many loyal Americans responded?"

"Fifty thousand, perhaps."

"Only thirty-two hundred. There were fourteen hundred regulars and eighteen hundred militia."

"I can't believe it."

"Go look up your history."

Bart pondered with his chin in his palm. "Doc, you should have taught history instead of coaching track."

"I wouldn't last one semester. Not the history I'd teach." Doc chuckled to himself.

"Are we really this bad as working patriots?"

"Most of us prefer to take our fighting like our other adventures—vicariously. That's why these moving pictures are so popular. How many spectators were here in Palmer Stadium today? Thousands. Just to watch a few athletes tear their lungs out for dear old Nassau. And how many more were sitting in the Polo Grounds in New York? I'll wager that if some promoter erected bleachers where spectators could watch a modern bayonet charge—without getting hurt—he'd have a sellout, day after day."

Crispin stiffened as the Princeton Flying Club biplanes clattered across the stadium.

25

Thoroughly enjoying himself, Doc continued the discussion. "If we do get into this European mess, as you call it, how many young men of college age will volunteer? Very few, Bartley. What few who have already volunteered are serving with the French Aviation or the Royal Flying Corps."

"I suppose you are right, but what would we gain if we did help the Allies to win the war?"

"Ye don't expect to gain anything in a war!" Doc bellowed, and stared in disbelief. "You can think yourself lucky if ye hold onto your sense of freedom. If that blasted Kaiser wins, what do ye think will happen to France and Britain?"

"I don't know, and I'm afraid I don't care too much—except it might conclude the Rhodes scholarships. I certainly want to go to Oxford."

"There should be plenty of space," the coach said solemnly. "Quite a few Oxford lads have gone under in the past couple of years. You might take over someone's bed and his seat in a lecture room."

"Damn it, Doc! I didn't start their rotten war."

"Of course not," Poultney said soothingly. "Alistair didn't either, but I hope he'll be around to help finish it."

"I hope so too, for your sake, Doc," Bartley said solemnly. "But I'll tell you one thing. They'll never entice me into that mess. I'm an American and my citizenship is worth more than all the phony glory or the medals any king can stick on my chest. I have other plans for my young life."

Doc adjusted a benign smile. "What about those boys over there in Britain? What will their citizenship mean if they lose the war?"

"I don't know, Doc. I just don't know," Bartley confessed, and picked up his suitcase.

CHAPTER THREE

While the coach and Bart were analyzing the tangled theories of patriotism and war, Ralph Macintosh was racing down the Princeton–Lawrenceville road astride his Indian motorcycle. He crouched over the fuel tank, goggled, breeched, and bundled up in a university sweater. The machine was a scarlet meteor, a scourge to all wandering poultry and the wheeled ambition of every small boy along the dusty road.

All the exhaustion of the relay had been swabbed away in the shower stall, and Macintosh was his aggressive self again by the time he had reduced speed to turn into the field of the Princeton Flying Club. Skidding up to the big wooden shed, he lowered the parking rack, removed his gloves with studied care, and folded them over the hydra-eyed speedometer.

He flicked a salute to a man in military breeches, golf stockings, and brogues. "Be right with you, Captain," he yelled, hurried inside the shed and headed for the slab-sided cubicle that served as the office.

"I want my logbook," he snapped at the indistinct figure seated at a disordered table.

The figure hunched its shoulders. "You know where it is, don't you? It's supposed to be in the activity rack."

"You're supposed to be employed around here, aren't you?"

"Yeh, as a mechanic, not a Goddamn flunky for you guys."

Macintosh considered the response, spat at the floor, and snapped, "I just hope Number 3 is in condition to get off the ground."

"It has been, all afternoon."

"It had better be. I'm trying to prove to this Limey inspector that I'm capable of getting a JN-4 off the ground and bringing it back again."

The man at the murky table turned and showed mild interest. "Don't tell me *you* are trying to get over there. I can't wait to read that in the *Daily Princetonian*."

"What else? Everybody's doin' it," Macintosh claimed, "and I don't mean the turkey trot."

"I'd give a month's pay to see them British guys putting you through the ropes. Something tells me you're about to start a real education."

"One take-off, two simple circuits, and a reasonably decent landing, and I'll be in line for a commission in the Royal Flying Corps." Macintosh began tightening the chin strap of his leather helmet.

"You mean you really want to go over there and fight those German Fokkers?" the mechanic asked incredulously.

"Sure. Why not?"

"You know that's one deal you can't buy your way into— or out of. They play for keeps over there on that Western Front. I can't see you in a setup where you ain't got it all lined up in your favor, mister."

Ralph selected a logbook from a shallow rack, checked over its entries, and tucked it in his breeches pocket.

"You got that all foxed up, too, I'll bet," the mechanic said with a sly grin. "You ain't bin out here doin' any flying for three-four weeks. Jack Morgan has put in more time than you, an' he's supposed to be workin' his way through college."

"What I have down has been attested by Major Morton. No one can argue with my flying time."

"Hey, wait a minute," the mechanic interrupted as Macintosh headed for the door. "How come you're joining the British? I din' know you had any Limey blood in you. What's the connection?"

"The Macintoshes are one of Scotland's most notable

28

families," Ralph snapped, and then proceeded to relate their history as he had memorized it from *The Scottish Clans and Their Tartans*. "They are among the foremost clans of the Highlands. Their first real chief was Malcolm Macintosh, who owned lands stretching from Petty to Lochaber . . . inclusive. His relations with the Lord of the Isles were most cordial and his son Duncan married Flora, the Earl's daughter. All this began back in 1430 and you'll find Clan Macintosh Societies all over the English-speaking world . . ."

"That line wins the lady's bicycle. If you're a Scotsman, I'm a Hungarian, an' my name's Sven Larsen."

"Now I know why you're just a mechanic. You're a dumb Swede," the collegian quipped with disdain. "Come on, let's get Number 3 twirling. The captain hasn't all day."

Outside, the British captain strode up and down beside the club's Number 3 Curtiss biplane. He had been a flight commander with Number 24 Squadron, flying DH-2 scouts, and had many hours of what was known as active service flying, registered in a logbook crammed with details of offensive patrols against the common enemy. There was little or nothing to show that he had destroyed fourteen enemy aircraft, for it was presumed that the two ribbons on his tunic would indicate that somewhere in his service career his devotion to duty had been suitably recognized. There was no necessity to go into details.

Captain Payne was glad to get into mufti whenever he was clear of front-line duty, for civilian clothes assured him of some privacy and filtered the embarrassing stares of people who wondered what "foreign" military service he represented.

"It's a bit of a ramp, you know," Payne said after the first three weeks of this recruiting program. "There are times when I wish I were back in France—where I belong."

Few of his social contacts could understand that wry reflection. Who could possibly want to go back "over there" and risk life and limb, fighting against those Germans?

"Well, we're ready, Captain," Macintosh announced as he strode up to the aeroplane. Observing the Britisher's casual dress, he asked, "Would you like a helmet and goggles? Gloves, perhaps? We can get you a set."

"Helmet . . . goggles? What for?" Captain Payne took another look at the biplane.

"I mean . . . you're going to fly with me, aren't you?"

"Yes, but I don't think we'll need goggles in this thing."

Macintosh resented the rebuff. "She'll do well over eighty. It might be uncomfortable."

"I don't doubt it, but not because of speed. What keeps it together in a high wind?"

Macintosh was uncertain of the meaning but decided finally that the captain was making fun of the club's machine. "I don't suppose it compares with what you have been flying over there, but we think the Curtiss is a fine aeroplane for flying club activity."

"Have they ever considered ballooning?" Captain Payne climbed up into the front seat. "It's fun, you know. Drifting about, dragging a grappling hook and pilfering old ladies' washing off the back garden clothes poles. Rare sport."

This type of humor escaped Macintosh, who could not apply the word "sport" to anything that was supposed to be amusing. He was glad when Larsen went to the nose and started easing the wooden propeller back and forth. He took a moment to walk around the aeroplane to check a few primary control cables.

Payne settled himself in the basket seat with resignation. "Let's get it over," he said over his shoulder.

"Be right with you, sir," Macintosh responded, and climbed up into the pilot's seat. He fastened his belt, took a quick glance at his wrist watch, and began the starting-up routine.

"Switch off—gas on—suck in!" he called to the mechanic.

The OX engine responded on the first twirl after the cylinders had been primed. The clatter reminded Payne of the bolts-and-nuts uproar of an old Renault engine mounted aboard an ancient Farman Longhorn he had once attempted to fly. Still, at a certain rpm there was a period of low vibration, and the comparative surge of smooth power was reassuring.

Macintosh taxied away and went to the end of the take-off strip. Captain Payne folded his arms and hunched behind the small curved windshield and checked the fluttering windsock on the top of the hangar. From that point on the Britisher had few complaints. Macintosh flew reasonably well for a club novice, and he went through a short program of banks and turns that satisfied his passenger. He headed toward the Delaware River, circled over Lambertville, and turned southeast until they encountered the industrial murk over Trenton. Payne was satisfied with that, and he waved his pilot off and indicated he could return to the field.

Macintosh's landing was fair, but the Curtiss, encountering a fractious gust, shivered from wing tip to wing tip. Payne twisted sharply in his seat and looked back at the pilot. The biplane rolled on and finally settled to a normal trundle. Satisfied that the undercarriage had not been damaged, the captain pointed toward the hangar. After the machine had been manhandled up to the cab rank, Payne climbed down, took another sardonic glance at the contraption, and walked clear of the wing structure.

"Sorry," Macintosh pleaded. "I guess that landing wasn't too good, but how did I do—on the whole?"

"Very well. You caught a gust that you might have spotted had you checked the sock as you glided in, but it was not important. You'll do. You can fly, but don't entertain any elaborate hopes. You'll have a hell of a lot more to learn before the R.F.C. will admit you can aviate. But I'm quite satisfied, Macintosh."

"Then you'll recommend me?"

"I think we'll be glad to have you."

31

The candidate exhaled in relief. "Whee! What comes next?"

"It may take a little time for the papers to go through, but I should think that by the end of July you'll be called to Toronto. After that you're in the lap of the gods . . . and the best of luck."

"The timing is perfect. I just can't wait."

"Well, you'll finish out your final year here at Princeton, won't you? You should do that, you know. In the meantime I'll see if I can get you into the first of the new R.F.C. training courses that are being established in Toronto—so don't figure on going to England right away."

"They're to have R.F.C. training courses in Canada?"

"Right. You'll probably be among the first of the X and Y squadrons. You'll get your ground school work in Toronto and then go to either Camp Borden or Leaside for your flight training."

"Great. I can't wait for school to close."

"Don't become too anxious. You'll get all the flying you can stand before this mucky business is over."

Later that spring evening the scarlet motorcycle took Macintosh out toward Hopewell, for he planned to call on Cynthia Pollard and relate his good fortune, hoping her enthusiastic reaction would lower some of the barricades she erected whenever they were alone. He had known for some time that he was acceptable as an escort, but on the doubtful side in a tête-à-tête situation. However, he hoped her unbounded enthusiasm for an Allied victory in Europe would respond rewardingly to an announcement that he had been accepted for a commission, and that he would soon be training to fly with the British air service. After all, this was the thing to do if one would stay in favor with the people who mattered.

He had selected a pepper-and-salt tweed suit, a checkered golf cap, and a plain white, soft-collared shirt for his ride out to the Pollard estate, hoping that he would find the family hosting an informal gathering of some kind. The track meet could have inspired a seasonable party for the entertainment of the visiting athletes. It was the sort of thing the Pollards were noted for.

But there were no automobiles anywhere in the long curving driveway that led up to the porte-cochere bulging from the elaborate front door. There was no extravagant display of lights, no small groups on the terrace, no strains of music from the french windows. If Cynthia was home, it promised to be a cozy evening.

He dismounted and pushed the motorbike close to the shrubbery banked up to the end of the broad front steps. It was then his hopes were disturbed. Someone had rested a bicycle in the convenient space. It was a black-framed affair with a red head beneath the handlebars, and had a New Departure coaster brake and a set of Vulcan nonskid tires.

"So little St. Crispin, Princeton's gift to the Horatio Alger series, is already on hand. He should be washing dishes down on University Place." Macintosh growled and shoved his powered bike beside Crispin's. "Well, he can soon be sent home to bed."

He hurried up the curved steps and poked at the bell. There was a faint light in the reception hall and he could see a plump, elderly maid coming to respond to his ring.

"Good evening, Mrs. Budge," he said courteously, as he always did to any of the Pollard servants. "Is Miss Pollard at home this evening?"

The apple-cheeked Mrs. Budge looked him over, considered the question for a suitable period of time, and finally decided the visitor was acceptable. "Yes, she returned late this afternoon."

"May I see her?" Ralph Macintosh went through the standard routine of admittance.

"Of course. Won't you come in? I'll tell her you are here, Mr. Macintosh."

"She has been away?"

33

"You know Miss Cynthia. Always on the go—somewhere," Mrs. Budge said in mock severity. "We never know where she is or when she'll turn up. It must drive her parents to distraction. May I take your cap?"

"I missed her at the meet today," Ralph added as he vetted his reflection in a pier glass.

"Perhaps that's why Princeton lost," Mrs. Budge said over her shoulder and padded away.

"You never can tell," he muttered as he combed his hair and straightened his tie.

"Ralph!" Cynthia Pollard's voice pealed along the reception hall. "Come along in. How nice to see you."

He hurried forward with both hands outstretched. "I'm sorry if I'm intruding. You have company?"

"Just Bart Crispin. He cycled over a few minutes ago. Wasn't that too bad about the relay? What happened?"

"Oh, you know." He would have given his version, but realized that Crispin probably had told the real story, and it would not be wise to create any false glory. "I was the culprit. I messed up the baton pass, and—well, that's how it goes at times."

"Come on in. I'm dying to talk to you, too. There must be wads of college gossip. I've been tied up in New York."

"Nothing startling, except . . . well, it can wait."

"You beast!" She took a mannish punch at his shoulder. "What have you been up to . . . and with whom?"

"It'll keep. I'm glad Bart's here. I think he's wanted back in town."

"He's in here."

The Pollard home reflected wealth, but there was a homey air about every corner. The room into which Ralph was taken was a combination den, lounge, family parlor. A broad-beamed fireplace was set as the focal point with bookcases buttressing both sides. It was faced by a deep sofa complete with down-filled cushions, and scattered about were three low tables that bore a terrestrial globe, an ancient nautical sextant, and an open dictionary. A

34

contemporary Victrola console in deep mahogany stood between two french windows while a baby grand piano gleamed wide-legged in an area offering floor-to-ceiling bookcases.

From the phonograph came the lovely soprano voice of Lina Cavalieri singing a solo from *Mefistofele*.

Bartley had risen to his feet and now stood with his back to the fireplace. He was wearing white duck trousers, a white shirt, a neat bow tie, and a university jersey.

"Ah there, Bart. Didn't know you'd be out here. Why didn't you tell me? You could have hooked a ride," Ralph suggested in greeting.

"Thanks. The biking did me good. It's a beautiful night."

"Wouldn't think you'd need any more exercise after this afternoon. I was dish-ragged out."

Cynthia was pouring lemonade from a large crystal pitcher. "Anyone for a thirst quencher, for a start?" she asked pertly.

"Just a minute," Ralph continued. "I don't want to shoo you out, Bart, but someone was looking for you outside Stanhope Hall. I'm not sure of his name, but it was Stratameyer, or Stosselmeyer . . . something like that. Anyway, I think it was about your Rhodes scholarship. You'll have to decide whether it is important."

"What name did you say?" Cynthia asked with a startled expression.

"I can't remember, but it was something like Stosselmeyer . . . or . . ."

Bart, who had been cudgeling his mind to place the names Ralph had brought up, broke in, "It wasn't Strathcona, was it?"

"That's it. I should have remembered such a Scottish name. Strathcona it is."

"Mr. Strathcona is a representative of the Rhodes scholarship committee in this area. I suppose I ought to hurry back to find out what is going on."

"You are a comic, Ralph," Cynthia said, handing out

glasses of lemonade, "getting a Mr. Strathcona confused with a name like Stosselmeyer."

"Damned foolish of me," he admitted.

"Why don't you call the Public Information desk and find out if your man is still in town?" Cynthia said to Bart. "It won't take but a minute and you could leave our number with them."

Macintosh damned the convenience of the telephone, and chided himself for bringing up the name of Stosselmeyer. It was maddening that his contrived ruse to get Crispin out of the house should coincide with a man named Strathcona. It was equally disturbing that Cynthia Pollard should pick him up on it.

Bart considered Cynthia's suggestion, and headed for the door.

"There is a telephone in the hall on the stand beside the coat rack," Cynthia called after him. "I hope you can catch your man."

"If he's around, he should be at Stanhope Hall. That's where he usually holds his consultations," Bart explained.

"He's probably on his way to the train, or he may be heading for New York by now," Macintosh said casually.

"But it's nearly nine o'clock," Cynthia protested. "Someone would put him up overnight."

"I shouldn't have brought it up," Ralph muttered, and sat down with his lemonade. "It's probably not important, anyway."

"Well, we'll soon find out," the girl said, and took a large lounge chair, spread out her multi-pleated skirt, and held up her glass in a cheery salute. "Here's to Mr. Stosselmeyer."

Ralph sipped his drink and studied Cynthia over the rim of his glass. He wondered why the vaudeville-like name should fascinate her. "To Papa Stosselmeyer," he responded, trying to go along with the joke. "I wonder where I heard that comic moniker."

The girl chuckled and confided to herself: I could tell you, but why spoil your evening, Mr. Macintosh. Instead, she sat upright and demanded, "Well, what's your news? I know you're bursting with something."

"Oh," He managed a hint of a smile. "I'm getting a commission with the British, the Royal Flying Corps. I passed a flight test late this afternoon."

Cynthia Pollard made no immediate response. An inner shock muffled all chords of speech. The Stosselmeyer flub was bad enough, but this announcement was a real stunner.

Her silence puzzled Ralph. "What's the matter? I thought you'd go into a rave at the idea. You're for the Allies, aren't you? You're always working for some British drive or fund."

"You're going into the Royal Flying Corps?"

"I'm practically in. I did a flight test with a club plane late this afternoon, and passed. Captain Payne, he's a British war flier, said he'd recommend me for a commission. That means I'll be going to Toronto for primary training right after commencement. With any luck I should be over there —at least in England—getting my final training before Christmas."

Cynthia probed and prodded to get the full story. This was something new. She had never considered Ralph Macintosh in the Allied column. In fact, she had never considered him anything but a typical college man who had no regard for the future, but was making the most of his four years of ivied walls and hallowed halls. But with this new move she realized that he was the perfect candidate for Herr Stosselmeyer's spreading net of intrigue. Her initial encounter with Captain von der Osten had opened the curtain on a frightening new world, and Ralph Macintosh was turning a blinding spotlight on a macabre pattern of intrigue.

"Well, what do you think?" he tried again, unable to account for her lack of enthusiasm. "I thought you'd . . ."

She came out of a mild stupor. "I'm delighted, Ralph. It's that I never put you in the American volunteer category, but now I can see why you joined the flying club. I thought it was just another of your social gambits. We never know what you are going to turn to next."

"Well," he confessed, "at first I did think of flying as a sport, and that all the well-to-do fellows who were taking it up would widen my undergraduate life, but then this war over there, and the stories about aviators fighting in the sky . . . I must admit I have some yearning for such a career. They say it's dangerous, but it must be a lot better than being in the trenches . . . all that mud, the barbed wire, and the awful discomfort. There's no future there for the individual, and I don't relish hand-to-hand fighting, so go ahead, tag me as a grandstander," he said with frank self-appraisal that astonished him.

Before Cynthia could reply or dig deeper into his plans, Bartley returned with an expression of uncertainty. "Couldn't get anywhere with anyone. Mr. Strathcona hasn't been in at the Information Office for several days. They can't understand how I thought it was he."

"Perhaps it *was* a Mr. Stosselmeyer," Cynthia said, and wrinkled her nose.

Bart fashioned a grin. "Give over. You'll have me using that comic name." He looked around for his drink. "Anyway, I guess there's nothing to worry about. I was afraid something had happened because of the war, and that the Rhodes grants had been suspended."

"Oh, don't say that," Cynthia cried.

"It could happen, when you consider everything."

"Well, sit down. We have some better news for you. Do you realize that you two may be in England for next term?" she said with some banality, but her mind was twittering like the type bars of a bookkeeping machine.

It was Crispin's turn to look puzzled.

"Ralph's joining the British Flying Corps after commencement," she explained with no particular enthusiasm. "He'll be an officer pilot. Wouldn't it be a coincidence if you did meet over there?"

Crispin stared at Macintosh.

"It's more likely than you think," Ralph said with an enigmatic grin. "They have a special school of military aeronautics at Oxford, and who knows, I might also wind up there. One taking a Rhodes scholarship, the other training for the skies over the Western Front. So it's three loud cheers for Princeton."

"And a locomotive," Cynthia added with a dull expression.

"You're joining the Royal Flying Corps?" Bartley asked, as though he couldn't believe what Cynthia had announced.

"I'm practically in."

He studied Ralph for several seconds. "I had no idea you were . . ."

"Neither did I," Cynthia broke in. "One can't tell what's going on anywhere these days. You're not secretly considering joining some British regiment, one that fights with those ugly-looking things called 'tanks,' are you, Bart?"

Here we go again, Bart said to himself. Out loud he spelled out his personal feelings. "I certainly am not. I'm not attuned to war. I hope the Allies win, but I wouldn't pick up a gun and shoot another man to uphold some political ideology. Military conflict is not in my make-up, I'm afraid."

He caught Cynthia staring at him as though she was having difficulty in interpreting his words.

"Wouldn't you like to fly over there?"

"No! Not to fight."

"Perhaps if you had been able to join the Princeton Flying Club you might have taken a different attitude." She selected her words carefully to avoid hurting Bart's feelings, or to infer she resented his attitude.

"I think I'd love to fly," Bart said impulsively. "It must be thrilling, but I couldn't shoot at a man who was flying another aeroplane simply because his carried a different insignia."

Macintosh exhibited a smirk. "Well, it takes all kinds. Frankly, I'm looking forward to it."

Crispin wagged his head negatively and tried to find an answer to this unexpected situation. "But what about your parents? What will they think of your abandoning your university education to join a foreign military force?" He looked to Cynthia for her support of this view, but she was idly adjusting the pleats of her skirt. "I should think the American chemical industry could use a hundred men with your training."

"Oh dear," Miss Pollard exclaimed, and put her fingertips to her lips. The reference to Ralph's having majored in chemistry was another shocker, for she had never taken any of his academic activities seriously. It suddenly occurred to her that he could be making a greater contribution to the cause by staying in the United States and helping in the search for the secrets of Germany's aniline dye products. What was the meaning of this Royal Flying Corps interest? "You know," she said pointedly, "Bart has a point there."

"I don't want to wind up in an explosive plant. I bruise easily." Ralph waited for a response to his quip.

"Bart's right," Cynthia began again. "You could fill any of several important jobs in the chemical industry." Then she as suddenly reversed her view, and picked up her line with "But you must know best, and you'll probably make a marvelous flier, Ralph. You have that sort of dash and élan."

Macintosh adopted a patronizing air. "There is another point, you know. We'll probably be in it eventually, and I was thinking that those of us with actual experience will be a great help in building up America's military forces."

"Then you'd complete the circuit and be back here teaching O.T.C. rookies." Cynthia Pollard wanted to dash her glass of lemonade in his face.

Crispin sat nursing a somber expression. "I wish you well, Ralph. I couldn't do it. I guess I don't fit into this war situation. I bruise easily too. Inside, I mean. Back home, I couldn't wring the neck of a chicken for our Sunday dinner."

"But you have marvelous competitive spirit," Cynthia broke in. "You've played basketball, baseball, hockey, and track. I always wondered why you never went in for football."

Macintosh had wondered about that too.

"But football's not a game!" Bart grumbled. "Not to me, it isn't. It's becoming nothing more than a Roman holiday. The whole spirit is savage and unhealthy."

"You can't be serious, Bart," Macintosh said, and appealed to their hostess. "Football supports all the other sports. There wouldn't be any extra funds for other games without the crowds that turn out for the grid schedule."

"That doesn't justify the overemphasis we place on football. I don't see why sports have to support themselves. Let those who participate, and enjoy them, pay for the pleasure, just as you do to fly with the club. Football is becoming very suspect. I'm told some schools actually recruit promising players direct from high school, regardless of their academic ability."

"So what?" Macintosh broke in, amazed that such a practice should be considered unethical. "Not that Princeton . . ."

"I consider sports a normal recreation outside the lecture rooms, not a circus performance to attract great crowds of paying customers. Did you ever stop to think what the money spent to build Palmer Stadium would buy in the way of laboratories, engineering sheds, or even scholarships for deserving students?"

Ralph Macintosh took up the rebuttal. "But how would you develop esprit de corps for your school without intercollegiate competition?"

Crispin shook his head. "I don't know. In fact I'm not sure how important any such abstract spirit is."

"Why did you select Princeton?"

"Proximity. It seemed logical to go to a college close to my home, in my own state. We always sang Princeton songs in assembly, and based our high school cheers on the Orange and Black. It never occurred to me to go anywhere else."

"You didn't get an athletic scholarship of any kind?"

"No. I'd never heard of any such sinecure. I passed my entrance exams and then went looking for a job to pay for

41

my tuition. I couldn't have been very bright because I had no idea what I wanted to learn, or become. I took the courses that were easiest for me, from the general science list. I was lucky in that, because when I found I wanted to build things, not tear them down, I was able to switch to architecture. Perhaps that explains my aversion to war."

"Obviously," Ralph said with a suitable smirk, "but you are not the typical college man."

"I agree," said Cynthia thoughtfully. "Most of them go for the social side. Some consult a college's football schedule before they decide where to go. The trips and fraternity contacts are more important than the academic ratings." She darted to the piano, tinkled at the keys, and sang:

> *"Though he sets the pace to kill,*
> *Father has to pay the bill,*
> *For he-e-e-e's a college boy!"*

When she returned to the couch, Ralph said with some feeling, "Bart, I'm afraid you're in for a rough time. You don't like commercialized sport, or war. Over the next few years there'll be few demands for architects because little or nothing will be built, except munitions factories, aeroplane plants, and warships. I don't know why you want to go to Oxford, even though they may teach classic architecture, for you'll be uncomfortably close to the war. Still," he added with a lip curled with contempt, "you may take up cricket, wear white flannels, and drink tea between innings. You'll probably like that."

"That's an unkind and pointless remark," Cynthia challenged. "I think it takes as much courage to ignore the emotions aroused by a war as to respond to them. I also think there is no way of knowing who will become a good soldier. I think I read somewhere that the greater percentage of British soldiers who have won the Victoria Cross were ex-choir boys . . . not gutter-fighting roughnecks."

"I don't believe a damn word of that," Macintosh growled.

"It's true," the girl insisted.

42

"I'm afraid I'm spoiling your evening, Cynthia." Bart stood up. "I'd better get along just in case Mr. Strathcona is in town looking for me. Will you excuse me, then?"

"Oh, Bart. Of course." Cynthia flashed to her feet. "But we'll see you before commencement, won't we? Father wants to talk to you about the scholarship. He's most interested. I'll see you out."

Standing erect, Bart focused a faint smile toward Macintosh. "Best of luck with the R.F.C., Ralph. If we do get to Oxford, we must try to get together, if only to improve my esprit de corps."

"All the best, Crispin."

"Thanks."

Cynthia found Bart's cap in the hall and handed it to him. "I'm sorry the evening ended this way," she said with concern in her eyes. "Ralph can be a dreadful oaf at times."

"But he has volunteered to fight," Bart said as he stood twisting his cap in his hands. "To be popular, one has to march with the mob. The day of the true individual is over. I can't help it if my conscience or sentiments separate me from the crowd. I can't expect other men to think my thoughts, echo my words, or applaud my stand. No man can have my sins, and I cannot have his virtues." He hesitated and broke into a boyish grin. "I guess I read that somewhere. It's not original, so don't give me too much credit for it."

"Oh, Bart, I do admire you." Cynthia suddenly gripped him by both shoulders. "You can't help being honest, can you? Even when you're taking your worst friends apart."

"Oh, Ralph's all right—in his own circle. He'll go a long way in the war, if he has any luck at all. He'll come back with a chestful of medals . . ."

"You are an amazing person," the girl said quietly. "No matter how people treat you, you're genial, openhanded, charitable in your judgments, and completely without rancor."

"What does it get you, being uncharitable?"

43

There wasn't enough light in the hall to illuminate the warmth of her expression. For a second or two she wanted to kiss him, but instead she simply increased the pressure of her fingers. "Don't ever give up your ideals, Bart. The war won't last too long—or so they say—and then we'll return to the times when people will again think with their heads, not with the headlines."

"Of course. Good night, Cynthia. Let's plan a long hike one of these fine afternoons, eh?"

"I'd like that. Let's."

CHAPTER FOUR

When she returned to the lounge-den Ralph was seated at the piano stroking with skill Gounod's "Song of the Golden Calf." She waited in a half shadow until he finished, and then glided forward and clapped her hands on his shoulders. "Well," she cried, "I didn't know you went in for the classics."

"Just for my own amazement," he quipped, and spun around to curl an arm about her waist.

"Always capable of some surprise. No wonder you're so popular at Princeton. Every week you come up with some new skill or promise. What next?"

"Who knows," he said, and twirled back to the keyboard. He fingered a few chords as he explained, "I try to please my friends with my modest contributions, hoping to keep pace with my more personable rivals. I'm not a great student. I'm only a fair athlete, and after all, how can a chemical stink merchant compete with an idealistic architect with a Rhodes scholarship?"

"Let's drop the competition line. Bart's more of a family friend, not my particular prize. Mother and Father are interested in him because of the manner in which he is overcoming his background. Dad admires men who can clamber their way up."

"I think he's in the wrong business. He should be an Episcopalian minister. He'd be perfect in that role. He's just masculine enough to make a commanding pulpit appearance, attract the young mothers, and draw a good congregation for the midweek matins."

"That's the masculine point of view. He's a fine young man who may go far, but he's not the person most girls would pick out for a husband. I'm afraid it would be a lifetime job trying to keep up with his ideals. Most girls want a partner with one or two faults . . . for them to work on. How would any girl keep up with the standards Bart represents?"

"Well," Ralph said with an exhalation of relief, "this is a new Miss Pollard." He rose and drew her toward the sofa. "I never believed I'd hear you take this line with our young Sir Galahad."

"Sir Galahad was a warrior, as I recall. Bart isn't geared that way. He'll never win any prizes for patriotism, but he'll never give the enemy aid or comfort."

Macintosh shot the girl an equivocal glance as they selected their positions on the sofa. Cynthia sat with her feet tucked under her skirt, and then looked around for her drink.

"You're quite right. Bart means well but his platitudinous attitude reminds me of a Salvation Army street gathering. He'll never learn to face reality, and for that reason I don't think he'll ever become a prosperous architect. You have to face uncompromising structural and material stress in that business."

"You may have a point. We'll probably never hear from him once he finishes school," she said somberly.

"He'll turn up for Alumni Week every five years. That crowd always does." He completed the denunciation. "By the way, what have you been doing with yourself lately? You've been among the missing for a couple of weeks. Your father keeping you on the treadmill?"

She sensed the probe, and searched his eyes for a clue. "Well, I'm the only one he trusts with certain phases of the firm's production. We have a lot of secret work going on at the Camden plant, you know."

"No, I don't know." Ralph produced an enigmatic grin. "Perhaps if I did I could make some nice pocket money— if I knew the right people in the German government."

46

She twisted her head to indicate puzzlement. "I had never thought of that," she said, spacing her words.

"Why should you?"

"Had you?"

"Not until just now when you mentioned the work going on down in Camden. By that I mean I can see how someone who was down on his uppers might see an opportunity to 'sell' a little information where it was in demand. After all, it wouldn't be . . . treason, or providing comfort to an enemy. We're not at war with Germany."

"Very interesting, but why did you think of selling information to Germany?" she inquired with an expression of faint interest.

"Well, anything your father's firm would be producing would almost automatically be made available to the British, wouldn't it? Of course, if you know of any firms that are producing war equipment for the Germans . . ." He produced a false chuckle. "I mean, how could they get it over there?"

"Ah, the British blockade!" Cynthia said with some sudden enthusiasm. "No, it would be very difficult to get war matériel into Germany from here, wouldn't it?"

He nodded somberly. "That is, unless someone produces something that would increase the efficiency of the U-boat menace."

"I'm afraid you're not making yourself clear."

"Simple. If the German submarine warfare program could be made as effective against warships of the British navy as they seem to be against cargo-carrying merchantmen, it would be comparatively easy to break through the naval blockade. There wouldn't be any question as to who would win the war then. England's life line would be severed, and Germany would be able to purchase vital stocks—rubber, copper, lubricants, and even food—from United States sources."

This was getting interesting, and Cynthia decided to pay out the skein. "But suppose . . . just suppose the British,

47

or the French, developed a device that would cancel out the submarine. I mean, some secret device that would make the U-boat a simple target . . . easier to find?"

Ralph gave her another searching glance as he finished his lemonade. "Don't get me wrong. Personally, I'm not interested. The spy game takes more brains than I have. But to someone vitally concerned, anything that would affect the submarine menace, or the information concerning it, would put a man on Easy Street for the rest of his life."

"But if he tripped over his own feet," Cynthia spelled out carefully, "he might wind up against a wall, a bandage around his eyes, and a firing squad rattling their rifle bolts." She studied the effect of her words, and then with a flash of pumps and silk stockings, she twisted to sit erect, glanced at her glass, and proclaimed, "Oh dear! This party is becoming too solemn. Let me go see what I can find in the way of more interesting refreshment."

Ralph eagerly held out his glass. "I was wondering when we were going to get off this Billy Sunday routine. I'll have a double scotch . . . some of your father's Old Antiquarian."

"Right. A double scotch, and I'll have a brandy and soda. Be right back."

With generous dollops, mixed to loosen a tongue and release inhibitions, the rest of the evening became a revealing experience, particularly for Cynthia, who had substituted ginger ale for the brandy and soda. Plying her wiles, and probing with casual indifference, she turned Macintosh into a puppet plaything. He was relaxed, content, and pleasantly satisfied with himself and the prospects of his future, but he thoughtlessly disclosed many of his inner reflections. Not that he made any definite statements or revealed any categorical intent, but to Cynthia Pollard there was no question that Ralph Macintosh was sailing under false colors.

She went to bed seething with indignation and fully determined to bring this treacherous man to her concept of justice.

48

Sunday morning brought a soft spring rain to bathe the faint dust from leaves, reeds, and blossoms. A low toneless tonk came from some country belfry, calling the righteous to their pews. There was no stirring in the air, but a few catbirds flitted back and forth across the pattern of the formal gardens of the Pollard estate, imitating their mockingbird relations and arousing the ire of the bluejays. Garlands of primroses were strung across the fronts of the flower beds, and the tulip-jonquil-narcissus parade was in full marching order.

Poppies waved their heads over abandoned trenches in Flanders and along the roads of the Somme area. That countryside too was filled with seasonal majesty. Mustard had spread a carpet of gold through the meadows, with patches of red clover that reminded one of the blood seeping through the muslin of a first-aid kit. The hedges of Picardy, drenched with early summer scents, also wore white patches of elderberry blossom. French women and children tossed sweet hay with wooden pitchforks, and then stopped to wave at men in khaki who marched along the bordering roads. The British army was moving up for another big push.

Shipley Pollard, a tall man with stooped shoulders, a flat stomach, and great, spatulate hands, sat at his breakfast. Between portions of sausage and sips of coffee he read from his newspaper or talked absently to Mrs. Budge.

"Has Mrs. Pollard been down, Mrs. Budge?" he inquired while he vetted the weather report.

"Yes, sir. She was early—smoked haddock again."

"Not again? . . . It's raining, I understand."

"Yes, sir. Has been since about half after seven, but it's only a light shower, you might say."

"I suppose we need it."

"The lawns and gardens do."

"Of course."

"A little rain never hurt anybody, sir."

"You're quite right, Mrs. Budge."

49

"It's good of you to say so, sir."

"Has Miss Cynthia been about?"

"She came back late yesterday afternoon. Haven't you seen her?"

"Not a sight or sound. Where's she been?"

"I don't know, sir, but she had some of the boys here last night. Mr. Crispin and Mr. Macintosh, it was, sir."

Mr. Pollard looked up and turned his pale blue eyes on Mrs. Budge. His face was work-lined, but years of good barbering had produced an aristocratic patina to his skin. A careful diet and regular massage had trimmed his figure to a tailor's delight. "Young Crispin was here? I wish I had known. I like young Bartley. Fine chap, that one."

"Yes, sir. He left early, but Mr. Macintosh stayed quite late."

"Ah, he would. Has my daughter been down?"

"No, sir, but I heard her taking her bath. She should be here any minute."

"I wish she would. I'd like to . . ."

"You sit still, sir. I'll pop upstairs and see if I can prod her along a bit."

"That would be nice, Mrs. Budge. Use the long poker in the den."

The maid drew to a halt, considered the suggestion, and after some thought concluded that Mr. Pollard was having one of his jokes. Still, one never knew in this house.

Five minutes later Cynthia, in a blue and white lawn dress, fluttered into the breakfast room. She darted to her father and embraced him affectionately. Mrs. Budge shuffled into her post at the buffet.

"Good morning, Dad." She cupped his face in her hands. "How's the big, bad, munitions tycoon?"

He drew back, looked his daughter over and, satisfied with the inspection, said, "I don't know. I haven't read all of the paper. It doesn't do to make any rash decision until all the reports are in. Who knows, I might find myself topping the obituary page."

Cynthia winked at Mrs. Budge and stroked her father's thick mane before she took her seat. "That reminds me. I came across a picture in the New York *Globe* the other day." She shook out her serviette. "It showed a criminal type, who looked startlingly like you, being hauled off to Sing Sing. I was just saying to myself, 'Well, they've caught up with the old boy at last. Now things should simmer down a bit,' but then I took another look and it was only someone involved in a mild case of body-snatching. Nothing really interesting."

Mrs. Budge stood in an attitude of frozen horror.

"Body-snatching? Not really my line," Mr. Pollard countered, and returned to his paper. This was standard dialogue when he and his daughter got together. They both delighted in gallows humor transposed into plausible conversation. "I've always had a yearning to secrete a jazz band in the foliage whenever some Tammany politico is being lowered into his grave. I think the idea has possibilities."

Mrs. Budge was taken with a spasm of hiccoughs.

"Here, here," Cynthia soothed, and bounced to her feet. "You pack off to the kitchen. We'll be going on like this all through the society pages. After all, we haven't seen each other for about ten days."

Mrs. Budge shuffled off, wiping a dewdrop from her nose with a corner of her apron. "Fair upsets me, it does, the way you two go on," she managed as her departure line.

"Poor Budgie. I believe she takes everything we say as gospel," Cynthia murmured as she doled out her breakfast. "Where's Mother?"

"I don't know. It's too unpleasant for gardening. She's probably raising hell at church."

"With smoked haddock on her breath as usual?"

"Probably. I hear you had young Crispin here last night. I would have liked to see him."

"He couldn't stay long. Had to pedal back to see someone about that Rhodes scholarship."

"A fine boy. He'll be a credit to Princeton."

"I agree, but don't hope to shove him into your business. He's going to be a great architect. He doesn't like the munitions business. He doesn't like war in any sort of a package," Cynthia explained over her fruit.

"Not many people do, but someone has to face up to it . . . and see it through. At least, I hope they do."

"Ralph Macintosh has volunteered with the Royal Flying Corps. He's getting a commission on the strength of his flying club training."

"Macintosh?" Mr. Pollard squeaked, screwing up his face in disbelief. "Why the devil would they take him? I wouldn't have him in a labor battalion . . . sweeping up the dugouts. Now if you had said young Crispin had volunteered . . ."

"Not Bart. He's very set against the whole business. We had quite a talk about it last night."

Mr. Pollard returned to his newspaper. "That's too bad. He's the one who should have put in for the Flying Corps. He'd make a damned good man. I've met several British naval fliers at the plant, and they're all out of the same mold as Crispin."

"He wouldn't think of it."

"I'd sooner have him in my squadron, if that's the word, than that faker Macintosh. I can't believe he's volunteered. If he has, I hope they watch him closely."

"Speaking of volunteering," Cynthia began with disarming abstraction, "I've decided to work as an agent for the German authorities—in this country."

The announcement made no immediate impression on her father. He said, "Oh? That should be very interesting."

"I think so too. You don't mind if I let the right/wrong people know that I am consorting with members of the German Embassy, do you?"

He looked past the edge of his paper. "No-o-o. As a matter of fact, it should be a good idea. Does the German Embassy know about this?"

"Oh yes. It seems they have learned of one Belle Goddard,

and some cute arrangements carried out in Sharon, Connecticut . . . some years ago."

He lowered his paper thoughtfully. "How interesting. I take it they approached you and threatened."

"It's the usual approach straight out of *Arsène Lupin*."

"Very funny."

"I had to put on a fast response, fake immediate shock, and gulp down a Bronx to register complete submission. All this in Peacock Alley."

"The poor devil—whoever he was."

"A Captain Gustav von der Osten. He followed me into the Waldorf, introduced himself in the best Ruritanian manner, and then I remembered we had met at the Consulate Ball a few weeks before."

"I must say you get around, considering you are supposed to be my confidential secretary."

"That's the point, Dad. You see, I'm supposed to be able to filch and present them with certain blueprints . . . under the threat of being exposed as spawn of Belle Goddard."

"But . . ." her father tried to expostulate.

"That is not the point. The point is the acoustic torpedo you are perfecting."

His face shimmered into a mild smile. "The acoustic torpedo? The damned thing doesn't work."

"Wonderful!"

"What do you mean, wonderful?"

"You're interrupting, Father," she remonstrated with mock severity. "All you have to do is give me a set of blueprints that have been doctored in the vital spots, and I'll hand them over to Captain von der Osten. They in turn will be turned over to German Naval Intelligence . . ."

Her father warmed up a faint grin. "Faked blueprints ought to drive them mad. How do you think of these capers?"

"It's easy. Von der Osten has it all arranged that German scientists will take one look at the drawings and immediately counter with a weapon or some device that will neutralize your acoustic torpedo. Are they that bright, Dad?"

"If any of them can neutralize what we've put together so far, they must be working over Druid cauldrons and chanting, '*Bubble, bubble, toil and trouble!*' I'm telling you the damn thing doesn't work. It is likely to pick out a whistling peanut engine three miles inshore, instead of the simulated target set out for it. The last one plowed through an amusement park at Penn's Grove, and was last seen heading up the shoot-the-chute."

"That'll be perfect for my first mission. You will have a set of faked blueprints made up?"

"Faked? We've got a kid in our drafting department who would drive Henry Ford batty. He'll give you a set that will have those Heinies gnawing on their slide rules."

"Wonderful. I knew I could rely on you."

He took up his paper again, and then a new thought arose. "By the way, what happens *after* you plant this fake on them?"

"Oh, they'll probably be months figuring out that they've been flummoxed, and in the meantime I can be thinking up some other didos."

"You're mixing up in a very risky business, you know. The war isn't being run by Quakers. These Germans are playing for keeps, not for marbles. You can get yourself in some very unpleasant situations."

"I can handle these squareheads, and besides, I don't like foreigners accepting our hospitality and using us to fight their horrid war. I'd like to show them we can be just as clever as they think they are. You know something? I never did like their Goddamn sauerkraut. It's damned good cabbage spoiled!" she raged.

"Your vocabulary is improving, I must say," her father concluded. "I think you'd make a fine confidential secretary. Should you ever think of taking it up, I hope you'll let me know."

"Please pass the marmalade."

CHAPTER FIVE

July 1916

*British and French attack north and south of
the Somme. . . . Deutschland, German submarine
freighter, arrives at Baltimore to deliver mercantile
cargo. . . . British use cavalry to penetrate German
second line. . . . Longueval and Pozières occupied
by British. . . . Royal Flying Corps establishes full air
superiority over Somme battlefield. . . . First aerial
operations carried out by combined British and
French air services. . . . Allies advance between Del-
ville Wood and the Somme.*

Bartley Crispin's path, following his graduation, took a
circuitous route. Returning home, he put in a few days repairing a cellar door, reflooring the front porch, whitewash-
ing the cellar, and putting new washers in several leaky
faucets. Over one weekend he returned to Princeton and
called on Cynthia Pollard, but the visit was hardly tumul-
tuous. Cynthia served him lunch, but seemed preoccupied
with pointless activities seen from several windows. She entertained him for half an hour at the piano, but never
finished her selections, and in the middle of "Melody in F"
she suddenly bounced from the piano stool and announced
they would go for a walk.

"I'll change into something—a light cardigan and skirt for
the woods trail. Be right down," she said tonelessly.

When she returned she had also wound a broad bandeau

about her hair, making her look like a gypsy fright. Bart was glad she had decided to avoid the open roads.

Once they were in stride Cynthia brought up the subject of Ralph Macintosh, who had departed on some vacation circuit that included New York City, Washington, D.C., and several resorts along the Eastern Shore of Maryland. It seemed he was making the most of his time before he reported to Toronto, or somewhere in Canada, for his training with the Royal Flying Corps.

"He says there has been some delay in setting up the necessary fields, camps, and schools," Cynthia explained. She had the story down pat and obviously had been in recent communication with the volunteer.

"You still have a warm interest in Ralph, don't you?" Bart said after listening to a long discussion of his itinerary and social stopovers.

"He's a very interesting man, Bart."

"Yes, I suppose he is, now that he has given up a promising career to go to war," Crispin agreed glumly.

"Father is interested in him too," she went on, but did not explain Mr. Pollard's particular curiosity concerning Macintosh.

"Is your father about to acquire some chemical interests?"

"I don't think we'd better discuss my father's business," Cynthia said offhandedly. "He's involved in many military projects of a very secret nature."

He stared at her for several seconds, and wished she'd remove that ridiculous bandeau. "I suppose you're right," he replied morosely.

"I'm not trying to put you off. You are not particularly interested in any phase of national defense, and, well, you'd have to get past the personnel manager. That's the way it is in the war matériel business."

He halted in stride, grabbed her arm, and made her face him. "You know," he began, and fashioned a grin, "for a minute I thought you were kidding me. I simply asked if your father was adding a chemical plant to his holdings,

56

and I wondered if there might be a summer job working on any new factory. Good grief! You don't think I'd try to spy on any of his munitions activities, do you?"

"It isn't what I think, Bart, but a short time ago you said you wouldn't work for a man who manufactured war products. Now suddenly you're seeking employment on one of my father's construction jobs."

Bart was unable to make sense of this attitude. He'd never seen her like this before. There must be some explanation. Or was this just a lead-up to close out their campus companionship? Not that that was important, but was she about to announce that she and Ralph Macintosh were to become engaged, and perhaps married before he went over to England? If so, good luck to them both. They'd all been friends for four years but he had never entertained the faintest idea of marrying into the Pollard family. It was completely out of the question.

"Look, Cynthia. Let's talk sense. My viewpoint concerning the right or wrong of war is something over which I have no control. None of us has. It has nothing to do with love of country, or whether the Allies or Germany win the war. You seem to be emotionally concerned, because of Ralph, and you think every able-bodied American should feel as you do. But you do not have to go over there and face machine-gun fire, clouds of poison gas, bursts of shrapnel, or even risk a trip across the ocean. All this maternal concern for anyone who volunteers to fight is creditable—understandable, but it doesn't emerge from logical thinking."

"Should we have one verse and a chorus of 'I Didn't Raise My Boy to Be a Soldier'?" she taunted.

"That's not fair. There are two phases to war, particularly this kind of war. At the moment you are enjoying the first . . . when with tossed flowers and gay laughter young girls send their loved ones off to fight the common enemy. That has been a standard recruiting lithograph since 1914 on both sides of the line. Everyone cheers that tableau, but

57

then they turn the page and come across the second phase when their heroes come home in ambulances, on stretchers, hobbling on rifles used as crutches, or being led by their companions because they have been blinded."

Cynthia stood firm and met his challenge, eye to eye.

"Now there is no waving of flags. No one tosses flowers into train windows. Reality has set in. No one wants to embrace a man who has had much of his face shot away. Who is eager to lead a blind man up to a church altar? What girl wants to take a crippled man for a walk through the woods? Who wants to share the lot of a man who for the rest of his life will have to live on a disablement pension?"

"You have apparently made a serious study of the situation," Cynthia said, and wrenched herself from his strong hands.

"I have thought a great deal about the war and the possibility of our getting into it. I have not ignored my responsibility. I just can't see any sane reason for getting into such a savage carnage. We ought to stay clear, avoid any foreign entanglements, and in that way make sure no decent, able-bodied American is killed, or maimed for life, in a conflict that has absolutely no justification. I tell you, we should be above war. Ever since the Revolution of 1776 we have shown ourselves as a nation far superior to any other—anywhere, and to share in this tribal bloodletting will only drag us down to their common level."

"Would you stand by and watch an enemy invade our country, ravage our cities, shell undefended areas, and mow down civilians as they are driven from their homes?"

"I don't know what I would do, but that is not the point."

"It is in France, Belgium, and Great Britain. That is what has happened over there. It could happen here."

"I don't see how . . . unless we stick our noses into a fracas that doesn't concern us."

"Humanity . . . our civilization concerns us, doesn't it? Isn't that worth fighting for?"

He rubbed his knuckles along the curve of his jaw. A partridge whirred up from a low thicket to distract their attention from her brood, which was fluttering in the opposite direction. A cottony cloud spread a filter across the golden sunshine. It was one hell of a way to enjoy a hike in the woods with an attractive girl. Humanity . . . civilization. How can people respond and share simple companionship when a blasted war, three thousand miles away, can set up such a disruptive field of influence? He tried to put the discourse aside by recalling what life was like back in 1912 when he had graduated from high school.

That was a glorious June, one designed for young love and promises of eternal devotion. Coupled off, they gathered daisies along the borders of the hayfields and decorated the Methodist Church for the graduation exercises. There had been one afternoon of breathless excitement while selecting their class rings, and then facing the problem of paying for them. There had been a ball game, and the girls served lemonade, gallons of it. One night they even staged a dance, just like the college crowd, at the Odd Fellows' Hall. They borrowed the dominie's Columbia phonograph and must have played the "Kerry Mills Barn Dance" a dozen times.

A teacher got up a trip to Verona Lake and some of the boys tried to paddle canoes. Two of the girls were dumped overboard, and a nice old lady on the other side of the lake took the bedraggled students in and found dry things for them. Within an hour they were screeching from the up-and-down horses of the merry-go-round in white voile confirmation dresses from another era. The class valedictorian, between licks of a taffy apple, declaimed they looked like equestrian Loreleis.

His montage of reverie was dissolved by Cynthia's continued insistence that the war was America's business, and that everyone ought to take a vital interest in it.

He tried to swing the subject into another channel; anything to switch from this gnawing crusade.

59

"By the way," he said, cocking his head to one side, "what do you intend to do if we get into the mess?"

Cynthia considered the question for several strides, hating herself for treating Bart so cruelly, but there was little choice if she was to carry out her commitments. "I have some incomplete plans," she said with deliberation, "but there are so many probables, and I won't discuss any of it at this time."

"You seem to be in New York a lot."

"Just shopping, mostly."

"Shopping? I thought you patronized the shops along Fifth Avenue. I saw you entering the North German Lloyd Line's shipping office down near the Battery the other day. I happened to be in that area getting a British visa on my passport."

"I'm afraid you made a mistake. You must have seen someone who looks like me."

"But I saw you. You were wearing that . . . what do you call it? . . . hound's-tooth check dress, your tam on one side of your head, and you carried a large brown cardboard folder under one arm. I couldn't have been mistaken."

"I haven't been in that section of New York for months and months!"

"I tried to call to you, but the traffic was particularly heavy. I would have followed you in, but I had an appointment with a British consular official. I figured you were on some business for your father."

"Ridiculous!" she snapped, her eyes sparking with her denial. "My father wouldn't have any dealings with a German shipping line. Why would I be going in there? I wouldn't be seen . . ."

Bartley was puzzled, for she had never behaved in such a deceitful manner before. What did it matter that she had been seen entering an office of a well-known German shipping firm? Dozens of people were hurrying up those steps, but Cynthia was a standout. He'd know her anywhere, particularly in that black and white checked dress. Why was she denying so vehemently she had been in that section of New York?

"Very well. I may have been mistaken—which is what you want me to say."

"Of course you were. I'm not likely to risk being seen in association with a German commercial firm, considering the standing of the Pollard industries . . ."

"*Risk* being seen?" he queried, completely off base. "You're making an ominous, spy-thriller situation out of nothing. Have we reached the point where no one can be seen in the vicinity of a German office building without being tagged as an enemy agent?"

"Well, that's how enemy agents work, isn't it? They have to gather information and turn it over to contacts working under cover of a perfectly legal mercantile establishment," she said as though trying to remember a recent dream.

"I wouldn't know. I'm not interested in such cheap melodrama. All I asked was what you intend to do if the warmongers get us into this European mess."

"You wouldn't be interested," she stated coldly, and wished she could tell him exactly what she intended to do if America found herself in the war. Bartley Crispin, she knew, was one person she wished she could confide in—except . . .

He rammed his clenched fists against his temples. "This is the damnedest, silliest, most unbelievable conversation I've ever been mixed up in," he charged. "Of course I'm interested. I've always been interested in you, Cynthia. We've had a long friendship, although our social levels are miles apart, but I can't help being interested in you. If you go into something to do with the war, I shall want to know where you are and what you are doing. That's natural, isn't it? Friends such as we just don't drop each other because of differences of opinion. I wish you'd take me into your confidence. I haven't many close friends, you know."

"I can't talk about my plans," she stated stiffly, and fingered the kiltie fringe running down the side seam of her skirt. "I think we'd better go back now."

"Yes, I suppose we should. We don't seem to be making the most of this refreshing hike. You probably have plans for the rest of the day."

"Well . . . I am expecting an important telephone call."

"I hate telephones," Bart snarled. "But let's head back. I should be starting for home anyway."

"You have quite some time before you leave for England, I suppose."

"I can use plenty. I hope to get a job of some sort. I'll need extra money for my passage . . . and suitable clothes for Oxford. I understand they're very clothes-conscious there."

"Very. In fact, nearly two-thirds of the student body is in khaki—taking various cadet courses to become officers in the British army. More than five hundred Oxford boys have given their lives for their country." Cynthia had no idea why she was reciting these harrowing statistics.

"Is that so?" he replied soberly. "I suppose that is the price of glory. I don't wish to die for *my* country. I want to live for it, and make my contribution to its future, its structure, and its standard of living."

The city of Toronto was a revelation to Ralph Macintosh. He found the spirit of battle at high pitch, and a determination to take part in some branch of the service was apparent in every man who could pass a physical or wangle his way into khaki or navy blue.

To those who experienced it, there never again will be such a period of national pride, patriotism, or trust in victory, though this universe continues to twirl for another million years.

By the time he had checked in, filled out the necessary papers, and considered himself in the baggy raiment initially supplied to all cadet volunteers, Princeton could have been ten thousand miles away. Already, it was little more than a vague memory, an indistinct dream, an experience with no touch of nostalgia. The war in Canada could lift a man from total obscurity to a bubbly sense of personal superiority.

Most of the candidates for the Royal Flying Corps were Canadians with a sprinkling of transplanted Britons who had crossed the border from the United States. There also were several Americans who had noted the writing on the wall, and a few United States Army and Navy personnel sent up to absorb as much primary training in military aviation as possible until their country could build a few air-training centers of its own. Although Woodrow Wilson had been re-elected to the presidency on the halfhearted claim that he "had kept America out of the war," German submarines were ending all hopes of peace. It would take only the impact of the Zimmermann telegram to tilt the United States into the conflict some months later.

The group that included Ralph Macintosh had been accommodated in the last car of the Montreal Express, and they eventually had arrived in Toronto. Before they had shucked out of their civilian clothes and tried on their first uniforms they had been quickly assembled on the parade ground of the University of Toronto for a sampling of British physical jerks. A Sergeant Trewarren, who boasted of some obscure association with the Coldstream Guards, and who later became widely known as Sergeant Tindrawers, took over this segment of their early training—and left his mark; one that would have shocked Rudyard Kipling. There were hours, weeks, and months of conditioning drill and footslogging between lectures where reams and reams of notes were taken, and immediately forgotten.

The early ground school program was made up of courses in military law, theory of flight, engines, rigging, machine guns, bombsights, aerial photography, and meteorology. Little of it was of any practical use, but the classes kept the cadets off the streets and under some military supervision. The courses were delivered from notebooks by totally bored Canadian and British officers who were presumed to have put in some service on the front line. What

63

the cadets were taught had to be completely unlearned once they reached flying schools in Great Britain, where they came under the supervision of instructors from the august Central Flying School.

Perhaps because of his previous exposure to an aeroplane, Ralph Macintosh was among those selected for an immediate commission, and with this subaltern preference "pip" he managed to evade most of the mud, ground school attendance, and parade ground discipline. He even avoided the discomfort of standard quarters, setting himself up in a small suite in the Queen's Hotel. The telephone kept him in touch with the training program, and he turned up whenever he felt it expedient to be on hand.

During his spare time he used his rank to inspect service files then being organized by NCO clerks, and because of his Sam Browne belt was able to take copious notes openly, remove photographs and ballistic charts on the premise that he was preparing new instruction books for the incoming classes of cadets. Ralph Macintosh's time brackets were perfect, and no one questioned his seemingly logical explanation.

In other instances he obtained permission to make a junior officer's inspection of several Toronto plants that were producing military equipment, ammunition, small arms, and component parts for aircraft. He was especially interested in anything relating to new planes that were being designed and built for the British aviation services. Because he was *Lieutenant Macintosh,* a surname held in solemn reverence throughout the Province of Ontario, he was shown more than the average junior officer would have been permitted to view.

He was welcomed into chemical plants and advised of the "secret" formulas for propulsives, smoke screens, lachrymatory gases, and the explosives used in trench-mining operations. The factory executives were fascinated with his basic knowledge in this field, and his "inside" information on what the enemy was doing in chemical warfare assured them they were entertaining a clever young man, one who would go a long way before the war was over.

Lieutenant Macintosh was Canada's white-haired boy when it came to providing important information—all of which eventually reached a man named Stosselmeyer in New York City. How it got there was an interesting point and proved that military espionage was not as intricate as readers of spy stories might assume.

Macintosh's routine was first to prepare his "cover," a class paper purporting to give full data on the latest British two-seater fighter; the new device for increasing the rate of fire of a Vickers gun; the prospects for a more compact wireless transmitter for aircraft use; or an advanced method of increasing the compression of a Hispano-Suiza engine. Watered-down versions of these various subjects were suitably mounted in folders and presented to the presiding instructor, who recognized that in this rookie Macintosh he had the ideal student-lecturer; and he willingly stood aside and permitted the young American to take over the afternoon's program. In a short time Lieutenant Macintosh was an outstanding figure in his particular course, and there was some inside talk that he was to be awarded the D.S.O. After all, a good many kiwi officers in the R.F.C. had received the ribbon for far less important contributions.

But while the administrative staff was enthusiastic about Macintosh's constructive interest in their preliminary training course, the man from Princeton was working in his small suite high in the Queen's Hotel on Front Street, preparing more detailed versions of his class papers. The hotel management accepted the explanation that he was engaged in highly technical work for the British government, and supplied him with a table and typewriter. He was an officer, and his name was Macintosh.

As soon as the larger brochures were completed, they were inserted in well-gummed and wax-sealed envelopes, and then—strangely enough—were placed in the charge of a pimply-faced dishwasher employed in the kitchen of the Queen's, who would then wrap them in a soiled apron and saunter along Front Street to the old Union Station where they were turned over to an Egon Kospsch, head-waiter of the Toronto Limited's dining car. When the train arrived at Grand Central Station in New York Captain von der Osten was always on hand. In this not too involved manner Macintosh's contributions were delivered to Stos-selmeyer, who was supposed to be a passenger executive with the North German Lloyd Line.

It was through these operations that Macintosh was able to maintain a suite at the Queen's, have a substantial ac-count at the Royal Bank of Canada, and remain a floating volunteer in the Royal Flying Corps's busy development of its air training center. When he had milked the ground school course of all available free time, he reluctantly moved out to the Armor Heights flying school where ground conditions, winter storms, and inclement weather afforded more opportunity for his "inspection" operations in the area encompassing Hamilton, St. Catharines, Brantford, London, Chatham, and Windsor. And so, while undergoing another primary flight-training course aboard joysticked Jennys or the Canucks with their monstrous wheel controls, he produced more than a dozen new pamphlets on modern military equipment "to be used in the R.F.C. training courses," while his more elaborate and revealing compila-tions warmed the Teutonic cockles of Herr Stosselmeyer's heart.

Because of his many contributions to the training pro-gram, Lieutenant Macintosh found himself delegated to additional training intended to turn him into a flight in-structor. In fact, he willingly volunteered for anything that would keep him from being transferred to the proposed Canadian-American fields in Texas where weather and ground conditions were more suited to flight training.

Had it not been for an urgent call for trained pilots from the Canadian schools to fill some of the gaps in the advanced training courses in England, Lieutenant Macintosh might have ended his war still milking Ontario factories of their research and development plans for Herr Stosselmeyer. However, Britain had plenty of new planes in reserve, but there was a critical shortage of pilots, so the Canadian program was combed for promising material, and to his secret dismay Lieutenant Ralph Macintosh headed a small contingent of rookie pilots who were shipped aboard the Royal Mail Steamer *Megantic* for Liverpool.

This upheaval threatened to disrupt the Macintosh-Von der Osten-Stosselmeyer network, but before the *Megantic* had taken in her hawsers at Halifax, it was appreciated that Macintosh was moving into a more productive heath. He was still a British officer in good standing; he would arrive in England wearing his "wings," although he had so far flown nothing more offensive than the Curtiss JN-4; he would be free to roam a new and complete pattern of aerodromes, factories, defense areas, and study at first hand anything new the British aircraft manufacturers were preparing to turn over to front-line squadrons. If he could continue his production of training pamphlets, he could double or triple his value to the German cause.

Before the *Megantic* had dropped anchor in the Mersey, Stosselmeyer had a new plan of action drawn up for Macintosh. One feature was that he should make a determined effort to become a recognized test pilot, one who would be transferred from factory to factory, so as to glean full and immediate details on every new plane that had reached the prototype stage of its development. In particular, it was desired that he check out a new two-seater that was said to be coming from the Bristol Aeroplane factory.

If the role of test pilot could not be managed immediately, it might be wise for him to volunteer for ferry pilot work, which also offered a wide range of "inspections" and study while ferrying new aircraft from the factories to the aircraft parks in France. There were many openings for a man named Macintosh, a man with a commission, a man who boasted quietly that he could fly anything if it had an engine in it.

At the same time Cynthia Pollard, who felt she had completed her task for Captain von der Osten, wondered whether she might use the contact to induce him to assign her to more important duties—in Great Britain, for example. Ever since the night that Ralph Macintosh had made his faux pas involving the name of Stosselmeyer, she had yearned to check on his activities, particularly since he eventually would turn up in England or on the Continent.

It would have been simple to arrange to go to Britain on some secretarial errand for her father. His firm was associated with one or two concerns over there through a number of manufacturing licenses, and these contacts would have permitted visits into various sections of the United Kingdom, but this would not have been in the spirit of her quest. She wanted to go over there as a bona fide German agent—at least as far as Captain von der Osten was concerned—to play a role that had first occurred to her that afternoon at the Waldorf.

She brought up the matter at lunch with the captain, and he considered the idea as he cut his grilled chop. The suggestion had considerable merit, he explained, but they would have to learn the outcome and value of her information concerning the acoustic torpedo before giving her another assignment.

"By the way," he said after some further discussion, "I'm somewhat puzzled by your continued interest. I asked only for a certain set of blueprints. You have produced them, and as far as I am concerned, the deal has been completed."

She pursed her lips, pondered, and selected her words carefully. "I rather like the inner fervor of this sort of thing. No, I am not taking it as some sort of game. Actually, my life is luxurious, but very tame. My parents are what are known as solid citizens, which means sedate and unspec-

68

tacular. This is all I have ever known, and when you brought up the Belle Goddard incident I experienced an amazing thrill. I found I was an entirely new person."

He sat listening, not quite certain what she was trying to say.

"It's like this. I have been to the best schools. I have had a sheltered, uninspired life with a staff of servants to take care of me. Suddenly, you come along and sever all those stodgy ties, and I find I am another person entirely. All my old associates mean nothing. I am in search of something or someone new. This whole prospect is bubbling up inside me, and I have . . . I simply have to respond."

"Don't you feel some responsibility to your father, or your family?"

She threw out her hands and overturned her water glass. A waiter moved in and dabbed at the damage.

"Dad and I are pals," she continued. "I love associating with him, but it's really not work. None of this can possibly hurt him. He will still make munitions and sell them where there is a demand. That is, he will as long as the war goes on, but I want to live my life. Many of my friends are going into various phases of war work—regardless of their background, education, or what their parents think."

"But for you to act as a German agent, that is . . ."

"Why not? I can't spy for the Allies. I don't speak German, and my French is fit only for the tourist circuit. Working with you, I stand some sort of a chance—particularly in England. I owe England nothing. I'm an American and I reserve the right to throw in my lot with either side."

"But suppose you make the one mistake . . . suppose you are apprehended? The Scotland Yard men are not fools."

"That's the chance I'll take. If I'm shown up, my parents can always shuck me off by explaining, 'Well, what can you expect from a spawn of Belle Goddard?' and that will be that. But I'm determined to have a fling at it."

"You are willing to take the risk?"

"I'll take the risk. I think it will be fun."

Over the next few days Captain von der Osten wondered what was happening to him. He had not expected this contact to work out like this. It was almost too good to be true, and yet, stranger situations had poured important information into his hopper on several occasions. One never knew in this exciting game.

CHAPTER SIX

January 1917

Turkey declares its independence of suzerainty of European powers. . . . Ivernia, Cunard liner, is sunk in the Mediterranean. . . . President Wilson suggests to the belligerents a "peace without victory." . . . Germany announces intention of sinking all vessels in war zone around British Isles. . . . Seaplane carrier Ben-my-Chree sunk off Kastelorrizon, Asia Minor. . . . British transfer responsibility of aircraft supplies to Ministry of Munitions. . . . Sergeant Thomas Mottershead, pilot of Number 20 Squadron, R.F.C., awarded Victoria Cross for gallantry while flying F.E. 2b pusher biplane.

Oxford was as much a puzzle to Bartley Crispin as Toronto had been to Ralph Macintosh. Not only did he find himself in a foreign country, one in the tragic throes of a continental war, but there was little academic atmosphere to provide the illusion of university learning. There was nothing of the American campus spirit, and over the first four months Bart walked through the motions of scholarship with the air of a man just aroused from a tangled dream.

Assigned to the respectable, if rather dreary, Aldrich College of the university, he soon realized that most of his fellow students were "civvies," undergraduates who were there for the special Architectural Association's course of municipal architecture. None was in the dominant khaki, for most of them lacked the physical requirements for the military, or they were more mature types who were determined to complete their education before the war snatched them from their drawing boards. Because of their interest in conjectural reconstructions of Assyrian gateways, or the transition from posts and lintel to the Gothic arch, they were the outcasts of the university, for, so it seemed to Bartley, Oxford had been completely reorganized for the education and discipline of the Royal Flying Corps.

Only the architectural students and the "swots" who delved in English literature, Greek hieroglyphics, and Latin translations moved about in mufti with academic gowns worn loosely on their shoulders. The dons in mortarboards and flowing garb cycled about the town, seemingly unaware of the khaki explosion that had shattered the centuries-old calm of the Isis institutions. A few divinity students, wearing thick-lensed spectacles, peered at the strange activities of companies of young men in khaki with white linen bands around the crowns of their hats as they marched in stiff cadence, doubled from lecture halls to dining areas, performed exhausting physical jerks, or dog-trotted through the streets with notebooks and drawing instruments under their arms.

Aldrich offered a good kitchen, a free and easy system of registration, kept merely by being in residence. There were no roll calls or required chapel attendance. It was also free of freshman college spirit. There was no hooliganism. It was a tolerant, civilized berth where one could lead whatever kind of life appealed to him. The buildings were nondescript and typical of a college that had been in existence since 1874 when it was endowed by Lord Wentworth, who had made a tremendous fortune erecting workers' cottages in the slag-smudged areas of the Scottish coal fields. It was ironic that his contribution to education should be funneled into a school to teach classic architecture.

During his first few weeks Bartley lived unobtrusively. He made few friends. Most of his associates were working hard, perhaps to ignore the militant activities going on around them. Now and then he was asked to tea by some lonely senior students. He tried going to church but the Anglican service bewildered him, so he turned to the regular sessions of reading in the Bodleian Library, or writing long letters to Cynthia Pollard. Few were answered, and she seemed to have no news of any interest or importance. Only Doc Poultney found time to fill him in on what was going on at Princeton.

Bart's rooms were modest, fairly comfortable, and reasonably close to the lecture halls. They were over a college bakery from where the haunting odors of hot dough, sardines and toast, and honey buns continually distracted him while he tried to read Kimball and Edgell's four-volume *History of Architecture,* or flipped through the *Architect's Journal.* One feature he found difficult to relish was the commons lunch, which usually consisted of bread, cheese, and beer—small fresh-baked loaves, wedges of ripe cheese, and a bitter ale drawn from the cask into silver tankards. Afternoon tea was served in the students' rooms by assigned "scouts." Most of the architectural students took their dinners in hall where the food, from the British point of view, was good—and cheap. Now and then when funds permitted, Bart tried dining out at the George Restaurant on the corner of George and Cornmarket streets, and once or twice he patronized the dining room at the legendary Mitre Hotel.

But these impulsive excursions often led him into groups of noisy R.F.C. cadets, most of whom were volunteers from every regiment in the British contingent. There were many lean, hard-bitten Australians; Scots from a score of clans, wearing bonnets, kilts, or trews; dour South Africans with Boer backgrounds, but more than willing to fight the

73

Germans if they could get into the Royal Flying Corps. There were tall, erect, pink-cheeked New Zealanders, the world's best-behaved warriors, who studiously avoided the bold, brash Aussies. There were hundreds of Canadians from Canuck cavalry squadrons, artillery batteries, or the engineers, but seemingly few native Englishmen.

Crispin pondered on this latter point, mentally approaching the general opinion that England was ever willing to have her blood relations fight her wars for her. He was sitting on one of the high benches surrounding the billiard room at the Clarendon Hotel. Beside him hunched a young soldier, wearing a county Yeomanry uniform, who watched the triangular paths of the balls under the glare of the overhead lights. He was broad-shouldered, lean of cheek, and determined of jaw. His responsive fingers telegraphed his keen interest in the progress of the match. He turned to Bart to state, "That chap has a nice touch. Ran up twenty-eight, if I figured right."

"A very nice run, I'd say," agreed Bart, and then asked, "are you English?"

"Right! Wiltshire, me."

"You've transferred to this flying service?"

"Bloody right. I've had enough of the trenches an' the back-area buggering about."

"Not many English lads seem to go for flying . . . I mean, they all seem to be from the colonies."

"You're an American, aren't you? Maybe a Canadian?"

"American. I'm over here on a Rhodes scholarship."

"Ah, that explains it. That's the way it looks. That I agree, mate, but you see it isn't easy for an Imperial soldier to get a transfer. Hundreds of 'em try it every day, but their COs won't hear of it. Canadians, South Africans, New Zealanders . . . anybody else can make it, but not Tommy Atkins."

"So that explains it," Crispin said after some consideration.

74

The Wiltshire lad with the tired eyes looked Bart over carefully. "What's it feel like to be in civvies?"

"It's rather uncomfortable here at Oxford, but I plan to stay in them as long as I can."

"It's been a long time for me, but I don't blame you for . . . er, staying in school. If you'd seen what I've seen, you'd be looking for a soft berth in Tibet, or one of them islands in the Pacific. That's why I bunged in for the R.F.C."

"But you managed a transfer. . . . How?"

"I don't quite know. Someone must have felt sorry for me, or else I was one bloke they could let go and never miss. Usually when one of our men puts in for a transfer, they argue that they can't spare trained men, or men with long experience at the front. Of course, if you were one of 'em who had slacked off until conscription"—he spat out the word—"you'd be welcomed into the R.F.C. mob. And don't forget, chum, a lot of these boys only put in just to get out of the bloody mud and thud. That includes me. Colonials, they can transfer just by asking, but not British Tommies."

Crispin watched a player go in off the red, and then added, "It's hardly fair, is it?"

"Fair? Nothing's fair with the English. You can be anything in this bloody war but an Englishman. The Jocks do all the bayonet charges. The Irish win all the V.C.s, and the Canadians get all the credit every time we take an enemy salient. Have you ever heard of an English regiment getting credit for even being out there, let alone winning a bloody battle? That's how it goes, mate."

Crispin agreed there was something to what the Wiltshire man said. Then he took up another angle. "Do you think you'll be any better off in the flying service?"

After some deep thought, the Englishman removed his cigarette. "It's like this. In the trenches you don't know what the hell you're doing most of the time. You wait for days for something to happen . . . and it seldom does, but the waiting takes all the guts out of you. That's part of

75

the grief. You're soaking wet and cold most of the time. You're lousy all the time. You're tired, weary, and you know you stink. There's nowhere to lie down, and when you do get a bit comfortable in a funk hole, they wake you up because it's your turn on the firestep. This goes on for fifteen—eighteen days at a time."

"You're in the trenches that long?"

The young Englishman spat again. "At least! But I'm a machine gunner and there's always a shortage of machine guns, or machine-gun teams, so when our mob is relieved, we often have to stay in and support the new blokes because they haven't any machine guns. When there's plenty of guns and ammunition, there's a shortage of machine gunners. War, somehow, is like that."

"Is that why you applied for a transfer?"

"That's some of it. Frankly, I bunged out because I know it'll take months for me to learn to fly. I'm a bloody good machine gunner, mind you, but I've got my napper screwed on right. I know there's something called the law of averages. You know about that?"

"Yes. I see what you mean."

"Well, that's it. I'm not really ducking out. I'm as willing to fight for what's right as anyone, but I think I've had my go at it, and it's only a matter of time before Jerry catches up with me. There's always one shell, one bullet, or one Minnie with your name on it, and if you stay around long enough, it'll find you."

Bartley nodded slowly. "You could be right, but isn't the R.F.C. something of a suicide club? I mean, I've heard the phrase used several times. It must have some element of danger. Just look at the casualty list every day."

The Wiltshire man screwed up his face and took out another fag. "Well, I'll tell you. It used to be, I suppose, when the aeroplanes weren't what they are today. You take it from me, mate, we're giving Jerry a real tanning in the air. I know what I have seen up at the front. It isn't like what it was back in late 1915. It's our turn now, an' while I shouldn't talk like this, we've got new planes that will make him scream bloody murder. Don't ask me about 'em, but you'll see what happens when the weather improves this coming spring."

"I hope so—for your sake."

"You wouldn't want to have a go at this, I suppose?" the young warrior said somewhat morosely, but kept his eyes on the caroming billiard balls. "Not that I blame you, if you don't have to go."

"I don't quite know," Bartley said, feeling a rapport with this stolid, honest Englishman. "Back home when I was in college, I swore I'd never volunteer to fight if my country got into it. I lost several friends because of my attitude, but that was the way I felt. Today, I'm getting a new perspective. . . . I'm reminded of what our track coach at Princeton said the last time I saw him: 'Bartley, I hope you get to Oxford. I hope you absorb all they have to teach you, but I think you'll learn more if you become personally involved in the war. In fact, I think a full-blown war would do you a lot of good.' Funny thing, my suddenly remembering his words."

"Ah, well. Of course he could talk like that, being over there. All the old gaffers pull that sort of line."

Bart looked the yeoman full in the eyes. "Don't get him wrong. A few weeks later he learned that his son, who had volunteered from the United States, had won the Victoria Cross while serving with the London Scottish."

"London Scottish? Then he must be Corporal Alistair Poultney. I know all about him." The Wiltshire man beamed, and then his eyes clouded. "Did he know the rest?"

"The rest?"

"Corporal Poultney was killed the next time he went out to the front. Only a few weeks ago. I remember reading about it in the *Daily Mail*."

"Poor Doc." Crispin stared at the green baize table and watched the marker spot the red.

"You see what I mean about the law of averages? You

have to try to break the sequence, but they don't tell you about that when you take the shilling."

Bartley looked puzzled. "Take the shilling?"

The yeoman smiled for the first time, and clapped Bart on the knee. "It's an old recruiting twist. When you join up, the Color Sergeant gives you a brand-new shilling. It's something of a token. It's like shaking hands with the King, I suppose. Anyway, we all get one, and try to hang onto it—for good luck, like. Most of 'em soon spend it for an extra pint, but I still have mine in the flap of my Pay and Mess book. Want to see it?"

Bartley fondled the silver coin that by now was stained and corroded with the brown dye used in the soldier's personal account book. He held it in the palm of his hand and said with a smile, "I hope it gets you through the war safely. It's done a good job so far, hasn't it?"

"You wouldn't believe it, chum. I've never so much as been scratched. Been in since the first Battle of Ypres, too. A lucky bob, that one." He tucked the coin back into its flap.

"I must remember that," Bart said. "Let's go have a drink."

"Thank you just the same, but I've got to get back and work on my Morse code. I'm a bit dud at the dots an' dashes. Don't seem to be able to cotton onto it at all. Have to keep trying, though. Some other time, eh?"

"Some other time. Perhaps next Saturday night."

"Right on the mark!"

Crispin wandered out of the billiard room, sauntered along a corridor, and found a small taproom. He turned in, ordered a half pint, and took his mug to a small settle, and in the dim wartime light found himself beside another young lad, obviously an undergraduate.

"How do you duck the proctors, being out at this time of night?" the youngster opened after he had studied Crispin for a minute or so.

78

"Oh, I'm at Aldrich. Rhodes grant, taking the architectural course," Bart explained for the second time that night.

The young man stuck out his hand. "American, eh? Well, shake. I think I am too. That is to say . . ." He took a long swig from his tankard.

Bartley tried to figure this out, and then shook hands, after the young man wiped foam from his upper lip. "What am I supposed to make of that statement?"

"My name's Bryce Melville. We're in London, but we have another place out in the Quorn Hunt country."

"Where does the American part come in?"

"Oh," Melville started to explain. He was a tall, well-built young man with a viselike handshake. He had yellow hair in tight curls all over his skull, olive eyes, a small nose, mobile mouth, and a square jaw. He could have been in his early twenties, but Bart sensed he was somewhat younger, for there was a youthful enthusiasm about his eyes. "It's like this," Bryce continued. "First of all, Dad and Mother are native Americans . . . full-blooded, as the saying goes. Dad came over here years ago . . . railroad man. Came over to take on the management of the London and Southwestern Railway to put in American ideas . . . things like that.

"You know how it goes," he explained with some note of apology. "He did damned well, and liked it over here. He became a British subject and old King Edward VII knighted him . . . one of the last things he did before he knocked off."

"Edward or your father?"

"The King. He died in 1910, you know."

"Oh yes. So your father is now a Britisher. Where were you born?"

"In Pennsylvania, Germantown. My sister Dianne was born over there too, so we're both Yanks—or we can claim American citizenship. I don't quite know what Mother is, but she makes the most of the old man's title and lets everyone call her Lady Melville. But, as you see, I'm an American."

"Well, good for you."

"Right now I feel very British, what with this bloody war and everything."

"Can they call you up?"

"Call me up? I wish they would. I've been trying to get into the R.F.C. for the last six months, but I can't get anyone to doctor my birth certificate. I'm a few months under age, and no matter how badly they need blokes for the flying business, they won't let you muck around with your birthdays."

"How old are you?"

"Hardly eighteen. I know I look well over twenty, but it's no good."

"But can't you get into one of these O.T.C. outfits they train at the various colleges?"

"O.T.C.? Who the hell wants that? All you do is drill, wear schoolboy uniforms, and mess about until you are eighteen and a half. That's the youngest you can be to get a commission. O.T.C. is a kid's game. I want to get into the R.F.C. and fly. It must be gorgeous. Bloody fine life, you know, but I have to wait about six months before they'll take me. Seeing all these fellows knocking about, wearing their cheese-cutter hats with the white cap bands, drives me crazy. I don't care whether I fly scouts, artillery spotters, or bombers. I'd even take balloon observing. But I'd love to have a crack at these blasted Zeppelins. Hellish business, that, dropping bombs on open cities, killing women and kids. Did you see the one that chap Leefe Robinson shot down last September?"

"No. I hadn't arrived here yet."

"I saw it. Bloody wonderful . . . blazed all the way down to the ground. That's the stuff to give 'em!" young Melville said spiritedly, and took another swig from his pint.

Bartley studied the youngster from his curly crop to his bottom waistcoat button. "Will they take you in the R.F.C.

if they find out you're really an American?" He knew he was wasting his words.

"Of course they will. They want the bloody railway to work, don't they? The old gent could put a lot of pressure on at Whitehall. The only thing, he can't get past that age-limit stipulation."

"Your father would pull wires to get you in?"

"Bloody right! Christ! He even tried to get in himself . . . in the Royal Engineers as a Railway Construction Officer. They wouldn't stand for that. They argued that he was more valuable here in England."

Crispin managed a faint grin and shook his head.

"By the way, how old are you?" young Melville asked pointedly.

"Old enough to know better. Don't try to ring me in on this joining up."

"I was just wondering."

"War does the damnedest things to people. Why don't you wait to see if America is drawn in? For one thing, the pay would be better, and . . ."

"Pay? What the hell has that to do with it? You don't join up for pay. Who needs pay in the army, or the R.F.C.? They give you your clothes, feed you, and provide the weapons. What more do you want? When you come back on leave, let the bloody civilians take care of your expenses. Who needs pay?"

"But suppose the United States comes in. I should think you'd rather serve in your own country's armed forces. I mean, how would you explain it years later . . . an American fighting in a British uniform?"

"Don't give me any of that 'What did you do in the Great War, Daddy?' You know as well as I do that they have voted Woodrow Wilson in again, and they'll ignore a few more submarine attacks, and still go on making and selling munitions. I'll settle for that too. Let 'em make 'em, and we'll use 'em to bang away at the bloody Jerries."

"You're a real firebrand, aren't you? By the way, who

will pay for all the munitions and supplies when it's all over?"

"Who cares, just as long as we drive the Germans back over the Rhine. The French and British have spilled a lot of blood in the war. Who's going to pay for that, and with what?"

There was a lull in the tirade while young Melville took their empty mugs back to the bar. Crispin winnowed through the paradoxical situation that had been offered in this Old World taproom with its ancient oak paneling, its age-old tang of hops, new sawdust, pungent pipe tobacco, and the ghosts of Oxford's greats weaving in and out of the smoky shadows. They had been discussing the greatest conflict the world was enduring, and he calculated that it was taking place a little more than one hundred miles away; in fact one segment of it was being fought at this minute—only a few thousand feet above the eaves of this hotel. He considered the Zeppelin incident Melville had mentioned, and cringed at the thought of a dozen or more human beings trapped in a grotesque framework, roasting to death as they fell through the flame-streaked sky. He tried to imagine an airship more than six hundred feet long, speeding at sixty miles an hour to deliver thirty tons of high explosive on a town like Oxford. He wondered what an aerial bomb sounded like when it exploded; what a bomb could do to a building like this, and how many of the present patrons would live if the Clarendon were hit.

He weighed the odds against a single-engined biplane flown by a lone pilot, attaining the same height as the airship and shooting it down with less than a hundred rounds of rifle-caliber ammunition. His mathematical mind was enjoying the pros and cons of the problem when his new acquaintance returned and was heard saying:

"What did you say you are doing here?"

"Architecture. I'm on a Rhodes scholarship. Went to Princeton. My name's Bartley Crispin . . . New Jersey."

"Architecture? I didn't know Oxford had such a course."

"It seems to be a tenuous connection with the British Architectural Association; probably arranged to fill in for the Rhodes scholarship grant. That's the best I can make of it."

"Oh, Lord! I'd be suspicious of that. They've packed up several of those temporary courses since they've had to give over so much space to the R.F.C. cadet program. You may not be able to complete . . . what is it, a two-year stint?"

"There are some such rumors, but until they toss us out I'm staying on. It's damned good, so far."

"You must be a top scholar to get a Rhodes deal. You have the odds of me. I'm already fed up with Oxford, but the old gent wants me to take up something that will help me move in and take over when he begins to slow up. What a hope!"

"The war seems to have put you off your stride."

"I'm afraid so, but I'll have to stick it until I can swing over to the R.F.C.," young Melville said soberly. "By the way, what do you do with yourself on weekends?"

"What is there to do? I mope about the town or the countryside. I have a bike, and try to get away from this parade-ground activity. There's really not much a civvy can do, but just keep his nose in the book."

"That won't do at all. What about spending a few days with us in London? My people would love to have you. They like to collect Americans. There's always one or two hanging around whenever I go home. What say, next week-end? I'll warn Mother to dig out her pancake recipe. She may even come up with some Philadelphia scrapple."

"Sounds great!" Crispin responded. "It's a date if your titled folks will have me."

"Forget the title. It made my old man a nicer guy to live with. Actually made him human. He was a bit of a slave driver before he was tapped with the ceremonial pig-sticker. There's something to this knighthood business. I guess they feel they have to act that way."

"This I must see," Bart said, and reclined in comfort.

CHAPTER SEVEN

February 1917

United States ends diplomatic relations with Germany. Count von Bernstorff is handed his passports. . . . Anchor liner California sunk off Irish coast. . . . British troops capture German positions on the Ancre. . . . Afric, White Star liner, sunk by submarine. . . . Laconia, Cunard liner, sunk off Irish coast. . . . British troops recapture Kut-al-Imara. . . . United States Government makes public Zimmermann telegram. . . . German submarines sink 134 vessels during February.

Lieutenant Macintosh's short stay in Canada had, to some extent, prepared him for the effervescence of wartime Britain, and he felt somewhat at home when he and his small troup of novice pilots arrived in London and reported to the proper authorities at Mason's Yard. The wartime capital was far more intense and alive than New York or Washington. The streets and squares seethed with spirited activity, and while there was some noticeable Zeppelin-raid bomb damage, it in no way hindered the progress of trade or transport.

The streets, shops, and hotels were full of men in uniform—every uniform worn by the men of the British Empire—and everyone was alert and charged with the wine of victory. True, Russia had erupted with her February revolution that would lead to the end of hostilities along the Eastern Front, but at the time few people realized that the debacle would release more than forty complete German divisions a few months later. In early 1917 the British felt they were at last moving with well-devised impetus, a force that would carry them on to ultimate victory. For a few weeks there was a period of hope and promise, for the horror of the Somme and the hopeless probes through the glutinous marshes of Flanders had been quietly shoved aside.

America was not as yet in the war, but there were some hopeful signs that her diplomatic relations would soon come to a spluttering close and that one day President Wilson would see the light and join the Allies in their grim quest for the freedom of mankind.

The British navy was safe, and supreme—except when one brought up the subject of the submarine menace. It was argued that the blockade was slowly starving Germany out of the war, and that if someone would only do something about a merchant-ship convoy system, the U-boats would have very slim pickings on the North Atlantic. Then, if America would come in . . .

The army was very pleased with the prospect of great improvement in the tanks, and felt that it was only a matter of time before they'd be charging all over France and Belgium, ripping up the barbed wire, straddling the trenches, and chasing Jerries up every side street in Picardy. Wonderful things, those tanks.

Only the flying services were in the doldrums. The success attained over the Somme had revived many faltering hearts, but to maintain such superiority to a depth of twenty miles inside the lines over a three-hundred-mile front was taking every man and machine available. The vaunted Fokker with its synchronized gun had been truly overcome by the De Havilland-2 fighter, but the Germans had absorbed the drubbing and were concentrating on a series of new Albatros aeroplanes that, fighting over the safety of their own territory, were gradually reducing the

British superiority. Dullard officialdom in Whitehall persisted in ordering and reordering types that were fast approaching the obsolescent level. At the same time three first-class, ultramodern machines, the Sopwith Camel, Bristol Fighter, and the S.E. 5, were, for some unexplained reason, being held in reserve. All three types were far advanced over anything being built or flown by the enemy. It was because of this shortsighted restraint that Bloody April became possible. Once these legendary machines were released from their bureaucratic bonds the German Air Service was again swatted down like flies.

Lieutenant Macintosh knew little of this when he arrived in England, but he gathered in much related material before he had seen any of the new planes. Again, he managed to move about in critical areas, collecting information that paid for his comfortable weekend suite at the Savoy and for a broad pattern of social pleasures. His funds permitted the entertainment of many staff officers from the Whitehall caverns, civilian officials of war equipment firms, and at times pilots and observers on leave from the front. All these welcome guests were willing to disclose what they had done, were doing, or were preparing to do. After all, Lieutenant Macintosh was the son of an American millionaire industrial tycoon; he himself was a commissioned officer in the British service, a flying man with a responsible background. The material often came in faster than Macintosh could handle it, and there were times when he wished he could get some reliable help; a clever girl secretary who could be trusted. But that was out of the question here in London. Back home it would have been easy. If only he could have contacted one of the buxom wenches who used to wander through the restaurants and hotels in the Yorkville section of New York City.

As a pilot trainee, Macintosh was posted first to a station at Hounslow where he and his Canadian cohorts were finally introduced to an aeroplane, the Avro 504K two-seater trainer. It in no way resembled the Jenny, for it responded to the controls and throttle like the thoroughbred it was. Although considered a primary machine, it could be put through all practical aerobatics and maneuvers with complete safety. Ralph soon felt he was flying a true military aeroplane.

"You're doing damned well," his instructor muttered, just before he sent Ralph off for his first solo. "I can't believe you were trained on one of those Curtiss grids."

"Thank you, Captain. Maybe I'm lucky. Maybe I'm one of those birds who takes to it readily. I really like to fly," Ralph replied, and taxied out for the turnaround into the wind.

His instructor watched him through the first circuit and then trudged over to the hangar to select another candidate. He had no concern for the young American. He was one of the few naturals.

In less than a week Macintosh was called in from his cubicle to report to the orderly room. He wondered what this was all about, and was glad there was no incriminating material anywhere in his room. Most of it had been transferred to a small tin trunk and left with a seedy tobacconist who managed a small shop on Wilton Road—a crafty gentleman who was playing as two-faced a game as Macintosh.

The base adjutant escorted him into Colonel Slatherwait's office.

"Lieutenant Macintosh, sir. You wanted to see him."

"Ah yes. Come in, Macintosh. By the way, do you have a sweet tooth for toffee? . . . Haw! Haw! Haw!"

"Not particularly, sir," responded Ralph, going along with the standard joke. "I don't have a side line of raincoats, either."

"Raincoats? . . . Er, oh yes, I see. Macintosh's rain gear, so to speak," the colonel finally responded, for he was completely taken down by the fast retort. "Ah well, we're here for business, eh?"

"I presume so, sir."

"Quite!" The colonel brushed his thinning hair back with

87

his long expressive fingers. He wore R.F.C. wings, and the ribbons of the D.S.O. and the M.C., indicating that he'd been in early and had more than done his bit . . . somewhere. There were two gilt stripes on his left sleeve to indicate how many times he had been wounded. There were no medals for such service incidents in the British army.

"Well, it's like this," he began again, after consulting a sheet of paper. "We've been asked to sort out one or two particularly good prospects for training on a new aircraft. Something special. A new Bristol. I should explain it's a two-seater, not a scout. I know how all you youngsters hope to get on scouts, but this, I might tell you, is something special. Have you ever heard of the Bristol Fighter?"

Macintosh hesitated, declining to commit himself.

"No. Of course not. Something very pukka, and jolly secret, for the time being at least. I don't want you to get it mixed up with the Bristol monoplane. No, this is a biplane fighter, powered with a new Rolls-Royce engine. Quite pukka, as I said. Now would you be interested?"

"Is this something in the nature of a test-pilot assignment, sir?" Ralph asked hopefully.

"Test pilot? Nao. Not really."

"I would prefer . . . scouts . . . single-seaters."

"Of course, but in this case neither of us has much choice. I have to select candidates, and they have to decide to make the best of it. You see what I mean?"

"Yes, sir. Clearly. Let's say I'm willing to take it on." Macintosh suddenly remembered he had been ordered to obtain certain information on an aircraft called a Bristol Fighter. What an amazing and fortunate coincidence!

"Good! Then I'll have your papers made out. I can tell you that you'll be part of a brand-new squadron, one that will be trained to fly these machines on a number of very special assignments. I can also say there'll be *beaucoup* promotion, and a ribbon or two, here and there."

"It may be very interesting," Macintosh agreed.

"Then you'll be ready to pack up and shove off by Thursday. I'll try to manage a few days' leave before you go to Bristol for the first part of this special training. That satisfactory?"

"It may be just what the doctor ordered," Macintosh said.

"Doctor? Are you under some treatment?" the colonel inquired, but the fog gradually faded and he choked off a guffaw as he spluttered, "Oh, I see. You mean it might be just what you are looking for. Is that right?"

"Exactly, sir," Macintosh said with a smile. "That's it exactly."

When the young pilot had returned to the adjutant's office the colonel tried the quip once more. "Just what the doctor ordered. . . . Just what the doctor ordered?" He shook his head in resignation. "Weird sense of humor these Americans have, I must say. Now what sort of doctor would . . . ?"

CHAPTER EIGHT

Almost two weeks had passed before Bartley Crispin could accept Bryce's invitation to spend a weekend at the Melville home in London. His studies were interrupted continually by the lack of a complete lecture staff and ominous reports that the course was to be discontinued and taken up again after the war. Once that prospect had been discounted, there was a tedious revision of plans and thought during which the days flashed by almost unnoticed. One minute Bart was studying the vague sailing schedules of the shipping lines, wondering how long it would take him to return to New Jersey—and what he would do when he got there—the next minute he was endeavoring to settle down to his work and pick up the loose ends once more.

Between these periods of uncertainty the war insidiously claimed his attention. A General Trenchard was making frantic appeals for more pilots, more observers, and more efficient aircraft. In his public statements he had pointed out:

> Owing to the unlimited space in the air, the difficulty one machine crew has in seeing another, the accident of wind and cloud, it is impossible for aeroplanes, however skillful and vigilant their pilots, however powerful their engines, however mobile their machines and however numerous their formations, to prevent hostile aircraft from crossing the line if they have the initiative and determination to do so. . . . The aeroplane is not a simple defense against another aeroplane. But the opinion of those most competent to judge is that the aeroplane, as a weapon of attack,

cannot be too highly estimated. . . . British aviation has been guided by a policy of relentless and incessant offensive. Our machines have continually attacked the enemy on his side of the line, bombed his aerodromes, besides carrying out attacks on places of importance far behind the lines. It would seem probable that this has had the effect of compelling him to keep back or detail portions of his forces in the air *solely* for defensive purposes.

Crispin read that and pondered on the sagacity of the opinion, but found himself hoping this General Trenchard, whoever he was, would get plenty of planes and pilots.

Now and then he talked to individual members of the R.F.C. cadet corps, and while quietly admiring their spirit, their buoyant sense of humor, and the previous experiences of those who had transferred from front-line organizations, he realized that these students represented a wide category of the volunteer. Some were Hun haters supreme; a few thought and talked of nothing but learning to fly; a great number, like the Wiltshire yeoman, heartily admitted they had made the transfer to get out of the trenches. Only a few had seen air action on the Western Front as NCO aerial gunners, and Bart remembered the Wiltshire yeoman's proclamation: "They'll never let you go, once you are trained and have had fighting experience."

On the train to London, he talked this over with Bryce. "There doesn't seem to be much logic to the recruiting for the would-be flying men," he ruminated.

"How can there be? Britain may be scraping the bottom of the barrel for men for any service," young Melville explained. "After all, they've been in this thing for nearly three years, providing military forces from here all the way out to German East Africa. When the war began everyone volunteered, willy-nilly. Expert mechanics joined cavalry mobs. Now they have to sift them out and send them back to England to build aeroplanes. They foolishly built up all the cavalry and mounted-infantry regiments, and then found there was no place for mounted men in trench warfare, so they wasted some of them in the Middle East; the rest were shunted into infantry outfits."

"Yes, I suppose the original enthusiasm did create some problems."

"Coal miners were accepted, trained for any of the services, and then had to be demobilized and sent back to the pits. They could have done much better with the cavalry lot. Most of them could have been drafted into the Flying Corps; cavalry officers, I've heard, make first-class pilots. Their machine-gun teams should have been moved into the two-seater squadrons and put immediately to work. Right now, I may tell you, the problem is not training pilots; it's the business of finding mechanics and machinists to work in the aeroplane factories . . . and engine plants. Do you know—but of course you don't—that Britain had to beg for two types of aeroplanes from the French to cover their military areas? They have good machines already designed and set up for production, but there are not enough trained mechanics and cabinetmakers to build them in any numbers. They're all out with some engineer outfits, or perhaps driving artillery teams. When the Ministry of Munitions requests that they be returned to Britain, the commanding officers refuse to let them go—or put up a large stink and delay the transfer."

"And all that holds up the aeroplane production," Crispin muttered, his mind well ahead of the conversation. "People like that don't deserve to win a war."

"It's not fair to take that view. . . . It will be interesting to see how the United States handles these problems, if they ever get into it. They'll be starting from scratch, remember. No Boer War situations to live up to. They should come in open-minded and not make the same mistakes that Britain . . . and France have. They will have millions of first-class men to select from, whether they rely on the volunteer system or establish some form of conscription. They should channel every available man into his proper niche, according to his basic ability. That's the way it should and can be done, but it will be interesting to see what bloody foolishness they will think up."

"I hope America never gets involved," Bart said, and stared out of the compartment window. "England's a lovely little country, and I'm beginning to sense what the British are fighting for . . . and good luck to every one of them. But what a dreadful waste—war."

Bryce lit a cigarette, filled his lungs, and exhaled slowly. "Right. You're right as rain, brother, but what do you do when a whole nation runs hog wild? Do you sit back and say, 'It's an awful waste'? Do you let the swine walk in, take over, and destroy everything your ancestors have built over the centuries? Germany won't even respect the Hague Convention, so don't tell me we should outlaw war. You can't outlaw the insane intentions of some imperialist madman. You can't write and adopt laws and expect the local maniac to stop playing Jack the Ripper."

"Well," Crispin said, somewhat subdued by the logic of the analogy, "I must admit the Germans have been cruel and ruthless. I don't agree with their submarine campaign— not for one minute. I don't endorse the bombing of undefended cities, but it must be a dreadful experience to serve aboard one of their Zeppelins."

"It's no use decrying the atrocities. The point is, would you volunteer to fly an aeroplane and willingly go up to drive off or destroy a Zeppelin that was bombing London, for instance?" Bryce demanded in boyish interest.

Bart looked around for his small valise and raincoat. "I don't know," he confessed. "I really don't know, but if you'll tell me who or what started this war, I might be able to give you an answer. Right now, I don't think I'm capable of a logical viewpoint, or could decide whether I would or would not shoot down a German airship."

"Listen, Crispin. I like you. You're made of the right stuff, but it would be foolish for me to try to tell you something you should have learned three or four years ago. I can give

93

you a very full and complete outline on the causes of the war; how Britain actually debased herself trying to bargain with Germany in order to prevent a war. After all, what did she have to fight with, other than a good navy? The Government Stationery Office has published a book, well over one inch thick, which presents in chronological order the letters, documents, telegrams, and all official messages that passed between London and Berlin. It's a revelation, but I wonder how many people have taken the trouble to read it. You can buy it for a bob—one small shilling."

"It's amazing what you can get in this country for a shilling," Bart said, remembering his conversation with the Wiltshire man. "I must get a copy."

"I'll see you get one before we start back to Oxford. The old man has a stack of them. Gives 'em out like cigars," Bryce promised. He glanced out the window at the passing semidetached dwellings. "Well, here we are."

Wartime London was a bubbling contrast to staid Oxford; the tempo and tone were higher in every respect, and Crispin caught this the minute they stepped from their compartment to the station platform. This was another world in his chronicle of travel and he devoured the sights and sounds with a strange enthusiasm. He halted in midstride and stared around the massive station. Although completed in 1841, Paddington was comparatively modern, with platforms more than seven hundred feet long, sheltered under three imposing spans of curved roof. His trained eye took it all in, but he could not know that since 1915 it had been a prime target for the raiding Zeppelins, and that the gleaming rails of the Great Western Railway provided a true course into the Hyde Park section of the city. He was to see office buildings in the vicinity that had suffered from the hurried aims of the bombers, but in the brittle light of that Saturday afternoon the Praed Street area bristled with buoyant activity. Traffic, in its gay colors of a happier time, wheeled, curved, and swept in and out of Edgware Road.

Despite the war and its relentless toll, its dismal failures, and its unfulfilled promises, the city was alive with restless gaiety. There were motley crowds everywhere. Some were in khaki, some in blue, and many in threadbare but well-brushed civilian attire. News vendors still hawked the latest editions while flaunting placards tied about their waists, that announced the latest bulletin from the front. Big Ben, silenced for the duration, glared in four directions, taking in the busy river as it swept under the Vauxhall, Westminster, and Waterloo bridges. Pink-cheeked recruits, marching through the Bayswater Road, still sang:

> "Here were are, here we are,
> Here we are again.
> There's Pat and Mac and Tommy
>   and Jack and Joe.
> Where there's trouble brewing,
> Where there's something doing,
> Are we downhearted?
> Nao! Let 'em all come . . ."

The hotels and restaurants were prospering although food supplies were limited. The theaters were full, as were the fashionable shops. It was still business as usual wherever goods could be gathered. There were flowers from the Scilly Isles, Perrier water from France, trays of gleaming fish from the North Sea, and oranges from Seville. A form of rationing had been established, but only the steady middle class took it seriously and queued for butter, meat, tea, eggs, and sugar. Others maintained they had no idea how the system worked or how it was to be carried out. Where ignorance is bliss, 'tis folly to be wise. On the other hand, if you had the money . . .

The man in the street could not comprehend the extravagant taxes or the fantastic principles of military expenditure. What he could not understand, he put out of his mind, or protested in illogical letters to the newspapers or *John Bull's* weekly firebrand sheet. The middlemen were enjoying a harvest. Military shirts bought during the Boer War for fifteen shillings apiece were purchased in bulk at less than six shillings, and resold back to the military for a few pence less than a pound. Price control was a convenient term to brighten a headline.

"You'll never again see a city like this," Bryce commented proudly as he bundled Bart into a taxi. "You have no idea what the war has done."

"Right you are, mate," the driver of the cab agreed over his shoulder. "Where to?"

"Come on, Hawkins," chided Bryce. "The blackout getting you? Twenty-six New Cavendish Street. It's your old pal Melville."

The taxi driver took another look. "Cor! I never recognized you, sir. My word, 'ow you are growing. The grub must be good up there at Oxford."

"It is, if you take enough with you," Bryce said with a grin. "How's it going down Bermondsey way?"

"The missus is orl right, considering. The bombing worries 'er, of course . . . bein' tied down to the 'ouse, like. It ain't like being up front 'ere where I can pop off down some side street if the gasbags come over. She 'as to stay there, under the stairs, of course, and stick it out, an' worry about the nippers. Bloody kids are all over the shop when the maroons go orf, or when the guns start banging. Nippers seem to love it. But, of course, what can they know? Nothin' much, really."

"It hasn't been rough lately, though," Bryce chided.

"No, but you wait an' see. As soon as the weather begins to ease orf, they'll be back. Take my word for it," Hawkins said over his shoulder, and gave Bart a searching glance. "I wonder when the Flying Corps blokes will begin shooting 'em down again. Seems like a long time between drinks where downing Zeppelins is concerned. Bloody wonderful sight, that. Zepps all alight, falling out of the skies. I'll never forget the night that Leefe Robinson chap got one. What a sight. Blimy, what a sight!"

"They'll give 'em a real beating this year," Bryce said, winking at Bart. "They say they're building them bigger, so they should be easier to hit."

"And they'll bring bigger bombs. By the way," the taxi bloke responded, "I see your sister now and then. She's joined up, I see."

"Dianne?" Bryce cried. "Don't tell me she made it . . . driving for the R.F.C.? She's been after one of those jobs for months."

"I've seen 'er. Drivin' a Crossley with officers in the front seat with 'er. Real nobby she looks in the uniform. An' yer mother, she's still in the V.A.D., or something. She had some wounded soldiers to the house a few days ago. You'll be lucky if there'll be any room for you. A proper Chelsea barracks she seems to be running."

Bart finally broke in. "What's he talking about?"

"Oh, this is Bill Hawkins. One of my pals. He's usually to be found around our way. We have known him for years."

"But about your sister . . . in the R.F.C. How can that be?"

"They're taking women who can drive cars and putting them in uniform to relieve manpower for more necessary work. She's been trying to get in for some time. I guess she's made it, according to Bill here."

"How old is she? I had an idea she was a school kid."

"No. Just about a year older than I am. A crazy tomboy. You'll like Dianne. A real whiz-bang. I'll bet she's giving those Whitehall Blimps some real trips."

"Right you are," Hawkins agreed. "I followed 'er down Oxford Street the other day. Cool! It was like three-laps-to-go at the old Brooklands. She can double-clutch better than that Frenchman, Louis Chevrolet."

Bart Crispin suddenly realized that he could not even ride a motorcycle, to say nothing of driving an automobile. But how could he? He'd never had that sort of money.

"See what I mean?" Melville mooned. "Even my sister has it over me, and Mother has been in uniform of some sort for months. The old gent must be chewing nails and spitting barbed wire."

"I see what you mean," Bart agreed moodily.

New Cavendish Street was one of the byroads off Great Portland Street, and the Melville home was near Portland Place. The homes were owned and occupied by merchant princes, members of the higher clergy, and financiers from Threadneedle Street. The house was a three-story residence with a distinct touch of Georgian architecture outside, but within it had been remodeled to fit an American gentleman's idea of space and comfort.

"You'll like it here," Bryce said for the twentieth time, after he had paid off Hawkins. "I just hope we don't have to toss out a few non-paying guests. If it's too crowded, we'll sign Father's name for a suite at Claridge's. It's not far from here."

Crispin couldn't help noting the similarity between the Pollard home in New Jersey and this town house in the heart of London's fashionable area. Both represented the reward of business energy, industrial success—and money. Both were the homes of first-class American families, regardless of the fact that Mr. Melville had, for personal reasons, changed his national status and returned to the land of his forebears. From all accounts, he was still an American in thought and spirit.

As they strode up the marble steps Bart reflected that he was once more being warmly accepted by an upper-class family, despite his lower-middle-class background. He wondered if this was due to a social change brought about by the war. He had already come to some such conclusion during his contacts in Oxford, but he dreaded the Melvilles' reaction to his viewpoint concerning the war.

The broad white door was opened by a man in neat, unobtrusive livery. He was of medium height, thick-necked, barrel-chested, and wore a medical discharge button in his lapel. The skin of his cheeks was sallow, and there was a brownish stain below his eyes, hinting that at some recent time he had been racked by pain and suffering. He clicked his heels, made a slight bow, smiled faintly, and then said in warm greeting, "Good afternoon, Mr. Bryce. We are so glad to see you." He turned to Bart. "And this is your colleague . . . Mr. Crispin?"

"Right! How are you, Jeffers? The leg coming along better?"

"Oh yes, sir. I had another examination the other day. They say I'm coming along . . . er, proceeding creditably, was the phrase."

"Bart, this is ex-Sergeant Jeffers. He's been invalided out. He was badly wounded at Loos. We're glad to have him back. Jeff, this is my friend, another American. He's also at Oxford, on a Rhodes scholarship. We're having him for the weekend. I hope there is room."

"Of course, sir. Your mother made sure of that. Your room is available and ready, and Mr. Crispin is next to you. We are expecting Miss Dianne any minute."

"Wonderful! Is there anything to eat . . . before tea?" young Melville bubbled on.

"I think Cook can manage . . . and how about a couple of bottles of stout?"

"You're a nine-day wonder, Jeff. I had exactly the same thought."

"May I take your bags, sir?"

"No. We can handle them. You take it easy with that game leg. Go tickle up Martha. We still have Martha, I hope."

"Oh yes, sir. Staff's much the same."

"Come on, Bart. Let's swill the first layer off. I'll show you your room. We're adjoining and have the same bathroom. A great arrangement, eh?"

"Better than home," Bart said, meaning every word of it.

Dianne Melville was all her brother had promised. She came striding into the card room as Bart and Bryce were finishing a ham tea that had been served by Jeffers. The Guinness from dusty bottles had taken the place of the oolong; the platter had been cleaned, and the two young men were making plans for the rest of the day when the slim, willowy girl in a military-gray uniform swept in from the reception lounge.

"Di!" Bryce cried. "Good God! You look marvelous!"

"Bryce!" the girl exclaimed as they rushed into each other's arms. "Lordy, how we've missed you!"

Flashes of admiration and affection lit up their greetings, and Crispin felt like an intruder. He had never encountered a brother-sister comradeship of this sincerity. He'd never had a sister, only a runny-nosed little brother not even a Santa Claus could warm to. He wondered if the fact that these two were still Americans, in an alien land, had something to do with their warm relationship.

"You look absolutely marvelous!" Bryce bellowed again, as he stood gripping her forearms. "Damn it all. It's not fair. Is that an issue uniform?"

Dianne stepped back and smoothed out her neat jacket. "No . . . that is, I had to have it made. I'm an officer of some sort, and the Motor Corps is not completely organized as yet, and we're sort of on our own."

"But what do you do, outside of making a race track of Oxford Street? Bill Hawkins tried to follow you the other day."

"It's rare fun at times, but they haven't drawn up any rules yet, so the schedule is rather flexible, but we do put in beastly hours. I have to be back at the Depot early in the morning."

Crispin had plenty of time to study the girl, who was of better than medium height with beautiful shoulders. Her loose uniform cap was tugged down over well-disciplined curls with the peak tilted at a jaunty angle. She had a healthy complexion that needed no artificial coloring. Her mouth was artistically bowed, and twitched with gaiety at the corners. She had a perky, proud nose, and her uniform fitted beautifully. The jacket was particularly smart, being hip-length with bellows pockets and agleam with well-polished military buttons. The skirt was comparatively short for the period and showed an intriguing length of khaki lisle stocking. Brown brogues and driving gloves completed her ensemble.

As Bruce and Dianne continued to compare notes and exchange compliments, Bart broke in. "I don't wish to interrupt but could anyone tell me how to get to the British Museum? I may as well take out a book."

"Oh, Bart." Bryce threw out his hands. "You must excuse us. This is Dianne, my sister, and we haven't seen each other for at *least* three weeks. She's crazy, of course, but we have to humor her."

"We have another American?" the girl responded. "Let's rally round the flag. Please introduce me, Bryce."

"Let's sit down. Jeff can get you a pot of tea and a bite if you pull the bell. This is Bartley Crispin . . . Princeton. He's at Oxford on a Rhodes . . . architecture. Bart, this is Dianne, the scourge of the Melville clan. Both of you are now on your own."

"Rhodes scholar? I thought they produced only hockey players at Princeton. But how wonderful. Wait until Dad hooks into you. He'll have you designing new railway stations for the G.N.W.—after the war, I mean."

"Nothing of the sort. Bart is going to build city halls, courthouses, and houses of detention for hoydens like you," Bryce countered playfully. "Besides, he's going back home when he finishes."

"What about the war?" Dianne asked, reaching to tug a tapestry bell pull. "Don't you think the United States will come in? They're ready to break relations now, so I understand."

"I hope not," Bart said, watching her as she tossed her

cap onto a leather settee. "I was awarded a scholarship, and I'd like to get the benefit of it."

Jeffers appeared in the doorway, and Dianne smiled at him and said, "Please, Jeffers, could I have a tea tray? I'm famished. Tell Martha I'd like one of her doorstep sandwiches, that thick." She held her thumb and middle finger apart to indicate the size.

"Yes, miss," Jeffers bowed and backed away.

"Now look, Di," Bryce interposed as he drew up a chair for his sister. "We're going to have a pleasant weekend, so get off your stump. Bart has the courage of his convictions. He's not the belligerent type. Wants to build things, not knock them down. It takes all kinds. I like him. That's why I brought him home. Actually, we're a couple of kindred spirits . . . both of us are frustrated. Me because I can't get into the R.F.C., and Bart because there's a possibility his scholarship course will be postponed until after the war. So don't rub it in because neither of us is in uniform."

Crispin smiled his thanks but couldn't think of anything to say. It was the same old situation all over again.

"All right, if that's how you want it," Miss Melville replied after some thought. "Later on tonight we'll take him out and show him wartime London. Let's agree it should be a change from Oxford."

As she sat and took her tea, Crispin studied her. She had a dulcet voice and a manner of speech that was new to him. She spoke well with an educated tonal quality, but it was difficult to say whether any of it showed the influence of her years in England. Whatever, it was fascinating, and her smile completely captivating. He found himself comparing her with Cynthia Pollard, another firebrand, but with Miss Melville he knew exactly what she thought and stood for. Cynthia was an enigma, and whenever she came to mind he recalled her walking up those steps in lower Broadway, and then later denying she had been in that part of the city.

"I'll leave you two for a couple of minutes," Bryce announced. "I have a telephone call to make. Please excuse me."

"That would be nice," Dianne said without looking up from her tea tray.

"What?"

"You're going to call Stacey Wallace, aren't you?"

Bryce glanced at Bart with resignation. "See what I mean? She even knows what you are thinking. Watch out for her. As a matter of fact, I *was* going to call Stacey to see if we could make a party of it. Perhaps get some theater tickets. What's good along Shaftesbury Avenue?"

"*Seven Days' Leave* is still running at the Lyceum, but that's about the war, so we'd better stay away from there. They're playing *A Little Bit of Fluff* at the Criterion. Delightful music. But let Stacey make a suggestion."

After Bryce left, Bart tried another tack. "You seem to be enjoying yourself, in whatever it is you're in. What is it?"

"It's a Motor Corps set up for the R.F.C. We drive officers about and do certain types of errands. Some of the girls are even driving lorries . . . big Leyland trucks, as you call them. They're jolly good, too. Me, I was lucky and was selected for lighter jobs . . . Crossley tenders. They're a sort of utility car, very useful for dashing about on all sorts of trips. Very fast, too, in top gear."

"Interesting. You must meet a lot of high-ranking officers, I suppose."

"Right. From generals on down. I'm not quite sure, but I seem to be assigned to an Intelligence group. I gather that from snatches of conversations I hear up front. I suppose they're always tracking some poor devil down to stick him in the Tower. I'm not sure, but I just sense it, and I often wonder what's in the sealed packages I'm sometimes carrying."

"Interesting," Bart said again. "You haven't picked up any German spies, have you?" he said with a grin.

"German spies? There aren't any Germans in Britain—not on the loose. The real troublemakers usually are Americans. They're really of German descent, of course, but they make the most of the protection of a U.S. passport."

"Funny, but I'd never thought of that. What stinkers!"

"One of our girls who drives a lorry had to take several of them to a court building for questioning. They certainly were stinkers. They were men who work on neutral ships, and they really were high. But there are several who are being watched, and they're quite fragrant. There's one young woman in particular. I have an idea they're letting her move about fairly free in the hope she will lead them into a complete group."

"Is she an American?"

"I think so. I'm almost positive. I had to take her and an R.F.C. officer round to Scotland Yard. I didn't get a chance to speak to her, but one could tell by her clothes and her speech. She's well educated and quite pleasant in her general manner. A girl like that can raise hob unless she's kept under careful surveillance."

"But if she's riding about in official R.F.C. motorcars, couldn't she be providing them with important information?"

"She could, but where would she get it?" Dianne said, and Bart was impressed with her sagacity. "She has been over here for only a couple of weeks."

"If she is an American she could have been in Germany recently. So far, Americans are free to move about over there."

"Ooh! I hadn't thought of that," Dianne said pensively, "but if she's working for us I don't think she'd be likely to be seen with R.F.C. officers—and sitting on the front seat of a Crossley. They try to blot out all such associations, you know."

"Yes, I suppose that would be considered unwise." He thought it amazing that he should be talking international intrigue with this girl, for it had never before entered his mind.

Bryce came back into the room with the announcement

that Stacey Wallace was free and that they were all going out to dinner at the Troc, and then go on to see Lee White in some American musical at the Gaiety. "How does that sound?" he asked with some pleasure. He winked at Bart as much as to say: Don't worry about money. We can take care of everything. Tonight is on the Melvilles.

Dianne looked at her wrist watch. "I've plenty of time to change."

"Change? You can go out in mufti?" her brother asked.

"Of course. I'm supposed to be commissioned. Besides, I don't want to be the only one in war paint."

"Wait and see. Perhaps Ralph Macintosh will pop along. I think he's in town this weekend. Stacey seems to think so."

"Who?" Bart broke in, suddenly aware of the trend of their conversation.

"Oh, he's another American. I told you we collect 'em here. Name's Ralph Macintosh, and he's a pilot in the R.F.C." Bryce stared wide-eyed at Bart. "By the way, he's a Princeton man too. Do you happen to know him?"

Bart wagged his head in the affirmative. "I know him. We were on the track team together. I know him very well. I didn't know he was over here. I presumed he was still in Canada."

"No. He's been here for several weeks. Seems to be on some special sort of assignment. I think he's something of a specialist as a pilot. But that's just my surmise. You can't get him to talk much about his work."

"It's a small world." Bart stared at the carpet. "Before we graduated we talked about the possibility of our meeting in Oxford. He thought he'd go there for the ground course while I was there on the scholarship."

Dianne looked up. "He may be on some sort of under-cover work. He goes all over the country—very often to look over plants that are under stiff security control. Dad thinks he may be working with the Intelligence Bureau, checking on unreliable workmen while posing as a military aircraft inspector. I have an idea he's doing a very valuable job."

"Macintosh?" Crispin cried with incredulity. "I can't imagine him in such a post. Still, I must admit he has a wonderful disguise. He was the last man in Princeton I thought would volunteer to fight for Britain."

Bryce studied Bart for a few seconds. "There's a strange thing," he muttered. "At times, I've felt the same way about him."

"Here! Here!" Dianne protested. "I'm positive Ralph's on the square."

"Mother isn't."

"I know, but you can't take Mother seriously. She's so soaked up with war work, she can't think straight. Every time she comes home from tucking in a wounded soldier she wants to go and throw bricks at the Albert Hall for offering musicians who play Beethoven."

Bart chuckled at the ridiculous picture Dianne had drawn of her mother. "I shall be interested in meeting Macintosh again," he said after some thought.

"Why didn't you try for the R.F.C. in Canada?" Dianne said impulsively. "It would have been easy for you . . . " She stopped and placed her fingertips to her lips. "I'm sorry, Bart. I forgot . . ."

"That's quite all right," he assured her patiently. "You see, Macintosh could afford to join and learn to fly with the Princeton Flying Club. That was a big help to him."

"Let's not get on that subject again." Bryce started to unknot his tie. "I hope he turns up, in a way. I have a few things I'd like to talk to him about. Flying Corps matters." He clapped Bart's shoulder. "I guess we'd better get a bath and be looking over our duds. See you later, Di."

CHAPTER NINE

Before being taken to dinner at the Trocadero on Shaftesbury Avenue, Bart had time and the opportunity for a quiet half hour with Sir John. His host was a pleasant, somewhat portly man, given to well-cut worsteds. Bart sensed that he in no way represented the massive, bellowing railway tycoon of popular concept. His hair had thinned and was brushed down over a pink scalp. As he talked he fingered a small mustache, and Bart decided that here was the type of American who admired the English social sphere and found no difficulty in adapting to the British pattern of good living. He spoke quietly but distinctly, with no particular accent. He had greeted Bart with a warm, friendly handshake.

"Well," he began, "so we have a scholar this time. Our American visitors seldom come up to the Rhodes standards. Architecture, too! You must have worked very hard, or are you a natural scholar?"

"I'm not sure, sir, but when I finally decided on my subject, I was fascinated. I even took three years of German, hoping I might one day finish up at Heidelberg. I was keenly interested."

Sir John twiddled with his mustache and gave Bart a keen glance. He liked his honesty. "But instead you wind up at Oxford. How is the course? You like it there?"

"It's very good, sir. It should be a great help."

"But are they up to American construction standards and methods, or do they pay more attention to basic design?"

"I wondered about that, but with each week I realized

they were stressing style, method, and the approach from the traditional European concept. It's not just skyscrapers, blocky railroad stations, and saw-toothed manufacturing plants. You get a full portfolio of up-to-date industrial ideas along with the classic designs. This results in a combination that should produce less stark monoliths. Who knows, out of this someone may create a brand-new American standard—a distinctive combination of the classic and utilitarian."

His host considered that for some time, and then pointed to a roomy armchair. "Sit down, son. This is very interesting. You'll be here for two years?"

"Unless the war intervenes."

Sir John went to a window and peered out at the darkening sky. "Ah yes. The war. It doesn't look too good—back home, eh?"

"No, sir. Still, Wilson has an obligation to the people who put him back in."

"Ah, but he's a politician. A very astute politician. You are not dealing with a university president now, you know." Sir John left the window, went to the fireplace, and rested his arm on the mantel. "Still, I don't think he'll have much choice if the Germans step up their submarine campaign. He'll be in a very difficult position. He doesn't want to go to war, but he may have little or no option."

"That's what I'm afraid of," Bart said quietly, staring into the glow of the grate.

"You don't like the idea, I take it. Well, we all have our views and preferences. Young Bryce is hell-bent to go in with the Royal Flying Corps. I wouldn't interfere. It might do him a world of good." He looked at Crispin for some comment.

"I don't like the idea of war, sir. It is such a waste of talent, money, science, and natural resources. Youth and young blood cannot be replaced after a battle. We may rebuild the towns and cities but we can't restore the men . . . men from fine families; with high ideals; with extensive educations. Who will rebuild all these countries after the war? There won't be any imaginative designers or builders left. This is the toll of war, page after page, in history."

Sir John selected a cigar from a mahogany humidor, took his time clipping the tip and lighting it with a fireplace spill. "I hope you can stay out of it," he said with quiet conviction. "You're the type we'll need when this is all over."

"But suppose I am . . . called up?"

"Unfortunately, the demands of conscription cannot be that selective. When you have a war thrust upon you, you are compelled to fight it with exactly the same weapons and recruiting demands as those of the enemy. But take my tip, young man. Stay out as long as you can. Britain can't touch you, and as an American I doubt that United States officialdom will bother to reach across the Atlantic as long as you are a legitimate student over here. Not unless the war goes on five or more years. That's one thing you country has . . . manpower. I don't think they'll bother you. You're in a very nice spot, my boy. The war will probably never touch you."

There was some high-spirited chatter outside the room, and Bart realized their party was gathering. As he contemplated what Sir John had said he found himself resenting such an obvious sanctuary.

"Well, it's been pleasant . . . getting your opinion, sir." Bart rose to his feet. "I'd better get along. Dianne and Bryce will be looking for me."

"Ah, yes. You're all going to the theater? Fine. Everyone needs a bit of gaiety these days. Have a good time. Perhaps we can have another talk in the morning. I like the ease and leisure of Sunday mornings. Always a good chance to talk."

"I would like that, sir. I'm not yet completely sure in my own mind—what I ought to do, if America comes into the war. I'd like to talk it over in more detail. There may be something I am missing."

"Perhaps. But, as of now, I'd plan to—finish your formal

education. The education of experience, in this case, can wait."

The Trocadero was a jovial madhouse. Men in khaki and field boots, with short-leave haversacks over their shoulders, jostled for positions at the Long Bar. There were Brass Hats, Red Tabs, and undistinguished men wearing green tabs. There were Defense of London pilots in from the network of aerodromes a dozen or so miles outside the metropolis. This was their night off, and they intended to make the most of it. God alone knew where they would be this time tomorrow if the Zepps started coming over again.

There were pink-cheeked youths from the training schools. Navy types with pale blue eyes, and Wavy-Navy gilt on their sleeves. There were Jocks in bonnets and kilts that were caked with Flanders mud. There were Aussies in wide-brimmed hats and with belligerency in their eyes. There were Canadians with puzzled expressions, all complete with the ubiquitous "Goddamn" in every sentence. Infantry officers looked tired and haggard. The Engineers appeared to have avoided ablutions for days. The Army Service Corps was round, rosy, and anxious to buy anyone a drink, knowing full well that DORA (Defense of the Realm Act) forbade even friendly treating. They gulped cocktails, brandy and soda, gin-and-It, shandy gaff, porter and small, and a dozen variants of the whisky *pahit*, ordered to prove the patron had been abroad and was not just a Kitchener campaigner.

Everyone laughed or talked against the chimes of glassware, the tonk of tankards, and the hiss of mineral waters. There was a definite whiff of new leather, old trench coats, hair oil, vermouth, Hollands, and the acid breaths of ancient brigadiers. There was a muddled change of scenery in the passageway that led to the dining room. There the martial masculinity was garlanded and pomponed with silk, fur, sequins, tulle, lace, ribbon, and honey-colored bobbed hair. The voices were dulcet or shrill, and the names were all boyish; Freddie, Marty, Jess, Mickey, Clem, Bobbie, Dinty, and Laddie, but they all answered in a high-pitched peal. Now there was music, the scent of bottled lilac and the click of heels. Canadian nurses in blue capes with linings of scarlet added a dash of regal color.

Bryce led the way while Bart steered Dianne and Stacey through the swirls of khaki and velvet. Obsequious waiters wore circular silver badges pinned to the mohair of their lapels, tokens of a service performed; permits from a benevolent government that allowed them to wait on others who had been spared to fight another day.

A pasty-faced man with an empty sleeve tucked into his jacket pocket led them to a reserved table. Bryce paid the assessment.

"Thank you, Mr. Melville. It is good to see you again."

"We may need an extra place, Bosworth. Mr. Macintosh may drop in and join us. Can you cope?"

"Most certainly, sir. I'll keep an eye out for him."

The dance band broke in with a crash of brass and percussion membrane: "When I Get My Civvies on Again!" The waiters went into their tripping minuets, crossing and crisscrossing the restaurant floor.

"Well, we made it. Damned lucky to get that taxi." Bryce looked round the table for an acknowledgment. "What a mob!"

Dianne had changed into a tailored dress that was only a few pleats less severe than her uniform. She had bowed to convention with a small spray of flowers at her shoulder. Stacey, a bouncy, auburn-haired girl with a pert, freckled nose, was in her element. An original flapper of the Bruce Bairnsfather days; one of a generation that was in school with hair in curls down their backs, but at six o'clock was brushed up and arranged in a mature style "to go out with young officers." She giggled and dithered like a molded jelly.

"Do you think we'll get through in time to make the theater?" she asked with wide-eyed concern.

"Of course we'll make it, unless you happen to be famished," Bryce said with a grin. "I know you. You can eat more than a cart horse."

Bart sat back taking everything in. He was amazed by the scene: the actors and the movement of this wartime tableau. It was impossible to imagine this was a city that, to a great extent, was under siege; that it had been through nearly three years of conflict, ceremony, and critical experience. He wondered how many who had recently drunk or dined here were still alive; how many here tonight would be back in civilian clothing when it was all over.

Someone was singing:

"When I get my civvies on again,
    And it's home, sweet home once more,
    There'll be no more bully beef,
    Or Mess Room tea,
    And nothing's going to put the wind up me."

The drinks were served with surprising speed, and the patrons' age was no consideration. Portions of the dinner were produced and snatched away between topics of conversation, or during aimless searches for friends. Lonely swains "sashayed" up to arrange future tea or cocktail parties. University men with grins from ear to ear came up to clout Bryce across the shoulders and pass intimate intelligence from behind cupped hands.

Just as the cutlets were being swept away, Stacey let out a squeal and pointed toward the door. "There's Ralph Macintosh! Here . . . over here, Ralph!"

"Don't fret," Bryce said. "Bosworth will get him here."

Somewhat annoyed, Bart twisted in his seat. He had been enjoying a pleasant exchange with Dianne. He had explained her father's views on his staying at Oxford, and after consideration she had agreed there was merit in the idea. From that they had gone on to her life in England, and how she had come to love this country, but hoped one day to go back to Pennsylvania and recapture many pleasant memories. Yes, she might even marry over there and settle down in her native land. Meanwhile there was the war to consider. No one could make plans of any importance until the war was over.

Bart agreed and wished there was an immediate solution to it; some magic that would return everything to its 1914 status and tranquillity. Still, there could be a future. . . .

Then Ralph Macintosh strode into the picture. "Bart, you old son of a gun!" he bellowed, gripping Crispin by both shoulders. "God, it's good to see you again."

Stunned by the warmth of the greeting, Bart tried to regain his balance and respond. He was fascinated with Ralph's appearance. "Great to see you again."

Macintosh was dressed in smart R.F.C. khaki with embroidered wings on the front of his double-breasted jacket. His Sam Browne belt gleamed with Kiwi boot polish and Brasso cleaner. His breeches were light Bedford cord, and his field boots obviously custom-made. He looked the typical British airman until one studied his face. There was no friendliness in his eyes. He looked tired and the tracery of weariness had stamped in a faint outline of the frantic mask he had worn that afternoon in Palmer Stadium. Bart suddenly felt a strange sympathy for him.

"You're looking fine, Ralph," and to make up for the lie Bart added, "Here, take my chair. The waiter's bringing another."

"Any day; to sit beside Dianne," he replied with a proprietary air. "Hi, Bryce . . . Stacey. What a wonderful idea, to have us meet like this."

"Have you had dinner?"

"Yes. At the Savoy. Had a meeting with . . . well, never mind. Let's drop business and make up for lost time. How's everything, Bart?"

"Fine, so far. I had no idea you were already in England."

"The Princeton Flying Club is the answer. It gave me a big lead in the course. Hear anything from Cynthia?"

"Not a thing. You?"

113

"Now and then. She's trying to get over here on some mission or other for her father. It's probably munitions business of some sort. Who knows?" Ralph beamed in a conspiratorial manner. "She may turn up next."

"Now who is Cynthia?" Dianne broke in. "I've never heard of her."

"Cynthia? She's a Miss Pollard. A very popular girl back home. The campus sweetheart, so to speak," Ralph explained as Bart took the added chair that had been placed between Bryce and Stacey. "The Pollards have always been partial to the college athletes . . . and you know, Bart was one of the best."

"No, I didn't know," Dianne said in mild surprise. "Did you, Bryce? He hasn't mentioned it."

"I haven't been here long enough to give you my full name," Bart said with a smirk.

"Oh yes, Bart is one of the immortals at Princeton," Ralph said, and reached for Dianne's hand. "In fact we were all surprised when he didn't go in with all the other star athletes who joined up in the Foreign Legion or the French Aviation back in 1916. But Bart had other ideas, and here he is, still deep in his schoolbooks. The perennial college boy."

Ignoring the silence that followed, Ralph turned to Dianne. "I hear you've joined up, Di. Hoped I'd see you in uniform. If I ever get enough rank to have a lady driver, I'll certainly put in a chit for you. Damned good show!"

From across the table Bart had to swallow this contrived scene, knowing it was being staged to point up his civilian status. He wondered why Macintosh had switched so suddenly from his warmhearted greeting to this obvious contempt. Certainly there was no necessity for it. He held the center of the stage. He was in uniform and was being goggled at by Stacey Wallace and admired by Bryce. There was no reason to make such a point of Bart's continuing his studies. Could it be because Bart was a guest of the Melvilles, and presumably was escorting Dianne this evening? If so, it could only mean that Ralph had previously marked her for his own. It was a situation that paralleled their association with the Pollard family back home.

Bryce was checking their bill, and then looked up to lessen the tension. "Well, let's get out of here. We'll make the Gaiety in good time if we move off now."

"The Gaiety? You're going to a show?" Ralph snapped like a sergeant major.

"Oh!" Dianne cried. "We didn't think."

"What asses we are!" Bryce stormed. "We could have reserved five seats just as easy as four."

"But you didn't know whether I'd get here," Macintosh said, and looked around the table. "But I probably can pick up a single. We can get together between the acts—and go somewhere afterward." It was clear he had no intention of withdrawing at this point.

"Wait a minute," Bart broke in. "I'd just as soon drop out. I'm not too enamored of the theater. I'd rather wander about London and see the sights. It's the first chance I've had."

"But there's so little to see at night. There's the blackout, remember," Stacey protested.

"There's no need. We can all get together after the show," Ralph added mildly.

"I could meet you anywhere you say, afterward . . . or back at your place on New Cavendish Street. I can find my way back," Bart explained.

Macintosh challenged the rest of the party with, "Well, what are we pondering about? If that's what Bart would rather do, I'll gladly fill in." He glanced at Dianne for assent, but she was looking at Bart as though trying to understand his decision to drop out from the group. She hoped he was capable of better manners, but deeper than that she sensed there was no love lost between these two.

"There's no use wasting time mulling it over. We should get out of here," Bryce said with resignation. "You sure you won't stay with us, Bart?"

"It will be much simpler for all concerned. I'd really like to ramble about the town." Bart glanced at Stacey, who was gathering her bag and gloves, and showing little interest in the quandary. Ralph, trying to act aloof, was straightening his Sam Browne, and then studied the inner lining of his cap.

Bart added, "I'm sure it is for the best."

"Well, it isn't what I had planned," Bryce said, and counted his change. "Still, if you want to go on your own . . . let's leave it this way. We'll all come back to our place, straight from the Gaiety. Di has to report in at her depot early in the morning, so we shouldn't dawdle about too late."

"Right. I'll see you about eleven or so."

Ralph had already started out with Dianne. Stacey was being helped into her coat, and she gave Bart a look of deep concern. Bryce shooed them toward the door, his face darkening with contempt for the manner in which Ralph had moved in and taken over.

"We'll see you later, Bart. Take care of yourself."

"I'll be quite all right. I hope it is a good show."

CHAPTER TEN

Crispin saw them into a cab outside the Trocadero and then turned toward the faint glow of Piccadilly Circus. After the comparative glare of the restaurant the busy theater street presented the gloom and shadowy silhouettes of a sinister melodrama. There was a strange quiet, and the coolness of the night refreshed him and soothed some of the indignation aroused by the appearance of Ralph Macintosh. Why did this unpleasant man have to dog his footsteps? Why had fate guided him to that taproom in the Clarendon Hotel where he met Bryce Melville? Why was he such a fool to back out and allow Ralph to take over in that peremptory manner? Would he always rule his life, simply by walking into the scene?

He tried to erase Ralph Macintosh from his mind and recount his short conversation with Sir John Melville. He liked this gentlemanly, honest man and his quiet manner. He respected his opinion and advice and hoped they could meet again in the morning when he could seek a more detailed explanation of Sir John's view that he should endeavor to stay at the university. Macintosh's "perennial college boy" jibe had left a welt that inflamed with every stride. There had to be a sound, logical rebuttal.

As his night sight sharpened, he saw there were stars in the sky and realized that lowering of street illumination made it possible to enjoy the evening and its astral marvels that were there without benefit of a man-made power station. Light wisps of cloud floated across the arch of night like scarves released by careless Pleiades. Before he had crossed the Circus and paid his respects to Eros atop his column, the bitterness Ralph had caused had largely dissipated. He would think only of himself and his own future. It was the kind of night in which to wander alone and sort out the dross from one's thoughts and planning.

He threaded his way through the swirling traffic of motorcars, taxis, and buses, all of which had deflector shields that directed the gleam of their headlights down in narrow slits that reached a few feet ahead on the roadway. There was no frantic tooting of horns, no screech of tires or snarl of brakes. Bicycles wove in and out like silent wraiths. Pedestrians were cloaked figures with light vees of shirt or blouse below indistinct faces. Long winter coats made it almost impossible to determine the sexes. Bart was spared the solicitations of the nocturnal street walkers, who reserved their appeals and slatternly charms for the bulky men who wore wide-brimmed hats turned up at one side. The Aussies were flush with money—and self-esteem. Civilians could be coppers in mufti and were therefore suspect.

The classic curve of Regent Street lured him on. He passed small knots of people who went about their own business. They exchanged comments on every subject but the war; there was no talk of France, Helgoland, the submarine menace, or the coming "push." Whether in civilian clothes or military uniform, the war seemed to be the last thought in their minds. Ration books, meat coupons, an extra dab of fish, the exorbitant price of chocolates—and soccer football. Who went down at Chelsea this afternoon? How did Sheffield make out? Tottenham Hotspurs would have to be watched. Everton scored six goals? . . . Cool The fortunes picked up in the football pools, ration coupons, the strength of the beer: anything but a reference to the hellish carnage that flamed across the Channel.

What amazing people.

Regent Street provided lighter shadows. The marble and granite walls of the great shopping area reflected the starry night down on the pavements and off the shopwindows.

New galaxies of stars appeared over the Oxford Street crossing, and then two slim, silvery beams of light swept back and forth, a manifestation of war Bart had not seen heretofore. He strode on, watching the crisscrossing blades of light that he presumed had something to do with London's defense against raiding Zeppelins.

He increased his pace, hoping to come upon the searchlight site. It would be interesting to see how this feature of the defense was carried out. Of course, it was only a routine practice. There were no Zeppelins up there. No guns flashed and spat shells into the sable night. There was no particular anxiety anywhere.

Another searchlight blade probed the eastern curve of the sky, and then a distant moan that began with a sepulchral tone gradually flayed itself into the bellow of a giant tuba. The warning spurred the pace of the gloomy figures, and they swirled in all directions, heading for familiar sanctuaries. The shrill whistles of policemen could be heard when the insistent sirens lowered their voices, as if to catch their breaths for another bellow.

After moving over close to a wall of a building, Crispin stood still. The siren wail continued and the searchlight blades increased their passage of arms. Someone hurried by, and Bart put out his hand. "Is this an air raid?" he asked.

The figure halted, turned, and strode back. "What did you say?"

"I'm new here . . . in London. That siren—does it indicate an air raid?"

"Right, mate! You'd better take cover."

"Do you know how I could get to New Cavendish Street?"

"It's a bit on from here. Over that way. I wouldn't try to make it while a raid is on. You must be bloody new here."

"A taxi? Would a taxi get me there?"

"Might. But not likely. Drivers usually pop into some nearby pub until the All Clear sounds. By that time they've mopped up most of the beer. If I were you, I'd bung in somewhere . . . a pub, or one of the Underground stations, until this is over. I wouldn't try to get to New Cavendish Street now."

"Where's the nearest Underground?"

"Just up the top here. At Oxford Street. I'm nipping along, mate."

"Thanks. Good night."

Uncertain what course to take, Bart stood there. It was hard to believe that on his first night in London he should experience a graphic wartime situation. He had read of air raids in the papers back home, but he had taken little notice of the accounts offered in the newspapers available in Oxford. With other matters that were important to him, he had tried to blot the war from his mind.

A thunderous juggernaut tore up Regent Street, which had seemingly swept all its traffic into the shadows of side streets. A Klaxon horn clawed at the eardrums while indistinct figures clung to the rails, framework, and the gray base of a mobile anti-aircraft gun. Farther on it screeched to a halt, and there was a clatter of metal as the support legs of the mount were lowered to the pavement. The gunners in steel helmets swarmed all over the impressionistic vehicle. The doors of the limber compartment swung open and the circular bases of the ammunition glinted and showed their percussion caps.

Despite all this fantastic furor, Bart had not yet accepted the fact that he had sauntered into an actual air raid. The whole scene; the lighting, the players were unrealistic.

"You'd better take cover, there!" a policeman on a bicycle cried from across the street. A shell burst high in the sky.

"Right away!" Bart yelled, and scurried toward a side street. He glanced up into the sky again, and to his amazement, amid the glinting stars, the fencing sword blades of light, and the frilly wisps of cloud, he caught the faint outline of a celestial insect. A searchlight beam speared it and held it seemingly pinned to the sky for the inspection of earthly onlookers.

"My God!" Crispin husked. "It's a Zeppelin. It's coming this way!"

A flood of revulsion swept through him as he stood transfixed on the street corner. The slender blade of light held the silver maggot in its beam as the sky beyond erupted with splintered explosions. The guns were alert, the searchlights had done their job, but where were the fighting planes?

He ran blindly along dark streets, stumbling over dustbins and stacks of refuse. The Zeppelin was almost directly overhead, and still in the glare of the pointing finger. "Room-oom-oom-oom!" continued the deep basso of the warning sirens. "Take cover, you fool!" someone yelled from the doorway of a dingy little pub.

A new tonal pitch was added to this mad symphony as something, piping the scream of a banshee, came wailing down. Standing wide-legged against the uproar, Bart stared about, trying to account for the new clangor. There wasn't another moving figure in the street. As he looked up again there was a deafening crash, and he felt himself hurled through the air. It was a foolish, unearthly feeling. There was a second explosion that set up a jagged wall of flame, and a building a few yards away took on the skeletal outline of war-area devastation. Great slabs of brick wall slammed across the street and stamped out the front of a habitation opposite it. Pathetic screams were blotted out by the rumble of toppling buildings. Great shards of glass were sucked through the air, and their points buried into frame-and-stucco house fronts. Chunks of chimney twirled flippety-flop down the middle of the street like slab-sided bowling balls.

Bart found himself in a sitting position under a low window. The air was mottled with smoke and mortar dust, and gave off the acrid tang of explosive. His shoulders ached, but he was able to get his palms under him and haul himself to his feet. Another crash erupted in a street beyond and chunks of masonry went sky high. Something had caught fire and the darkened street was immediately as garish as a cheap melodrama set. Bart swayed slack-kneed and watched gouts of flame surge from what had been windows. A door lay at an angle across the gutter. The glare of light illuminated a cross section of a block of cheap flats, putting open interiors on display. There were brass bedsteads, puny fireplaces, wardrobes at a crazy angle, floors that were preparing to collapse, and items of bedroom furniture were slithering down tilted hallways to tumble into the street.

"My God!" Bart breathed again.

Nothing seemed real. Everything was a garish impression, simply brought up to size. It reminded him of the old exhibits of the San Francisco earthquake that were offered at Coney Island. But that was a diorama that one could walk around. The buildings were only the size of Grape-Nuts boxes. Sections were tilted to give the illusion of a major eruption, and the flames were only patterns of scarlet and gold paper.

But this was real. The shattered houses were real. The tragedy itself was pitifully real. He hurried along past the open doors and saw two children lying in the rubble of a balustrade. He reached down to pick one up, but a new burst of flame pointed out gushes of blood, and he knew they were beyond help. He let out an earthy curse, and then pulled off his overcoat and laid it over the two youngsters. An ambulance wheeled up and the driver yelled something unintelligible. Bart pointed to the mounds under his coat.

"What condition?" the driver yelled.

"Bad. Probably dead."

"What are they?"

"Two little kids. Little girls."

"Ahr-r-r-r! Well, let's get them out of that mess, eh?"

Another roar of explosion went off some distance away, and Bart turned and looked back. The airship seemed to stand still. The searchlight blades were held erect like ceremonial lances along a parade route. The Zeppelin took on the glow of a Chinese lantern, and then gushed flame and smoke. A tiny biplane, a veritable midge with a ruled line of sparks spitting from its nose, curled around the stacked elevators of the raider. It was then that another spasm of reaction swept across Bart's shoulder blades. His eyes widened and his lips parted. "He got him! He got him! That Flying Corps guy got him! Wonderful! He got him!"

The ambulance man with a dead child in his arms said, "An' about bloody time! Too bad we don't 'ave more of 'em up there. Give me an 'and with that other one, will you, mate?"

As Bart picked up the broken body of a little girl, her head fell back over his elbow and a gush of blood trickled over her pale cheek. He staggered to the rear of the ambulance and someone took the child from him.

"Is it always like this?" he asked the indistinct figure.

"Sometimes it's worse. They can identify and put a name to something like that. Wait and see what we pull out from under them walls. They'll look like somethink you see 'anging in the butcher's window on Saturday nights."

"God!"

"Well, let's get on with it. You're not too done in to give an 'and, are you, mate?"

"Not at all."

"Need all the 'elp we can get. When it starts we 'ave to rush orf, whether there's anybody to 'elp or not. It's a bloody awful game."

"But they got that one—up there," Bart persisted. "It's all in flames!"

"Poor buggers. A rotten way to get it, I always say."

Someone offered Bart a cigarette. Someone else shoved a mug of coffee into his hand. He helped with the stretchers, tugged at fragments of masonry, crawled up sets of demolished stairways, and carried moaning heaps out to the ambulances. His blue serge suit was a mottled fawn by now, streaked with plaster dust, blood, dirty water, spilled

123

coffee. His hair was matted with sweat and soot, and stained with something blue that had spilled out of a kitchen cabinet. He didn't remember giving his overcoat to a woman in a shawl and a nightgown.

The battered street was now filled with policemen, fire brigade men, St. John's Ambulance workers, and a few figures in khaki who scrambled and tore in frenzy at the devastation.

A girl in some sort of uniform with a first-aid kit over her shoulder came up to Bart. "May I help? Are you hurt? Do you live here in any one of these houses?"

Bart shook his head wearily. "No, thank you. I just happened to be here when the first bomb hit."

"You mean you were out in the street?"

"Wandering about like a fool, but I'm very lucky. I'm not hurt. I look like this from trying to help. Very foolish of me."

"I just want to make sure you are all right. You're certain? So many are in shock, you know, and aren't aware they've been hurt. We had one woman walking about looking for her husband. She was unaware the lower part of her arm had been blown off until we grabbed her and applied a tourniquet. She then looked at the stump in amazement, and with that, toppled over."

Bart tried to put things in some sort of rational order, as the girl sought a casualty on whom she could apply her ministrations. Completely exhausted, he breathed hard with his arms slack at his sides, but a strange glow of accomplishment flickered within him. It was like the physical expenditure following a quarter-mile run, but more complete and serene.

The clatter in the street seemed to cease. The ambulance gongs no longer jangled their authority; no more questions were asked; the policemen tucked their notebooks away and went back to their beats. All the violence had dissipated, the street was again gloomy, stark, and the bare beams and jagged masonry stood out against the starry sky. It was not an important street. Those who had been killed or maimed were not in Debrett's or entitled to coats of arms. The patch of battered habitation was obscure, but during that agonizing period of blinding illumination Bartley Crispin feared that he had seen briefly the future of his world— of mankind.

He pulled himself together, brushed the dust and mortar flecks from his shoulders and coat front, and walked away. He remembered that he had to get back to New Cavendish Street, and that someone had told him it was over in *that* direction. He had better hurry to get there before the others returned from the theater. They would want to wind up the evening in a suitable manner. He wondered if they had heard the raid. What did they do in theaters and other public places when the Zepps came over? Perhaps the theater had been emptied and the audience sent home . . . told to take cover. If so, they would all be at home by now. He wondered if the Gaiety Theater was anywhere near where the bombs had fallen.

Zigzagging through the streets, he headed in *that* direction. His shoulders were stiff and his thighs ached with the clambering and crawling he had done, but he reflected that the experience was one he would never forget. He'd tell about it over and over for as long as he could remember; how he'd been in London, wandering about the streets during a Zeppelin raid. How he actually had seen what happens when a bomb falls in an area of dwellings; how he saw a Zeppelin in the sky attacked by a lone man in a little warplane, and how the Zeppelin had caught fire and tumbled in a shapeless mass to the ground. Wait until he got back to tell Mr. Pollard; he'd keep him talking through all hours of the night. He wondered if Mr. Pollard's factory had turned out anything that had been used in the raid tonight. Perhaps a gun, an anti-aircraft gun. Maybe he had made and shipped over the searchlight that had speared the German airship. He may have provided the shells, or the cartridges the pilot had fired from his machine gun. It was something to think about; that someone back home had contributed some one item that may have helped in trapping that raider.

If so, wouldn't Doc Poultney be pleased? Doc would question and probe until he had savored every word of it. He must remember that girl with the first-aid kit and the matter-of-fact way in which she went about her business, carrying on as she was supposed to. Doc would love that part of it.

As Bart moved on his stride shortened, his pace reduced. He stared about wondering if it would not be a good idea to find a pub, get a drink and a sit-down. He came up to a sidewalk pillar at the base of a set of murky steps. He stood there, his hand on the top of the column steadying himself, resting. He waited for some minutes with his chin on his forearm, and then he glanced up the stone steps. There was a dull glow under the edge of the door where years of footsteps had gouged out a hollow. There was a paper notice fluttering under the front window sill. He glanced upward and his eyes caught the fabulous words: ROYAL FLYING CORPS. Muscular reaction forced him to grip the top molding of the pillar, and gradually his eyes took in smaller lettering on a sign pasted to the lower half of the door.

He lowered his forehead to the cool surface of the stone balustrade. It felt good. He looked up again and was able to make more sense of the sign on the door. He wiped the back of his hand across his mouth, stood erect, and muttered, "Okay, Doc."

With some effort he forced his legs to take him up the steps. He read the notice again, and fumbled drunkenly for the doorknob. It took some effort to force the warped portal open. He stepped inside and found himself in an unfurnished hallway, but to the right a doorway opened on a small former reception room.

"We're about to close," a man in khaki said from one end of a table made of planks and sawhorses and covered with a gray military blanket.

Another man, an officer, sat at the center of the table, shuffling a sheaf of papers into some general order. He was a flying officer with a blue and white ribbon below his pilot's wings. There was a narrow bar of gold at the lower end of his left sleeve. He stared at the weary, stained man who stood before him.

"Are you hurt?" he inquired with consideration in his voice. "Were you involved in the raid?"

Crispin looked at the wings on the man's tunic. He wondered what the blue and white ribbon represented. "No. I'm all right. I was in that street . . . helping out with the wounded."

"There's a washroom in there," the sergeant said, "if you'd like to get some of it off."

"No, it's not that."

"What can we do for you?" the officer inquired.

Bartley Crispin heard himself say, "I . . . I want to take the shilling."

There was silence. All movement ceased. A figure on a recruiting poster stared down on the tableau.

"We're R.F.C. here, you know," the officer finally said.

"The Royal Flying Corps," the sergeant explained.

"Yes. That's what I mean. I saw that Zeppelin shot down. I want to do something about what I have seen tonight."

The two R.F.C. men exchanged glances. The officer said with renewed interest, "Well, I must say we can use you."

Crispin put his hands on the table and went on, "I want to fly and fight those swine. Until just now I wanted no part of it, but after what I have seen tonight . . ."

"Yes, we know what you mean."

The sergeant leaned over and muttered, "He probably means the aerial gunner list, sir."

"Exactly."

"Farnborough isn't full up as yet. We can send him right on."

Crispin understood the words "aerial gunner" to mean they were accepting him to fly an aeroplane. The British always seemed to use formal phrases. It would be a plane fitted with a machine gun. A fighting plane. "That's what I want. To fly and fight. . . . Shoot those blasted airships down."

A new form was produced. The sergeant went into the next room and spun the handle of a wall telephone. The officer took out his fountain pen, looked up at Crispin, and in a businesslike manner said, "Your name, please."

Bryce Melville went to the front door for the third time. Macintosh was pouring a drink and studying the eyes of Dianne. Stacey Wallace was trying to make a phonograph work.

"We should have insisted that he stay with us," Dianne repeated for the third or fourth time. "It was ridiculous to let him wander about on his own."

"He's a big boy," Ralph remonstrated. "He should be capable of taking care of himself."

"He's never been in London during an air raid. It's easy to become bewildered and get into trouble."

The phonograph finally opened with "If You Were the Only Girl in the World."

Bryce came back into the room, morose and concerned. "If he headed in this general direction from the Troc he could have walked smack into that bombed area. God only knows what could have happened. He might not have known enough to duck into any doorway and ask for shelter. You mooch about in the street and you can get it in a dozen different ways."

"I still say he should be able to take care of himself. I don't know what all of you are so worried about," Ralph repeated.

"He's our guest, and we're responsible for him," Dianne continued. "We should have insisted . . ."

A bell tingled and Bryce rushed from the room. The rest turned and stared, awaiting some assurance that the wanderer had returned. Macintosh said, "That must be he. Who would be at the front door at this hour of the night?"

There was some excitable conversation and then Bryce came back in with his hand gripping Bart Crispin's elbow. "Well, here he is," Bryce cried as he led the gutter-stained figure into the center of the room.

"Bart!" Dianne cried, snapping to her feet. "Whatever happened?"

Macintosh waved his glass in Crispin's general direction. "Ladies and gentlemen, I give you the man who wanted no part of the war."

"What happened? Are you all right, Bart?" Dianne inquired anxiously. "Wherever have you been?"

Bart wiped the back of a clenched hand across his eyes. "I got caught in the raid. It was pretty bad, but I tried to help. Dozens of people . . . and little kids were killed. Awful."

"All right . . . all right, but are you hurt?" Bryce demanded.

"He's all blood and dirt. He must be," Stacey almost whispered, hurrying to the phonograph.

"I'm all right. I saw the aeroplane shoot down that blasted Zeppelin. I was right there where it happened. It was the most glorious night I have ever seen . . . and after that I went and took the shilling." He turned and glared at Ralph. "I'm going to fly with the R.F.C. I'm to be in Farnborough on Monday morning."

"You *what?*" Bryce Melville grabbed Crispin's arm. "Say that again. You took the shilling?"

Bart grinned like a gargoyle, opened his clenched hand, and held out a bright silver coin. "On the way back I found a recruiting depot and I went in. There's the shilling."

Ralph moved to the center of the room and stared down at Bart's open palm.

"You took the shilling . . . enlisted?" he demanded.

Bart nodded. "Right. I just had to after what I saw tonight. Some of it was dreadful . . . hellish; but seeing that airship go down in flames . . . that was glorious, just glorious."

"But, Bart." Bryce yanked Bart around and stared into his eyes. "Do you know what you have done?"

"Of course. I've joined up. I'm going to fly a warplane . . . a battle plane with machine guns on it."

Macintosh let out an indistinct exclamation, turned on his heel, and went back to his chair. "Well I'll be damned!" he concluded in amazement.

"Bart, are you sure about this?" Bryce began again.

"There must be a mistake," Dianne said. "Taking the shilling means you have enlisted—in the ranks. They'll make you a mechanic, fitter, motor driver, or just someone who sweeps up the hangar."

"They said I'd be flying in a very short time," Bart insisted.

"You crazy, Goddamned fool!" Ralph bellowed.

"Don't you see?" Bryce said in a kindly manner. "You have enlisted. Over here, it means you have signed up in the ranks. If you wanted to fly you should have applied for a commission. You would have become a cadet like those kids at Oxford. Then, after a certain amount of training, you would have been awarded your commission. By that time you would have been well on toward finishing your flying courses. But as an enlisted man there's no such chance."

Dianne said, "Maybe Dad can do something for you."

"But he's signed up. He has his shilling," Ralph insisted with some undisguised glee. "He has to go through with it now. He's a Second Class Air Mechanic . . . in charge of spare parts."

Crispin took it all in, standing stock-still in the middle of the floor. He stared at Dianne and then at Bryce. "But I thought . . ."

"I know what you did. I know exactly," Bryce said. "You saw what happens in an air raid, and you were disturbed. Then you came upon a recruiting depot. It has happened many times. I almost did it myself, once, but I want to fly, not clean spark plugs."

"Wait a minute," Macintosh broke in. "I think I know what happened. He went barging in, the savior of the British Empire, and bellowed something about wanting to fly and shoot down Zepps. Well, who knows, he may. I'll bet they've signed him up for the aerial gunner course."

"What's that?"

"He'll be an NCO flier. A machine gunner aboard the old pushers . . . sitting out there in a bathtub nacelle in a sky full of Albatros scouts and Fokkers. He'll see all the flying and fighting there is to be seen. It's a real suicide club!" Macintosh ranted on, and burst into a tuneless chorus of "Oh, Oh, Ain't It a Lovely War?" "They'll have him out in France in a few weeks. There are no gas-filled Zepps out there. Only Fokkerinos. All he'll get at Farnborough will be a short course on Lewis guns, and then it will be two patrols a day . . . as long as he lives."

"Is this something new?" Bryce asked.

"It started a few months ago. They needed gunners on the two-seater fighters and they kidded guys to volunteer from the trenches. The idea worked well, so they decided to set up a new NCO gunner course. That's what Bartley boy fell into. Not only that, but it's cheap. He'll get one and six a day rank pay, and four shillings a day flying pay. Had he done the right thing from the start he would be drawing nearly a pound a day. That's what he gets for 'taking the shilling.'"

"It's too bad," Bryce commiserated. "If you had only told us what you . . . but it's too late now, I'm afraid."

Bart made the best of it and took a drink from Dianne. "I don't mind about the commission, just so long as I can do something . . . something with flying and fighting in it."

"Oh boy!" Macintosh ejaculated. "Listen to the fire-eater now. The last time I saw him in Princeton he was blubbering about the waste and horror of war, declaring he would not fight and kill some mother's darling boy. After seeing a modest sample of what war over London is really like, he wants to roar off and blast Germany off the map. Even I don't feel that belligerent."

"That is quite evident," Dianne agreed, anger rising in her cheeks. "I don't think you do. But you can't be expected to. You seem to be having a rather good time—here in England. There seems to be plenty of London leave for some commissioned officers."

"Oh, come off it, Di," her brother remonstrated. "That's not fair. No one can decide whether he will, or will not, go out to the front. Right now Ralph's involved in very important work in a new squadron that is training on a brand-new plane. He'll go out when his squadron is ready."

Macintosh studied Dianne in this new mood. Who could figure young women? He accepted the possibility she was disturbed over Bart's mistake, but all evening she had been most concerned about his flying this new aeroplane. She had heard that it was very fast, and that the first squadron would soon be sent out to France to establish a new airfighting formula. Now she was bestowing her solicitude and sympathy on this dope Crispin who suddenly wanted to fly and fight the Huns. Well, he'd need all the concern and sympathy he could get if he went out to the front as an aerial gunner. He might survive a couple of weeks, but damn the man, was he always to blunder into these high-level social circles and grab the prize?

"I know all about Ralph and the new aeroplane, and the special squadron he's assigned to," Dianne snapped, "but that does not give him the call to lord it over Bart. I think it took courage to do what he did tonight. Good luck to him."

"He'll need all he can get," Ralph said over the rim of his glass.

Bryce led Bart to a settee. "Let's get this straight," he probed again. "You signed a paper?"

"Yes, and I took the oath to serve for the duration of the war."

"Any question about your nationality or citizenship?"

"None. They said lots of Americans had joined the Royal Flying Corps. I did not renounce the United States. I simply agreed to serve King George—for the duration."

"Did you take a medical?"

"No. It was too late for that. The doctor had left, but I can take one when I get to Farnborough. There won't be any concern along that line."

"Yes, damn it, you'll pass if they only look at your teeth. But what a shame. You could have become a cadet and had a commission in a few weeks. Not only that, your Rhodes scholarship probably goes down the drain."

"That's not all-important. Right now I still feel I must do something. You should have seen those people. Game as they come. No one complained. A few moaned with pain. There were some amputations, and those ambulance workers and nurses would make any man sign up then and there. Only those who were not involved stood about and swore—and then shuffled off to the nearest pub."

"It takes all sorts. What are you going to do now?" Bryce asked.

"I suppose I'd better take the train back to Oxford early tomorrow. I can clean up everything there and then swing down to Farnborough. That's all I can do. I've signed in, and I'll have to go through with it."

"I'll talk to Dad and see if he has any influence anywhere. He might be able to annul your enlistment and have you transferred to the cadet course."

"No! Don't do that. I talked to your father earlier in the evening. I wouldn't want him to think I wasn't sincere. I think a lot of his opinion. I'm going through with it, Bryce."

"I almost wish I was going with you. They'd take me in the ranks, you know."

"Don't. One damn fool on the team is enough," Bart said.

Macintosh was on his feet, preparing to leave. "Anyone going my way—toward the Savoy? I'll get a taxi and drop you off."

"Good night, Ralph," Bryce said over his shoulder. "I'll

133

walk Stacey home. It's not too far from here. Get your things, Stacey."

Bart sat with his drink between his knees. He just looked up at Macintosh and allowed him to walk out of the room without any response. He had to admit Ralph looked smart in that R.F.C. uniform.

Dianne came and sat beside him. "You've had a rough night," she said, and put her arm across his shoulders. "One of the bad ones."

He nodded and stared down into his glass. "It was my own fault. No one else to blame. Not that I regret it now. It is something I'll remember as long as I live."

"I'm sure you will," Dianne said, and stroked his head.

"It's very good of you," he said, appreciating her sympathy. "I'm sorry I caused this trouble for the family."

"No trouble. I think we're going to be proud of you. You must come and see us whenever you get leave. You're always welcome here." She twisted his head so she looked straight into his eyes. "Come on, chin up," she ordered, and kissed him with warmth.

"Chin up!"

Dianne hooked her arm in Bart's and took over. "Listen to me. You *want* to come and see us, don't you? I mean . . ."

"Where else would I go?"

"Don't put it that way. I want you to come to London whenever you can." She turned and waved to Stacey, who was being led out by Bryce. "Good night, Stacey. Keep in touch.

"Nice girl, that," Dianne went on. "Perfect for Bryce."

"Everyone's nice," Bart muttered, and flicked his hand toward the couple.

"You're the best yet," Dianne said. "We've never had one like you. You will come . . . for me?"

"I'm just an air mechanic," he said with a grin.

"I don't care what you are, Bart. I'm thinking about you, not a uniform."

"You mean that?"

"I mean it. Now listen to me. When you get any leave, don't come here. This damned place is always cluttered up with leeches . . . like Macintosh. We saw him at his worst tonight. We can't be alone, or talk here."

"Alone?"

"Of course. There's so much to do, and talk about."

Bart took the rest of the message from her eyes. It was the first time he had enjoyed true affection. Not even Cynthia Pollard had reached within him like this.

"Listen, Bart," Dianne went on. "Don't come here. I'll give you the address of Mrs. Cartwright. She used to be with us, but when her husband died she bought a house in Keppel Street . . . number 26 Keppel Street. It's behind the British Museum, Bloomsbury area. Mrs. Cartwright will do anything for me. I'll have her reserve a room for you whenever you are in town. Consider it your leave home. I'll arrange to see you there."

"Is this . . . er, conventional?" Bart asked, no little puzzled by the turn of the conversation.

"Damn conventions! We can't get together here."

"This Mrs. Cartwright. She won't mind?"

"I told you, she'll do anything for me."

Bart was astounded at her plan, and suddenly realized she was offering everything she had. "Is this what you want?"

"It's the only way."

"But I don't want you to take any risk—with your good name."

She smiled and kissed him again. "Now you know why. . . . I've never met anyone like you."

"But there are some rules . . ."

"Keep that in mind, but follow your heart. Always do exactly as you did tonight. You can't go wrong."

"Boy." Bart shook his head slowly. "I did everything wrong. I just hope I don't tarnish you with my unstable emotions."

"Stop talking. You're driving me frantic. Leave the shilling business to me. We can take care of that."

"I don't want you to get your father into this."

"Father? What influence has he with the R.F.C.?"

"I don't know, but . . ."

"I told you to leave it to me. I'm in the middle of it all."

"I don't know what you are talking about, but I don't want to crawl out. I got myself into it and . . ."

"Forget it. Just remember number 26 Keppel Street. Mrs. Cartwright. That's your London home from now on."

"Just as long as you are not besmirching your name in any way."

"Go to bed. I won't see you tomorrow. I shall be at the Depot by the time you and Bryce are having breakfast."

She kissed him once more and led him to the stairway.

"Number 26 Keppel Street . . . remember."

CHAPTER ELEVEN

March 1917

*British make good advance toward Bapaume. . . .
Mexico repudiates offer made in Zimmermann tele-
gram. . . . Count Ferdinand von Zeppelin dies. . . .
Baghdad captured by British forces. . . . Revolution
moves started in Petrograd. . . . Czar Nicholas ab-
dicates. . . . Germans withdraw on an 85-mile front.
. . . Three more American ships torpedoed. . . .
British advance moves toward Cambrai.*

The Nissen hut was fairly new and had windows of oiled
linen. Naked bulbs hung from the splintery arches, spreading a weak glare on wall charts and drawings that presented
the working parts of rifles and machine guns. A long, greasy
table stood in the center of the room with uncomfortable
benches along each side. A portly corporal with a stop watch
in his hand sat at one end, and at the other a man in a baggy
uniform stood behind the spade grip of a Lewis gun. He
had been blindfolded with a soiled gray muffler. Along each
side of the table sat ten or a dozen other rookies in the art
of warfare, none of whom displayed more than tepid interest
in the proceedings.

"Now the h'idea 'ere is," the corporal was explaining, "not
to 'ave you strip this gun and put it orl together agayne wiv
yer eyes tied up. That ain't the h'idea at all. It's just a way we
'ave of learnin' yer 'ow to remedy stoppages in case you 'ave
any in the air."

The man behind the gun scratched his nose and then started to finger the latch of the ammunition drum.

"Now 'arf a mo' there, Crispin. We don't try beatin' the watch. 'Ands orf the weapon!"

"Yes, Corporal."

"Now wot this trainin' is intended for is that if ever you are h'engagin' an h'enemy h'aircraft, an' you 'ave a Number Two stoppage, for instance, there ain't any good takin' yer h'eyes orf the enemy plane, is there? Nao! You must keep yore h'eyes on the enemy, even while you're remedying a Number Two stoppage, an' to do that you 'ave to learn 'ow to strip an' assemble yore weapon while ye're blindfolded. You h'understand wot I mean, of course. You see, while yo're keeping your h'eye on the 'Un, you are practically remedying the stoppage wiv a blindfold on. That's right, ain't it? Any questions?"

The sooty-eyed trainees made no audible response; they were too tired to interpret the corporal's parrotlike patter, having endured this sort of tuition, fourteen hours a day, for several weeks.

"Nao? Well, get on wiv it, Crispin."

The blindfolded figure behind the gun snapped off the ammunition drum, selected a cartridge from the circular container, and inserted the bullet end into the prong of the spade grip. The Lewis gun required only a round of ammunition to dismantle the weapon completely.

"I remove the spade grip," he began, explaining the stripping sequence. "The trigger group is drawn out, which lowers the pinion casing for removal. The body cover comes off . . . and now the feed arm is free. The cocking handle is withdrawn and I can now take the bolt from its mount on the piston rod."

As he spoke his dextrous fingers carried out each movement with precision. He spoke quietly, selecting his words carefully, and placed the parts on either side of the table. The corporal watched him with official interest, and consulted his stop watch at intervals. Now and then he raised his eyebrows, signifying his disbelief in the speed of the performance.

"Great care must be taken in this particular operation," Crispin explained. "Threads on the gas-pressure parts are not to be damaged in the slightest. On reassembling, see that the barrel band is replaced correctly. While I can't see, I must feel to make certain that the letter *F*, indicating 'Front,' is set square with the gas chamber . . ."

"Roit!" the corporal agreed. "Carry on, Crispin."

There was a creak of a door and the thud of official boots. The corporal snapped to attention and bellowed, "Class . . . 'shun!" The blindfolded man halted his test with his expressive hands over the weapon. The others jerked to their feet, turning over one of the benches, which fell with an outraged clatter.

"At ease!" someone bellowed. "Carry on!"

Crispin tried to fathom the interruption, but continued his race against time. A tall man in G.S. (General Service) uniform with wings and a row of ribbons on his tunic tucked his stick under his arm and watched the performance. He checked the parts that had been removed, and when Crispin began the reassembly test, he reached over and took the stop watch from the corporal. He studied the flickering second hand for a minute or two and then handed it back.

When the gun had been reassembled Crispin removed the blindfold and was surprised to see that their visitor was the station adjutant, Captain Donegal.

Donegal looked at the stop watch again and said, "Very good. An excellent show. What's the man's name, Corporal?"

"That would be Crispin, sir. Air Mechanic Crispin."

"You have any others up to that mark?"

"Well, sir, not quite. Crispin's one of the good 'uns. Still, there are several who will do it well under time."

"That's what I came in about. Pick out your five best men and have them report to Personnel Office at eleven o'clock. I want their training course records, also. That's all. Carry on."

"Class . . . 'shun!" the corporal bellowed to accompany his salute.

As the orderly sergeant left, he gave the instructor a knowing wink and then slammed the door after him.

"Cool!" the two-striper said, blowing out his mustache. "Now 'ere's a pretty kettle of fish. Looks like some of you are not a-goin' to finish this course. I am told that five of you are to report to the Personnel Office. You know wot that means?"

"You can put me down, Corporal," someone broke in.

"'Ere, one thing at a time. I ain't through explainin' yet."

"Anything to get out of this place. Like jail with hard labor."

Still under the squint-eyed influence of the tight muffler, Crispin was uncertain what was taking place. He sensed his test had gone well, and assumed the Adjutant had picked him out for some new phase of instruction. He hoped he had been selected for the cadet course, but there had been too many disappointments over the past few weeks.

"There's worse places than this, I can tell you," the instructor continued, scowling. "All I can say is that there must 'ave been a few cas-u-al-ities somewhere, an' they probably need several—five at least—new aerial gunners. The ones I select will undoubtedly be picked to go. Now wot was you sayin' about puttin' you down, 'Artwell?"

"If it means gettin' out of 'ere, put me down. I'll go to-night!"

"You'll go early this arfternoon . . . as soon as you can pack up, if I know anythink. Any other volunteers?"

Crispin looked around the training group. They had been together for about four weeks, and all they had been taught was to march about a parade ground, how to clean, load and drill with a Lee-Enfield rifle, wear the R.F.C. uniform, and dismantle and assemble a Lewis gun. Not one of them had so far fired a single burst. The only aircraft they had been introduced to was a decrepit B.E. 2c biplane that had been fitted with a new Scarff mounting. Aboard this hulk, set up in a drafty barracks hall, they were shown how to climb in and out of an aeroplane and to test out the movement of the gun mounting. Only a few men who had displayed some personal initiative had attempted to learn the difference between British and German aeroplanes. They knew nothing of aerial cameras, the Morse code, or what made a Cooper bomb explode when it hit the ground, but as men who were to fly against the enemy they had certainly been taught how to march on a barracks square.

"But we ain't nowhere near finished the course, Corporal," someone complained, "an' there's the matter of draft leave. We're entitled to seven days before going over to France."

"Who said you wuz goin' to France? It could be you'll wind up in Mes-o-po-tamia."

"Where's that?"

"'Ow the 'ell do I know? It's somewhere orf Africa, ain't it? Don't you remember any of yer 'istory?"

"So we don't get no draft leave?"

"One thing at a time. Now . . . er, Crispin, you don't seem to 'ave much choice. The Adjutant picked you. Now what about four others? You're all about the same as far as Lewis guns are concerned. Good, but not extra-ordinary."

"I'll go, if I can get a few days at home."

"Put me down. I ain't got no 'ome."

"It's a bloody ramp—no draft leave, but anything's better than friggin' Farnborough. Put me down."

The required number was finally coerced by innuendo, false promises, and guile to volunteer for this vague assignment.

"All right, then," the corporal said as he sucked the end of a pencil. "You five be on time at the Personnel Office. I'll be there wiv yer trainin' records. You'd all better bung orf now an' get your kit together—just in case. The rest of yer will stay 'ere an' we'll go over the immediate h'action to remedy a Number Three stoppage."

"Do we 'ave to wear our puttees, Corporal?" one of the volunteers bleated.

"Puttees? Of course you do. You're goin' afore the Adjutant, ain't yer? D'yer think turnin' up wivout puttees is accordin' to *King's Rules an' Regulations*? Gorblimy! A bloody good job we've got a navy!"

"I just wondered, Corporal."

"Stop wonderin' an' get on wiv it. You wear puttees!"

The relieved quintet stormed out of the training shed, decided on a circuitous course that would avoid the barracks square, and made for their quarters. During the Farnborough course the volunteers had been accommodated in temporary Nissen huts. They might just as well have been quartered in Greenland.

In the center of the elephant-iron structures stood a sheet-metal stove, complete with built-in inadequacy. It devoured all the fuel that could be scrounged, but refused to deliver one degree of creature comfort. To cope with the Hampshire spring the recruits seldom took off their uniforms, removing only their military boots when they retired. This custom produced a level of masculine effluvium rivaling that to be encountered in any collection of Lascar seamen. In contrast, the floors were continually scrubbed and swept. Equipment was arranged with meticulous formality, and the beds made to the precise order and compactness of those in a hospital, but there seldom was any warmth or an extra degree of comfort. The orderly officer, on his daily search for a fluting of dust or a nailhead of mud, was usually wrapped in his heaviest British warm, fur-lined gloves, and a woolen scarf to face these arctic conditions.

Bartley Crispin pondered on the unexpected upheaval in his training. In one mind he realized he would see air action before Ralph Macintosh, and in the next he wondered how his limited training would fit him for the front. How soon would he be out there? What kind of squadron would he be posted to? Would there be any leave before being sent across the Channel? That is, if they were to be sent to France or Belgium.

There were some letters and rolled-up periodicals on his bed, a regular feature that placed him well above the status of the other aerial gunners. Crispin was a plutocrat as far as mail was concerned. He received books, food parcels from Selfridge's, magazines, and, most unusual, considerable mail bearing United States postage stamps. The others received a murky envelope now and then, and sometimes pitifully small packages that might contain a bar of chocolate and two packets of cigarettes.

"You must 'ave a lot of friends—everywhere," the man called Hartwell said, looking down at the colorful stack.

"Help yourself," Bart replied. "That big one is probably a food package. We might as well celebrate."

By the time he had opened a letter from Dianne Melville, Hartwell was munching on a hefty pork pie, and a little Derbyshire man, Bowen by name, was drawing contentedly on a Gold Flake cigarette.

"You *must* 'ave a lot of friends," Bowen agreed, "but do they expect you to read all that stuff?"

Bart grinned, and then plunged into Dianne's letter while sharing a box of cream-filled wafers.

> Dearest:
> How are you? When do you think you can get away again? Mrs. Cartwright just adores you. I shall have to watch her. Isn't your room perfect—for us? I almost feel like taking it over myself. The weather in London is improving, and there are some little yellow flowers blooming in the back garden.
> Had a letter from Bryce and he feels that they'll take him almost any day now. He is so excited about you, too. Father continually asks about you and intimates he may see someone named Henderson, in your behalf. Ralph Macintosh came around last Saturday, but he was brushed out with the wilted flowers. He wanted to take me to the Royal Automobile Club for dinner,

143

but I produced an excuse with no trouble at all. I just
don't trust him.

You should be due for another weekend leave,
shouldn't you? If you need anything—money, or
clean things—Mrs. Cartwright will take care of you. I
have it all arranged. Please get "home" soon.

All my love,
Dianne

After some thought, Bart tucked the letter back, and then
riffled over the others. There was a note from Doc Poultney,
another from Mr. Pollard with no news of interest, and
some shaggy newspapers from Princeton. Doc was still on
his soapbox, lauding the "successes" of the Allies and offering some faint belief that America would eventually get
into it. He, of course, did not know of Bart's "taking the
shilling" so could not crow or comment. There was no
news of any sort from Bart's parents.

"You think we'll get any draft leave?" Hartwell spoke
through a mouthful of currant cake.

"I hope so."

"Got a girl over here yet?"

"Well, I have some very good friends in London."

"Friends ain't the same. Do you 'ave a bit of fluff?"

Bart grinned and explained. "Well, I have a nice old lady,
Mrs. Cartwright, who takes good care of me and sees to
it that I don't want for anything."

Hartwell produced a quizzical grimace. "This Mrs. Cartwright don't 'appen to 'ave *two* daughters, does she?"

"No. I'm sorry . . ."

"No 'arm in arskin', is there?"

"None at all. Try the lemon curd," Bart invited.

"We'd better start packin' up," said Bowen. "I'll 'ave one
more gasper, if you don't mind?"

Hartwell grumbled as he reached up to a shelf for his
kit bag. "I didn't think we'd be off as quick as this."

"Anything's better than Farnborough," Bowen stated with
spirit. "Coo! Don't they put you through it 'ere?"

"I just 'ope we get some draft leave," Hartwell repeated morosely.

There were no ifs, ands, or buts at the Personnel Office. It was stated in unintelligible military jargon that there was an immediate need for aerial gunners at the front. . . . No, there would be no draft leave since this could not be considered a draft. . . . It was an emergency. . . . The two-seater squadrons were carrying the bulk of the fighting now, and aerial gunners were not volunteering from the trenches in sufficient numbers. . . . "You men are quite capable, and will receive further instruction once you join a squadron. . . . Have no fear, you won't go on a patrol until you are completely familiar with your weapons, your aircraft, your front, and your over-all duty. . . . As for leave, flying personnel are entitled to fourteen days every three months. . . . You'll be surprised how quickly three months will pass out there—once you start regular patrols. . . . And remember, your flying pay starts the day you set foot in France."

"That's all!" the Regimental Sergeant Major bellowed. "You'll parade with your equipment at two-thirty this afternoon. Service tenders will take you to the station. From that point on you'll be in the hands of the R.T.O.s (Railway Transport Officers), and you'll be sorted out at the Pool and assigned to the requesting squadrons. That's all! 'Shun! About face! Quick march!"

Crispin reflected this was totally unlike any standard wartime farewell to departing troops. There were no bands or bunting. No one made encouraging speeches with high-sounding references to home and fireside, to King and Country, to the confusion of the common enemy. There were no mothers drying their eyes with the corners of their aprons; no wives or sweethearts reaching up to train windows; no little boys or girls waving tiny flags . . . not even a mongrel pooch to entangle the underfoot proceedings. Just "'Shun! About face! Quick march!" But more regrettable, there would be no return to Mrs. Cartwright's bed-sitting room seclusion where Dianne would greet him and share his wonderment and joy. He wondered how many Mrs. Cartwrights there were in the world. He tried comparing her to his own mother, and gave up.

The five-gunner draft, wearing standard serge maternity jackets, breeches, puttees, and new military boots, shouldered kit bags and stood by for the service tenders, light utility cars that were used for these movements. From Farnborough they were carried to Waterloo. There was not enough time to make a telephone contact with Dianne at that time of day, since she would be out on her driving assignments. The best Bart could do was to scribble a telegram and advise her of the sudden change in his training program. It would have to do until he was in France and had a definite squadron address.

"My tart will raise bloody 'ell," a gunner named Meakins observed over a cup of tea in the station restaurant. "She'll blame it all on me, of course, as though I can go and come as I like. Gals just carn't understand the military, but then, who can?"

From Waterloo they were shunted to Folkestone, where they spent most of the night in a drafty convenience under the eye of the Military Police and the R.T.O. They were allowed to remove their British warms and tunics to wash and shave, but any digression for a breakfast was out of the question. The cross-Channel packet, the old *Victoria*, would tie up at the quay at any moment. She was only seven miles off Folkestone . . . or so it was reported.

"You can get a breakfast on board—perhaps."

"As I awlus says," proclaimed Hartwell after some serious consideration, "there's only one thing they carn't do to you in the army. Not that they won' 'ave a try one of these days."

"Fancy bein' on light duty for nine months," observed Bowen.

Hartwell took a long look at Crispin, who was staring at

his reflection in the flyspecked mirror. "I suppose orl yore relatives are over in America," he said with some friendly concern.

"What few I have, or know of. They seem to be scattered all over."

"A funny way to live."

"Well, it's a big country, you know."

"Ah, so I've been told. You can go thousands of miles in any direction, eh? Must be nice in a way, though."

"Wot-yer come over 'ere for?" Bowen broke in.

"I was awarded a scholarship to Oxford, and while there I decided to join up. The scholarship can wait. It won't be any good if Germany wins the war," Crispin said, and wondered how he came up with that idea.

Bowen and Hartwell exchanged glances. "You think Germany *can* win the war?" Hartwell asked in amazement.

"You 'adn't ought to talk like that," Bowen chided.

"Were you ever in a Zeppelin raid?" Bart asked bluntly.

"Me? I've never even seen one in the sky," Hartwell replied with some left-over amazement.

Bowen thought it out. "They don't come round our way. I've read about 'em in the papers, of course, but I've never seen one."

"Seems like they're always trying to blow up London."

"You have no idea what war is like until you've been in an air raid," Crispin chided. "I was in the middle of a bad one, just a few weeks ago. I don't think I shall ever forget it."

"Ah. It must be bloody awful. But when you only read about 'em none of it seems very real."

"Trench warfare must be pretty bad at times, but in an air raid civilians are involved. Women and little kids. That's the part that turns your stomach. Men fighting men, one can accept. It's like a rough football game," Crispin explained, staring at the floor.

"Is that what made you join up?" Hartwell said suddenly.

Crispin shoved his cap back. "It had a lot to do with it."

147

"You could 'ave waited, you know."

"Waited? For what?"

"America will be comin' in soon, won't she?"

"You could join up in your own mob then."

"I don't think America will come in," Crispin snapped in mild anger. "Wilson was voted in again. That means they don't want any part of the war. I don't think America will come in."

"It's something I carn't understand," Hartwell mused, and lighted a Gold Flake. "I mean, what can they be thinkin' about? Do they like the Germans?"

"You must remember one thing," Bart tried to explain. "People think differently in different parts of the world. You are either in it or you are neutral. When I was at home this war seemed like an insane affair, and I swore I would never have any part in it, whether America went in or not." He grinned at Bowen. "I argued that I was an architect. I said I was going to build beautiful buildings . . . not blow them down with bombs. I actually said that because I hated the thought of war."

"You carn't take no notice of war, like that."

"You can't over here." Bart nodded in agreement. "The people know all about war, and they know it has to be won. It's not like that in the United States. There it's just something people read about in the newspapers and see on the Pathé News picture screens. Do you want to know something? You don't have any idea about war until you've smelled it."

"Smelled it?"

"Right. War has a stench of its own. I first caught it that night in London. There's the whiff of gunpowder, smoke, and first-aid solutions. You first smell the stench of your own dread: that's when you begin to sweat. Even the motor-cars and other vehicles smell differently. When the front of a building collapses it releases all the smells of bedrooms, kitchens, dusty passages full of old clothes. It's not what you see when a house topples in, it's what you smell. I

148

don't think I'll get some of the stinks out of my nose until I get into the air and have it all blown out of me. I think that's why I joined up—without knowing it."

Hartwell sat with his long horse face in the palms of his hands. Bowen was reading the gilt lettering on the Gold Flake. Finally Hartwell mumbled, "Wot was that they used to say about old war 'orses sniffin' the battle afar?" He turned and looked at Bart. "You ain't makin' any of that up, are you?"

Crispin looked up puzzled. "I suppose I am making it up as I go along. I hadn't thought about it in that way until this minute but, take my word for it, it is the smells that remain with you."

As they sat considering their reflections in the mirror, a bulky man with a red band on his arm came up and poked Crispin's shoulder. "You chaps had better get yourselves together. Rise an' shine. Out to the quay."

The Pool for aerial gunners was set up in a disused French barracks where the temperature was several degrees lower than that at Farnborough. The food was considerably worse, but there was much more of it, reflecting the rule of supply and demand. Although they had been rushed out of England with commendable speed and military efficiency, all factors of a grim emergency dissolved once they stepped off the *Victoria* at Boulogne. They spent most of that day searching for an R.T.O. who had some idea what an aerial gunner was and where they were supposed to report. They had wandered about chestnut-lined streets and found an estaminet near the Pont de Briques station. They had tried to get into the bar of the Folkestone Hotel, but because of the stain of their lowly NCO rank they had been imperiously shooed away. "For Officers Only," the sign read, and there was a platoon of sadistic M.P.s standing by to enforce the edict.

They toiled up a hill and found a transient camp where more spoiled food was available, and then finally stumbled into a transport officer who remembered something about aerial gunners being connected with the R.F.C.

"I have an idea you chaps are expected at Hesdin," he said after some cogitation.

"Where's that?"

"It's a new deputy-area headquarters of the Royal Flying Corps. They'll probably know what to do with you."

There was considerable business in getting back to the station, still hauling their gear, and getting aboard a train that was scheduled to get into the Hesdin area. There were hours of sitting in freezing third-class compartments, hours of shunting back and forth, hours of standing at remote sidings, and very few minutes of halt wherever food or refreshments were obtainable.

Hesdin turned up two swills and a shave later, and after some basic interrogation in another Nissen hut set in the orchard of the memorable château that housed the R.F.C. staff, they were given a cursory medical examination. No details of the findings were announced. It seemed to be against the rules for a medical officer to converse with or even admit the existence of any transient individual. A terminal case of leprosy might have raised one eyebrow— but nothing more.

"'Ow did you make out?"

"'Ow do I know? No one said anything all the time I was in there. Wot about you?"

"Same thing. I could 'ave sent me mother in, an' they'd never 'ave noticed the difference. Bloody funny, ain't it?"

"Bloody funny."

"A bloody funny war, if you arsk me."

The quintet was enjoying a basin of tea and a can of salmon sopped up with chunks of bread. A sergeant, wearing an observer's wing, the ribbon of the D.C.M., and three wound strips on his sleeve, broke in to present their final orders.

"Who is Clark?" he demanded with a squint.

"I am," one of the five responded.

"When you get to your squadron see about 'avin' them two teeth out."

"Wot two?"

"'Ow do I know? You've got to 'ave two teeth out. The rest of you are orl right."

"What's next, Sergeant?" Bart asked. "Are we posted to any squadron?"

"You are. Let's see now. Clark, Meakins, and Bowen are to go to Number 11 Squadron. F.E. 2bs, for your information."

"Pushers?"

"Pushers, an' you can be thankful it ain't Sopwith one-and-a-half strutters, chum." The sergeant flicked a finger-nail across the three wound stripes. "P.B.O. . . . Poor Bloody Observers."

"Wot about us?" Hartwell broke in.

"All in good time, my boy. Crispin an' 'Artwell are down for Number 20 Squadron."

"What are they flying?" Bart inquired.

"Same thing . . . Fees."

"They're two-seater pushers?"

"Right. Offensive patrols, two or three times a day, you lucky dogs. I do 'ope you can remedy a Number Three stoppage."

"If I may ask, Sergeant," Crispin broke in, "what squadron were you in when you got that D.C.M.?"

The three-striper looked very pleased. "Number 22 Squadron," he said, and folded his papers. "An' mind you, when I've said that, there's nothing more to say. Number 22 is the best bloody squadron anywhere in the world."

"What were you flying?"

"Wot were we flyin'?" The sergeant stared in amazement at such ignorance. "If you're the best bloody two-seater squadron anywhere in the world, you can be flyin' only one bus . . . the F.E. 2b. The bloody old Feel"

Crispin decided it might be politic to display further interest in the sergeant's career. "You have been taken off flying, Sergeant?"

"Taken orf? 'Corse I ain't! I'm just 'avin' a bit of a rest. I 'ad done more than four hundred hours over the line . . . when they decided I needed a change. So I drew this job. But I'm goin' back. In fact, I'm still on flyin' pay. They ain't bloody well a-goin' to bury me 'ere on this blasted desk job."

"Aren't you entitled to a commission and a chance for pilot training?" Bart continued.

"That's wot they tell you when you volunteer for aerial gunnery. But wot they tell you and wot 'appens are two different things. Anyway, there ain't bin no aerial gunners goin' back through 'ere to take commissions or for flying schools. Not since I've been 'ere, there ain't."

"And you still want to go back . . . as an NCO gunner?"

"Christ! Who wouldn't? That is, if you'd ever 'ad a packet of the trenches. I don't want no more of that bloody game, chum. I'll do flyin' any day . . . on Fees, mind you, rather than another dollop of wot we went through on the Somme. I ain't balmy, I ain't."

The newcomers exchanged glances, sniffed, and swilled down the rest of their tea. There was no further argument with this bloke. Still, it was comforting to know that all five were going to squadrons that were flying pusher fighters. None of them had the slightest idea what a Fee looked like, what engine it used, or how many guns it carried. Had one been drawn up outside the mess hut with its Beardmore engine ticking over not one of them would have recognized it.

CHAPTER TWELVE

April 1917

*Aztec, American armed ship, sunk in submarine zone.
. . . United States declares war on Germany. . . .
The Missourian, American steamer, sunk in Mediterranean. . . . Austria-Hungary breaks with the United
States. . . . Germans retreat before British on wide
front. . . . Cuba, Panama, and Bolivia break with Germany. . . . Vimy, Givenchy, Bailleul, and positions
around Lens taken by Canadians.*

Hartwell and Crispin had said, "Well, so long," to Bowen,
Clark, and Meakins two weeks before as they climbed into
their respective tenders outside the château at Hesdin.
Bowen was to die of wounds within ten days, on his second
patrol. Meakins went down in a mid-air collision during a
frantic dogfight in which at least sixty planes took part.
Clark, minus two teeth, was to be awarded the Military
Medal for downing two Albatros scouts long before he had
put in enough patrol hours to claim his observer's wing.

The Warloy aerodrome was totally unfit for flying. It
was so small, the hangars had to be set up on one side
of a road and the landing area patched out amid a tangle
of ditches and drainage areas on the other. As a result,
sideslip landings were routine when the wind was so in-
clined. During flying operations a French gendarme was
assigned to flag down road traffic when planes were being
taxied from their shelters to the take-off area. It was hardly

worthy of a kite-balloon base, but the Fees of Number 20 Squadron had to make the best of it.

Two days after reporting in at Warloy, Hartwell and Crispin were assigned to "C" Flight, replacing a gunner who had been wounded and another who had gone on leave. There were two NCO airmen in each of the three flights, and they were accommodated in a war-weary Adrian hutment set up a short distance from the hangars. They were fitted out with standard flying equipment and told to report to the armament officer twice a day for further instruction in the Lewis gun.

Early in the second day Hartwell was given a few minutes in the air with their flight commander, who explained that he was going up to test an engine. On the way down the new aerial gunner was given a chance to fire a few rounds at a ground target. Evidently satisfied with his performance, the pilot put his name down to go on a patrol immediately after lunch.

"What was it like?" Bartley asked when a green-tinged Hartwell returned, after turning in his gun.

"Don't ask me." Hartwell slumped down on his cot and cupped his chin in his greasy hands.

Crispin was concerned about Hartwell's vacant stare, his troubled expression, and the hopelessness of his attitude. "Are you all right?"

"I'm all right, but I'll never be the same."

"It isn't that bad, is it?"

Hartwell took time to think it out. "It ain't going up that bothers you," he explained. "It was that bloody gun. Frightened me half to death. I'm tellin' you, Crispin, you 'ave no idea what a noise it makes. Then when we started to dive toward the ground, I thought I'd spew my guts out. It was worse than the swing boats at Scarborough."

"You fired at something on the ground?"

"Don't arsk me. I really don't know whether I fired at the ground target or at a bloody big haystack."

"No stoppages?"

154

Hartwell peered up like a betrayed spaniel. "Stoppages? I don't remember. I suppose not. I should 'ave remembered, shouldn't I?"

"I should think so," Bartley mused. "Well, let's go get something to eat."

"Not me. I couldn't face it."

"Perhaps you're wise. I'll tell them to save something for you in case you feel more like it later on."

"That's very good of you," Hartwell muttered, staring down at his thigh-length flying boots. At the moment he looked like a man who was wondering how he had got there, or whether he was in the middle of a six-reel nightmare. His long face was pitted with cordite, his hands were soiled with gun grease, and his thin, lank hair stood up in uneven tufts. "I couldn't eat anything now."

"Well, stretch out until we have to go to another lecture," Crispin suggested. "I'm going to get my meal. I'm famished."

Crispin took down his mess kit from a shelf over his bed and headed for the mess shed. Passing along the row of Besseneau hangars, he could see the Fees of "C" Flight being dragged out to the line. There were six of them, broad-winged biplanes, each with a bathtub-like nacelle mounted on the spars of the lower wings. The engine was set aft with the propeller twirling inside four bamboo tail booms that carried the tail assembly. The pilot sat in front of the Beardmore engine, reasonably well sheltered, but the observer or gunner had to make himself comfortable in the low front nacelle, the side of which—when he stood up—reached to a point an inch or so below his knees.

A machine gun, mounted on a telescoping tube, was fastened in the coaming between the two cockpits. This could be raised to fire over the top plane at any enemy aircraft attacking from behind, but the gunner had to stand with his insteps on the rim of his cockpit and manipulate the gun while holding onto the telescopic mounting. It could be done, but it took a certain amount of in-air experience, agility—and nerve.

The second weapon was bolted to a short length of gas pipe, pivoted to the center of the cockpit floor, and could be moved about and locked in any of a series of brass prongs around the semicircle of the nacelle. The gunner used this weapon most of the time, or whenever his pilot was able to give him shots from any of the segmented positions.

It was aboard this so-called fighting plane that the R.F.C. was continuing its aerial offensive deep within the enemy lines. Surprisingly, it was giving a most creditable account of itself, and had Fee squadrons been limited to fighting above the enemy trenches, their casualty rate would have been better than negligible. Unfortunately, the British attitude was that "offensive" meant intruding as deep into enemy areas as engines, fuel, and weather would permit. Thus, if some damage was inflicted on the Beardmore, there was no choice but to go down and land in German-held territory. A turn in the weather could also be tragic, for the science of meteorology was in its infancy. If it was decided that conditions were unfavorable, it was impossible to recall planes because wireless was not the two-way convenience it later became.

When Bartley returned to their hut he found Hartwell talking to one of the mechanics.

"You Crispin?" the visitor asked, wiping his nose on his coverall sleeve.

"That's right."

"Get your kit on. You're on patrol . . . fifteen minutes."

"You've drawn the job I was supposed to do," Hartwell explained with a long face. "I probably didn't 'it the bloody haystack!"

Outside on the field several engines were being run up for tests. Bart looked at the mechanic for further confirmation. "But I haven't been off the ground as yet—or fired a machine gun in the air."

"You're an American, ain't you?"

"What's that got to do with it?"

"It's like this, chum. This Mr. Prance—'e's an American—or a Canadian; something like that, an' 'e arsked if he could take you on your first flip. This bloke 'ere don't 'ave to go. You got fifteen minutes."

"But . . . don't we get *any* sort of training?"

"Of course." The mechanic grinned. "I'll show you 'ow to get dressed. You do 'ave some flying kit, I suppose?"

Bart pointed to the stack of secondhand leather and rubber piled at the bottom of his bed.

"Good! First, take orf yer boots an' loosen yer puttees. That eases the circulation, an' yer don't get frostbitten feet. Pull yer flying boots on an' hook 'em to yer trousers buttons, some'ow. 'Ere, let me show you."

This instruction took fully three minutes, and by that time Bart was trussed up in leather gear that covered him from his head to the soles of his feet. His helmet bore a deep flounce that was tucked inside the collar of his flying coat. His gloves, with high gauntlet cuffs, had additional mittens that could be pulled over the fingers when manual dexterity was not all-important.

"Now, there you are," the mechanic concluded, looking Crispin over from top to bottom. "Make sure you keep your 'ands warm. That's important. All you 'ave to do now is to go out there and climb aboard. You're a P.B.O. . . . Poor Bloody Observer, chum."

"But what about machine guns?"

"Don't worry. The blokes in the armament shed will bring your guns out. You *do* know 'ow to bolt them to the mounts, don't you?"

"How should I? I've never seen a military aeroplane, let alone a gun mounting. We have just had some instruction on the Lewis gun in a shed. We've never even *heard* one of them fired. We used wooden bullets to learn about the feed and stoppages."

"Chum," the mechanic explained with little solicitude,

"you'll be amazed at 'ow much you'll learn over the next 'our or so. Now let's get on wiv it."

"Good luck, Crispin," Hartwell said with no enthusiasm, as Bart followed the mechanic out the door.

Lieutenant Prance was a bouncy New Englander, a graduate of Dartmouth, and a real war hawk. He was of medium height with bold brown eyes, a broken nose, and a mouth of strong yellow teeth. He loved to fly and hunt Huns. This much was evident during the first few minutes of their association. He was delighted that Crispin was also a Yank, and a Princeton man at that, but was much puzzled by the explanation of how Bart had become an aerial gunner.

"Ah, well," he said thoughtfully, "we'll see that you are broken in slowly. It's really fun, and I know you'll enjoy it." He started to climb up over the wing, and then suddenly bellowed, "Oh, by the way. Have you heard? Old Wilson declared war on Germany yesterday morning. We just got the news in the officers' mess."

"America is in the war?" Bart gasped in disbelief.

"Right, and about time, too, I say. By the way, you *do* know something about the Lewis gun, I suppose," the lieutenant rattled on.

"A little. I can dismantle and reassemble it, but I've never fired one."

"Never mind. You'll have plenty of opportunity later on."

The mechanic, who had been dogging Crispin's footsteps as though he feared he might attempt to bolt from the scene, helped him up into the front nacelle. This was completed without Bart's stepping through any panels of fabric. The guns were already on their mountings, and he had simply to try them out to learn how one could be raised and lowered, the other moved from prong to prong.

"Take my tip," the mechanic whispered. "Don't load either gun until you approach the lines. In that way you won't shoot anyone here on the aerodrome . . . by mistake, like."

Two other mechanics, who stood inside the tail booms,

swung the prop and the Beardmore engine started with a bold surge. Bart was startled by the general uproar, but Lieutenant Prance sat nonchalantly tightening his safety belt while watching the activities of the other pilots. He offered no advice to Bart, nor did he seem interested in the uneven chatter of the engine.

As he settled down in his drafty nacelle Bart began to sense that war flying aroused a complete catalogue of noise and odors. Engines roared, propellers screamed, guns screeched at nearby gun butts, fuel tanks clanked, and men bellowed commands and responses. There was a tang of new leather, damp clothing, lubricating oil, petrol, linen dope, cordite, and cigarette smoke. It would be like this as long as he had any association with an aircraft, and he would be years blanking out the sounds from his ears or the combined stenches from his nostrils.

In his loneliness, he could not interpret the strange signals, hand waves, mouthed messages that were inaudible but always brought an immediate response. The ground crew had one set of signals, not one of which made sense to the flying men unless they were intended for them. The figures on the ground seemed to move through a series of curved slots, actuated by means of a mechanism hidden below the tarmac. They were all alike in the same grease-encrusted coveralls, the same shapeless, murky caps, the same hobnailed boots, and the identical masks of oily stain on the same portions of their faces. They walked alike, stood alike, and moved through their mysterious duties in exactly the same manner, whether they carried Lewis guns, wrenches, ball-peen hammers, or scarlet cans of gasoline. There always was one oldster with a dragoon mustache who stood slack-kneed guard over a pail of water. No one ever saw him use the liquid for anything. It was never poured into a radiator or on a fire. It was always there between his polished boots and was carried back and forth from the hangars with all the ritual of an ecclesiastic processional. There was one fable that he had been a full colonel in a

posh regiment, but an indiscretion with his general's lady
had brought about his downfall. He was cashiered out and
deprived of all honors and decorations. With the outbreak
of war he had joined up again under another name and
found refuge in the Royal Flying Corps. It was a fable
that was to be found in every Wing. No one believed it,
but it wasn't wise to question it, either. After all, the "other
ranks" had to have their small measure of pious fraudu-
lence.

In contrast, the flying personnel was a giddy gang of
individualists, and each seemed determined to renounce
any item of equipment that in any way corresponded with
that worn by any other member. Beginning with helmets,
they outdid themselves. There were the soup-basin crash
covers saved from the Pre-Cambrian era of 1914. Some
were daubed with designs said to be replicas of their earlier
regimental badges. One carried the skull and crossbones of
the 9th Lancers. Another, painted a bright yellow, bore an
advertisement for a noted vermin ointment. The newest
member of the flight was crowned with a brand-new Burberry helmet, complete with ear flaps, pressure pads, and
a furry chinpiece that made him look like an aerial Sir
Walter Raleigh. The flight commander, who had been "out"
since Loos, was perfectly content with a Highland bonnet,
a pair of motoring goggles, and a voluminous scarf.

The flying jackets ranged from extra long to short. A
Canadian from the upper reaches of Hudson's Bay still re-
tained a gay Mackinaw that would have made a Coster's
donkey bolt. One diminutive pilot was bundled in a raccoon
coat several sizes too large for him, and once he was en-
sconced in his cockpit he looked like a rowdy cherub nes-
tling in a bed of moldy meringue. Most pilots wore short
coats with fur collars filched from every type of animal
from an Australian wallaby to a mangy hyena. They wore
tartan trews, infantry slacks, posh riding breeches, Black
Watch kilts, and corduroy bags usually found only on mem-

bers of the Chinese labor battalions. One or two late risers scrambled into the cockpits still wearing the pants of their pajamas hurriedly stuffed into the tops of mismatched golf stockings.

But it was in the area of footwear that these birdmen predominated. Some wore fringed-tongue brogues below neatly pressed slacks; some preferred knee-length flying boots, designed in the manner of hunting boots. Where these came from no one would explain. They were passed on when a wearer was hospitalized, posted to Home Establishment, or invalided out of the service. The standard thigh-length flying boots made of sheepskin, and finished off with red rubber soles, were perfect for these imaginative innovators. The boots were hacked off at various lengths with inept skill and clumsy instruments. Some were scalloped at the top, some were defaced with a hit-and-miss design in which bunches of wool were allowed to blossom out in odd places, but no two pairs were anywhere near the same length. There was one frantic period when everyone ransacked the shops in Amiens for American galoshes that were buckled over bedroom slippers "for convenience." A few men with morbid foresight dressed for Prussian prison camps—just in case. Besides extra shirts and socks they stuffed their pockets with shaving kits, oil-silk maps, compasses, jackknives, and Lifebuoy soap.

This personality parade was restricted, of course, to the officers. NCO aerial gunners were expected to maintain some regimental discipline and decorum; there were enough ragtime fliers among the officers. The noncoms carried out their duties in regulation helmets, Triplex goggles, full-length flying coats—with no fur collars—and they wore flying boots that would have passed any choleric sergeant major on the Farnborough parade ground. Only in rare moments of official rapt meditation could a gunner add a civilian scarf or some item of personal comfort to his flying clothes.

The Fees of "C" Flight rumbled across the road and gathered in a covey on the take-off turf. They reminded Crispin of a small flock of mourning doves working up the courage to waddle toward a patch of unexpected grain. He sat huddled on the floor of his cockpit, wondering what inverse twist of intent had placed him here. The aeroplanes bumped and bored about, seemingly with no basic aim, until he finally saw they had formed into a flying wedge behind the leader, who flaunted two green canvas streamers from the king posts of his elevators. Beyond this identification, there was no difference in any of the machines. All displayed blue, white, and red cocardes on their wings, straight blue, white, and red stripes on their rudders, and small, indistinct factory numbers across those identifying stripes. There were no gaudy squadron crests, no individual markings or challenging names across the noses of the nacelles. Such childish display was for the French. To daub individual aircraft in distinctive colors was "Hunnish" and simply asking for individual attention by the opposition. Anonymity was much preferred by the R.F.C.

The low rumble of the engines suddenly opened up into a concerted, savage roar. Bart felt his cockpit tremble, and then seemingly nose down, and the plane began to charge toward the one ahead. He stiffened, with his feet rammed against the three-ply nose of the compartment, fully expecting to smash into the plane ahead. Instead, all six Fees began to move away together, still maintaining some flying-wedge format, and when the rumbling and thud of the wheels finally subsided, Bart realized they were in the air and that much of the noise had diminished. The forward movement was smooth, even, and entrancing. Ahead spread the farmlands of northern Picardy, and the loops of the Somme sparkled in the high afternoon sunshine.

The experience was nothing like what he had expected, and the higher they climbed, the smoother and more effortless it seemed. He risked looking around, and sensed that Prance's plane was on the outer point of the rear row, and that if he looked to his left he could see all the other planes of the flight. But there was no sense of violent movement, no sense of their one-hundred-mile-per-hour speed, no feeling that they were rushing headlong toward the front lines of the war. The aircraft seemed to be dangling there, hanging by invisible wires. At times one would swing gently and slide back into position. Now and then one would tilt its nose up and take a slightly different position, or move to make the V more precise. There were none of the preconceived notions of flying.

Then came an ominous thumping somewhere behind and fear crept into the scene. He turned his head slowly, hardly daring to risk learning what had gone wrong. The pounding continued and Bart finally hunched up and stared back. His pilot was punching at the top of the cowling that separated their compartments.

"Come on! Get off your rump!" Lieutenant Prance seemed to be bellowing. He pointed out toward the other planes. Bart looked around again and saw to his amazement that all the gunners were sitting on the edges of their nacelles! They might just as well have been enjoying an afternoon ride in a wicker donkey cart.

He nodded and made an attempt to follow the general pattern, but as soon as he had cranked to his hands and knees he found himself peering over the edge of the nacelle and staring down at the ground several thousand feet below. To rise above that position and scotch on the edge of that frail three-ply bathtub was obviously a deliberate attempt at suicide. He'd be blown over and go tumbling . . .

"Come on!" Prance insisted. "You haven't loaded your guns yet. Get on with it!"

The idea of doing something with the guns offered some hope of being able to carry out part of this insane game. He took a drum from the rack on the floor and managed to get it clamped down on its peg and securely latched. But the aft gun had to be loaded too, which meant he would *have* to get to his feet because it was well above his head. Prance leaned over, grabbed him by the scruff of his neck, and hauled him to a near upright position, but Bart could only cling frantically to the gun mounting.

"Get that bloody drum on!" Prance bellowed. "We've got some Huns up ahead!"

"Huns? . . . Where?" The suggestion was ridiculous. Still, there was a possibility. Bart reached down and brought up a second drum, but what with fighting the slipstream, the full effect of the dizzy height, and the fact that his eyes were blinded with tears, he had considerable difficulty in forcing the ammunition pan on the rear gun.

"Your goggles!" Prance yelled. "Pull your goggles down!"

"Goggles? What goggles?" Not until then did Bart realize his goggles were still up on top of his helmet. To hide his embarrassment, he slipped his thumb under the elastic and drew them down, cutting off the blast. Almost immediately he felt unexpectedly comfortable amid familiar surroundings, and then realized that he was actually sitting on the edge of the nacelle. The goggles blanked out all his dread, the fear of height, and the unfamiliar discomfort. He felt part of a new world. Before he had been oblivious of much of the exciting movement around him; now he was suddenly part of the team.

Prance beamed with a grin as broad as a Halloween pumpkin. "Now you're in the game. Keep your eyes open. We can be in for some fun."

The wedge of Fees headed east and clambered for working altitude until the broad gray and green smear of Saint-Quentin came into view. Crispin had no idea where they were, since he had no map, nor in fact any concept as to where they had started from. He learned how to make himself reasonably secure by hooking one foot under the front gun mounting. He watched the other gunners and tried to analyze their movements and the reasons for their intense study of a segment of the sky.

Crump! Crump! Crump!

Three black blobs of smoke suddenly appeared dead

ahead, and then the concussion of a dull explosion. For a few seconds Bart looked about in mild wonder and then saw they were being fired at from the ground. He remembered that night in London when the Zeppelin had come under the rage of the ground guns, until someone in a small biplane had put the torch to the glistening dirigible.

He turned to look at Prance. His pilot was ignoring the smoke balls and seemed to be searching for something out of range to their rear. The Fees dithered through the smoke and more concussion, and then, for no apparent reason, broke up their wedge formation and swung into a silly childish circling movement.

Prance, his eyes agleam with expectation, was bellowing something and pointing at the front gun. "Use your sights!" he was yelling. "Don't fire on the tracers, unless they are very close. Use your sights!"

Bart nodded, but wondered why there was such a change in maneuvers. Why he needed to get on the gun he had no idea, but while getting down on one knee to take an alert position he saw that all the other gunners were firing in short, staccato bursts—at something. He glanced at his pilot again, who was staring upward as they continued their tight-banked circle. The anti-aircraft fire had stopped, but the machine gunners continued to hammer in what seemed to be some pattern of design. Their tracer bullets sparkled and erected a cone of fire directly above the center of the circle.

"Oh!" Bart gasped. "I get it."

"Come on! Come on!" Prance was yelling. "The ammunition is free. You won't be charged for it!"

Amid the excitement, noise, the scream of props, and the tang of cordite smoke Bart suddenly saw a number of broad-tailed biplanes nosing down into the scene. They were diving on the whirling circle of Fees as intermittent spurts of sparklet fire spat through the sheen of their propellers. The Fee gunners took them as they came.

Finally Bart risked pulling the trigger and was astonished

to find he was pouring a stiff burst straight into the V-strut of one of the attackers. He saw something flash in the sunlight but did not know what it was. He was breathless with the slipstream and stiff with excitement. He waited, and then saw another come down the chute. He fired again. His tracers seemed to be pounding into the rear section of the enemy's fuselage, but he had no idea what damage had been done.

He looked about to see how the other gunners were handling the situation. All of them were in the same position as he, each taking his turn as the Albatros biplanes came in. Then, to his dismay, he saw one of the front men snap his left arm across his chest and grip his right shoulder. His head dropped, and he clawed at the rear gun mounting with his free hand.

An enemy aircraft, gay with black crosses, a bright red tail assembly, and a lozenge design in green and brown across its main planes, was almost in the middle of the Fee circle when it suddenly exploded, gushed a splintered pattern of flame, and seemed to stumble over its landing gear and break up while still on its back.

"Don't look at it!" Prance screamed at Bart. "Keep the other swines out of the picture. Don't look at it! I know what type it is and where it is falling. Leave that to me. You shoot!"

The pilots continued their circle of death for the German planes to plunge into. The gunners set up the cone of fire whenever the enemy aircraft came down, and by now Bart was taking a full role, as though he had been doing it for months. The clatter of the guns was a mere obbligato to the mad music and dance of the conflict. The sky was littered with slabs of fuselage, portions of wing panels, a loose wheel, and twisted scarves of smoke. Bart glanced around to check on the gunner who apparently had been hit. He was now on his knees, his head cradled in one arm, which was resting on the top of the spare parts locker. His pilot was showing no concern for him, but continued to hold his aircraft in its proper segment of the circle, and fire the rear gun with one hand on the pistol grip.

"And don't look at him either!" Prance roared. "Keep the swines out of the action. You're doing swell!"

"It's wonderful," Bart tried to yell, but the slipstream devoured his words before he could screech them. He watched another fish-tailed Albatros start down, and he held it in the sight until the engine nacelle and cockpit filled the outer ring. He pressed the trigger. Nothing happened. The drum was empty. He heard himself swearing like a proverbial trooper, but his pilot was roaring with laughter. "You'll learn! You'll learn!"

Bart snatched off the drum and looked about for a replacement, but by the time he had latched it to the stud the Fees were back in their normal wedge formation and evidently heading toward the west. He wondered about that and looked at Prance for an explanation.

"We beat them off. Two went down . . . one in flames."

Bart nodded.

"We're taking Darlington back toward Albert. His gunner has been wounded. Then we'll have a pot at the balloons," he explained with exaggerated mouthing and bellowing.

As they approached the British lines, Prance vetted his machine carefully. He pointed out one burst that had perforated the wing fabric near the port aileron. There was another tear through the three-ply walkway near the engine mount. He seemed very pleased with the evidence.

"Take a look back and see if we have any damage to any of the tail booms. Make sure, now. The tail booms, and anything around the elevators. They're important," the pilot explained.

Bart stood up, gripped the rear mounting, and ran his eyes along the bamboo tail booms. There seemed to be no damage on either side, but there was something fluttering off the starboard elevator. He explained this to Lieutenant Prance.

"Is it a strip of green?"

Bart nodded.

"Come on! Wake up! That's our streamer. We're the sub-leader. The leader carries two. See . . . on the leader's tail?"

Bartley felt like a fool, but was appreciative of the responsibility placed on him to search for serious damage. He was quietly pleased with his showing, and hoped Prance was satisfied with him. He settled down again on the edge of the nacelle, by now able to note things that before had evaded him. He watched the gunner aboard the leader's plane and realized that he was continually on the move, checking the sky above, below, and keeping his pilot advised of any unusual situations on the ground. At times he jotted notes on a small pad and showed them to his pilot. Then he would check the positions of the other Fees and flip certain signals at which someone would move in closer or take a more protective position off the wedge. Bart decided he would get a notebook and take more interest in what was going on.

The leader's gunner suddenly stood erect, raised one hand high above his head, and then started a series of choppy swings with his arm. He pointed to the patch of demolition that was Albert, and the plane that was carrying the wounded gunner banked clear, nosed down, and headed for the sanctity of the British lines. In a few minutes the pilot, called Darlington, would land at an advanced dressing station, deliver his wounded gunner, and, after loading on a couple of sandbags for ballast, would take off again and return to Warloy.

Prance was banging on the cowling again. "Fix your gun into a prong on the right-hand side. We're going balloon-busting."

This made little sense, but Bart did as he was ordered and went to one knee again. The Fees were heading north and were obviously losing altitude fast. The panorama of the war below was more distinct. The back areas presented supply dumps, horse lines, transport concentrations, marshaling yards, and small gatherings of troop shelters.

The anti-aircraft fire became more intense and accurate. The concussion of the shells thudded against their ears, and the stench of the burned explosive swept past their noses and made everyone cover his face with a glove. A strange streak, seemingly composed of several greenish missiles chained together, came up from the ground at a languid pace, and for no apparent reason disappeared.

"Flaming onions," Prance explained laconically. "To protect the balloons."

"Balloons?" Bart was once more disturbed by his air blindness. He peered about, looking for something large, bulbous, and Hun-gray. There was nothing to be seen anywhere but the blobs of smoke from the anti-aircraft fire. Prance pointed down toward the ground, but Bart could see nothing; just trenches cut out of the lime-packed soil, some zigzag communication lines, M.G. posts, and areas of heavy shellfire, but no balloons.

The leader's gunner dropped to a kneeling position and gave his attention to his Lewis. Bart wondered about that, and then the Fees broke up once more, and before he could compute exactly what had happened, he saw that the leader had shot ahead into a sharp dive, and the rest were following in single file.

"What are you waiting for?" Prance screamed.

Completely bewildered, Bart stared around. There were no balloons anywhere. The steepness of the dive had disconcerted him for a minute or two, but he hung onto the base of the mount, and then, to his amazement, saw a burning balloon not fifteen yards from him. The big bag had gushed a gout of smoke, and this was followed by a belch of scarlet flame. Something dirty white blossomed out below, and he realized that a balloon observer had jumped and taken to his parachute. The basket of the balloon was being slung about like a weight on a string with the parachute cone and rigging lines stretched taut as the burning bag bucked and twisted under the quirting of the inferno.

"Hang on! There'll be another in a minute!" Prance screeched.

The in-line Fees were racing along the German line to give the gunners a chance to shoot at the big bags. Two went up in flames, but as the alarm flashed along the front the rest were hauled down as fast as the motor winches could twirl the cable drums. Bart got in a few short bursts, but the bulbous targets were too close to the ground and well out of range and he had sense enough to desist. The ground fire was heavy in patches, and he noticed a few more single perforations here and there, until their leader nosed up again and sought a safer level. Only the flaming onions came up, but these soon died out, and they were once more in the wedge formation and slipping through the stinking smoke of the three-inchers.

He looked at Prance again for instructions. His pilot smiled and nodded his approval, as Bart checked his ammunition drum, changed it, and then returned to his seat on the edge of the nacelle.

"Fine!" Prance yelled, and pulled his gunner closer to him. "You did all right. Just remember all you did today, and you can fly with anyone. Just keep your eyes open, watch the leader, and keep a full drum on the stud." He grinned and shoved Bart back into an upright position.

They stayed aloft for another thirty minutes, but there was nothing to draw their immediate attention. A flight of Sopwith Pups came up, and the pilots exchanged impudent signals. Two R.E. 8s plodded up and down, flying an artillery-shoot pattern, and Prance pointed out where the British guns were dropping short salvos into an enemy transport concentration. Crispin felt he had learned more in the last hour than he had gathered unto himself in all his years of formal schooling. He reflected that all the drivel about teamwork and school spirit he had absorbed on the athletic field was a mere primary introduction to what he had seen and taken part in today.

This was LIFE.

CHAPTER THIRTEEN

May 1917

Russian Council of Workmen's and Soldiers' Delegates demand peace conference. . . . Liberia breaks with Germany. . . . General Pétain succeeds General Nivelle as Commander-in-Chief of French armies. . . . Bullecourt captured by British in Arras battle. . . . Conscription bill signed by President Wilson. . . . Italians advance on Corso. . . . Germans make first aeroplane raid over London. . . . German U-36 sunk in North Sea by British flying boat. . . . U. S. Government decides to send an army division to France. . . . Twenty-one Gothas attack London in daylight, causing more than 200 casualties. . . . Captain Albert Ball of R.F.C. killed. . . . Zeppelin L-22 destroyed by British aeroplane pilot.

The meeting was a shocker, particularly for Lieutenant Macintosh. To Cynthia Pollard it was what she expected, for she had been instructed to use this tobacco shop for her particular role . . . one suggested by the man at Scotland Yard. She had sauntered around from her hotel to the Wilton Road doorway to deposit a squarish envelope that had been sealed with scarlet wax and stamped with the imprint of an old signet ring. The contents purported to disclose some details of plans for a British naval raid to be carried out against the submarine-assembling dockyard at Ostend.

The little bell above the door tinkled its mild alarm as she walked in, and she was over the threshold before she saw there was another customer at the narrow counter. The cadaverous-looking proprietor displayed concern, but quickly returned his attention to the tall man in khaki who was accepting a flat tin of Navy Cut tobacco with one hand and pocketing a reddish-brown envelope with the other.

"Thank you," the man in khaki said, and almost clicked his heels as he turned; he had started to step aside when he noticed the girl who had just come in.

"Oh . . . pardon me."

"Good heavens! Ralph Macintosh!" Cynthia pealed.

Ralph was caught completely off balance, and for an instant had to restrain an impulse to throttle her. "Cynthia! My God! Whatever are you doing here . . . here in London?" he added quickly. "I didn't know. . . ." His voice gurgled into a streak of unintelligible croaking. He turned to get some explanation from the man behind the counter, but the tobacconist just nodded, dropped his eyes, and then looked up to await Cynthia's approach.

She had her response ready. "Same thing as you, I suppose. Buying cigarettes. I've picked up the wartime habit." She turned to the proprietor. "A packet of De Reszke, please."

The man in khaki was in a panic. This had to be a trap of some sort. He grabbed her wrist and twisted her hand so he could read the address on the envelope she held. Cynthia gave him an oblique glance and a sly smile that took most of the tension out of the encounter. The tobacconist offered the packet of cigarettes, and with the same gesture took the envelope and with skilled sleight of hand passed it under the counter. Cynthia gave Ralph a raised eyebrow.

He was plainly relieved. "Well, well, well," he said. "How long has this been going on?"

"Since the day you dropped the baton at Palmer Stadium."

He took her elbow and they walked out of the dusty

172

shop into the mellow sunshine. He still had to make certain that matters stood as they seemed. "You are staying—where?"

"Over at the Grosvenor. It's very convenient."

"Very," he agreed, and managed a weak smile. "Shall we drop by? I suggest we munch a bun and have a spot of tea. That's what everyone does in London."

"A *cup* of tea," Cynthia corrected. "Fancy meeting you on Wilton Road!"

"Fancy meeting *you!*"

"I should have thought you would be with one of the Home Defense squadrons taking on the new Gothas. I understand they are to replace the Zeppelins."

He glanced at her in some admiration. "How fast you learn. Home Defense squadrons, new Gothas . . . my, my, this is all very interesting."

"We have to learn fast in this business, don't we?" she said, drawing him on.

"I wouldn't know. Perhaps we're not talking about the same thing." He led the way into the hotel corridor. "I think we can find a spot down those stairs."

"Right. I'm there quite often."

"That's good to know. I may not be around London much longer."

Cynthia showed some mock concern. "You don't expect to be picked up, do you?"

He looked worried, but said, "I mean, I'm to go over to France. My squadron . . ."

A waiter came up and took their order while they chatted about everyday topics. When the tea had been set out, Ralph leaned forward and said, "Well, tell me. How did you get into this business? I mean to say . . . the daughter of Shipley Pollard."

"That's just how," she said with a piquant smile. "It seems there's some question as to my lineage, and—well, Captain von der Osten has cleared it up."

"Von der Osten? Who's he?"

173

"A lackey for your Mr. Stosselmeyer. Remember Stosselmeyer?" she quipped with a twinkle in her eye.

"I'll never forget him," he reflected. "No wonder you picked me up that night when I tried to get Bart Crispin out of your place."

"Wasn't that funny? I thought you were about to strangle, but I couldn't help plying the prod. It was then I realized what you were up to . . . and where your pocket money came from."

Macintosh was obviously worried. "Let me get this straight. This Von der Osten found out what?"

"That I am *not* my mother's daughter. It seems that Father was once involved with a notorious Broadway theatrical star whose morals were not all they should have been. I was the natural result, but now your Mr. Stosselmeyer and Co. feel this is the right time to disclose Father's indiscretions and toss a monkey wrench into the Pollard munitions assembly line. They have a point, of course."

It took a minute or so for Ralph to clarify all that. "They threatened, and you agreed to sell out?"

"I first gave them the blueprints of a new acoustic torpedo."

"Holy Cripes! What's that?"

"A new weapon. You fire it in the general direction of an enemy submarine, and it guides itself to the target through the sound set up by the thrashing propellers. Quite a piece of work."

"Jesu! You did more in one jump than I managed in three or four months."

"Oh, then," Cynthia rattled on, "I gave them the general plans of a new aerial cine-gun-camera. They loved that one. What next did I give them?" She patted a lip with her forefinger. "Oh, it doesn't matter. It's so easy for me . . . particularly over here where I am *really* Cynthia Pollard, confidential secretary to Shipley Pollard. I have them eating out of my hand."

Macintosh leaned over his teacup. "Do you really hate the

British this much? I mean, you don't *need* the money. You can't possibly love the Germans. What's the story?"

"I'll need all the money I can get if they ever betray my father, and they may, you know. We can't trust these people."

Macintosh glared at her. "Of course we can trust them."

"You have it your way. I'm taking care of Cynthia. If one day I fail in some mission, they'll drop me so fast I'll bounce." She rubbed her thumb and forefinger together. "Money. That's what makes the world go round and enables young ladies to look continually pretty. I'm after as much as I can get . . . just like you."

"It's unbelievable." Ralph stared at a Banbury bun. "Only a year ago we were in Princeton, miles from all this, and enjoying college life to the full. Now here we are in London smack in the middle of the war, and both of us scheming and plotting for the Kaiser."

"And Bart Crispin is in France, an aerial gunner with the Royal Flying Corps," Cynthia announced with the air of a town crier. "That's even more improbable than our situation."

"Bart's in France? How do you know?"

"I've had a couple of letters from him."

Macintosh was completely mystified. These incidents, and their telling, rammed a new jolt of dread into him. "I mean . . . how did he know you were over here? I didn't."

"I wrote to him at Oxford, but he had left, and my letter was sent on, finally reaching him. I received a reply a few days ago."

He worked out the time brackets in his mind and satisfied himself that she was telling an acceptable story. "Well, look here. I saw him some time ago. Actually, the night he joined up. We were all at the Melvilles'—they're an American family here in London. He had gotten mixed up in a Zeppelin raid, and that did it. He enlisted right away, without bothering to apply for a commission, but I didn't know that he was already in France. That was fast!"

Ralph filled Cynthia in regarding the Melville family, and retold the "shilling" story several times with rare zest. "You ought to meet the Melvilles," he interposed. "You'd like them, and who knows, you might pick up some hot items. Dianne is a driver with the R.F.C. and her old man is the top railroad authority over here. You should be able to twiddle him around your fingers."

Cynthia sat musing over the situation. "I think I may have met that girl. They had her take me to"—she had to get this story straight—"to one of the factories that is aligned with the Pollard interests. I remember deciding that she was not *exactly* English. She had certain mannerisms, but very pretty. She was driving one of those Crossley utility cars."

"She's probably the one," Ralph said thoughtfully. "She's going off the deep end for Crispin. By the way, you're not still mooning over him, are you?"

"Mooning? Oh, come now. He's a fine fellow, but I never could take him seriously. We're just not in the same league. There's another thing. Bart once caught me in a lie and I can never hope to win his confidence again. You know Bartley Crispin."

She related the incident of being seen entering the offices of the North German Lloyd Line on lower Broadway, and denying that Bart had ever seen her in that area.

Macintosh listened with rapt attention. "Has he brought it up since?"

"Not directly, but I sense it in the tone of his letters."

"Does he ask leading questions? Goddamn, he could give us both trouble," he ranted on, pawing nervously at his jowls. "Do you have his address?"

"You want to write to him?" she asked in some surprise.

"I may. I'd like to know where he is . . . how I can get in touch with him, just in case. I can't fraternize with him. He's not an officer, you know. The damn fool could have been, though."

Cynthia said: "He gave me '1st Class Air Mechanic B. H. Crispin, c/o Number 20 Squadron, Fourth Wing, Royal

Flying Corps, B.E.F., France.' I can't remember his regimental number, but that address should reach him."

"That's all I'll need."

"He seems to be doing very well," Cynthia continued. "He likes the flying and the air fighting. He can't say much about it, of course, as all his letters are censored by his superior officers. He has an American, a Lieutenant Prance, as his pilot, and he's quite taken with him. A Dartmouth man, from all accounts. Isn't that nice . . . for Bart?"

The routine at Number 20 Squadron went on at the tempo of the war. They coursed over the area between Saint-Quentin and Arras, and carried out their offensive patrol assignments with what the daily communiqués called "vigor and determination." Crispin learned fast and became a valuable member of "C" Flight. Before he had put in fifty hours over the line to win his observer's wing he found himself in the flight commander's bus, practically in command of their patrols. Their Captain Blount went on leave and Lieutenant Prance took over the point of the wedge. Together they worked as an efficient team, and during the two weeks Blount was away they did not lose a machine.

Hartwell also became a workmanlike performer, but he was not capable of assuming too much responsibility. He was at his best during the air fights when he blazed away with wild enthusiasm; in fact he destroyed two enemy planes before his first week had been completed; but he had no idea where his flight had been or where any particular action had taken place. What went on down on the ground was a complete mystery to him, and his patrol reports were total blanks, unless he had engaged a few enemy scouts. Then his imagination went into high gear, and some of his reports made enjoyable reading at Wing Headquarters.

Hartwell also assumed another role. He was the comic of the squadron and the life of the hut where the half dozen or so NCO gunners bunked. He could sing a hundred popular music hall ditties, tell bawdy stories by the hour, or relate the amazing adventures of his mother who, from all accounts, was the chief character of her neighborhood.

"Did I ever tell you of the time my mother took on to 'elp out our local undertaker?" he would begin within minutes of returning from a particularly hazardous patrol. "Well, it seems that some old gaffer in our street 'ad died in the night, an' when they got to 'im it turned out that 'e 'ad snuffed it wiv 'is knees up. Mother and the undertaker went in an' the undertaker told 'er to press 'is legs down flat like, so they could get 'im in the coffin. Well, you know Mother. She just leaned over and started to press down, but when she did, the old bloke sat straight up, because of 'ow 'is legs 'ad been, you know. Mother thought the old bloke 'ad come to life. She let out a scream, bolted down the stairs, an' kept on runnin' until she pulled up in the Market Square about a mile away. She never even went to a funeral after that."

Then there was the day Hartwell had been taken on as a motorman of a suburban tramcar. Someone had set the wrong switch and he took his passengers on a hilarious joyride, ending up in a gravel pit miles from the carbarn. One night he had stolen a full card of Boy Scout whistles and hidden them carefully in the cellar. The next morning he was aroused by earsplitting alarms from the street. It seemed a younger brother had found the card and made sure every kid in the street got one—and learned how to use it.

Crispin was the only gunner who could put a "cease fire" to Hartwell's monologues. He would say, "Hartie, old boy, you ought to save all those stories, write them down, and put them in a book. You'd make a fortune."

That did it.

Hartwell was a prime example of the talkative type who was the perfect storyteller. He could turn the simplest incident into a major production, continuing on and adding features and asides that kept the other aerial gunners in stitches. There were times when they couldn't raise the strength to pull off their flying clothes, but just sat down on their beds and howled. Not that they believed a word of

Hartwell's tales, but they all nurtured some inner hope that the most outrageous yarn was absolutely true.

But any suggestion of a written composition stilled his voice. He was incapable of writing a legible letter or producing two grammatical sentences in sequence. He would sit for an hour or more, sucking on a short stub of pencil, a forlorn, completely frustrated soul, praying someone would suggest a game of cards, a scrounge through some shell-pocked area, or even devise a new idea for a petrol-tin shower.

He worshiped Bart Crispin and would do anything the American suggested. He followed him about with the yearning and affection of an idolatrous schoolboy.

There were afternoons when they wandered through some of the nearby towns. Crispin would study the architecture and sit among the debris sketching any remaining building forms, columns, chimneys, arches, or mullions. Hartwell would kneel beside him and watch with fascinated eyes, convinced Bart was a genius.

"But they are only rough sketches," Bart would explain. "I'm only doing this to keep my hand and eye in."

"Bloody marvelous!" Hartwell would breathe. "I don't know 'ow you can do it wiv just a bit o' pencil and a sheet of paper from a book. Cool"

Although assigned to one of the three flights of any squadron, aerial gunners were not limited in their activity to any particular flight. For instance, a "C" Flight gunner might fly with his own formation in the early morning show and return in time to gulp a meal, buckle his gear on again, and fly the midday patrol with "A" Flight simply because "A" Flight was short a man. But this did not relieve the "C" Flight gunner from going on a late afternoon patrol with his own pilot later in the day. In other words, aerial gunners might fly as many as three patrols a day, but no pilot was expected to assume such an exhausting program.

Because of these unfair conditions and one-sided rules,

Bart Crispin soon logged his fifty hours over the line, which entitled him to wear the flying "O" insignia, but the accomplishment did not bring the reward of a commission and pilot training in England. He was simply an NCO aerial gunner. Instead, to his bewilderment and Lieutenant Prance's outrage, 1st Class Air Mechanic (Aerial Gunner) B. H. Crispin was suddenly "struck off strength" and posted to Number 86-SS Squadron, R.F.C.

"'Ere. Wot's the idea?" Hartwell roared when they read the item in the Squadron Orders tacked up on the mess hut door. "It don't include me. We came together. . . . 'Adn't we ought to be transferred together?"

"I don't know what it means," Crispin said, puzzled. "I'll ask the squadron clerk after supper."

"'E's probably in 'ere. Let's look around."

Blenkinsop, the squadron clerk, had his nose in a big mug of tea. He withdrew his beak to glare at Crispin. "Bin lookin' for you all over the shop," he said with routine belligerency.

"You didn't look far. I've been in our hut ever since we got back from the afternoon patrol."

"You seen the orders?"

"Yes, I noticed them outside."

"Well, you'd better be packed and ready arter breakfast in the mornin'."

"Wot abart me?" Hartwell broke in.

"You? What about you? You ain't transferred, are you?"

"No, but why not?"

"You weren't spoke for. Crispin 'ere was."

"Let's start from the beginning," Bart said as he squatted on the long mess bench. "What is Number 86-SS Squadron? What kind of planes do they fly, and where are they?"

"It's like this," Blenkinsop explained as he smothered a slice of bread with marmalade. "Number 86-SS is a new Bristol Fighter squadron—from all accounts. They're somewhere up near Arras . . . somewhere in that area. They sent a signal asking that you be sent on to join them. I don't know why. That's all I know."

"Cool!" Hartwell exclaimed, and sat down in despair.

"I mean this Number 86-SS. What does the SS mean?"

"It's something new. I think it means Special Service. They probably are to carry out special patrols, since they have the first lot of the new Bristol Fighter."

"Wot the 'ell's a Bristol Fighter?" Hartwell asked with no especial interest. He was looking at Crispin as though Bart were being banished to some foreign strand.

"Ah, now you've arsked a question." The sergeant clerk beamed. "They're the new two-seater fighters, just comin' out. Very fast, very pukka, with Rolls-Royce engines. They'll be raisin' merry 'ell once we get a few squadrons of them out 'ere. You ain't 'arf lucky, you know, Crispin. You must 'ave friends up that way, to be arsked for. Lieutenant Prance put up a lovely row about it, but when you're arsked for there's no gettin' out of it."

"I was asked for? By whom?"

"'Ow the 'ell do I know? But you've read the orders. Right after breakfast, in the morning, remember. I've warned you."

"Who the 'ell would arsk for you?" Hartwell pleaded.

Crispin rubbed his chin. "I haven't the slightest idea. I don't know anyone of importance in the R.F.C."

"I just 'opes you've still got that lucky shillin'."

Bart slapped his pal across the shoulders. "I'll never give it up. It has worked wonders so far."

CHAPTER FOURTEEN

June 1917

General Pershing, Commander-in-Chief of American Expeditionary Force, arrives in England. . . . Messines-Wytschaete ridge taken by British troops. . . . Senator Root arrives in Russia at head of commission appointed by Wilson. . . . New draft army registers in the United States. . . . British aircraft used in organized attacks on ground targets. . . . First large-scale daylight attack by German aircraft on London. . . . War Office recommends that Royal Flying Corps be expanded from 108 to 200 squadrons. . . . General Allenby appointed to command Egyptian Expeditionary Force. . . . U. S. Aviation Section becomes the Airplane Division of the Army Signal Corps. . . . Lieut. Col. William Mitchell relieves Major T. F. Dodd as Aviation Officer, American Expeditionary Force.

It took but a short time to learn who had "spoke for" 1st Class Air Mechanic Crispin when he arrived at Number 86-SS Squadron's field at Serny, which was convenient to Arras. On reporting to the Adjutant, he was greeted warmly and told that the squadron was still undergoing its formation, but that trained aerial gunners were in short supply.

"I understand I was especially requested, sir," Bart said while still standing at attention. "May I ask by whom?"

"Whom? Aren't you a friend of Lieutenant Macintosh?"

"Lieutenant Macintosh? Ralph Macintosh, sir?" Bart said in surprise. "I didn't know he was out here."

"Oh, I thought there had been some sort of collusion." The Adjutant smiled. "You were university mates, I understand."

"Well, not exactly. We were at Princeton at the same time, but we were not bosom friends. However, I am glad to be selected for Bristol Fighters. I understand they are . . ."

The Adjutant stared down at Bart's papers again. "Just a minute. I must have a word with the major." He rose and hurried toward a doorway that was covered by a brown army blanket. In a few minutes he returned and beckoned. "Come in, Crispin. The major would like to talk with you."

Major Horne was a squat man with broad shoulders. He had merry eyes and a bluish chin, and was well scrubbed and shaved. He wore wings above a broad row of decorations, and looked the typical career soldier who was enduring the tortures of paperwork. He greeted Bart pleasantly.

"Good morning, Crispin. That's a good British name for an American. I thought they all came as Mazzinis or Rappaports."

"There are a few Anglo-Saxons left, sir."

"Very good." Major Horne beamed. "Oh, er, break off—easy. We're a trifle ragtime here. Now about this transfer. You did not apply for it? You did not volunteer for Number 86-SS?"

"No, sir."

"But you do know Lieutenant Macintosh?"

"We were at college . . . Princeton together. He joined up in Canada. I was in England on a scholarship. I had no idea he was out here—or would want me here."

"Strange that he should request you, and stranger still that the request should be granted. It's not usual, you know."

"He seems to have many important connections, sir."

"Yes. Were you particularly good friends in America?"

"No. Not particularly, sir."

Major Horne was puzzled. "Strange. You of course know nothing about our work, or the new aircraft?"

"No, sir. Nothing."

"Well, we fly the new Bristol Fighter. We have great hopes in her. She's nothing like the Fee you've been flying."

"A tractor biplane, as I understand, sir. Rather fast and very maneuverable."

"Very adaptable in many ways, and because of these qualities this squadron has been organized for special types of work. You may as well know—co-operation with the Intelligence chaps. Some of it will be a bit sticky, but most necessary. I tell you this because you do not have to take it on unless you wish. Of course, if you are willing to volunteer, we have to let you in on certain phases of the work, and you, in turn, will be expected to keep what you know very much to yourself."

"I understand, sir."

"We have investigated our flying personnel thoroughly, which is why I am puzzled about your being lifted from a Fee squadron to join us without going through the wringer, so to speak. But for that matter, I was puzzled about Macintosh, who is also an American, being selected for this particular work. We usually confine it to British subjects. However, you're here now, and if you're willing, we may as well keep you on."

"One question, sir. Does this mean I will be flying with Lieutenant Macintosh?"

Major Horne turned and stared out the window. "That's a bit of a puzzler too. Since he applied for you, I assume he'll want you as his gunner. Still, then we'll have *two* Americans in one Bristol. It's hardly sound operations. Would you have any objections to flying with Macintosh?"

"No, sir, but I don't understand why he would pick me out."

"He's a damn good pilot, you know," Major Horne assured him. "He has to be to carry out some of the games we're down for. I wouldn't worry about that. Pukka pilot, Macintosh."

"Then I suppose there's nothing more to question. I think I'd like to stay on, sir."

"Good! It probably won't be for long. If you do any good

at all, you'll be sent back to England for pilot training. They won't expect anyone to stick at this bloody game for very long."

"It might be very interesting."

"Oh, quite. Now bung off and the Adjutant will arrange to have you in on the afternoon talks, explaining the work. When you get settled somewhere, you might go out to the hangars and look over the Bristols. In particular, I want you to go over the dual-control system. It's a bit tricky, putting the bits together, but if you ever need to take over, it is well to know how it all works. That's all, Crispin. Good luck!"

Bart clicked his heels and said, "Thank you, sir."

Serny was no better, and no worse, than any wartime aero-drome. It was laid out in what had been agricultural country with small patches of woods nearby, some gently rolling hills, and a few villages that had not been completely wiped out. A short distance to the west lay the smudge of Doullens. To the north was the old fortified town of Arras on the right bank of the Scarpe. It was the ancient capital of Artois, and now the chief town of the Pas-de-Calais Department. In peacetime it pulsed as the heart of the grain trade, although centuries earlier it had been one of the centers of the woolen industry. Arras, at one time, produced some of France's greatest tapestries, but the best of them were sold and taken to Britain and America by those who could afford such luxuries. Symbolically, Arras was the birthplace of Maximilien de Robespierre and of Joseph Le Bon, a curé who organized the Terror in that city and was long remembered for his cruelties.

Six Besseneau hangars had been set up in an "L" at one corner of the field, and accommodated two squadrons. The other squadron was an Australian R.E. 8 artillery observation outfit that served the Aussie divisions in the Arras area. Number 86-SS was gradually taking over three of the shelters and filling them as fast as the new fighters were delivered.

After finding the Nissen hut provided for the aerial gunners, and scrounging the materials to construct another bed, Bart wandered through the tangle of sheds, bell tents, and Adrian hutments where the officers were accommodated, and finally wound his way past a mobile power lorry and a machine-gun butt until he came to the hangars. A flight sergeant nodded to him and went on about his business, so Bart took Major Horne's tip and went in to inspect one of the new machines.

Right from the start the Bristol Fighter entranced him. It was a smart but rugged-looking biplane, powered by a Rolls-Royce engine. It was only slightly larger than an S.E. 5 scout fighter, but once he climbed up on the wing root and studied the cockpit layout, Bart realized that this was a thoroughly modern aeroplane. The workmanship was first class, and the compact arrangement of the two cockpits had been so well thought out, Bart saw, that it was the ultimate in a two-seater fighter. Gone were the gaspipe features of the Fee and the shallow nacelle accommodations. Aboard the Bristol the pilot sat in a comfortable, efficient cockpit with a fixed Vickers gun in a most convenient position. There was a very complete instrument panel, and a generator to provide current for the new Sidcot electrically heated suit.

But it was the gunner's pit that most fascinated Bart. In the first place, it was set close to the pilot's seat and was provided with the new Scarff gun ring on which a Lewis gun could be mounted and swung through 360 degrees and fired over a very flexible arc. There was convenient space for six ammunition drums and the spare parts bag, and a seat that could be folded back out of the way when any action arose. The feature that took his immediate attention was the dual-control equipment that was provided in case the pilot was killed or knocked out of action. There was no such provision in the Fee. If the pilot was eliminated, there was little hope of taking over his stick, throttle, or rudder to get the aircraft down.

Aboard the Bristol Fighter there was a control stick set in a convenient pronged rack. This could be pulled out and inserted in a pivoted socket set on the right-hand side of the cockpit floor. Thus, while sitting on his seat facing forward, the passenger could operate the elevators. His rudder control consisted simply of a wooden handle bolted to one set of rudder cables running along the left-hand side of the aircraft. Although he had no aileron control he could fly the plane with the stick and control the rudder with his left hand. A rudimentary throttle control was also placed on the left-hand side.

Crispin tried the equipment and decided that he would get his pilot to let him fly the plane whenever possible. It was not as efficient as the dual-control system on training aircraft, but in an emergency the gunner could make an attempt to get the plane down with a certain degree of safety. Bart was positive he could at least make some kind of pancake landing, should the occasion arise.

He was climbing down when a familiar voice echoed through the hangar.

"Get out of my aircraft, Crispin!"

As he touched down he saw Ralph Macintosh striding into the hangar.

"Hello," Bart responded. "Major Horne told me to get acquainted with the machine, so I . . ."

Macintosh came forward with an oily grin. "First, you salute me and address me as 'sir.' It's not my decision. It's rules and regulations. We may as well get that straight, right off the bat."

"Yes, sir," Bart responded, and snapped a regulation salute.

"I'm only trying to keep the status quo. You know how the British are about this sort of thing. We're old pals, but as long as we are here we have to recognize the difference in our ranks. You're a ranker. I'm an officer. This is the way it is."

"Yes, sir. Now will you excuse me?"

"No. You withdraw when I so order."

"Yes, sir."

"When did you get here?"

"A short time ago, sir."

"Well, you're to be my aerial gunner. I see you have got your 'wing,' so you ought to know something by now. We may be down for a special agent show any night."

"Night? We fly at night?"

"On these special jobs, yes. You'll hear about it at the afternoon lectures. That is all we're doing at present. Later on we'll go on regular patrols. Right now we're something of a side show for Intelligence. You'll find out."

"It sounds very important . . . sir."

"I hear you're still writing to Cynthia. I met her in London just before we came out here." Macintosh lighted a cigarette. Bart made no comment.

"I also saw Dianne Melville."

"Has Bryce made it into the R.F.C. as yet?"

The officer pilot trod out his match without answering. "We had quite a party at the Savoy. I suppose she told you about it."

Bart held his tongue.

"We should get plenty of leave in this squadron," Macintosh went on. "Too bad you took that shilling. We could make it a foursome in London, but as it is . . ."

"I'm quite satisfied . . . sir."

"Sure . . . sure," Macintosh agreed, flipped his half-smoked cigarette through the hangar door, and strode out.

Three nights later Bart Crispin made his first night patrol with Ralph Macintosh as his pilot.

Night had fallen across the war-torn levels of Artois. It had rained late that afternoon and there were reflective pools in the depressions of the tarmac. There was some seasonal warmth, some relief from the dreads of the day, and for those not assigned to a patrol, there were prospects of a run into Amiens.

The clank of a wrench, the rasp of a hacksaw, and the grind of a device used to test spark plugs could be heard inside the dimly lit Besseneau. A sooty figure shuffled about moaning a recent music-hall ditty that was some jeremiad by Marie Lloyd explaining why she was late. The figure dropped its hands and released an asthmatic guffaw.

What little light there was took on life and movement, throwing faint triangles of gleam, as a Bristol Fighter was wheeled out and dragged to the cabrank. The illumination churned out by a mobile power lorry flashed unevenly off the yellow struts, glossy wing panels, or from the bow and ratchet arms of the gunner's Scarff mounting. There was brief activity beneath the wing tips as a crouched figure bolted black metal brackets, bearing phosphorus cartridges, to a main rib just in front of the ailerons. None of the cast of characters spoke during these operations, but glumly carried out their duties with somnolent motions, and when the tasks were completed they gathered beneath the gray engine cowling to renew the break in communications.

"Wot are they doin' tonight?"

Someone touched a glowing wick to a cigarette.

"Who knows? Anything to bugger up somebody's hour or so orf."

"I'd like to go on one of these shows—just once. Just to to see wot they do do."

"They never say."

"Bloody mysterious to me, it is."

"'Ush! 'Ere comes the major."

"Everything all right here, Nethersole?" he mumbled, and kicked at a wheel tire.

"Yes, sir. Flares all wired in an' the back seat properly looked at. The dual-control gear is all there. Everything."

"Good! This is a dicey show, and we want everything right —shipshape. Chaps who go on these jobs are entitled to the

189

best. Let's get her warmed up. They'll be out in a minute."

Before the big Rolls-Royce had cleared her throat, two muffled figures in tan leather jackets, thigh-length flying boots, and helmets appeared out of the darkness. An armorer also turned up, cradling a Lewis gun in his arms. The aerial gunner climbed up, dropped down inside the Scarff ring, and leaned over to take the weapon.

"If I get a Number Three stoppage," the aerial gunner said with a pleasant grin, "I'm coming back and rough you up with the spare parts bag."

"If you get a Number Three stoppage, you may not come back, chum."

Lieutenant Macintosh and Major Horne were talking near the wing tip. "Now remember, you're not to go down unless you get the proper signal. Two whites and a red. You have that clear? Two whites and a red, in that order."

"Two whites and a red. Right!"

"Well, good luck, and don't take too many chances."

"Two whites and a red," Macintosh repeated as he went to the stirrup on the fuselage and climbed up. He looked back at Crispin. "Everything all right with you?"

Bart peered around his office, felt for the gun drums, the dual-control lever, and his Very signal pistol. "Seems to be," he concluded.

"Well, it's your problem. You took the shilling, remember."

"I'm not likely to forget."

"I didn't, and I had a commission before I crossed the Atlantic," the pilot retorted after a contented guffaw.

"Let's get on with it," Bart growled.

"Let's get on with it, *sir!* Remember who's in command here."

"Yes, sir."

Macintosh turned back to the controls. He checked the compass, the clock, and then ran the engine up for a rev test. He throttled down, raised both arms, wigwagged his satisfaction, and watched while the mechanics yanked the

190

wheel chocks away. Crispin lowered his folding seat and sat down facing the broad back of the pilot. He had time to ponder on the strange circumstances that had placed him here, an aerial gunner for this hateful man. "So I took the shilling. I had to win my wing over the enemy lines, not in some English flying school," he muttered to himself with understandable satisfaction, and then returned a cheery wave from one of the mechanics.

Macintosh taxied the Bristol Fighter out to the long strip of take-off turf. He handled the two-seater with rare skill. A three-quarter moon slipped from behind a cottony cloud, bathing the field in a pewter gleam. Ralph hoped they would be as lucky in their foray into enemy territory.

Crispin steadied himself for the take-off run and checked his wrist watch for the time. Time was all-important, and he jotted the figures down in a slim, brown-covered note-book.

The Bristol was nosed into the slight breeze, and then every wire, cable, and strut stiffened as the big prop slashed in whirling fury. They scraped a skid gash for a few yards, then the tail came up and there was a concerted rumbling from below as the big two-seater spewed fire and hot carbon from her nostrils. They were away in less than one hundred yards. The pilot curled her into a climbing turn to circle the field twice before heading for their rendezvous.

Crispin adjusted his goggles, tightened the wrist straps of his gauntlets, and peered over the side, studying the field with its slabs of Adrian huts, Nissen shelters, and bell tents as they took on some distinct pattern. Gradually, his eyes gained their night sight and he caught a semaphore lamp flashing. He studied the message for a minute and sensed the letter "M" was being repeated over and over. He stood up and gripped the pilot's shoulder, then spoke clearly against his helmet.

"We have a 'Return' signal, sir. A letter M. I see it clearly. They are using the Aldis lamp instead of the daytime ground strips. We have a 'Return' signal . . . sir."

Macintosh listened, and caught the meaning. He turned again and looked down at the field. The lamp continued to flash, but he glanced back to Crispin and then waved one hand in a "washout" signal. He cut back on the throttle and yelled, "That's not for us. Must be for one of the R.E. 8 boys. It's not for us."

"But it's coming from the apron of our 'C' Flight hangar, sir," Bart protested.

"I tell you it's not for us. Why would we have been sent out, if they want to recall us?"

"It seems clear to me, sir."

"I'll decide whether it is for us. I'm in charge. Sit down and leave matters to me."

"I just want you to remember I advised you . . ."

"All right. Now forget it."

"Yes . . . sir." Crispin was in no position to argue.

Bristol Fighter A7107 climbed to six thousand feet and headed for the Ypres–Courtrai road. A few tatters of fleecy cloud fluttered past the silver moon, and when the aircraft attracted a few desultory anti-aircraft shots, Macintosh turned northwest and headed toward the shapeless patch of Roulers. Crispin felt for the cocking handle of his gun to make sure it was loaded, and then he stood up to carry out a more complete watch over the area.

As they approached Bourlon Wood the pilot assumed a more intense attitude, snapping his head from side to side, and then apparently watching for evidence of opposition from below. The air became colder with the increase in height, and Ralph buttoned the throat flap of his flying coat. Crispin noticed this unusual vigilance, for in his previous flights aboard old Fees his pilots had shown more interest in what was ahead or slightly above, but this could be the mannerisms of an airman who was more familiar with a plane in which the propeller was up front.

Suddenly, apparently from nowhere, the aerial gunner saw two fishtails of flame slightly below, obviously from the twin exhausts of an aircraft engine. He tapped his pilot on the shoulder again, pointed down to the twin glares, and placed his forefingers together to form a cross. "Could be a Hun," he said distinctly against the pilot's ear flap. It paid to be suspicious of everything in the air, especially at night.

Macintosh shook his head negatively and reached for a flashlight fastened in a set of prongs screwed to the instrument board. "It's not a Hun!" he bellowed back. "Leave him to me."

Crispin looked down again and remembered that no present-day enemy aircraft carried two exhaust pipes. He jerked back and explained, "That's an S.E. 5 . . . one of ours. What's he doing up in this area at night?"

Macintosh put on a sneer. "Well! You finally caught on. Of course it's one of ours."

Somewhat chagrined, Bart studied the machine that was climbing toward them at a good speed. As it approached, he made out some detail from the glare of the exhaust flames. He grabbed his pilot's shoulder, squeezed hard, and shouted, "Watch out! It has German markings. It's an S.E. 5 all right, but with Jerry crosses!"

"I know. I know all about it." The pilot poked his flashlight over the edge of his cockpit.

Crispin was completely puzzled. "Is this part of the patrol . . . the contact?"

Macintosh glared at him in anger. "Will you shut up and do your job? I'll do mine!"

Crispin was disturbed and puzzled. No S.E. 5 had been mentioned in the instructions they had been given in the squadron Recording Office. He divided his attention between the strange behavior of his pilot and the approaching single-seater. He had no idea what to do. Here was a British plane well inside the enemy lines, daubed with German markings, and Macintosh was behaving as though this was a routine occurrence. As he watched he saw a number of signals flash from the plane below, and Macintosh responded with a short message. It was difficult to transcribe either signal since they were just a series of letters in standard Morse code. He watched the pilot below give a concluding signal and actually wave a farewell.

Convinced this exchange of code messages required an explanation, Crispin finally demanded, "What's the idea?" He was swinging his Scarff mounting around so that his machine gun would be positioned to fire down on the intruder.

Macintosh caught the move and threw his arm over the back of his seat and grabbed Bart's left forearm. "Lay off! Don't fire on him. I'll explain later. No shooting, Crispin! That's an order!"

The aerial gunner lowered the spade grip of the weapon and watched the S.E. 5 curl over and drop away. He was convinced now that Number 86-SS Squadron was assigned to very strange missions. No wonder it was designated a Special Service unit.

As they continued to head northwest, Bart decided to make a note of the area in which this puzzling contact had been made. He concluded that the plane could have come up from any of the German aerodromes around the Rumilly Forest. He scribbled a notation in his book and continued his rear-seat vigil.

Macintosh circled over the Cambrai road, taking in Graincourt and Fontaine. Twice he glared back at his gunner, and then he, too, made a keen study of the ground below. He throttled back the Rolls-Royce, almost to idling speed, and the altimeter needle began to drop slowly. He jabbed his elbow into the gunner's shoulder and yelled, "Keep your eyes open for a ground signal. It will be two whites and a red, remember."

"Two whites and a red," Crispin repeated, and in the next breath cried, "there they are. Flashing from that hedge alongside that field." He pointed to where some faint signals were winking in the prearranged sequence.

"Good! Plenty of room," Macintosh said. "They picked a good strip for a change. Get ready to climb down. You remember the passwords?"

"I remember . . . sir."

"Right. Sit tight. I just hope it is as level as it looks."

The Bristol Fighter went into easy S-turns with the engine just ticking over. Crispin had to admit his pilot was remarkably skilled and professional. He studied the surrounding area and marked it as level agricultural country. A few cottages could be noted, but none offered a friendly light. Either they had been abandoned, or the inhabitants were observing wartime blackout rules. While checking the landscape, the roads, and the distinctive topographical features—for future reference—he sensed that the plane had leveled off and was gliding in for a landing. There was no movement, no sign of life anywhere. It could have been any section of southern New Jersey, as far as the rural pattern was concerned.

Then came the faltering approach as, with stick and rudder, the pilot eased the Bristol Fighter down for the first touch. There was a low moan of undercarriage frame and the gasp of depressed tires; a slight bounce, and the flutter of anxious wing tips, then a long shudder of relief as she finally settled down and dug in her tail skid. The Bristol rolled up to a position almost opposite the section of hedge from where the faint flashes had been noted.

"Right!" Macintosh ordered. "Pop out . . . but first help me swing her around for the take-off. Take an outer strut."

Crispin vaulted over the Scarff ring and dropped lightly to his feet. He ran to the wing tip, grabbed the lower portion of an outer strut, and dug in his heels. The pilot held his rudder over, opened the engine, and in that manner fanned the tail around for the getaway. There could be no hoping for an into-the-wind take-off. In these situations one was satisfied to get down safely and have a good engine to get away again.

Crispin took a signal from Macintosh and then darted

toward the hedge. The flashlight was still snapping its white and red signals. He halted a few feet from the foliage and spoke his line. "Kitchener is dead."

From the shadows came the response. "But Lloyd George lives."

"Righto," the aerial gunner replied as he moved forward and waited for his contact to emerge.

A tall, angular man, wearing a peasant's smock and a crushed felt hat, appeared from the shelter of the hedge. In his hand he held a short cardboard tube at each end of which hung a trigger cord that, when pulled, would ignite a low-combustion powder—just in case.

"You have everything?" the gunner whispered cautiously.

"Yes. Everything is here." The man spoke with a cultivated British voice.

"Splendid! Best of luck to you, sir. Good night."

"Good night, and the same to you. By the way, if you get back to London, on leave, get in touch with . . ."

Before the man in the smock could complete his suggestion, a spurt of fire screeched past the gunner's head. There was a low, choked scream and a throaty gasp. The British agent fell flat on his face. The gunner threw himself sideways, still clutching the cardboard tube, as another burst slashed through the hedgerow.

"You dirty swine!" Bart Crispin screamed. "You filthy . . ." He now realized that the gunfire had come from the Scarff ring on the Bristol Fighter.

From a crouched position on his hands and knees he saw the Rolls-Royce spurt flame from its exhaust. The propeller raged and the two-seater hoiked its tail, but the pilot was ready for the bucking and he eased the stick forward. Then, light and free, the biplane roared away, the unmanned Lewis gun pointed to the moonlit sky.

The gunner crawled to the side of the fallen agent. A burst of bullets had crashed into his chest, and he lay vomiting gouts of blood. Bart got to his feet, glared at the fleeing Bristol, and husked again, "You filthy swine, Macintosh!"

He slipped out of his flying coat, laid it over the stricken agent, and with a final glance around, tried to pick up his bearings. Deserted, and seething with rage, he darted through the hedge and began running to his right.

Thirty-five minutes later Bristol Fighter A7107 made a perfect landing at the Serny aerodrome. Some primitive ground flares had been laid out but were quickly doused as soon as the Fighter had touched down safely. Macintosh rolled the two-seater up to the hangar apron.

Major Horne, no longer taking comfort from his briar, came up and glanced at the unoccupied cockpit. He peered over the Scarff ring, as if expecting to see a wounded gunner hunched up on the floor. He sniffed at the muzzle of the Lewis gun and then in a quiet voice said: "I take it you ran into trouble."

Macintosh wondered about the gun muzzle business, and then said: "It was a bad contact. Crispin just got to the hedge to give the password when a machine gun opened up—and he went down. I heard him scream and realized we had been trapped. I thought of getting out to drag him back, but he was too far away from the plane. It was hopeless, so I decided to take off while I could."

"Didn't you get our 'Return' signal? We recalled you before you had made fifteen hundred feet."

"No, sir. But Crispin should have seen it. He made no such report to me. I was too busy getting my night sight," Macintosh said as he climbed down and began to peel off his flying gear. "We were recalled? Why?"

"Actually, the order came from London. Something official. Also, we received another, ordering Crispin to London. He was to be commissioned and given pilot training. I can't understand why neither of you saw the 'Return' signal. He was a good man and knew his job."

Macintosh considered that and then said: "He said very

little all the way to the contact area. He saw the agent's signal before I did, and he did everything right from that point on. But he just walked into a murderous ambush."

"You're sure he was hit—out of action?" Horne demanded.

"Positive! I saw both Crispin and the agent, who was wearing a peasant's smock and a crushed hat. I think I saw a cardboard tube, but both went down screaming. They were both badly hit."

"I shall want a complete report on the whole flight," the major growled as he searched his pocket for his pipe. "I don't like any part of this show."

"I relied on Crispin to keep the time brackets," Macintosh mumbled. "I'll do the best I can from memory."

"I shall want to know every detail. Was the ground signal correct? Were you intercepted in the air by any enemy aircraft on the way?"

"We saw absolutely nothing in the way of aircraft. There was some anti-aircraft fire, but nothing too accurate. The field was adequate but not ideal. I had a tough time getting down without damaging the undercarriage or the wing tips."

"That's strange. From the photographs it looked like a perfect strip."

"Photographs can lie at times," Ralph argued.

"Well, it's too bad. I shall want that report as soon as possible. Wing will want full details. Everything."

"Yes, sir."

CHAPTER FIFTEEN

July 1917

> *American Expeditionary Force arrives in France. . . .*
> *Russians begin an offensive in Galicia. . . . Canadian*
> *House of Commons passes Compulsory Military Serv-*
> *ice Bill. . . . Constantine of Greece abdicates in favor*
> *of his second son, Alexander. . . . Bethmann-Hollweg,*
> *German Chancellor, resigns; succeeded by Dr. George*
> *Michaelis. . . . Russians retreat on a front of 155*
> *miles. . . . Winston Churchill becomes Minister of*
> *Munitions. . . . General J. C. Smuts appointed to*
> *Cabinet Committee on Air Defense and Air Organiza-*
> *tion. . . . Drawing of draft numbers for American*
> *conscript army begins. . . . Franco-British attack*
> *penetrates German lines on 20-mile front in Flanders.*

Early one morning a bedraggled man slipped out of a railroad carriage at the Burs Station in Rotterdam. Standing aside while passengers more familiar with the platform hurried past, he finally reached a decision and turned toward the flight of broad steps that led down to the street. Again uncertain, he studied the early morning workers before he moved from the shadows of the stairway.

Of medium height, the stranger was stooped and moved like a man who had worked at hard labor for many years. He wore a Dutch-type seaman's cap, a stained smock, baggy corduroy trousers, and hobnailed boots that were streaked with mud and farmyard dirt. Under one arm he carried a cardboard tube. He seemed to be a rustic who was ill at ease in a busy city.

He made his way in short hurried spurts across the busy street and headed for the Exchange. Once he stopped and referred to a square of smudged paper on which an address had been scrawled. He turned to his right and crossed over two narrow streets from which dozens of workers and shopgirls whirred on bicycles. He turned to stare into a sooty window as a man who looked like a policeman passed by, and then he scurried through the traffic and down a side street until he reached Noordblaak 47, a building that bore a number of small brass plates. He read them in turn until he found one that carried the name of the Zeeland Coastal Transport Company.

Glancing around with indecision, he suddenly hurried up the stone steps and finally found the offices of the Z.C. T.C. He pressed a small button twice, opened the door, and went inside. On the walls of the room were weather charts, dusty navigation sheets, ancient posters that offered excursions to Delft, and framed lithographs of coastal steamers. Anyone would have taken the layout for a standard shipping office, and had one inquired for freight rates to Antwerp or Flushing, the information would have been given immediately.

Here a small staff of British Intelligence agents carried on an undercover program of operations. It was headed by a short portly man, known only as Colonel Outerbridge, who had organized a network of lesser operators who reported all train movements in occupied Belgium and northern France. Outerbridge and the famous Henry Landau had developed this dreary toil into a fine art and just recently they had gained possession of a brand-new copy of the German Field Post Directory that had been bought from a deserter. This volume had a complete list of every unit in the Kaiser's army. It indicated where every regiment, battery, flying squadron, and other units—some still in the process of formation—were located. With this valuable book any Intelligence operator could make an exact estimate of the strength of the whole German army, for it included forces on both the Eastern and Western fronts, and gave the location of each field post.

The man with the cardboard tube under his arm went to a small reception window and to the inquiring face that appeared he dangled a small red fiber disc on which was stamped, "B. H. Crispin, 18963, Royal Flying Corps, Presb." It had been strung on a loop of commercial cord and was usually worn around the neck.

"You are an escaped prisoner?"

Bart Crispin nodded and put the disc back in his pocket.

"Come in. Take that door to the left."

In a few minutes Bart Crispin was sitting at a small table, relieved to find someone who spoke English. The man who had appeared at the reception window asked a few more pertinent questions without a change of expression, no matter what answer Bart gave to his inquiries.

"I assure you I am an aerial gunner with the Royal Flying Corps."

"You'd better be, or you may never walk out of here," the man said, barely moving his lips.

"I hoped you could help me."

"Don't worry. We've been expecting you."

Bart had no answer to that and decided to hold his tongue.

"Come this way, please. Colonel Outerbridge will see you."

In a smaller office a chubby man with pippin apple cheeks greeted him with the same friendliness that he might have extended to a company salesman. "I'm Outerbridge," he explained. "We're very glad you got through. I suppose it was a bit sticky at times, eh, Crispin?"

"There was little chance for rest, or to view the scenery," Bart answered, somewhat puzzled over this turn in his reception.

"Let's hear about it—from the time the British agent was

killed until you walked in here," Outerbridge said, and took up a massive cigar. "I have two reasons for this. One, to make sure our underground is reasonably efficient and, two, to correlate the information you absorbed during your escape. This is usually typed up and turned into small booklets distributed to service squadrons for the information of others who may be forced down in enemy territory. I'm sure you understand."

"I understand."

"We of course know the agent. He was in and out of here regularly. We did our best to head you off, but there was no response to the 'Recall' signal. If we could have stopped you, the poor devil would still be alive, and you would by now be in England taking pilot training."

"I caught the signal, but my pilot refused to obey it."

"His name is Macintosh?"

"Yes, sir. Ralph Macintosh. I knew him at college . . . Princeton."

"There are times when such coincidences are unbelievable. There you were, a university associate acting as an aerial gunner, fitting into Macintosh's plans perfectly."

"I am still a trifle bewildered, sir."

"Let's unravel it slowly," Outerbridge began again. "You escaped Macintosh's attempt to kill both of you. You cleared off with the tube. By the way, you haven't opened it?"

"No, sir. I had no idea what it contained, and that trigger cord worried me."

"You worked your way into the clear and moved about carefully for three days and nights, or until you were able to get aboard a canal barge just south of Ghent. Now let's get all that down step by step. What route did you take, and why? What means did you devise to avoid being picked up by the police or enemy soldiery? How was the contact made with the barge captain? What were the Belgian civilians like? Did you notice any unusual groupings of enemy troops, supply dumps, or heavy traffic over any main road or transport artery? I want every item you can remember. It's important."

"The barge captain was most helpful," Bart began with a wry smile. "I was puzzled about that at first, but I soon sensed he was part of . . . well, some sort of a system. He sheltered me whenever the police or customs men made an inspection."

Colonel Outerbridge studied the ash of his cigar. "He should have. We pay him one hundred pounds a month for such services."

"He did his job. He gave me some Dutch money and the address of your office. I'm beginning to understand the working of this escape system. But why were we recalled, sir? That incident has intrigued me ever since I broke into the clear and had time to cogitate."

"Weren't you intercepted by a British plane with German markings?"

"Yes, we were."

"And didn't your pilot exchange signals with that machine?"

Bart nodded, and waited for the explanation.

"We learned, just too late, that you were to be intercepted. Something went wrong there and Macintosh, who is a German agent, knew he had to take matters in his own hands. By the way, his name is not Macintosh. It is Mackensen, and he's a nephew of Germany's Field Marshal August von Mackensen, the man who set up the breakthrough in Serbia and finished off Rumania."

Bart sat listening intently and caught himself flipping his English shilling from hand to hand.

"Now you're wondering why, if we know all this, Lieutenant Macintosh hasn't been picked up and given the Tower of London ritual."

"There can be only one answer to that," Bart said thoughtfully. "You are allowing him to move about for some particular reason."

"Correct! We hope he will guide us to the whole organization."

"Is the tube of any importance?"

"The tube? Oh yes. It contains the blueprints of the German Siemens-Halske engine. They may be valuable, perhaps worthless. That is not for me to decide. Outside of my jurisdiction. But let's get on with your escape story."

"Well, from my particular experience the first important thing to remember, once you are down and if you are capable of moving about, is to keep full control of yourself. Never lose sight of the fact that you are still a free man and that your future is in your own hands. I can see how one might panic immediately, and blunder straight into trouble. But if you keep your head, several moves should be clear. You must get as far away from your aeroplane as possible, because the enemy will begin a patterned search for the downed airman. This must be done whether one goes down in daytime or at night. In my case it was faintly moonlit and I had no trouble in following the hedge to a road and then along the shadowy side until I found a culvert . . . you know, a drainage ditch going under a road."

Outerbridge smiled. "You must have been brought up in the country to use such a word."

"I was. I wanted to creep inside, but then realized that was where they would look first, so I continued on until it was almost dawn. I found an old stone bridge and turned in there and got some sleep. I stayed there all through the next day and did not move until darkness fell again."

"What did you do all that time?"

"Well, first I slept and when I awoke I was naturally hungry, but I found that I was more keenly alert. I had a dozen thoughts and ideas—and plenty of time to work them out. This is a point worth recording."

"Go on."

"I next cut my flying boots down to ankle height for easier walking. The rest of the fleece I hid under some loose rocks. I had my flat cap in my tunic pocket so I did not need my helmet. I had left my flying coat so I turned my tunic inside out, and the lining made it look something like a peasant's work smock. At any rate, I didn't look too much like a man in uniform."

Colonel Outerbridge nodded, and Bart continued.

"I had little trouble moving about at night, but to maintain the direction in which I wished to travel I often had to make wide detours to avoid villages or towns. I had a map which, like all airmen, I had stitched into the lining of my jacket, so I had a general idea where I was and how I was progessing."

"What made you head for a canal?"

"That idea came to me during one of my periods of intense thinking. So far, I had subsisted on brook water and anything I could find that was edible. I found some eggs in an old barn that were practically newly laid. I sucked them raw—another country-boy trick—and they nourished me. Food wasn't much of a problem. Then I began to catch a whiff of cheese—dairy products—when I moved through the farm lands at night. That brought up old geography lessons and I remembered that this part of the country supplied large amounts of cheese for the market. Something else told me that cheese in bulk would have to be moved to the big cities for sale and distribution, which brought to mind the idea of canals and barges. If I could get aboard one and become a stowaway . . ."

"Good! Now let's get it clear, just how you managed that. I should explain that all this is being taken down in shorthand by my clerk on the other side of that screen," Outerbridge said, and grinned.

Bart continued to flip his shilling. "I had little to do with that, actually. A barge captain simply impressed me. I mean, he grabbed me from where I was hiding among some empty crates and to my amazement said, 'For God's sake, how long do I have to hang around looking for you? You're a regular Pimpernel'—whatever that means. He hauled me across the towpath and shoved me aboard.

Captain Vandervelde was a very large man and I didn't have much chance of resisting him. As it turned out, however, I was in good hands."

"Did he explain?"

"Gradually, bit by bit. I now knew I had stumbled into an underground system set up to get Allied soldiers and downed airmen into Holland. Seemingly, Vandervelde had known I was probably heading in his direction and he had been looking for me while pretending to haul a cargo of cheese to Moerbeke. It was from there that he went through the motions of getting me across the border, and then keeping me out of the hands of the Dutch police, who I understand would have interned me. I think that is all I have to tell you, except to repeat that an escapee must first get into the clear, and from that point on, make every effort to think logically. He must keep under cover during daylight hours and move fast at night in a planned direction. Whenever he comes across a suspicious situation he must go to earth again and use all caution."

"What about the uniform?" Outerbridge asked, and rubbed his chin.

"I suppose there are times when you can procure civilian clothes, but that can be dangerous. If you are captured and are wearing civilian disguise, you are breaking the rules and might wind up against a wall. That's the Hague Law as I understand it. I figured that since I intended to travel only at night I would be no better off in civilian garb."

"But here you are in Rotterdam wearing a Dutch cap, a peasant smock, and corduroy trousers."

"Yes, but they were provided while our barge was going through the locks on the Belgium-Holland border. They were worn chiefly to help me get to Rotterdam by railroad."

The colonel nodded and smiled. "I know all that, but I want to get it into the typescript. After all, you may help many others to work their way through the same situation. You may, in fact, have to do it yourself sometime."

"I hope not. If I never smell Limburger cheese again it'll be too soon."

"Well, you've made your story very clear," Outerbridge concluded.

"What do I do now, sir?"

"Oh, we'll soon start you on your way back to England. You were booked for Reading, but we have new plans. You'll return with no fanfare, and will probably have a new name for a short time. You will be given individual instruction by a couple of specialists from the Central Flying School. If they can't make a pilot of you, no one can."

"Wonderful!" Bart beamed.

"But you will not join any particular squadron. You will be put on a special assignment devised to bring Lieutenant Macintosh to heel. Macintosh and the whole crew, as a matter of fact."

For the next hour Colonel Outerbridge drilled an amazing plan into the mind of 1st Class Air Mechanic B. H. Crispin. He had to learn it word for word and memorize it completely.

"Splendid. You have a fine mind," Outerbridge boomed when the lesson had been learned. "Then too, while you have been fiddling with that shilling—the one you took on joining up—I have thought up an idea that may help us put Lieutenant Macintosh off his feed. Let us suppose that from this point on . . ."

The crafty colonel outlined an addition to the Crispin plan and Bart had difficulty in suppressing a real guffaw.

"He'll go crazy, sir. He'll simply go off his rocker."

Through the course of events Lieutenant Ralph Macintosh was given what was listed as Technical Service leave and sent to England to provide the Bristol factory with some final suggestions for a standardized model to be put into high production. None of the suggestions was of a secret nature, but there was some singularity of phraseology to provide evidence of treasonable intent if he ever attempted to advise German technicians of these features of the new Bristol Fighter. In particular, there was a suggestion for a substitute engine mount, one to take the Sunbeam Arab in case an alternate had to be found for the Rolls-Royce.

He sat in with the designers and engineers at the Bristol plant and airily told of his exciting experiences on Intelligence agent pickups and routine fighter patrols. These technicians listened patiently, asked a few relative questions, sketched some rough designs of the proposed engine mount, and went through the motions of showing their appreciation for his keen concept of military requirements.

Ralph Macintosh was in his element.

This went on for several days, and following each luncheon, the relaxing beverages were increased in potency with Lieutenant Macintosh responding perfectly. He gave three different versions of what happened the night he had gone into Hunland to pick up some important material from a British agent. When he had completed his technical conferences he hurried back to London to make his drop at the tobacconist's in Wilton Road, renew his association with Cynthia Pollard, and pick up the loose ends at New Cavendish Street.

He had no idea that Cynthia Pollard had followed him into the dusty tobacco shop and had exchanged one packet for the one Ralph had delivered but half an hour before. His contribution was to be delayed until British counter-intelligence men could suitably revise the "information" Macintosh had provided for German technicians, and substitute other material that would keep them puzzled about a totally fictitious engine that was supposed to be under development by the Sunbeam Motor Car Company of Wolverhampton. In this manner the net was being laid and the snatch strings lined out, awaiting Macintosh's con cluding moves.

Later that Saturday afternoon he arrived at the Melville home and rang the bell.

Bryce, who was now in R.F.C. uniform, was sprawled out on a deck chair set in the sunshine of the garden. His sister Dianne sat nearby scribbling a letter on a stationery tablet. Her uniform was showing the evidence of its weeks of service.

"Lieutenant Macintosh, miss," Jeffers announced with a decided sniff.

"Macintosh!" Bryce cried. "He's supposed to be in France." He glanced at his sister and then said, "Keep him occupied for a couple of minutes, will you, Jeff? I want a word with Di."

"Yes, sir. A couple of minutes."

"Now listen, Di," Bryce warned. "I want to question this cove. I'll tell you why. I have an idea—and it's only an idea—but I think Bart is somewhere in England."

"But he has been reported as missing in action."

"I know, but there's something queer about it all. Listen to this. The other day we were given small booklets—something about how to act and what plans to follow, if you are shot down in enemy territory."

"That's a standard part of your training, isn't it?"

"Yes, but this was a new booklet, supposedly set up on the experiences of a man who had recently escaped. I read it over and over and I suddenly realized that I felt I was reading a letter from Crispin. The sentences were like Bart's. The thinking process was exactly Bart. In fact, I could actually hear him reciting this stuff to some stenographer. That's how it read. Bart Crispin to a T."

"I don't quite understand."

"Look. Let's suppose Bart did get down, somehow, and then escaped. The first thing R.F.C. officials would do would be to get him to tell how he did it, just to provide material for anyone else who might have to make the same

he got through, they'd take his story and put
et for the rest of us to study. This darn book
like Bart . . . when he talks. I have an idea he's
but for some reason they are keeping him under

Dianne sat staring into space.

"Now remember this when I start questioning Macintosh. There's something queer going on."

They were back in their staged positions when the American airman strode into the garden. His uniform looked war-weary too, but he wore it with the air of the "intrepid birdman." All he lacked was a row of oil-smudged decorations and a wound stripe or two.

"Well, well, well!" Bryce cried in greeting, and leaped from his deck chair. "Don't tell me you've finished the war already."

Ralph approached Dianne and took her hand. "Not quite, but it won't be long now. I see a token American Expeditionary Force has arrived in France."

"Lafayette, we are here! . . . At six per cent!" Dianne chipped in with a smirk.

Macintosh turned to Bryce. "And how does this young fledgling like the R.F.C.? Do you know the difference between a pusher and a tractor yet?"

"Oh, I'll be months sorting that out. Right now I'm taking physical jerks, Morse code, interior economy, and learning to tell a B.E. 2c from a Leyland lorry."

"Fantastic! Don't tell me they're still serving up that kindergarten stuff?"

"We go step by step. It's all something one must absorb before approaching an Avro during the molting season. What brings you back to London so soon?"

"Oh, a little matter of a conference on the new Bristol Fighter."

"Very hush-hush stuff, I take it."

"Well, we don't know how a plane will perform until we fly it against the enemy."

"Have you flown—against the enemy?" Dianne inquired with simulated little-girl wonder.

"Of course! I've done about a dozen regular patrols, and one—which was something special. Unfortunately, that was the one on which we lost Bart Crispin. He was my gunner, you know."

"Lost?" broke in Bryce. "He's just listed as missing in action in the *Gazette*."

"I'm sorry," Macintosh said, and opened a camp stool. "No such luck. I saw him killed. You might as well know. We were trying to pick up a wad of information from a British agent—well inside the German lines. Bart and the agent were killed. We were caught in an ambush, and I was very lucky to get away . . . with the aeroplane."

Bryce twisted in his chair. "Let's get this straight. You can tell us, can't you? Bart was your observer?"

"Aerial gunner. He wasn't an officer, remember. He had to jump out, run to the hedge, and take a wad of information from this agent. I was still in my cockpit and saw the whole thing."

"I take it this was a night show. How could you see if either one was killed?"

"It wasn't completely dark, and there was the gleam from the machine-gun fire . . ."

"They used a machine gun from an ambush?"

"Of course. They had to make sure of getting both of them."

"But wouldn't it have been more logical to capture both at gunpoint, say, and then have them to interrogate, and learn all they knew?"

"You're second-guessing, Bryce. All I can tell you is that both were cut down by machine-gun fire. No question about it. They were both killed."

"But the *Gazette* report has it that Crispin is missing in action. I would take that to mean that he has been taken prisoner. That's what it usually means. If you reported that both were killed, why would Crispin be listed as a prisoner . . . or words to that effect?"

Macintosh sat pondering on the theory, and much of the high color of his cheeks had drained away. "I can't help how they interpret my report. That's how I saw it and how I wrote it. I still believe both were killed."

"But how can you be so sure if you were still aboard the Bristol Fighter? You say Bart had to jump out, run to a hedge, and take the information from another man. How far away was he when they were shot down? He could run fifteen or twenty yards in a few strides. How could you see so distinctly—at night?"

"You are setting up a situation to fit your own conclusion, Bryce. I can't remember how far it was to the hedge, but it was nowhere near twenty yards. You must realize that I was concerned with waiting for Bart, hoping for a clean getaway, and finding my way back to our aerodrome. The distance, visibility, and what went on at the hedge were outside my scope of concern. I just did the best I could . . ."

"It must have been a horrible experience," Dianne said gravely.

Bryce prodded again. "What happened after the flight?"

"Nothing. What could happen? I just wrote out a full report and it was sent up to Wing."

"Were you kept on these Intelligence flights? After all, it must have been something of a shock . . ."

"Yes, it was. Remember, I considered Bart a close friend, a university pal. We were on track teams together, and though he was only an NCO gunner I tried to make things as pleasant for him as possible."

"Like picking him as your gunner on a dangerous night show?" Dianne said with raised eyebrows.

"I can't remember whether I picked him or whether Major Horne selected him. He was a good man and Horne liked him a lot. I think it was Horne who picked him, not I."

"Why was Bart transferred from Number 20 Squadron to yours?" Dianne continued relentlessly.

"We needed trained aerial gunners, so it was decided to draw a few from all the two-seater fighter squadrons in the area. I had nothing to do with that. There is a shortage, even now."

"What did you do after that disastrous night show?" Bryce began again.

"Oh, I had a couple of days off, and then Major Horne put me on working out new bombing sites . . . for what is called strategic bombing. You know, hitting German war plants."

"Have you spent any time in Germany? I mean, before the war?"

Macintosh flushed. "Well, no. You just take an encyclopedia, and an atlas, and work out targets from such sources."

Dianne said, "How nice for you."

Ralph dropped his eyes and then rose to his defense. "What do you mean by that?"

"Poring through old books must be cushy compared to picking up Intelligence agents."

"Well, I have done more than my share."

"You mean you have carried out other pickups at night?"

Macintosh was becoming angered by the inquisition. "No, damn it! I've been taken off that sort of job—at least for the time being—but I have made a number of what are called offensive patrols. We are entitled to a break now and then. You'll find out, Bryce, if you ever get out there."

Ignoring Ralph's explanation, Bryce said, "It sounds very interesting. How soon do you go back?"

"I have a couple of days left, but I have been considering putting in for a transfer to the American forces; now that *we* are in the war."

"Oh, you should," Dianne cried with fervor. "You'd be accepted as a full-blown aviation expert by *our* people."

"It's not that," Macintosh protested.

"Don't you think you owe something to Britain for your training?" Bryce inquired with a firm jaw.

"I don't see anything wrong with transferring. My training will still be contributed to the Allies, but I'd feel I was fighting under my own flag, for my own country."

"You would as soon as *our* country had anything to fly. In the meantime you'd be safe from the agent pickups and offensive patrols. That's what I mean by owing something to Britain. As I see it, the United States has nothing in the way of warplanes, and damn little in any sort of military equipment. But of course you could go back home and show them how to build Bristol Fighters, I suppose."

Ralph Macintosh got to his feet. "I can see I turned up on the wrong day. I'm just as sorry about Bart Crispin as either of you. I witnessed what happened to him, and I am not likely to forget it for a long time. Don't think I'm callous, but at the front we have to face up to such things almost every day. I realize that his death has touched both of you, but it is something you will have to accept."

"We've lost a number of friends since the war began," Bryce said quietly, "but Bart Crispin was someone special."

"I'm not giving him up," Dianne said, staring at her tablet. "I'm certain he'll come back."

"There's not a chance," Ralph said in a dull mumble. "However, we can't let these setbacks blight our young lives, can we? I wonder if I could induce you to make up a foursome and weave about the town tonight?"

"No. Dianne is due back at the Depot in an hour or so, and I have too much School of Military Aeronautics bumpf to digest. I thought I'd ended swotting when I left Oxford," young Melville explained, snatching at a convenient notebook.

"Well, so be it," Ralph said with little regret. "I'll have to look up some other playfellows."

When their visitor had left, Bryce poured himself a whisky, and while squirting in a dash of soda, said to his sister, "That devil lies like a drunken trooper. I'm positive Bart Crispin is somewhere here in England."

"If so, why doesn't he write to us?"

"I don't know, but I am positive he is being kept under cover for some special reason."

Dianne took a sip of her brother's drink. "If so, no wonder Ralph wants to transfer to the American forces. Maybe he has some quiet suspicion too."

"I think there's some sort of a move on to worry Mac. That *Gazette* notice stating that Crispin is missing in action must puzzle him. You know, there is such a thing as playing on a man's mind, rather than on his physical being, to attain a certain end. . . ."

"I'd love to be in on such a scheme," Dianne said with cold fury.

"You did all right here. You needled him properly."

As Ralph Macintosh left the stately home on New Cavendish Street, he sensed his world was beginning to totter. He saw it in Jeffers' attitude; in the fact that neither Sir John nor Lady Melville had appeared. There was a sinister air in every corner of the home, particularly in the interrogation Bryce and Dianne had subjected him to.

Because of the Bart Crispin affair he had become a pariah in the Melville household. Before, he had nurtured a hope that through Dianne he might move into the family circle and one day have access to a large share of the fortune, and a place in a respectable society. Such an association would quickly erase any taint that might become public if his enemy-agent activities ever were uncovered. It was just a matter of evading detection until the war came to an end. The letdown of peacetime would ignore all previous mistakes, digressions, falsities, and even treasonable acts. The blood-lust generals would become national heroes, the inept admirals take on the stature of Nelson and Drake. The public would bow before the statues and monuments erected to the military heroes, and their memoirs would be published in gilt-edged volumes and displayed in the Empire's great libraries. All their mistakes would be forgiven, the casualty lists would be removed from the front pages of the newspapers and hidden in Books of Remembrance, tucked away in seldom-visited chapels erected to the Heroic Dead.

All this Ralph Macintosh conceived in his bitterness.

What living heroes were left would be quickly forgotten, discarded, and left to rot in a poverty-stricken world that no .303 cartridge, no trench mortar, no automatic weapon, no canister of poison gas, no military aircraft, no dreadnought could ever wipe out. A few would walk the streets seeking work. A few would display their medals on velvet pads, resting on the fronts of hurdy-gurdy barrel organs from which would twang once popular tunes of their war days. A few would pack up what rags and tatters they had and take their ambitions and skills, honesty and courage, determination and ideals to make a living in some faraway colony or commonwealth with new blood, new interest, new manhood that rightfully belonged to their homeland. But perhaps this is the inevitable pattern of the spread of civilization, the state of human society for which they had fought so bravely. Perhaps this is the true reward of all war heroes.

Instinctively, Ralph Macintosh knew all this, and prayed silently he could hold out until the bells of peace chimed. To drench some of the dread and concern from his mind, he took a taxi to the Royal Automobile Club, which occupied the site of the old War Office in Pall Mall. Before he ordered a drink he put in a telephone call to the Grosvenor Hotel and asked Cynthia Pollard to join him.

"I'm so glad you called," she responded. "I have something important for you. I'll explain when I see you."

"I'll be in the Wolseley Lounge," he said laconically, and hung up.

Within twenty minutes Cynthia breezed in, light-footed and wreathed in smiles. He wondered how she could maintain such gaiety under the stress of the work he believed she was doing. Again, she was smartly dressed and drew the attention of several other R.F.C. men who envied the Bristol Fighter pilot, and reflected that some blokes have all

216

the luck. They wondered if it would be possible to wangle an invitation to join him. Perhaps he'd be catching the boat train from Victoria later in the afternoon. Chaps do have to go back at the close of their leave.

Cynthia sat down, asked for a Bronx cocktail, and then fumbled with the catch of her handbag.

"I heard you were in England," she began, and then looked around the lounge with a careless air. "I was afraid I'd miss you."

"I have a couple of days yet. You said you had something for me?"

"There was a slip-up on Wilton Road."

"My God, no!" he gasped, and blanched.

"Nothing serious. I happened to go in after you left this morning. I had something for the drop too."

Macintosh took a drink in relief. "For a minute there, I thought . . ."

Cynthia thanked the waiter for her drink, and then let out a gay peal. "No, nothing went overboard, but Hugo was supposed to give you this package. The ghost walked, as they say." She handed him a squarish envelope that bore only his initials. It was sealed with red wax and was almost an inch in thickness.

Ralph took it, weighed it thoughtfully on the tips of his fingers. "This is all mine?"

"Yes, of course. Anything wrong?"

"No. It just seems more than generous, if this is in five-pound notes."

"Just figure they're satisfied with your work, but you'd better put it where it is safe. Looks like a lot of money."

"How did you know I'd be in London?" he asked, and unbuttoned the flap of his pocket.

"Hugo said you had just been in and that he'd forgotten to give the packet to you. I knew you would call me, eventually, so I decided to take it and hope you would. I just took a chance, I suppose, but I knew you could use the money. I mean, you're so out of touch in France."

He accepted her explanation. "They take care of you this way?" he asked, slipping the envelope into his tunic pocket.

"No. I never see or touch any of it. They put it to my account in American funds—in a bank in Holland. I have to move very cautiously, you know."

"I see. You heard about Bart Crispin?" Ralph lowered his eyes and stared at his hands.

"Yes. I saw a note in the *Gazette* . . . and the *Times* casualty list."

"About his being missing in action?"

Cynthia peered into his face. "Yes, I also read, somewhere else, that he was 'missing, probably a prisoner of war.' Have you heard anything official?"

"He's dead. I was with him," Ralph said quietly. "We were working a pickup show together."

"So I understand." Cynthia sat erect but showed no further interest in the Crispin incident.

"You know? Don't tell me you were in on the whole deal? You're covering a lot of territory."

"It came up in a recent interview with one of my contacts."

"Well, I was in a spot. I had to get rid of both of them . . . Crispin and the agent."

"Yes, you were in a very difficult position," Cynthia agreed, and finished her cocktail.

"Bart knew I had ignored a 'Recall' signal. Then he would have reported the air contact which let me know that the agent was to be taken care of—I don't know what happened to that part of the deal; it slipped up somewhere. So I just had to do what I did, whether it was Bart or some other aerial gunner. I had no choice," he said in dismay. "If he had gotten back he could have crucified me . . . perhaps the whole espionage unit."

Cynthia nodded, and sat tracing the details of the whole affair, as she had been told it at Scotland Yard. In that version, she had no idea that Crispin had escaped Macintosh's treachery and on that premise was even more determined to play her part in bringing him to earth.

Finally she said: "I don't see what else you could have done." She nodded at the waiter, who had brought a second drink. "All's fair in love and war, they say."

"I'm sorry it had to be Bart, but as you say, 'all's fair.'" Macintosh straightened up as though the subject had been closed. "What are you working on now?"

"Something rather involved. A matter of rounding up a great deal of important information in one sweep." She smiled in her old form again. "Something about a new force being organized by the R.F.C. Have you heard anything about it?"

"Not a thing, but of course my line is more in the technical field," Macintosh said with smug satisfaction.

"Have you as yet run into a man named Hugh Trenchard?" she asked cautiously.

"Trenchard? Oh, that ass. He's trying to fight the Smuts Air Board. They'll be tossing him out of France any day. No one would take that wild man seriously."

When Macintosh arrived back at his hotel he found that a small, bedraggled envelope had been slipped under the door of his room. His name had been scrawled on it in a careless manner. Inside was a square of cardboard in which was inserted a new silver shilling . . . nothing more.

CHAPTER SIXTEEN

August 1917

Pope Benedict XV issues plea for peace on a basis of no annexation, no indemnity. . . . Commander S. H. Dunning makes first successful aircraft landing on HMS Furious. . . . Czernowitz captured by Austro-Germans. . . . Canadian troops overrun Hill 70, dominating Lens. . . . General E. B. Ashmore takes command of London Air Defense. . . . Zeppelin destroyed off coast of Denmark by aircraft from HMS Yarmouth. . . . Saint Quentin cathedral destroyed by Germans. . . . Germans make last daylight aeroplane raid on England. . . . Italians cross the Isonzo and take Austrian positions. . . . President Wilson rejects Pope's peace plea. . . . General Smuts submits proposal to create separate air force in Britain.

The man who had taken the King's shilling had been transformed into a smart, trim lieutenant in the Royal Flying Corps. During his weekends he strode the streets of Edinburgh with the silken wings of a pilot on his breast, and, equally important, the gleaming red and blue ribbon of the Distinguished Conduct Medal. Crusty majors greeted him with cheery "Good mornings." Poker-backed sergeants and kilted privates of the Highland regiments threw him especially snappy salutes when they spotted that particular decoration, for one and all recognized the ribbon as one that could only be won in action by a noncommissioned soldier; one who had once taken the King's shilling.

Bart Crispin glowed with pride now that he was a real flying man, a pilot, a true airman, and more particularly in being honored with a position of great trust. It was a long stride from the ivied halls of Oxford. He was to be trained as a free-lance airman, while keeping the secrets of the Allied armies. His training had been fundamental, intense, and then augmented with special instruction in the varied skills of the Intelligence operator.

Once he had been secreted out of Holland and quietly welcomed in England, he was escorted up to Cranwell, at the time a Royal Naval Air Service station, where he was provided with an R.N.A.S. uniform, a new name, and another identity disc. He immediately began dual-control tuition aboard an Avro 504K trainer, a two-seater biplane, powered with a Le Rhône rotary engine. This machine was selected because it would give him experience with a rotary, for he was slated to fly the Sopwith Camel, a scout powered with the same type of engine.

His first training phase at Cranwell was taken over by a specialist from the Central Flying School at Gosport, who found the young American an ideal pupil.

"You have had just enough flying to be at home in the air," his instructor said after their first dual-control lesson, "but not too much to have developed ill-conceived notions about piloting. We get a number of Bristol Fighter observers who are so accustomed to high speed in the air that when they come home for flight training it takes us a couple of weeks to tone them down and make them realize that they do not have 250 horsepower up front, and that they can't make split-ass turns as soon as they get ten feet off the ground. You're one of the few in the happy medium category. You'll do very well."

The C.F.S. instructor was right. Bart took immediately to the Avro. He applied to each dual-control lesson all the caution developed in his journey across Belgium to Holland. He approached each problem with an open mind, respected the intent of the instruction, the laws of aerodynamics, and the limitations of the aircraft. The primary maneuvers and the fundamentals of flight were worked out in his orderly, mathematical mind before he put the machine through the required evolutions. His turns were almost perfect examples of speed, bank, and direction; the three stabilities, directional, longitudinal, and lateral, were all combined in the required formula.

After five hours of intensive dual-control instruction, Bart was sent aloft on his first solo. The decision was made after he had completed a first-class, if routine, landing. His instructor ordered him to turn the Avro around for another take-off. While they sat watching for other incoming planes, the instructor flipped his belt, climbed over the side of the cockpit, and stood on the wing root. Bart wondered what had inspired this unexpected move.

"You're on your own," his instructor said, and flipped off his helmet. "You're to take off, make two circuits of the field, and land. If I like what you do, I'll send you off again. You can buzz about for twenty minutes, just working out your school figures."

"All right . . . if you say so," Bart said, and faced the test with interest and determination.

"Remember, now. You're alone, and she'll respond somewhat faster to the control stick. Also, she'll glide in farther for the landing, being lighter, so don't try to force her down. Let her come in on her own, but give yourself plenty of room. Off you go!"

"Yes, sir."

Bart's first solo was better than adequate. He took off in a straight run, held her nose down until the air-speed indicator showed enough to allow her to fly herself off. He then climbed easily to six hundred feet. He banked gently into the turn, keeping her nose on the horizon, and then straightened out to fly the down-wind leg. By that time he knew he could fly. The two circuits of the field were made, and then he throttled back and glided in for the landing. She was thistledown light, and he was glad his instructor had warned him, but he remained calm and put her down with little over-control. As he turned around again and started toward the line-up of trainer aircraft, a white Very light signal was fired from the tarmac, and he knew he was being sent off again to put in twenty minutes on his own.

The instruction period passed quickly. From the Avro Bart moved on to the Sopwith Pup, a lighthearted single-seater that only a few months before had been a front-line fighter. It was the ideal machine for the novice, for it handled beautifully in the air and could be put through any standard maneuver with very little trouble. He reveled in the sense of aerial freedom the Pup provided, and because of its sound design he was soon able to perfect himself in all fighting maneuvers. In fact the Sopwith Pup turned Bart Crispin into a very complete airman as far as flying was concerned.

During these weeks he was also given instruction in aerial navigation, some primary meteorology, the design features of all enemy aircraft, and a comprehensive study of the Western Front, at least as far as the British responsibility ran. Various types of signaling were taken up, including the Aldis lamp, and ground-strip markings used by the infantry. He also spent considerable time becoming familiar with night flying and the secret "lighthouse" signal system being devised for the new night-flying bombers.

Once all this phase of his program was completed, he was moved up to the Sopwith Camel, a fierce, bad-tempered, single-seater that was being adopted as a medium-level fighter. This stocky, short-fuselaged machine had a dozen faults and half a hundred advantages. It was fast, highly maneuverable, wicked in right-hand turns, until the pilot learned to employ her vices to his own ends, but a tough, bulldog type of plane that, once mastered, could become the scourge of any enemy formation. Few people knew it at the time, but the Sopwith Camel was to prove to be the most effective fighter of World War I.

Crispin sensed that here was his true test. The Clerget rotary engine gave out 130 horsepower. The pilot's seat was close to the rear of the engine, and the fuel tank was directly under his seat. Thus, the weight was highly concentrated and provided a center of gravity that permitted extreme maneuverability. Because of the short fuselage and the stubby wings, the torque effect of the whirling rotary engine set up a condition in right-hand turns that could be either deadly or advantageous, depending on the skill and reactions of the pilot. If he was careless he might find himself in a fatal spin before he was barely off the ground. But the same flying characteristic could be turned into a fighting asset, for the Camel could outfly any aircraft on the front if the pilot persisted in doing right-hand turns, and maintaining safe flight by the use of top-rudder.

It had two Vickers machine guns that fired through the arc of the propeller, and as a daylight-operations machine was unquestionably the finest aeroplane on the front right up to the end of the war. When it was employed in night operations in defense work against enemy bombers, its tricky maneuverability did reduce its tactical value, but it was a splendid aircraft nevertheless.

Once Bart was reasonably competent aboard the snarling bulldog-like machine, he was ordered to put in some flying at night to carry out his projected operations across the Channel. In the midsummer of 1917 few airmen had flown at night. Prior to that a handful of Home Defense pilots aboard ancient B.E. 2c biplanes had gone into the air to fight off Zeppelins, but there was a tremendous difference between the stodgy B.E. and the Camel. In the first place, the single-seater was not equipped for night flying; there was no instrument illumination on the panel; there were no luminous dials, and ground lighting was little more than a row of oil drums, filled with blazing waste, set along the level area of the field. There were no flares or landing lights on the wing tips.

For his first attempt after dark, Crispin was given a pocket flashlight to check his instruments while the engine was being run up. Then, pocketing the torch, he taxied out to the center of the field and took off, guided by three blazing drums that were set to indicate the direction of the wind. For a minute or so he was terrified during the take-off, for he realized he was roaring into a black nothingness, and wondered how he could possibly get back on the ground.

With a doubtful mixture of a pilot's illogical trust and stoicism, he skimmed through the streamers of oily smoke that almost immediately reminded him of that horrifying night in London when he was involved in an air raid. He sat tense, tight-throated, but in a few seconds he had climbed up into an area of quiet assurance. True, the Clerget engine was roaring, and his propeller was in full song, but the dreaded darkness magically became a definite landscape, an ink-wash illustration of a familiar area. He could see the gleaming metal of the railroad that wound into Sleaford. There were dark fields, bounded by light gray roads. Little villages he had walked through became tiny scenes from a storybook. He banked over, feeling no need to check his instruments. The Clerget was humming its satisfaction, and the pressure on his cheeks seemingly checked his air speed.

The fairy scene below broadened; the little houses threw back faint gleams from their angled roofs; small lakes and ponds twinkled, and a Puffing Billy crept north along the rails, heading toward Lincoln. He climbed to six thousand feet and by then could identify the pewter indentation of The Wash and the blurred design of Boston. Looking back over his shoulder, he spotted what he thought was Nottingham—and was right. He circled that area for twenty minutes, secretly hoping he would come across a formation of marauding Gothas. No such interception was enjoyed, so he returned to Cranwell and prepared for his first night landing.

By that time his night sight was at its keenest, so he had no difficulty finding the gleaming baubles that marked his flare path. It was on this first night flight that Bart discovered what flying was really like. Out in France as an aerial gunner he had been only a passenger aboard a magic vehicle that left the ground, climbed into the air, and moved about in a three-dimensional journey, but he had had no sense of being in control. There had been only the quaking thrill of being taken off the ground and put through the same maneuvers as the aircraft. As an aerial gunner he might just as well have been one of the struts, a leg of the undercarriage, or even a length of fabric that covered the wings.

As a pilot—particularly flying at night—he gulped deeply of the joy that came with the command of this graceful bird. To feel the responses to his will or whim at the stick, to sense the surge of power that came with palming the throttle, or the deliberate change of direction following the delicate pressure on the rudder, produced a glow of satisfaction he had never known.

Night flying was totally unlike the pleasure of skimming about the sky in daylight. There was a velvet smoothness, a calm path from one point to another, a caress of comradeship that no other man-made motion afforded. There was an instant or so when Bart remembered a summer job he had had aboard a cargo bark, her high masts strained by the tug of taut canvas, her yards scarcely discernible, and her shrouds as shadowy as a cobweb. Gliding out of a New England port, the bark had moved like a phantom across the surface of the black water. The lights of the port had flickered and a railroad engine had sent up a pillar of yellow flame that daubed the mottled sky. Below him now were the same dim lights from indistinct buildings, and with them came the assurance of friendly sounds and clamor.

The sailing vessel and the aeroplane chanted the same siren song, each promising new experiences ahead. Both revived half-remembered dreams, the sounds and cadences of other voices. There was a warm frenzy within him, an ecstasy he could not explain—and never would. It was a tumult of personal accomplishment.

There was no time to pursue the flight of imagination further. He found himself putting the fractious Camel down with hardly a bump. He taxied up to the group of ghostly mechanics who seemed to emerge from the sable gloom of the ground to stand wide-eyed in the glare of the Clerget's exhaust.

"Are you all right, sir?" one of them asked breathlessly.

"Fine. Those flares were wonderful. They're all we need, really."

"Cor! We couldn't see you up there. We could 'ear you, of course, but we couldn't see you. Bloody tricky 'ow you could get down again . . . all in one piece, like."

"It's not bad at all," Bart explained when he had climbed down, "but I'll tell you one thing. They can order all the blackout precautions they like, but once you get used to the night, everything's just the same as it is in daylight. I don't see how bombers can miss anything they go for, if they take their time to study the area carefully."

"Coo! No wonder the blasted Germans can 'it London whenever they like. I didn't think you'd see anything."

"Well, never mind," Bart said as he rolled up his helmet and stuffed it in his jacket pocket. "Our turn will come, if we ever get planes that will fly as far as Berlin." He winked, and slapped one of the mechanics on the shoulder. "That will be the day, eh?"

Another month of intensive training carried Crispin through the Air Fighting course at Ayr in Scotland where he was given special instruction on machine guns, the Constantinesco gear that synchronized the weapons to fire through the whirling blades of the propeller, and the types of ammunition used for various targets. But, most important, he was able to try his skill with the Camel against several types of enemy aircraft, machines that had been captured, put into first-class flying condition, and were flown by experienced pilots. In this manner he learned the merits of the different types, their blind spots, weak structural areas, and capabilities under various conditions and altitudes. At Ayr he became a highly skilled airman, one who was far better trained than the average novice who was rushed to the front with fewer than ten hours solo on the plane he would fly over the enemy lines.

During all this time Bart never went near London, or in fact very far from his present training depot.

CHAPTER SEVENTEEN

September 1917

New American National Army to assemble at various cantonments. . . . SS Minnehaha torpedoed off Irish coast. . . . Germans stage first big aeroplane night raid against England. . . . Argentina dismisses Von Luxburg, German Minister, on charges of improper conduct. . . . Paul Painlevé becomes French Premier, succeeding Ribot. . . . Russia proclaimed a republic by Kerensky. . . . General Tasker H. Bliss named Chief of Staff, U. S. Army. . . . Georges Guynemer, famous French flier, missing in action. . . . General Smuts becomes Chairman of British Aerial Operations Committee. . . . Zonnebeke, Polygon Wood, and hamlets east of Ypres taken by British. . . . William D. Haywood and 100 members of I.W.W. arrested for sedition. . . . British capture whole Turkish Mesopotamian Army. . . . Brig. General Wm. D. Kenly appointed Chief of Air Service, American Expeditionary Force.

Ralph Macintosh spread his weekend leave into several days of pointless, riotous living, but enjoyed few hours of his illicit absence. Unkempt, husky, with bloodshot eyes, and his pupils slack in picking out varied distances, he returned to France by Channel steamer. On his arrival at Boulogne he sidestepped the Transport Officer and took a train to Paris, rather than the squadron tender that would have run him back to his base area. Having visited the

French capital in his university years, he knew his way about and soon located the offices of the New York Guaranty Trust Company, where he changed some money and rented a safe deposit box in which he stowed a wad of British bank notes. He felt relieved when they were out of his possession, for with every stride they had seared an inflamed patch across his thigh.

Once outside, he stood and watched the swirl of passersby, the inhabitants of a city that had maintained their courage and dignity through three years of war. Paris was unlike London or New York. It had been on the fringe of the carnage but bore none of the scars of the Zeppelins. Instead, it flaunted its gaiety, femininity, and determination to bear up and provide a haven for the heroes and heroines who hopefully returned to its boulevards, bars, and restaurants. There was a dash, an élan, a rowdy spirit that only a few could sense, taste, or smell, but it was always there for those who had escaped from the front. What Paris contributed to the war in the practical sense was debatable, but there was no question that the City of Light could offer romance, fellowship, camaraderie, and a broad, encompassing warmth of esprit de corps.

None of this welcome reached Ralph Macintosh. He was a pariah in an alien land. He had no time for pleasure, joie de vivre, the handclasp of an almost forgotten friend, the hallowed communion of views along a bar or across a café table. Instead he made his way to a dingy office in a building on the Rue de l'Opéra, and following almost the same pattern as that of Bartley Crispin when he had arrived in Rotterdam, Ralph studied two vertical rows of brass plates. The concierge came to the top of the steps, flipped the end of a cigarette, and spat into a corner. Ralph caught his eye, pointed to one of the brass plates, and put on a questioning grimace. The shabby doorman spat again and nodded.

The airman climbed the steps, passed the doorman, and then turned and looked back. There was no further advice forthcoming, so he pressed on and sought Suite 204 on his own. He knocked on an ancient door in which the glass window had been replaced by a square of sheet tin painted black. The number was in bluish-white chalk, and a small piece of paper had been pasted to the lower right-hand corner. In a blotchy script he read, "Franco-American Import Cie." The door opened an inch or so and a slice of ugly face was disclosed. A set of three fat fingers held the portal secure.

"Ugh?" came out of the thick-lipped mouth.

"Mackensen."

"Ugh." The door opened another three inches, revealing a chunky man in an unpressed suit and heavy-soled shoes.

The airman turned the lapel of his tunic back to reveal a small metal disc that bore concentric red, white, and black circles.

"Ach!" The door was opened wide enough for a slim man to slip through.

The interior was in determined competition with the slovenly entrance and musty corridor. The office equipment comprised an ill-treated Louis XV *bureau du roi* with most of its moldings and gilt plaques missing. The opened desk panel presented a turmoil of dog-eared catalogues, sheaves of dirty paper, a cluttered ash tray, a tilted telephone, and two empty tobacco packets. A telephone directory hung from a rusty nail that had been pounded into the wall nearby, and below it was a slatternly settee from which most of the cushion padding had long since billowed out and been swept into some convenient dust heap.

The ugly man, now fully revealed, had a distinct bullet-head, a warty nose, and a set of yellowed tusks that showed streaks of blood beside the canines. He looked like a man who would relish a dogfight. With another grunt he pointed to the settee.

After Macintosh, with evident disdain, had seated himself, the man finally sprawled in what had once been an office swivel chair. As his great form filled the seat, the rusty mechanism emitted a growl, followed by a squeak that set Ralph's teeth on edge.

"So?"

"I understand you wished to see me."

"Who do you know in New York?"

"Oh, come on! There's Stosselmeyer, Von Reichenau . . ."

"Von Reichenau is in Washington!" the bulletheaded man growled, and then belched.

"He's in New York as often as he's in Washington. Then there're the people at the North German Lloyd Line office. I have met most of them."

Bullethead took some greasy photographs from a drawer, riffled through them, studied one, and compared it with the airman. He tossed them back again and elbowed the drawer shut. He did nothing with ease or dexterity.

"Goot!"

"I haven't much time. I'm overdue at my squadron now. What do you want to see me about?"

The ugly man picked up some dirty papers from his desk. "How are things going?"

"Fine, as far as I know. They pay me well, so I must be producing what they want."

Bullethead nodded. "The material on the Bristol Fighter was very good. Who would have thought of a two-seater fighter?"

Ralph put on a snide grin. "Now they've got a two-seater bomber that can fight almost as well as the Bristol. You're in for trouble if this man Trenchard has his way."

"We know all about Trenchard."

"You'd better. He'll be raising hell soon."

"Then you'll have to stop him."

"Me? How? I'm just one man aboard a Bristol Fighter. You surely don't expect me to shoot . . ."

"Imbecile! Of course not. We have to use methods that cover the whole bomber idea. Now listen to me." Bullethead reached inside his jacket and drew out a sheet of

232

typewritten paper. "You have drawn up a list of German targets?"

"Right. I turned in a copy to the London man. They should be able to take immediate precautions and have defense Staffeln alerted—for night-raider defense." Macintosh nodded his head with each word.

"Bah! It is almost impossible to stop aircraft raiding at night," the ugly man growled. "Look how we struck at Dover a short time ago."

"Dover is not London."

"There is no difference."

"Have it your way. I'm just a working airman."

"Now you listen to me!" Bullethead continued, and they sat talking for more than an hour—until the telephone rang.

Early in September Bart Crispin enjoyed a five-day leave spent at the home of a University of Edinburgh friend with whom he had become acquainted through his C.F.S. instructor. There he met two other civilians who were in the architectural field. The change of scene and subject acted like a tonic.

When his instruction time was up he was ordered to take a certain train south and to put up at a small hotel in Surrey. After he had unpacked he was picked up and taken out to the Sopwith Aviation Company plant at Kingston-on-Thames. London was still out of bounds for him and he spent the next few days watching the erection of Sopwith Camel B-1497, a Clerget-powered machine that was fitted with night-flying equipment, including wing-tip flares and instrument-panel lighting. It was a beautiful aircraft, gay with national markings, gleaming varnished struts, with two Vickers guns under the cowling and small bomb racks beneath each wing. The taut fabric shone, and the aluminum engine cowling sparkled with an engine-turned finish. At first Bart saw none of this standard dressing-up but his eyes were immediately caught by a silver medallion artistically painted on each side of the fuselage just ahead

233

of the blue, white, and red roundels. He stood off and studied the unusual insignia—a gleaming English shilling.

Two days later, after several test flights with the new
Camel, he checked out from the Griffin Hotel and hauled
his light gear out to the hangar. His field valise was sent on
to cross the Channel by sea. His personal gear was stowed
in various sections of the scout. No one of importance in
the company came to see him off. As far as the Sopwith
staff knew, Bart was another ferry pilot assigned to fly a
new plane out to the Aircraft Park at St. Omer. That business
of painting on a replica of a shilling seemed like the childish whim of some brand-new flight commander. Obviously
one of those crazy Canadians. Still, it took all kinds.

Bart settled down in his cockpit, fastened his belt, and
went through the ritual of starting the engine. The Clerget
responded well since it had been artfully doped by the chief
mechanic. Bartley gave it plenty of time to warm up, and
then ran it up for revs. He could tell by the expression on the
chief mechanic's face that it was more than satisfactory, and
they exchanged knowing nods as the chocks were pulled
away. He rolled out to the runway and took off with no
gaudy display of aerobatics, but held her in a straightaway
climb until he had enough room to make a wide circle of
the field. He crossed over the hangars, fired a white Very
light, and received a wave from the chief mechanic below.

He then headed southeast for Hythe, and from there
picked out the aerodrome at Port Lympne distinctly marked
by a fifteenth-century castle, long the residence of the
Sassoon family. He landed and checked in, as did all pilots
before making the Channel crossing to France or Belgium. After all formalities, and a drink in the Administration
bar, he took off again, climbed to twelve thousand feet, and
then took the chance and headed across The Streak, as the
Channel was known to experienced pilots.

He landed, according to his written instructions, at an
advanced field a few miles southwest of Furnes, which was
about fifteen miles east of Dunkirk. He had to circle about

for ten minutes before he spotted his area, and then realized he had been assigned to a simple turfed strip that had a one-plane hangar, a fuel dump, and vague ground signals. There was a small wind sock fluttering from a staff above the hangar, and nearby a stack of sandbags that evidently were used for a gun-test butt.

Bartley dropped in, made a careful landing, and ran the Camel up to the hard-packed earth in front of the canvas shelter. A sergeant and a lank-haired mechanic appeared from nowhere and stood staring at the unusual silver disc on the fuselage of the Camel. The mechanic scratched his head; the NCO simply looked bored. Sergeant Crosby had been in France since the retreat from Mons and was inured to all kinds of personal affectations, but 2nd Class Air Mechanic Harry Husbands was fascinated by the reproduction of what would buy a pint of bitter in any regimental wet canteen.

"Good afternoon, Sergeant," Bartley greeted Crosby, after he had climbed down and unbuckled his helmet. "I'm Lieutenant Crispin."

"Ar-r-r, yes, sir. We were told to expect you, sir. We haven't much idea what this is all about, but I suppose you do, eh?"

"I'm supposed to," Bart replied, and took off his flying coat, revealing his wings and the ribbon of his decoration.

"Oh, I see," Husbands gulped. "That's why you've got a shillin' painted on there."

The sergeant took another look, and forced a mild smile.

Husbands was rattling on. "You was once one of us," he said with pride in his interpretation. "I mean, since you 'ave the D.C.M. you must 'ave taken the shillin'. That's why you 'ave one painted on your bus, like."

"Well, or words to that effect," Bart admitted. "I used to be an aerial gunner, first with Number 20, and then with 86-SS Squadron."

"Bristol Fighters!" Husbands said, the name coming out like a cork from a bottle. "Coo! That's what I allus wanted

235

to be . . . an aerial gunner, but they wouldn't let me. Said I was too important as a mechanic."

"Must 'ave been balmy," the sergeant broke in with a smirk. "I can't see you up there trying to shoot down 'Uns. You'd more likely blaze away at the wrong planes. I know you."

"'Ow can you know, if they never gave me the chance?" Husbands appealed to Crispin.

"That's the only way to find out," Bartley admitted. "Now perhaps you'd be so good as to show me around here. I presume I am to operate from this strip. Not much room for more than one, is there?"

"Some days we 'ave 'arf a dozen when things get 'ot," Husbands began again, running his fingertip around the insignia of a shilling.

"He means, sir, we often have planes drop in for fuel or ammunition, or even for more important emergencies— like someone being wounded, and we have to see them off to a casualty clearing station. We have an old Crossley for things like that," the sergeant explained.

"But am I the only one who stays here?"

"Right, sir. You 'ave a billet in the village down the road. 'Usbands and me 'ave quarters behind the 'angar. Nice an' snug, like, and no one bothers us, sir. It's really an old bell tent but, as they say, any port in a storm."

"Well, I suppose it will do as long as the weather is mild, but we'll have to find something better than that when it turns."

Both Crosby and Husbands appreciated the thought, and with that started to unload Bart's light gear and transfer it to the Crossley tender. Over the next half hour Bart noted that the sergeant was most interested in the new Camel and it's mechanical features. He went over the machine from prop to tail skid, while Husbands seemed intrigued with the pilot; his every gesture was a quiet but obvious compliment to the young American who not only had volunteered to serve for Britain but had joined as a

236

ranker and won his commission in the field. To Harry Husbands no one could show a greater depth of friendship. Here was a man who deserved the same in return.

The Camel was hauled tail first into the canvas shed where Sergeant Crosby began a routine check of the engine, guns, and gun gear, the ammunition and controls. He double-checked through the data on the inspection sheet and logbook while Husbands took Crispin on a tour of their little establishment.

"We keep a supply of Cooper bombs over 'ere under that tarpaulin," he explained. "We 'ope to dig it in deeper, because, who knows, they might 'ave a go at us one of these nights, but so far they've given us the miss, so to speak, sir."

"Their night bombers must fly directly over here on their raids on Dunkirk, St. Omer, and Boulogne," Bart said, and stared up into the sky as though he expected to see a course drawn across the lowering overcast.

"On their way to 'it the 'ospitals, you mean. That's right. We 'ear 'em go over regularly."

"And what about ours? I haven't been out here in some time so I've rather lost track of what's been going on."

"Well, you know, sir, the DH-4s have been very busy, and I believe they're beginning to do night shows against important Jerry targets, but a lot of it is just talk. We don't 'ear much that can be relied on, and it don't do to take much notice of latrine rumors, does it, sir?"

Bart smiled. "You've got yours screwed on right, Husbands, but I think we can look forward to considerable night work by the bombers soon. In fact, we've already established a special field down at Ochey—that's near Nancy—on the French front. From there we hope to attack important German munitions centers. It's called strategic bombing."

Husbands assumed a bewildered look and remained silent.

"We'll have some of it up this way eventually, when we get the planes that can do the job," Bart assured him.

"Well, I 'ope so, sir. It's bin a long time comin', ain't it?"

"That's the way it looks to us," the young pilot agreed. "Well, you seem to have everything shipshape here. There's a field telephone in the hangar?"

"Yes, sir. A direct wire to Wing 'Eadquarters. That's for you an' your work, I suppose."

"Well, someone has to tell us what to do," Bart said with a grin. "I better go have a look at my billet. Where is it?"

"Just down the road. Not too far, but I'll run you down with your gear, and tell the madam who you are. They seem to be expecting you."

"That's good to know," Crispin said, and then made a quick decision. "By the way, do we have a hand drill in the hangar?"

"An 'and drill? Of course, sir. I'll get one in a jiffy."

"No. I'll come along. It's just a silly idea perhaps, but . . ."

Bart took his silver token from a flap in his wallet and then bored two holes in the coin with the hand tool. He fingered about for a couple of short brads and went back to the Camel. "Here, Sergeant, tack my lucky shilling on the instrument panel, will you, please? Just there between the air-speed indicator and the watch."

"Well," Sergeant Crosby said with a benign smile, "you'll always have a bob with you, so you'll never be broke. Now there's a nice thought."

With this pleasant co-operation, Bart Crispin set out his stall at Furnes and prepared to carry out the plan devised by the man in Rotterdam, a plan that had been further improved by officials in London. By this time, too, Cynthia Pollard had been recruited into the widening net, and at the suggestion of a one-armed man at Scotland Yard, she began a series of journeys that took in cities in northern Ireland, Denmark, Italy, Gibraltar, Greece, and two ports along the southern shore of the Mediterranean. The tobacconist in Wilton Road continued his faceless trade with a number of equally silent patrons who brought in or took out wrapped packets of varied sizes and shapes.

In the Midlands of England, Bryce Melville had been posted to Number 128 (Camel) Squadron, which was being organized at Castle Bromwich for an overseas assignment. At the Serny field, Ralph Macintosh, now a first lieutenant, received another shilling wrapped in a bedraggled envelope. It had been mailed from Douglas, on the Isle of Man. Two days before, a third such coin had arrived from Copenhagen.

Confused, enraged, and giving way to an ungovernable fit of temper, he hurled them into a corner of his cubicle, hoping to rid himself of the taunting symbol. Then, after a minute or two, still seething with wrath, he dropped to his hands and knees, crept about the floor, and retrieved them. He sat on his haunches holding them in his palm, morbidly fascinated by the gleaming discs of silver.

"What bastard game is this?" he whimpered, and began pounding the floor with his fists.

After a long searching speculation which provided no logical answer, he got to his feet, washed up, changed his shirt, and selected a new knitted tie. He wandered into the Administration shed where he intercepted Major Horne.

"Anything new on the board?" he inquired, and turned to the Squadron Orders sheet thumb-tacked to the wall.

"Things are much the same. We are to continue our routine offensive shows, of course, but we have another pickup on Thursday night."

"We're back on that? Who has it?"

"I'm trying Trowbridge—and young Martin. They're a good team."

Macintosh nodded moodily and then asked, "Where?"

"That area we call Number 3-B, south of Courtrai. You've never been there, have you?" the major asked in a conversational tone.

"I haven't been given a pickup job since I lost that gunner—Crispin."

"Crispin? Oh yes. He was a college mate of yours, wasn't he? That was most unfortunate."

"By the way, has anything more been reported on him? In London I got the impression they felt he had been captured and was a prisoner of war. There's nothing to that, is there?"

"Why should there be? You reported he was killed, didn't you?"

Macintosh studied Major Horne's eyes, but there was no hint of suspicion there. "I certainly believe he was killed. I don't see how anyone could have survived that first blast. He took it full in the chest. A ten-round burst, at least."

"I don't know why anyone would question your report or assume Crispin is alive—a prisoner of war," Horne muttered with an air of disinterest.

"But why would anyone think otherwise, and why did the *Gazette* in London report him missing in action?" Ralph persisted.

"I haven't the slightest idea," the major said without looking at the junior officer. "Of course, London may have a contact with someone on the other side of the line, someone who may know what actually happened that night."

Macintosh took a deep breath. A shiver rippled across his abdomen, and he found himself standing slack-kneed.

"Both sides do this sort of thing, you know," Horne went on, pottering about the office as though looking for something that had been missing for hours.

"Do you mean to say that if Crispin didn't die . . . if he was captured, and let's say placed in a German hospital, his capture and condition wouldn't be reported by someone —by the International Red Cross, for instance?" Macintosh was taking the attitude of a man who was appealing for a special dispensation, pleading for a reduction of a court sentence. "I mean, why would anything like that be kept secret?"

"There could be all sorts of reasons." Horne continued to mope about the office, apparently searching for something—a tobacco pouch, his pipe, a box of matches, a pipe cleaner.

"But it isn't as if he is anyone of importance. He's not some general's son, a member of the British aristocracy. He's not a noted 'ace,' as the French call them. Crispin was just an NCO aerial gunner. Who and why would anyone want to keep his whereabouts or condition a secret?"

Horne appeared to ponder thoughtfully. "Well, he is, or was, an American, wasn't he? That may have something to do with whatever is going on. I'm not responsible for the views or action of British Intelligence. They do their job as they see it, and we have to do ours."

The words "British Intelligence" startled Ralph Macintosh for a few breaths. He hadn't considered Bart Crispin important enough to excite the interest of British Intelligence, but if he was still alive—no matter where—he'd be able to talk to someone. Even if he talked only to a German interrogation officer there was no telling what he would say or what explanation he might have for his being captured when his pilot and plane were not. But surely, if he told that much, German Intelligence would make certain none of that would get back to London. They would never allow anything to get out that might menace the German espionage network in Britain. That much was certain.

But suppose Crispin had lived, and had tried to get back into his own lines, or even into Holland? To erase that possibility as quickly as possible, Macintosh said, "Do you think London would keep Crispin's situation, whatever it is, a secret, Major?"

"As I said before, they could have one of several reasons."

"I don't understand. Such as—what?"

Major Horne set up a series of wrinkles in his brow. "Well, now you ask me, I really can't name one, but then I am not an Intelligence bloke." He shuffled about with the papers on his desk and then changed his mien. "Ah, here it is. I knew it was here somewhere. A funny little chap, wearing an American uniform, stopped in here the other day while you were in Blighty, and left this for you." He handed Ralph a weary-looking envelope on which was scrawled his name and squadron number.

Ralph gave the missive a thumb-and-finger inquiry, and without tearing the flap, knew it contained another silver shilling. He forced a smile and a "Thanks," and then, as if to close the conversation, added, "By the way, Major, could I have some transport in an hour or so? I'd like to run into Aubigny. I understand there's a small American party in that area. They're taking instruction from the British on poison-gas prevention. I believe I have a couple of old friends in that outfit. I won't be gone long."

"By all means, Macintosh," Horne said, "but you'd better take a map with you. Aubigny is pretty close to the line, you know. Don't go barging into trouble, old boy."

Half an hour later Lieutenant Macintosh, slouched in the front seat of the squadron tender, ordered the driver to take him to the center of Aubigny. They rumbled into the little town, listened to the distant thunder of the guns, and caught a faint trace of phosgene gas.

"We should have brought our gas masks, sir," the driver said with some concern. "We're up bloomin' close in this area."

"Never mind. We shan't be long."

"Good! I've had too many whiffs of that stink."

Halfway through the town, Ralph instructed the driver to turn right, and they headed down a road and could see the Scarpe glistening ahead in the crisp sunlight.

"Stop at that church over on the left," Ralph ordered. "I have an old friend, a priest, there. I shan't be more than a few minutes."

"I thought we were looking for an American gas-course party."

"That'll come later. Be right back."

CHAPTER EIGHTEEN

October 1917

> *Franco-British attack takes Poelcapelle.* . . . *Antil-les, American transport westbound from France, sunk by submarine, 67 lost.* . . . *An aircraft is flown from gun-turret launching gear aboard HMS* Repulse. . . . *American artillerymen fire first shot in their war against Germany.* . . . *French troops advance north-east of Soissons.* . . . *Palestine Brigade of R.F.C. formed.* . . . *Austro-Germans begin big offensive against Italian positions.* . . . *British organize new 41st Wing to bomb German industrial targets.* . . . *Gorizia captured by Austro-Germans.* . . . Beersheba, *Palestine, occupied by British troops.* . . . *Peru, Brazil, and Uruguay declare war on Germany.* . . . *Italians in full retreat to Tagliamento River.*

That Thursday night Captain Angus Trowbridge, with Corporal Jonathan Martin, took off for the pickup strip known as 3-B, south of Courtrai. The arrangements were much the same as had been set up for Macintosh and Crispin many weeks before. A British agent was to appear at a certain time, make contact with the aeroplane, and pass on a cardboard tube of information. This time, it was presumed it would be the details of a new Fokker biplane that rumor said was to replace the triplane produced by the same company. Several good contacts had already been made at the Courtrai strip, and Major Horne felt it would be a simple operation this time. For one thing, the night was clear, and there was a promise of a good moon at about the time the landing would be attempted.

Horne gave similar instructions: "You will not start into your glide until both of you have spotted the correct signal. Tonight it will be two greens and a white. Unless both of you see, and clearly identify the flashes, you are not to go in for the landing."

Captain Trowbridge nodded.

"Now remember, Martin," Major Horne continued, "until you see that signal clearly you are not to give your assent to Captain Trowbridge. This is a two-man deal—regardless of rank. Until you both agree you are seeing a clear signal you are not to go down for the pickup. Understand?"

"Yes, sir!"

"Right! Off you go, and the best of luck."

The Bristol Fighter got away with no trouble. Trowbridge, long a flight leader of daylight offensive patrols, enjoyed the take-off, and after making two circuits of the field in case a "Recall" signal was flashed, he climbed to five thousand feet and headed across the lines. The course was simple, for the clear night plated the Lys in dull silver, and he followed it all the way from Comines until the shapeless splotch of Courtrai in northwest Belgium spread itself across the silver-gray countryside. Trowbridge made a diversionary circuit around the town, drew a few bursts of anti-aircraft fire, and then boldly cut across the built-up area and headed for his rendezvous strip.

As he approached open country he began losing height and searching for some evidence of the wind speed and direction. Near Lauwe he noted a small flax mill, and smoke from its low stack gave him some idea of wind conditions, and with that he made his zigzag course over the undulating countryside. The moon rose to a level that spread a wide carpet of garish light, and the 3-B strip appeared as if by a wash of a photographic chemical. His gunner tapped him lightly on the shoulder and pointed out the site. Trowbridge nodded and circled the area.

As the Bristol lost more height and her engine was throttled back to almost idling speed, a flash signal snapped from a small cluster of leafless shrubbery. Both the pilot and the gunner saw it, and watched for the color sequence. It came . . . two greens and a white.

"What do you see?" Trowbridge asked.

"Two greens and a white, sir."

"Correct. Two greens and a . . ."

That was as far as their agreement reached. A double burst of machine-gun fire converged, with splintered chains of tracer fire overlapping; and then seemingly pinwheeling in all directions. There was a heavy clangor about the engine cowling, and the propeller ran wild, screeching its agony. A segment of brass-tipped blade slashed through the upper wing, baring a great triangle of ribs and spar. The Rolls-Royce engine clattered to a halt.

"Damn and blast!" Trowbridge swore. "A bleeding ambush."

Young Martin tried to bring his gun into action, but it took seconds to swing it through 180 degrees to draw a bead. By that time the Bristol was wallowing in a soggy glide for the field below. The gunner got off only a short burst before the big fighter began bumping across the autumnal turf.

Another burst from a scraggy hedge spattered into the Fighter, and Martin let out a low cry.

"Both legs, sir," he gasped, and hooked his elbows over the Scarff ring. "You'd better nip off . . . on your own."

A third burst, from the opposite side, convinced the pilot that he hadn't a chance to get to cover on either side. The ambushed team had to sit and take it.

Two nights later another attempt was made on a strip south of Thourout. A pilot named Lieutenant Thisby and a Sergeant Gunner Malcolm took off to find a man who would make his position known with the same signal. This time an entirely new situation was experienced. It was a beautiful moonlit night without a cloud in the sky; ideal for take-offs and landings, but a condition that offered little or no cloud cover in case of an emergency.

Thisby and Malcolm had hardly crossed the lines when they were picked up by three aircraft that could not be identified. The gunner stood an alert watch while his pilot headed for the rendezvous. As they gradually approached the Thourout-Cortemarck area, the three aircraft moved in and came close enough for Malcolm to identify them as Albatros D-IIIs. He noted the French-type V-strut that had been adopted by Robert Thelen, the renowned Albatros designer. This strut permitted a narrower, single-spar, lower wing that afforded a wider view downward. Sergeant Malcolm had had considerable experience against the D-III during the previous Bloody April when many British airmen had mistaken the German V-strutter for the French Nieuport scout.

The pickup operation was held in abeyance while the gunner gave his attention to the Albatri. His first burst was concentrated on a D-III that had started down to pepper their tail. It wrapped a tracer design around the sleek engine cowling, and Malcolm saw the pilot's arm swing up to shield his face. The German scout snapped up in a sharp zoom, and a wheel went skimming across the sky as the plane came to a stall. Malcolm then turned to a second that was coming in level but at a sharp angle. He took aim and waited for his wind-vane sight to steady itself . . . and then saw the Albatros break up in mid-air. A top wing panel folded back and slapped down on the whole tail assembly with a smack that sounded like two wet planks being banged together.

Sergeant Malcolm, squinting along his gun, stared in amazement. "What the . . . ?" He watched the D-III break up and roll itself into a ball of structure and torn fabric.

Thisby was as bewildered, but as thankful as his gunner. While Malcolm prepared to take care of the third D-III his alert eye caught still another machine. A Sopwith Camel!

"Now where the hell did he come from?" Malcolm grumbled to himself, chiefly because he had been denied a welcome target. "Never knew they'd try night flying with Sop Camels. The bloke must be proper wonky!"

"Proper wonky" in Sergeant Malcolm's vernacular meant this Camel josser was off his onion . . . a bit tapped in the noggin . . . up the bloomin' pole. He actually meant the pilot must be crazy. An American of the same stripe would have had it that the guy must be nuts.

The Sop Camel was split-ass turning through the tangle of aircraft, chunks of wreckage, a long streamer of gasoline flame, and inky smoke. The remaining Albatros took the bait and hoiked over to get on the Sop's tail. The Camel went into a tight, right-hand turn.

"You bloody fool!" Sergeant Malcolm bellowed in the Hun's direction, and then took a quick glance around for evidence of a ground strip. Before he could find anything that looked like a long, flat surface, the Camel was moving in for the kill, its blunt nose bearing almost dead-on for the broad tail of the Albatros.

Malcolm stood watching the one-sided contest, and then his eyes widened. "Now there's a funny thing. That bloody Camel has some sort of medal, or something, painted on its fuselage. I wonder what that's for?"

The guns of the British plane spat twin streams of tracer bullets, and almost immediately the German plane burst into flame. The glare bathed the Camel with its tragic illumination, and the insignia was outlined in considerable detail.

"Cor!" Malcolm gulped. "It's a shillin' the bloke has painted on his bus. What the hell next?"

The Camel pulled out of its dive as the Albatros threw away its tail assembly. The port side V-strut snapped off and zipped across the sky like a giant boomerang. What was left was quickly devoured by the fire, leaving only a tubular body that spewed flame like a blowtorch, and some fragments of skeletal wing structure.

The Sopwith banked over hard and came roaring to clear the Bristol Fighter by less than a dozen feet. Thisby and Malcolm looked up and saw the pilot wave at them.

"A nice helpful chap to have handy," Thisby said.

"I think he's waving us off, sir. I think that's what he meant—for some reason."

The Camel turned and came back toward them, and as it approached a red Very signal was fired from the cockpit. It arched up, spluttered, and broke into its scarlet glare.

"You're right," Thisby agreed. "He's probably part of the system. We'd better buzz off."

The Bristol Fighter turned to the west, picked up Ichteghem, and crossed the Allied line. The Camel held a position off the right elevator until the Fighter was well into the clear. Then, with a final wave, it tilted over and went into a steep dive toward Nieuport.

"Now there's a funny thing," Sergeant Malcolm reflected. "What was that Camel doing up there all alone, at night? Another thing, how did he know those Jerry Albatri would be up there looking for us? But what puzzles me more that anything is that shilling painted on the side of his fuselage. They don't usually allow that sort of game in the R.F.C., they don't."

When they had returned without making the pickup, Major Horne listened to their story until Malcolm brought up the matter of the unusual insignia painted on the side of the aircraft that had driven off the intercepting Albatros D-IIIs.

"Oh, I see," he said, and his eyes glistened. Then he did an unusual thing. He put the tip of his forefinger to his lips and slowly shook his head.

Both Thisby and Malcolm nodded.

"That'll be all. I'll see you in the morning," Major Horne concluded.

As they left the Recording Office Lieutenant Thisby threw an arm across his gunner's shoulder. "He means it, you know, Malcolm. We'd better forget we ever saw a Sop Camel with a shilling dangling on its watch chain."

"Never heard of such a thing, sir," Malcolm agreed. "Besides, no one would believe it, would they?"

After Bart Crispin had seen the Bristol Fighter safely over its own side of the line, he dropped to three thousand feet and zigzagged back to his strip southwest of Furnes. He made a perfect landing down the upright of an "L" laid out with three oil-waste flares and a number of reflective plates that picked up the glare from the moonlight. The system was primitive, but under favorable conditions it at least indicated where the smoothest stretch of turf lay.

As he rolled the little fighter scout up to the hangar, Husbands was dousing the flare glare with old metal dustbin tops. Bart slipped over the side of his cockpit and dropped lightly to the ground.

"Everything all right, sir?" Sergeant Crosby asked in almost a whisper.

"Everything's fine, but I shall want four 20-pound Coopers at once."

"Bombs, sir?"

"Right . . . four high explosive, not those shrapnel things that are used against moving troops. This is something— bigger."

"Cool!" Crosby emitted, and ran toward the bomb trolley. "When Husbands comes back, have him check your petrol and ammunition, sir."

"I'll just need fuel, and the bombs."

While his instructions were being carried out, Bart went into the hangar and unfolded a large-scale map of the Vimy Ridge area. He checked out several farms and then found one that bore a particular, conventional sign—a circle with a small cross straddling its upper curve. He marked it clearly on his own map. "Let's see," he concluded to himself. "I fly directly south for about fifty miles. Just before I reach Arras I turn right and pick up Aubigny. If I take a line running between Aubigny and Vimy I should spot it . . . less than five miles from Aubigny."

He tucked his map away, then flipped through his School of Military Signalling notebook and checked out an unusual heliograph instrument. He went over the notes he had taken during the course.

"We're all ready, sir," Sergeant Crosby called. "How long will you be gone *this* time?"

"Just about an hour, perhaps a little more."

"Ah, well. We'll be here waiting for you. By the way, did you have any luck, earlier?"

"Let's say two Jerry Albatros D-IIIs won't bother us again . . . three in fact. A Bristol Fighter gunner got one too."

"That's the stuff to give 'em!" Harry Husbands crowed. "That's what I wanted to do, but they said . . ."

"Not agayne, Husbands!" Sergeant Crosby interrupted. "Mr. Crispin can't waste all night listening to your prattle."

"I just wanted to say I'd love to be an aerial gunner."

Bart evaded the issue by going out and making certain his bombs had been placed in the wing rack, and that they were the type he had requested. "Let's get on with it. I haven't had any supper," he said, and grinned as he climbed back into his cockpit.

In ten minutes he was in the air again, heading south, with the smoke, sparkle, glare, and eruption of the front line snaking past on his left. A resounding salvo of anti-aircraft shells was fired at him, but he pressed two buttons on his instrument panel; slim-beamed signal flashes snapped from a small glass-covered aperture in the bottom of his fuselage, and the gunnery halted immediately. Ahead, a series of narrow searchlight blades stood erect like great twin-edged swords, providing guidance for a formation of DH-4 bombers that were heading for some target near Thielt. This was another Belgian weavers' town with a Cloth Hall in the manner of Ypres. More ancient architecture was due for a pounding, but such is the wage of war.

The night was glorious as far as flying was concerned. The air was heavy enough to provide almost perfect carburetion, and his engine literally sang as it swept him southward past Armentières, Bethune, and Bullecourt. Then the river Scarpe gleamed along the Aubigny–Arras road, and he eased back on his throttle. His hand fingered the Bowden controls that ran down to the bomb racks, and he checked the position of his hydraulic gun-gear handle and pulled it up to assure the proper oil pressure for the synchronization line.

He dropped down fairly low as he approached Aubigny, and noted there was a large stone-towered church outside the eastern side of the town, standing on the road that in happier times ran through to Vimy. The juggernaut of war had practically obliterated the pastoral highway. From that point Crispin began a zigzag search for his unusual target. He was very close to the lines, and once or twice sensed that light machine-gun fire was being directed at him, but he had to find his objective and make certain it was the same one he had noticed earlier when he first began his evening foray.

He switched back and forth over what had once been a picturesque and valuable agricultural area. There were the remains of little cottages, barns, ancient haystacks, cattle ponds, and open sheds. Gunfire from enemy sources had raked the countryside regularly, and there were few trees or fences left. Singularly, there was one item of agricultural interest that remained unscarred, and it was this that had attracted his attention earlier.

At last he found it again and, circling low, he moved away and zigzagged in several directions, always watching for the telltale factor that had caught his eye. Then he saw it. A penetrating beam of light, two beams, in fact, each flashing from opposite blades of a lowland windmill.

He wasted no more time. Guiding the Camel at the

target as a horseman would put a hunter to a five-barred gate, he put his eye to the Aldis sight, his left hand to the bomb-release toggles, and said, "Damn you, Macintosh. Your stinking mob will never again use this setup for your treachery."

The outline of the windmill came into the cross hairs of the sight, and when he could determine distinct features of the great hub bearing the four arms of the mill, he yanked two toggles. The Camel jerked with the release of the two 20-pounders, and he had to hoik over the tiled dome of the tower. As he banked hard and curled around again, there was a muffled explosion, several great splinters of flame, and then a widening glare. The two Coopers had pierced the upper wall of the mill, bored inside, and the delayed-action igniter triggered the explosive. Both bombs burst inside the mill tower.

As Crispin came round he saw the main portion of the tower collapse, and the four great arms of the vanes go end over end across the open field. A jagged wall of flame rose from the base of the tower, and in minutes there was little to indicate where the picturesque old mill had stood.

"No wonder the Germans never tried to shell that thing," Bart muttered to himself. "It was perfect as a heliograph station from which to send messages across the line toward Douai. Well, let's make certain no one will crawl out and explain what happened."

He heeled over again, slammed at the burning pyre, and lobbed two more Coopers into the inferno. "Nothing like getting plenty of practice," he decided and climbed away, turning north. When he arrived back at Furnes he had no explanation for the empty bomb racks; just a friendly request that the Camel be put away and given a thorough examination in the morning.

"I think it will be wise," he added, "if we keep the hangar closed whenever there are other aircraft on our field. We don't want to risk having to answer too many questions, do we?"

"No," Sergeant Crosby agreed, "not even if we had an idea what *we* are doing."

Bart winked and said, "Let's keep it that way."

Air activity, with many objectives, continued all through that month at increased pressure, although the weather was beginning to take its toll. Low temperatures at high altitudes unsheathed the talons of frostbite, causing personal discomfort and increased respiratory ailments. The mechanics, responsible for aircraft maintenance, worked with split fingertips, abraded knuckles, and suppurating blisters. Clothing suitable for such working conditions had not been thought of. The new electrically heated Sidcot suit was made available to the pilots and a few officer observers, but the NCO airmen had to make the best of extra sweaters, cardigans, scarves, and knitted helmets that had been sent from home. Odorous whale oil was smeared on every inch of exposed flesh, but men's cheeks bore frostbite scars for months.

The inclement weather played havoc with the machinery of aviation. Engines refused to start, lubricating oil had to be heated before being poured into the sumps, ignition systems choked up, and the flexibility of undercarriages' springing was seriously affected. Guns froze and fired erratically, bomb racks refused to release their missiles, and control cables either jammed in their guides or snapped under the subzero temperatures. Frozen ruts on the flying fields flipped tires from wheels with the facility of a schoolboy removing the top from a cooky jar.

But technical progress was bringing some rewards. Aircraft, in particular, were bigger and better. The new Handley Page 0/400 twin-engined planes were in high production, and many of them were going to new squadrons being organized for night bombing operations. This big aircraft had proven its worth earlier in the hands of the Royal Naval Air Service, first in daylight naval patrols over the North Sea, and later on counter-bombing attacks against the Gotha bases during the daylight raids on London. By September 1917 the Handley Page was finally turned over to a few R.F.C. squadrons for night bombing against important German bases, augmenting the DH-4 single-engined machines that had been assigned to the 41st Wing. The first true night bombing force was Number 216 Squadron (formerly Number 16 Naval), which began operations with four Handley Pages in October 1917, flying out of Ochey near Nancy on the French front. This was to become the nucleus of General Trenchard's proposed Independent Air Force. In the meantime night bombing was the main assignment of several DH-4 squadrons, operating out of fields in northern France and Belgium. The "Fours" were reinforced later by the DH-9 and 9a models.

Another innovation was established by the R.F.C. to meet anticipated military conditions. Sopwith Camel squadrons were ordered down from the safety of their altitude capability and re-established as low-level attack units. This situation was conceived when it became obvious that as soon as German ground forces could be driven out of their elaborate trench emplacements, attack-type aircraft would be needed to keep them on the run, to destroy their dumps and supply bases, and to harass all types of ground transport. The new tanks that were to show much promise in the Battle of Cambrai were expected to initiate this breakthrough.

At this time of innovations, changes, and developments, Bryce Melville, now a novice pilot with Number 128 (Camel) Squadron, arrived at Serny and was intrigued to learn that Ralph Macintosh's Number 86-SS Squadron was quartered on the same field. For a few days he tried to avoid meeting his fellow American, but eventually Major Horne's airmen were invited across the field for Number 128's first Guest Night, and Macintosh seemed pleasurably surprised to find himself sitting opposite young Melville. He reached across the table to shake hands and express his amazement that Bryce had become a front-line pilot in such a short space of time.

"It's a trick," Bryce explained in a stage whisper. "I told them I had done my School of Military Aeronautics when I was at Oxford. They swallowed it whole, and the next thing, well, I was taking dual control on Avros. In that way I cut more than six weeks off my training."

"But I thought . . ."

"When you last turned up in London? Sure, I told you I was taking the S. of M. A. course. I had to. I didn't want you to squeal on me. Judas! I'd never have gotten out here; messing about with carrier-pigeon husbandry, interior economy, and those damn silly social behavior courses. Besides, they need Camel pilots and a few of us were picked out of the Cranwell list without our taking Aerial Gunnery and School of Air Fighting instruction. They figured we'd get all that quickly with the new low-level program to which all Camel squadrons have been assigned. It's damn good fun, you know."

"Boy, oh boy!" Macintosh muttered. "How many hours have you had on Camels?"

"Oh, ten or a dozen," Bryce said airily. "They're wonderful to fly if you have the touch."

"It's murder!"

"Nothing of the sort. I'll get in ten or so more before I go on patrol. After all, I'll not be up at fourteen thousand chasing Fokker triplanes or Albatri. We'll be down low strafing roads, trenches, fuel dumps, and railroad traffic. Any quirk can do that. Judas! We were doing that sort of caper as soon as we went on Pups. . . . Up and down the beaches above Skegness. What a lark! The silly bloody mayor put in a complaint almost daily."

Bryce bubbled along in that vein for most of the evening. There was the ubiquitous phonograph grinding out "If You Were the Only Girl in the World"; the rugby scrum with a rolled-up flying boot for a ball; a small group huddled in a discussion concerning the relative merits of the S.E. 5

and the French Spad; a would-be pianist picking out the Dead March from *Saul;* a bridge foursome manfully trying to play in rotation and keep an accurate score.

Then Bryce abruptly changed his tone and manner. "Here, tell me again about that pickup flight when you lost Bart Crispin." He handed Ralph a whisky and soda. "My treat," he added.

"Damn it all, I didn't lose him! We were ambushed, and he was cut down while trying to make the pickup from the British agent."

"I'm not questioning your point, Mac," Bryce continued. "I'm still puzzled why R.F.C. officials refuse to admit he was killed. In fact, you can't get anyone to admit he's even missing in action."

"How do you know all this?"

"I've been making personal inquiries."

"Why?"

"Why? Because I'm interested in the guy. I want to know what really happened to him, and I can't get a reasonable answer."

"You don't believe me when I say I am certain he was killed?"

"How can you be certain? You admit you were occupied with making your getaway."

"But I saw him fall; heard him scream under the first burst of gunfire."

"First burst? How many were there? You didn't mention that before. I thought there was only one burst."

"Look, Bryce," Ralph turned on a new level of conversation. "How can you tell what is a burst? It might have been one long burst . . . twenty, thirty rounds. I might have decided that all that noise and muzzle glare was one long burst, or a series of short bursts. It all depends on the man with the trigger."

"I can't believe anyone with a machine gun would fire twenty to thirty rounds at one . . . or even two men. I'm

256

not a machine-gun expert, but I would think that two five-round bursts would quickly cut down two men."

"You weren't there. You were not in my unenviable position, Bryce. I tried to be calm and rational, but I was Goddamn new, remember. You won't believe it, but today I can scarcely remember any of the salient details of that pickup show. I've done so many other things since."

"But Crispin was a friend. You were in college together. You'd known each other for more than four years. Don't you have some continued interest in his, er, what happened to him?"

"Look," Macintosh pleaded, sensing they had gone over much of this before, and positive Melville was trying to trip him into a glaring contradiction. "I was terribly upset, and, as you say, we were long-time college friends, and saw a lot of each other, moved in the same circles a great deal of the time, but when it happened I knew I couldn't let it break my morale. That was it, morale. You have to learn to take these things. Not let them get you down. If I seem callous now it's because I have had to shove that night out of my mind. You'll find out what I mean when you've been out here for a while."

Bryce nodded, and then said, "When you went to London the last time did you make any inquiries on your own to find out whether anything more had been learned about Bart?"

"No. Why should I? I believed he was killed. I still can't understand why you persist in thinking otherwise."

"Well, let's forget it for now."

"Yes. Let's talk about something pleasant. How's Dianne?"

"She's fine. Still loves her job. Gets about all over the place."

"A wonderful girl. Too bad I couldn't gain her interest, but that's how it goes."

"Dianne's never been the same since she last saw Bart Crispin. I don't think . . ."

"Saw him? When?" Ralph spilled some of his drink in his anxiety. "What are you talking about?"

"I mean . . . well, she saw him several times while he was at Farnborough before he went out as a gunner. He used to come into town on weekend leaves."

The explanation brought some relief, but the Bristol Fighter pilot sensed there was more to this conversation than Bryce was making apparent. "How many times did Bart get to London?" he asked.

"I don't know. I was too busy wangling my way out of school and into the R.F.C. It wasn't easy, you know."

"I didn't know you had any trouble."

"Remember? I was under age, and we had to tug a few vital wires. Fortunately, Father was in a position to have some influence. It's a long story, but that's why I don't know much about Bart after he started his training. I mean, about how often he saw Di."

Macintosh wrinkled his brow, took another gulp from his glass, and said, "You know, you keep talking as though Crispin had been popping in and out of London for weeks and weeks. You probably don't mean to make it sound that way, but in one breath you are arguing that he wasn't killed over there, and in the next you're talking about him as though he is still . . . alive; in circulation. To me, who saw him go down, it is, to say the least, somewhat disturbing."

Bryce stared at Macintosh. "Me? Isn't it the other way round? I say Bart was in London once or twice while he was in training at Farnborough, and from that you decide he has been bowing in and out every weekend. I know you were rather interested in Dianne, but you shouldn't allow your personal feelings to set up situations that have not occurred. It's ridiculous when you are so certain in your own mind that Bart was killed on that pickup patrol."

Macintosh finished his drink. It tasted like bitter aloes. He lighted a cigarette with cold deliberation and tried to outstare Bryce. For the first time he tasted the dread that

Bart Crispin had not died that night; that it was the scream of the agent he had heard. But more disturbing was the fear that Bryce Melville somehow knew that Crispin was still alive—somewhere. All this cross-purpose talk could be only another probe in that damned shilling business. He wondered how many others felt as Melville did.

It was obvious that Bryce Melville's name would have to appear in the *Gazette* casualty list as quickly as possible.

"How soon do you think you'll be sent out on patrols?" he asked.

Bryce shrugged his shoulders. "Who knows? If they need me, they'll send me out tomorrow."

"It's quite possible, you know," Macintosh said, and got to his feet, "that our squadrons may cooperate on any of the special shows."

"That could be very interesting."

"Well, I've had enough of this binge. I think I'll go back and turn in. It has been nice meeting and talking with you again, old boy. Toodle-oo!"

Bryce raised his glass. "Same to you, Mac."

CHAPTER NINETEEN

November 1917

Germans abandon positions along the Chemin des Dames. . . . Americans in trenches for first time, suffer 20 casualties. . . . Italians retire on wide front, abandon Tagliamento line. . . . Canadians capture Passchendaele. . . . Battle of Cambrai opens with successful tank attack. . . . British Mesopotamian forces reach point 100 miles northwest of Baghdad. . . . Russian Bolsheviki under Lenin and Trotsky seize Petrograd and depose Kerensky. . . . Italians retreat to Piave. . . . Clemenceau replaces Painlevé as Premier of France. . . . Ribecourt, Flesquières, Havrincourt, and Marcoing captured by British. . . . Italians repulse Germans on whole Piave front. . . . Cambrai menaced by British who approach within three miles. . . . British Air Force Act receives royal assent. . . . Brigadier General B. D. Foulois becomes Chief of Air Service, American Expeditionary Force.

Just as Ralph Macintosh had predicted, three nights later Numbers 86-SS and 128 Squadrons were assigned to an escort show for a formation of DH-4s of Number 18 Squadron that was to bomb an important dump behind Hoogelede. It was known that this supply point was to support an enemy attack along the Belgian Yser.

Bryce Melville was included in a six-plane Camel element that was to take off with the Bristol Fighters, stay with them as far as Staden, from there fly a diversionary patrol, and then await the return of the De Havillands and the

Bristol Fighters. Melville was allowed to go along, chiefly because he seemed to be the most ambitious pilot, practically demanding the assignment. Some thought he had been booked to give his CO an evening of comparative peace. Earlier in the day he spent a few hours firing several hundred rounds of machine-gun ammunition against the squadron's ground target.

"He'll never be more ready than he is now," Major Ian Glamis, an ancient from the Farman-Shorthorn days, muttered moodily. "It's either that, or another night of that blasted phonograph torture." So Second Lieutenant Bryce Melville was assigned to his first war patrol.

Lieutenant Ralph Macintosh found himself as acting-leader of the Bristol formation, and as such had to be fully informed of the details of the proposed raid. He made another quick trip to Aubigny, where he learned that the windmill heliograph base had been mysteriously destroyed. The village priest had no clear idea how this had happened, but he accepted Macintosh's package of cigarettes and a small wad of American newspapers and said he would do the best he could.

"You'll like those fags," Macintosh said pointedly. "They're American. I picked them up in an American YMCA recently."

The priest nodded knowingly and tucked them under his cassock.

"You haven't much time. We shall be leaving by nine o'clock," Macintosh told him, and turned back to the Crossley tender.

"We may be able to use the organ system," the priest said. "If it is not too windy."

"If it were windy, we wouldn't be going."

This mixed-bag raid was the first attempted by strategy experts of the Fourth Corps, and was arranged to give all concerned some experience in night-flying attacks carried fairly deep into enemy territory. It was hoped that the bombers would be able to find their target, move into a line-astern bombing formation, and then re-form for their return. It also meant that the Bristol Fighter escorts would have to organize and fly a very flexible patrol in order to take care of the bombers during the flight out, the in-line attack when the DH-4s would be strung out over a wide area, and then during the frantic period of re-forming.

To take care of much of this, Macintosh devised a Very light signal system by means of which he would order his eighteen Bristol Fighters to take up the required defense positions. These colored signal flares could also be used to communicate with other interested groups.

Hoogelede was about twenty miles inside the enemy lines on the road that ran northwest from Roulers to Corte-marck. Staden was a small pastoral town a short distance west of Hoogelede. All formations were to rendezvous a short distance north of Ypres.

Comparatively speaking, it was a quiet night. The cloak of darkness had been spread, but there were all the usual areas of unexpected illumination. The Lys and the Yser dragged their dull neon blues across the Belgian landscape. From the industrial areas behind Lens intermittent glares were thrown up when furnace doors were opened. Locomotives, objecting to the cheap fuel they were expected to consume, spat clots of smoke that bore eruptions of heated carbon, sparks, and scorched splinters of slate. When their firemen threw on more coal great triangles of glare fanned up into the sable night. There were dull glows of tarnished gold here and there, and at times an unexplained spatter of light lit up the edges of lacy cloud. There were long minutes when the soggy, water-soaked lowlands of Flanders gave off a luminous glow that might have been some latent chemical reaction of ancient vegetation or decayed mounds of prehistoric flora and fauna. Could the guns be turned off, one might imagine he had entered a vast anchorage of peace and tranquillity.

The Bristol Fighters were lined up in strict military

formation, as though arranged in a three-sided box for a decorations investiture. Sooty mechanics, armorers, fitters, riggers, and kiwi office personnel crisscrossed through the bluish glow created by the steely glare from the exhaust tubes. A few electric torches poked into open inspection panels, aped childish curiosity when withdrawn, and flashed off the natural finish of the interplane struts. Hunched figures moved about inside the Scarff-mounting pulpits like hooded clergy fumbling for their notes. Groups of threes scuffled with recalcitrant engines, yanked at propeller blades, twisted and turned, and then finally joined up in a three-linked unit to pull the airscrew through the energizing punch of high compression.

There was the usual formula of stenches, whiffs, and odors; wet leather, hot lubricating oil, damp serge, cough syrup, cigarette smoke, decayed teeth, and spilled petrol. Someone went through a belated gun test at the sand-bagged butt, and the dazzle of cordite and silver tracer played against the night like the beam of a runaway projector. The clatter seemed to whip the actors of this moody tableau into action, and more figures hurried into the scene from all sides, wrapping billowing scarves around their necks, buckling helmets, and adjusting chin straps. A few stood in low conversation as they drew on long gauntlets or leaned over to tighten the knee straps of their flying boots. Discarded cigarettes were flipped away, setting up scarlet arcs of hot ash, and then spattering their sparks into the frizzy, frozen turf.

"Remember, you still owe me eighteen bob!" someone cried.

"Double or nothing when we get back. Let's see how lucky you are."

"Watch him. He tucks aces in the tops of his golf socks. He'll have your eye-teeth before you go on leave."

"Listen to who's talking!"

Someone broke into a wartime ditty:

"When this bloody war is over,
Oh, how happy I shall be.
When I get my civvy clothes on,
No more soldiering for me."

Ralph Macintosh, who was gathering a handful of pilots around him, wore a brand-new Sidcot suit, a Burberry helmet, and a pair of woolen gloves that were lined in heavy silk. Under one arm he carried a neat prison-camp roll—just in case.

Major Horne strode up and down with a short swagger stick under one arm, and as he stepped out he stared down at his polished brogues, but was reliving his earlier days during the Somme blood bath when he flew DH-2s, single-seater pusher scouts. That was fun, he reflected. Today it was all buggered up with planning. In 1916 none of it had been designed to any projected doctrine, or some unwritten law of tactical operations. You just went out, day after day, took on whatever turned up, and had a hell of a good time . . . and damn the Keir Hardie pacifists. If it became too hot, you buzzed off. If the Jerries funked it, you chased them all the way back to Bohain or Busigny.

No one bothered about how many you shot down, because you really didn't know. It was a bloody good game to mix it with them, but it didn't do to take the outcome too seriously. After all, how could you know whether that blighter in the Albatros was "swinging the lead" or not? You couldn't follow him home and jot down the extent of his injuries from his medical report. Only when the buggers went down, tossing their wings away, or in flames, could you be anywhere near certain. If they cleared off, dragging a long smoke plume, what did it mean? You can make any engine smoke, if you know how. Who could tell how many tinkers had cleared off with a smoking engine to pack up and sit it out in some Jerry prison camp? Who knew, or dared make such an accusation? Look how many of the craven had disappeared, and then turned up in

Switzerland to enjoy full parole and take up skiing or bob-sledding at Cresta. They say it's very pleasant in Switzer-land—especially when you can keep drawing your pay, or if you have a devoted mater who will send you food par-cels from Selfridge's. You can pull queer tricks with a smoking engine.

He about-faced and strode toward Macintosh's group. Mac was saying, "Now I want everyone to watch my Very signals. This is most important. I intend to get every bomber to Hoogelede and bring them back again. I also want to see every Bristol here safely in its hangar when I get back. We can do it, if you'll obey my signals."

Major Horne packed his pipe and put a match to it. He didn't have much faith in Very signals, but that was the best they could do on night flying. There had been a rumor that the Royal Aircraft Factory had been experimenting with wireless sets . . . *telephone* sets that would allow the leader to convey his spoken orders direct to his pilots. Sounded a bit like Jules Verne, but who knew? Fancy talking to a bloke flying another aeroplane, yards and yards away! It was all right to do the dot-and-dash business with a telegraph key, but saying, "Form fours. Right turn. You're a trifle out of position, Number Three. Move in closer," over a wireless set was a bit too thick. Still, no telling what this bloody war would turn up next.

The nocturnal nightingale picked up his ditty:

"Roll on when we go on furlough,
Roll on when we go on pass.
We will tell the Orderly Sergeant
To stick his passes up his . . ."

Major Horne wished he could go along on this show. He'd even be satisfied with a subleader's streamer, but the nobs up at Hesdin had decided otherwise. They'd even in-sisted that Lieutenant Macintosh lead the escort show. Why, knowing Macintosh's history, he had no idea. Then there was the amazing report from young Crispin a short time ago that explained how the Jerry agents were getting Macintosh's reports through by means of a specially controlled-beam heliograph mounted in a windmill down near Aubigny. How that kid had figured that one out was a bit of a mystery, but the nobs at Hesdin were highly satisfied, and someone had gone through the battered mill and brought out an instrument that had proved his contention. Damn good work, that. Perhaps it was wise to keep Macintosh occupied in this manner. He was certainly providing plenty of leads toward picking up the Jerry agents. They'd been quietly nabbed all the way from Toronto to Paris . . . and it must be admitted he was proving to be a wide-open funnel into which went tidy amounts of misinformation. Still, Major Horne wished Macintosh could be "relieved" of this bomber-escort job.

The Bristols stood throbbing lightly on their wheels and tail skids like sprint men anxious to get off the blocks. The airmen sat awaiting Macintosh's signal to rumble away and move out for the take-off. At that point a number of Clerget rotaries hissed and clattered into power, their exhausts belching flame and sparks under the fuselages. The six-plane flight of Camels from Number 128 were being run up and checked. They would take off shortly after the two-seaters had cleared the field.

Young Melville was elated. The fact that he had drawn a night-escort show as his first front-line patrol disturbed him not at all. After all, such matters are relative. So far, he had not been on a daylight patrol so there was no particular anxiety connected with the assignment. He just hoped his damned engine would start. What was the difference—day or night?

Crusty, dour, and favoring a right leg that had been badly battered in a crash some time before, Major Glamis came up to Bryce, who stood beside his cockpit while a flight sergeant took over the starting sequence of his engine.

"Now look here, Melville," his CO began, trying his best

to be officious. "You're sure you want to go on this show . . . this night job?"

"Certainly, sir. Why not?"

"That has nothing to do with it. You're a damn good pilot —over the aerodrome, but you've had no experience of any kind. I don't like sending or letting you go, and I wish I hadn't allowed you to talk me into it."

"But, Major . . ."

"All right. Remember I'm giving you the chance to step down. You don't have to go if you have any qualms about it."

"If I did, you'd have to select someone else, and it's much too late for that, sir. Besides, I *want* to go. That's what I joined up for."

"Joined up? You young devil. Your father pulled every blasted wire of any importance at Whitehall. Joined up? You totally ignored the whole introductory training program. I've just been getting some facts about your capers. I ought to send you back home and make you start from scratch. I would, if I had any sense. Joined up, bah!"

"Please, sir . . ."

"Climb up. And report back to me the minute you land. That's an order!" Major Glamis growled, and stalked away.

"That I will, sir," Bryce said, and tapped the flight sergeant on the shoulder. "That's enough, Flight. Let me in there before Old Bull Whiskers takes another look at my logbook."

By this time the Bristol Fighters were taking off in ones and twos and climbing into an ellipse above the aerodrome. Major Glamis stood on a hangar apron, resting on a knobby buckthorn stick and watching the gradual assembly above. When the two-seaters had gathered and turned northward, he let out a bellow that could be heard above the ripsaw snarls of the Clergets.

"Move off! Get on with it!" he ordered.

The rendezvous was made on schedule over Boesinghe. The bombers, loaded with 112-pounders, took the lead up the Boesinghe–Cortemarck road with the Bristols sitting above them in three six-plane flights. The Camels trailed behind to keep watch on enemy fields in case planes were sent up to intercept. They stayed with the main formation until they reached Staden and then broke off, went down, and put on their diversionary show. Two enemy airfields were attended to with light Cooper bombs and token contributions of machine-gun fire. The little snub-nosed Sopwiths came down out of the midnight blue and made for the rows of German hangars. No great damage was done: two small hangars burst into flame, and there was a lot of smoke. Some low-flying gunnery was carried out, but most of it was put on to make a noise and attract German night-flying planes out of the Ostend or Bruges sector and keep them from the main target area.

Bryce Melville had a riotous time streaking over the tops of sheds and yanking on his bomb toggles. He had no idea what he had hit or whether his bombs had actually dropped from the rack. He skimmed in and out, banked wildly, and fired hosing bursts at anything that stood three feet or more above the ground. He was the last to leave when his flight commander began firing signal flares to re-form and clear off.

Farther east the DH-4s were forming their in-line approach while their leader sought out the dump they were supposed to destroy. It had been arranged, after consulting the meteorological information available, to cross the target at fifty-five hundred feet. All bombsights, such as they were, were set for that altitude, and the in-line attack began.

Flying about fifteen hundred feet above the bombers, the Bristols were dispersed to provide as much protection as possible. For reasons best known to himself, Ralph Macintosh took a position somewhere above the middle of the chain of bombers. As they approached the Hoogelede dump he started firing a series of green Very lights. These were supposed to order his Bristols to open their V-formations wider in order to provide a greater coverage of defense.

Three green flares sizzled up into the sky, and seconds

later the lead De Havilland slammed into a salvo of anti-aircraft fire and exploded in mid-air. The second, which was flying fairly close to the leader, banked through the smoke and glare and straddled the target with its four 112-pounder. There was a minor explosion below, but it was blotted out by another salvo of anti-aircraft fire. This time another DH-4 took the shock of the shells, tilted up on one wing, and then seemingly burst in two, its tail assembly fluttering away, end over end.

The pilots and gunners aboard the Bristols looked down on this unbelievable destruction with awe and outrage. Some felt that with such an unexpected interception there must be enemy aircraft in the vicinity. Macintosh fired three more green flares, a display that completely bewildered his aerial gunner, a Belfast boy called Marty Killane.

"An' what the 'ell is all this Guy Fawkes Day show about?" Marty asked himself, and then turned to study the sky above.

Two more DH-4s got through and one of them laid two 112-pounders smack on the dump, creating a monumental explosion that spread a blanket of gold against the sky. But while the Bristol fliers restrained their cheers, two more of the bombers went down under the gunfire from below. The rest made halfhearted attempts to get their bombs into the inferno but must have realized that anything they could do would be only an anticlimax. Finally one of the bomber pilots had the courage to take over and assume command. He fired a recall signal, took what was left of the bomber force out toward Cortemarck, and then turned toward the sanctuary of Dixmude. By that time he had only three DH bombers behind his tail. They had started out with nine.

Macintosh fired another Very signal, a red and white display, and gathered his Bristol Fighters together and assumed his original position to escort the bombers home. He glanced around to check on his own force and noted that every Fighter was present. He could hardly believe that, and he studied the three flight vees. No question about it. Only DH bombers had been lost, but of course they had been ordered to fly at fifty-five hundred feet.

It was very interesting, and very satisfactory, considering what means had been taken to get those figures and the target pinpoint across the line. This sort of thing could be carried out raid after raid with no risk of any kind . . . to the Bristols. As he turned back to check the position of the remaining bombers, his eye caught the flash of a new aeroplane. He saw its outline over his right shoulder. He elbowed Marty and cried, "What's that bus up there? Can you make it out?"

"A Sop Camel, sor."

"A Camel? One of Number 128's? We're not supposed to pick them up until we get . . ."

"Not a 128er, sor, but it's a Camel."

"Keep your eye on him, and if he turns his nose toward us, give him a warning burst. He's not supposed to be anywhere near this formation."

There was a strained silence for a half minute, then the Camel in question eased in closer. A flashlight was held over the side, its beam bringing out a distinct insignia . . . a silver shilling.

"Did you see that, sor?" Marty bellowed. "It's got an English coin painted on its side."

"A what?"

"A silver coin. Looks just like a shillin'."

Macintosh felt a cold shudder flit across his shoulders. He looked back at Killane again just to make certain he had said those words. It was that damned word again that jolted him. There was only one thing to do. He'd never have another chance like this.

"He's an intruder. Give him a good long burst! That's an order!" Macintosh said very distinctly.

"But, sor . . ." Killane hesitated just long enough. The Sop Camel tilted over on one wing and skimmed away into the darkness over Cortemarck.

Macintosh turned and glared at his aerial gunner. "Forget it. I didn't mean you to fire at him."

"I'm glad I didn't, sor."

"I said, forget it. We never even saw him."

"But the others must have done."

"Forget it!" the pilot screamed.

The Camels of Number 128 rejoined the DH-4s and Bristols as they made the turn for Dixmude. So far, since leaving the Hoogelede dump, there had been no opposition, but as they approached the line there was desultory anti-aircraft fire, a few flaming onions, and then unexpectedly a small flight of light Brandenburg W-12 seaplane fighters, probably out of Ostend. These unusual aircraft, mounted on twin floats, had performed well in coastal engagements with British naval planes, and were so satisfactory that small formations were assigned to night-flying defense in the coastal areas. Unquestionably this small force had been alerted to intercept the British bomber formation that was trying to get back to its own lines.

"My God!" Macintosh muttered, still disturbed by the appearance of a Sopwith Camel bearing a tantalizing insignia. "I hope these German navy guys have been properly informed. Otherwise we may have to put on a front of some sort."

The chunky Brandenburgs came charging into the British formation. The DH gunners took them on with broadside bursts, and the German naval pilots used their fixed guns in reply. The effect of streams of tracer-laced fire at night is most impressive. For a few minutes there was a sparkling exchange. Macintosh fired two red Very lights—and swore. His gunner practically emptied a full drum at one snag-toothed seaplane, but the German navy men continued to fight for their cause. So far, Macintosh had not given a definite order to the Bristols, but he knew that he had to make some move to keep the ledger straight.

He curled off to the right, giving the impression he was

moving out to cut off the interceptors, but before he could bring his flight into range again, a covey of Camels came down from above and poured short, snappy bursts into the German biplanes. Macintosh swore again, went charging into the melee, and then, for no apparent reason, turned away. His experienced eyes had picked up a Camel that bore the shilling insignia. It was slamming into the dispersed pack of seaplanes.

There was considerable glare from a burning Brandenburg, and he could see the distinctive Camel pilot waving to another who was flying a Number 128 Squadron Camel. For a few minutes these two Sopwiths were flown side by side, the pilots exchanging enthusiastic salutes and waves. Macintosh did not miss one feature of this revealing intercourse, but he could only swear—and ponder.

Marty Killane wondered when his pilot was going to give him a shot at those Jerry seaplanes.

Macintosh rammed his throttle forward and charged into the fray. He put his eye to his Aldis sight, drew a tight bead on the shilling insignia, and pressed the Bowden trigger. At that same instant the target Camel pilot gave a final wave, pulled into a sharp climbing turn, and Bryce Melville's Sopwith took the full burst of Macintosh's insane hatred.

"Wot'jer do that for?" Marty Killane demanded. "You biffed one of Number 128's planes!"

Macintosh turned and bellowed, "It was an accident! I didn't mean to . . ."

Within an hour after the bombers had been escorted back, and all returning planes were in their hangars, Major Horne received a telephone call. He took it over a three-way hookup that included an Intelligence official at Hesdin. The call was made from Bart Crispin's air strip near Furnes.

"I saw most of what took place," Bart explained. "For one thing, I'm pretty sure Lieutenant Melville is down safe. I followed him, and would have tried to pick him up . . ."

"You'd never do it with a Camel."

"Well, I might have been able to get him out . . . over the usual route. I mean show him how to . . ."

"Not without specific orders, you won't. We don't want that system cluttered up with people who are not expected," the man at Hesdin said with authority.

"Well, I might have flown him out but the area was badly shelled and typical of the marshy parts of Flanders. I'm pretty sure Melville pancaked in safely. His plane didn't nose over or catch fire. Beyond that, I wouldn't wish to state. If he was badly wounded he wouldn't have been able to make such a landing."

"You know they lost five bombers—right over the target," Major Horne said, and coughed.

"It was amazing. They seemed to run dead into prearranged salvos as they approached the dump. I don't know how to account for that."

"Remarkable! We shall have to put someone on a study of German anti-aircraft fire control. That, or what type of range finders they are using," the man at Hesdin said.

"It would be easy if they knew in advance at what altitude the bombers would approach the target," Bart Crispin said, as though conversing with himself.

"We've got to put Macintosh where he can't do any further harm. The gamble is becoming too one-sided," Horne broke in.

"No, not yet," Crispin pleaded. "We must accept a certain percentage of losses, but we still need him to set up our one big prize. I think it will be worth the gamble."

"But he's in a vicious, dangerous mood. He probably shot down young Melville intentionally."

"It's a question," Bart said. "He could have been firing at my plane, the one with the shilling insignia. But I must have hoiked out just in time, and Lieutenant Melville took the burst instead."

Major Horne agreed dismally.

"This shilling business will make him break, one way or another, sir."

"Oh, no question," Major Horne admitted. "Each time another arrives he goes quietly loopy. Misses meals, won't talk to anyone, and goes off by himself, wandering all over the countryside. The one that came in from Malta made him break out in a bad case of hives. I wonder who posted that one."

"I wouldn't know, sir. The shilling idea was set up in London—I think."

"Well, whoever thought of it is either a genius . . . or a devil," the man at Hesdin muttered, "but we shouldn't allow Macintosh to lead any more important escort jobs of this sort."

"We can," Bart broke in, "if we use the navy trick. Place his orders in a sealed envelope—which must not be opened until he is at five thousand feet. In that way, he'd have no chance of communicating the information in advance."

"It's still a risky business," Horne said. "Who would trust him not to open it before he left the ground?"

"You don't give it to him until he is in his cockpit and ready to take off," Bart explained.

"I think you're right, Crispin," the Hesdin voice came through. "There's one more very important bomb raid to be carried out; one that, well, it might make a lot of difference to the outcome of the war."

"I know what you mean, sir," Crispin responded.

"Well, we'll hang up, and we'd better have a more detailed talk here at Hesdin tomorrow. Shall we say in time for a good lunch?"

CHAPTER TWENTY

December 1917

*German East Africa completely conquered. . . . Al-
lies' Supreme War Council holds first meeting at Ver-
sailles. . . . Russian Bolsheviki arrange armistice with
Germans. . . . British relinquish many gains in Cambrai area. . . . American destroyer* Jacob Jones *sunk
by enemy submarine. . . . Steamer* Mont Blanc *loaded
with munitions explodes in Halifax harbor; 1500
persons killed. . . . United States declares war on
Austria-Hungary. . . . General Allenby captures Jeru-
salem. . . . Conscription confirmed in Canada. . . .
Russia and Germany sign armistice at Brest-Litovsk.*

Early in December, about five weeks after his being reported missing in action, Dianne Melville received a POW
letter from her brother Bryce. It was written and posted
from the Holzminden camp, the infamous German laager
to which many British airmen were confined after capture.
She was puzzled that he should write first to her rather than
their father or mother, but on second reading of the letter
she thought he had a definite reason. It read:

Dear Di,
    First of all I am quite all right. No damage to speak
of. The Red Cross food packages are so well packed
we often have to make holes to get (the stuff) out. We
are treated fairly well but have an idea we may get
pushed around at any time. There's a lot I would like
to tell you but I can't write it here. The Germans are

too smart to let us get away with anything like that. I can say that the toffee maker was responsible for my going down. A German officer who was nearby when I was taken told me his battery had full details of the raid and particularly the exact height at which the bombers would approach the supply dump. Aren't they clever? Give my love to Eva James. She will need a lot of attention. Am certain the *Gazette* has Crispy all wrong.

Your loving brother,
Brugo.

Dianne was intrigued with the cryptic wording, especially his signing himself "Brugo." He had never used that name before, and who "Eva James" was, she had no idea. But "Crispy" obviously referred to Bart Crispin. Had Bryce found out something that had not been officially announced in London? The "toffee maker" referred, of course, to Ralph Macintosh.

To satisfy herself she showed Bryce's letter to the first British Intelligence officer she met at the R.F.C. depot. She had been assigned to drive him to the International Red Cross office near Birdcage Walk.

The officer glanced over it quickly and smiled.

"Your brother has picked up the prisoner-of-war lingo very quickly," he said. "I like the way he flatters the Germans. That's always a good trick to get a key sentence past them. They love to be told how clever they are."

"My brother is a bit of a devil. He'll drive them crazy."

"That may be, but his letter contains some interesting points, some of which we know, and some we are glad to know about."

"Can you tell me about it?"

"Don't see why not. You're a uniformed member of the service and, as such, are responsible for service security. That means you don't share it with outsiders. Understand?"

Dianne nodded as she wove her Crossley skillfully through the Regent Street traffic.

"First off, the reference to holes in Red Cross packages indicates he has joined a tunneling team and is trying to dig his way out. That's good!"

"That's typical of Bryce."

"Next, the reference 'we may get pushed around' indicates he has heard something of a new German push. That confirms something we already know. This toffee maker . . . ?"

"Oh, he means Ralph Macintosh. You know, Macintosh's toffee."

"Of course! Well, we know plenty about that bloke, but giving the Jerry gunners the exact altitude of the approaching bombers explains the deadly accuracy encountered over Hoogelede. We chalk that one up to Macintosh," the Intelligence man said, and sucked the end of a pencil. "Now what about Eva James? Is there such a person of his acquaintance?"

"Not that I know of."

The Intelligence officer pondered, staring straight through the windshield. "Eva James . . . Ev James . . . Everja . . ." He let out a low chuckle. "Of course! He refers to Everghem! That's a key point on the Bruges Canal. He must mean something important is taking place there. Everghem. I must jot that down."

"I wondered who Eva James was," Dianne said, dodging around a brewery truck.

"Now who is Crispy?"

"That must be a nickname for Bart Crispin. You probably know about Bartley Crispin. He was an aerial gunner and was . . . well, lost on the other side of the line."

"Bartley Crispin . . . an aerial gunner? No, can't say I've ever heard the name," the Intelligence man said, and studied his reflection in the windscreen.

"Oh," said Dianne. "I had hoped . . ."

"Of course, there may be such a person, but your brother hasn't made the point very clear, has he?"

"No, I suppose not. Then there's the business of signing himself 'Brugo' instead of Bryce. That puzzles me too."

"Brugo . . . Brugo. He could be referring to Bruges." The man stared at his driver as if he expected her to come up with a complete solution. "Bruges . . . that could be the key point . . . the supply base—I mean for any future push. In other words, if we tie all these hints together we might decide that Jerry plans a big push. He has something relating to it at Everghem, but the main point of attack can stem from Bruges. Any in-force move out of Bruges would, of course, threaten the Channel ports. From this we should plan a counterattack that would put the stopper on the proposed German offensive. That's what I get from your brother's letter."

"You have nothing for me on Bartley Crispin?"

"I never heard of him, Miss Melville."

"Lieutenant Melville, sir," Dianne corrected.

"Of course! I remember now. You're to be the first driver to go out to France. You're to be Wing Commander Southgate's special chauffeur. Congratulations!"

Dianne winked knowingly.

"You don't mind if I keep this letter? It may turn out to be very handy. I'm glad you inquired about it."

"We're always ready to please," Lieutenant Melville responded, pulling smartly up to the curb.

As the wintry days passed, air operations continued when weather permitted. There was considerable fog in the early hours of daylight, but it usually dissipated before noon when patrols were hurriedly sent into the air. Unfortunately the same condition returned by early afternoon, and most of the airmen were fortunate to get down safely anywhere inside their own lines and await clement conditions before returning to their own aerodromes. All this cut down on the all-around service efficiency and considerably reduced flying time.

Bart Crispin continued his security forays, acting as a

winged sentinel over the formations of De Havilland bombers during their daylight attempts on targets in the back areas. He joined the coveys of escort scouts and tracked the Bristol Fighters that maintained their pressure against flights of Fokkers and Albatri. Equally important, he watched for any willful digressions from patrol duty during heated air action. His special Camel was noted on several fronts, but it seemed always to be in the air when the Bristol Fighters of Number 86-SS Squadron were on patrol. Ralph Macintosh, in particular, noticed this ominous biplane whenever he was leading his flight into action. He usually spotted this distinctive Camel sitting above his formation when enemy planes appeared on the horizon.

He fumed silently while trying to determine who was flying the gadfly machine and why the pilot seemed to be so interested in his Bristol Fighters. He made several attempts to edge in closer to the single-seater but the Camel was too tricky to be caught by such a maneuver. What bewildered him most about these contacts was that no one in his flight would admit to having seen a Sopwith bearing a silver coin insignia.

"But the damn thing was sitting above us all the way from Roubaix to the line at Armentières!" Macintosh bellowed one day as they were scribbling out their patrol reports. "You mean to stand there and tell me that none of you saw it? The swine was up there—practically all the time." All his tirade aroused was a half circle of blank, incredulous faces. Major Horne had explained previously that this was all a game—a little joke he was playing on Lieutenant Macintosh.

But as the weather cut down flying time, Bart Crispin became edgy and anxious to get on with his job. After a short discussion at Hesdin, it was agreed he might follow Bryce Melville's suggestion and try an intrusion into the Everghem area to find out what could be of such a threatening nature.

"I could go over for four or five days," Bart explained. "It wouldn't take me long to learn what they have there, and if I could get the sort of delayed-action explosives they showed me at Cranwell I might be able to give them a bad time."

"Well," the man at Hesdin reflected, thumbing the bowl of his pipe, "anything we can do to hinder their planned push will be well worth the risk. If you're willing to chance it, I don't see why we can't oblige you."

"Then," Bart continued, "if we find out something definite, we can use our Macintosh foil for one last decoy or, better still, completely confuse the enemy regarding our plans."

There was some pursing of lips, some wrinkling of brows, and some deep breaths, but it was agreed finally that Lieutenant Crispin should make his second visit into enemy territory.

"By the way, do you speak any German?"

Bart suppressed a grin. "Fortunately, I took that language during my first three years in college. I had an idea that one day I might go to Heidelberg to finish my architectural course, but I went to Oxford instead. I remember some of it."

"Let's try you out." The man at Hesdin took a test card from his desk drawer. "See if you can read a couple paragraphs of that."

Bart took the card and began laboriously to read aloud. It was from an essay in German by Heinrich Heine. After a few sentences he showed he could pronounce words fairly well. He also translated well enough to make his questioner reach over and take the card from him.

"That'll do. You're not exactly fluent, but we can set you up as a Swiss national trying to speak German. We'll have a passport, an area identity card, and some suitable letters and documents made up for you. I think we can even provide a suit of clothes."

"Could you put me in touch with that barge captain—Vandervelde? He might be a big help."

"We will if there is time, but don't rely on it. It just occurs to me that this trip can be worth while. We'll have you deliver the plans for our next big offensive."

Bart looked puzzled.

"I mean a set of plans and details of a British push that is supposed to break through from Arras to Douai. Now just suppose such information was picked up in an authentic envelope. What do you think the Germans would do about it?"

"Probably move twenty or thirty divisions into that area to stop it."

"Exactly!"

"But . . ."

"We haven't the slightest notion of starting a push toward Douai." The Hesdin man reached for the telephone.

It was a questionable night for agent-dropping. The day had been beset by fog, and there was no air movement to disperse the pus-yellow vapor until late in the afternoon. It still hung in the low sectors and blotted out the marshes and waterlogged fens and flat acres of Flanders. However, Major Horne took off from Serny and found his way to the strip outside Furnes where he was greeted by Harry Husbands, who looked longingly at the unoccupied gunner's cockpit.

"Lieutenant Crispin on hand?" the major inquired.

"I couldn't say, sir."

"What do you mean, you couldn't say? Don't you know whether he is or isn't?"

"Well, sir, it's like this. When Lieutenant Crispin is in uniform we *can* say . . . but when he ain't we just don't know what to say."

Major Horne let out a guffaw. "Got it in a nutshell! You mean you have a funny-looking bloke hanging about waiting for a bus. Is that it?"

"Yes, sir."

Before the pointless conversation could proceed further a man in civilian clothing came out of the hangar. His ensemble was topped by a felt hat, at least one size too small, that sat on his head somewhat precariously. A high, starched collar was held together by a stringy necktie of atrocious colors. His coat was a dreadful imitation of a Scottish tweed, with two of the buttons missing. His trousers may have been well-pressed flannel at one time, but in the deceptive light looked more like a garment that had been discarded by an itinerant bricklayer. His shoes, when new, had been bright yellow and box-toed. Now they were well scuffed, oil-streaked, laced with commercial cord, and needed new heels. He carried an ancient attaché case in one hand, and a weather-stained raincoat was draped over one arm.

"You're not overdoing it, are you, Crispin?" Major Horne smothered a grin with his gloved hand.

"I don't expect to occupy a box at Albert Hall," Crispin countered, trying not to look at Husbands.

"You have that—that envelope?"

"Everything. A few sample watch movements, and an item that looks like something out of Jules Verne. I was told not to drop it."

Major Horne took another long look at Crispin as he pulled on the raincoat. "You know," he concluded, "at last I know what they mean by the horrors of war. I don't know whether you are coming back, but this is how I shall always remember you. An officer . . . and a silly-looking gentleman. Climb aboard, Mr. Crispin."

Harry Husbands edged up to the cockpit. "You wouldn't want me to go along, an' come back as your gunner, would you, sir?"

Major Horne gave him a rewarding smile. "It's a bloody nice idea, but it just can't be managed tonight. But I'll remember that. What's your name?"

"'Arry 'Usbands, sir."

The major winked, waited until Husbands had moved to grab the outer strut, and then eased the throttle up the quadrant. The Bristol Fighter roared off into the dank, fog-streaked night.

"Bloody rough game, that," reflected Harry Husbands. "Still, it would be all right, goin' as a gunner."

Horne steered a westerly course until he had crossed the line, and then sought the confluence of the Bruges and Ostend canals. There was a large triangular area due south of it, and he circled twice to identify clearly his planned touchdown. He turned to Crispin, who had tied a long scarf over his hat to afford some protection for his face. "Well, how do you feel? Quite ready?"

"Everything is in order, sir."

"Good! Here we go then."

"You'll pick me up at the Thourout strip on Friday night?"

"Right! Alternate red and white flashes."

"Red and white. Right."

The big Bristol lowered her voice and her nose, and started down toward the dull gray panorama below. Crispin tried to blot out the memory of his previous night landing, but the details kept sweeping through his mind. There was the same sigh through the wings and wires, the same warning whistle of the propeller. He ran his hands over his pockets to make sure he had brought everything necessary. There was a flat automatic, the round electric torch, the wad of decoy plans with their bright red sealing wax. There was a shapeless wallet stuffed with a mixture of bank notes, another containing his passport and identification papers. In addition, he carried a wad of letters, all bearing Swiss addresses, which proved he was Gustav von Moos, dealer in Swiss watch movements with an office in Geneva. He also had a British half crown that had a deep "V" filed into its milled edge.

The Bristol sucked in her breath, leveled off, and dropped down as light as the proverbial feather. It was a beautiful landing but there was no time to offer a compliment.

"Good night, sir," Bart said, and vaulted over the side before the aircraft had come to a halt. Seeing his passenger

283

leave in that slick manner, Horne rammed the throttle up; the Bristol raised her tail and roared into an immediate take-off.

The instant he landed on his feet, Bart flattened out and remained prone until the plane had flown well beyond his hearing. He waited several minutes to make certain no one had planned for his arrival or had decided to find out why that aeroplane had touched down in that manner. Ghostly wisps of fog drifted across the field. Gradually, he rose to his feet and moved toward a boundary hedge. A few raucous birds raised a chorus of warning, and he flattened again. When no one responded to the alarm in the hedgerow he moved on until he came to the thicket. He peered through and sensed there was a well-paved road on the other side. He parted the shrubbery and forced a path through with his elbows, and then encountered a single strand of barbed wire that caught him about knee high. He snarled quietly, stepped over, clambered down a low bank, and had just regained his balance when he heard a grunt. He felt for his automatic, but was grabbed immediately from behind by two great arms. He caught the odor of stale beer and vinegar. There were some indistinguishable German words and another grunt. Whoever his captor was, he was evidently drunk.

Crispin hastily remembered one important axiom taught him in his brief Intelligence course. "All German soldiers are slaves to higher authority. Try to plan your moves on that stifling inhibition."

"*Achtung!*" Bart bellowed. The command had much the same effect as the legendary "Open Sesame!" The man, whoever he was, released his captive, stepped back, and tried to pull himself to attention.

Playing his role to the limit, Crispin stiffened, and held his head proudly erect. The indistinct figure before him stood rubbing the back of his hand under his nose. In a flash, Bart uppercut the man with his heavy attaché case. There was a thud, a strangled gasp, and the figure toppled

284

backward. Bart stared around, expecting opposition from other quarters, but the night was still. His opponent remained spread-eagled and made no further effort to get to his feet. Tugging his hat down hard, Crispin moved off silently, gradually increasing his speed as he hurried toward Stalhille, which he knew was only four miles away.

After a breakfast of ersatz coffee, crusty rolls, and a bowl of bluish oatmeal at a small pension in Stalhille, Bart moved boldly on, inquired for the nearest German military headquarters, and was directed to Hauptmann Hans Knoke, the local town major. Explaining that he had been in England trying to interest British artillery officials in a number of new nose-cap mechanisms, but had been brusquely ignored, he had returned to Bruges and had been misdirected as to the location of a German artillery depot that he believed was in this area.

The town major was unimpressed. Civilians were a damned nuisance, particularly at this time of day.

Bart showed some of his papers, his passport, and finally some of his watch movements. "The British are not interested in Swiss products, but then they weren't interested in Herr Fokker's aeroplanes, were they?"

With that reference the German officer took a new view. "Of course. Of course. Please forgive my seeming indifference. I am seldom called upon for anything more important than a quarrel between drunken soldiers and ungrateful shopkeepers."

"But your job is important," Bart insisted.

The town major managed a smile at Bart's difficulty with the German language. He looked down at the spread of letters. "Ah, yes. You are Swiss. I know how difficult it is for you who must adapt to both the German and French languages. Then, before the war, you were expected to take up English . . . for the tourists. It must be very difficult."

"Very," Bart agreed, and then presented Hauptmann Knoke with a simple watch movement. "Any good watchmaker will mount it in a suitable case, for a small sum."

The Hauptmann was delighted. "Now what you want," he explained, "is the artillery repair depot at Eecloo. That is about twenty-five kilometers east of Bruges. See . . . here on the map."

"Do you know the name of the officer in charge?"

"That is easy. Let me show you the Army Depot Directory. It will be in there."

In a few minutes Bart had obtained the name of Colonel Erik von Teuchtmann, commanding officer of the Eecloo depot. Eecloo, it turned out, was a town of more than ten thousand inhabitants where the Bruges–Zelzate–Lokeren line diverges to the right. It was all there clearly on Hauptmann Knoke's wall map.

"There is no convenience, such as an omnibus, running in that direction, I suppose?" Crispin said while still devouring details on the map.

"No, but I could get you into Bruges. We have a motor truck going that way in about an hour. I could give you a permit to ride with the driver. After all, you are on military business, eh?"

"I hope so. I would like to show our improved nose caps. I'm sure Colonel von Teuchtmann will be interested."

"You must be assisted, by all means," Knoke decided.

"By all means," Bart repeated, still studying the details of the East Flanders canal system. He made certain, too, that he could easily make his way to Everghem, Bryce Melville's particular point of interest.

Just before noon he was dropped off near the Waterloo Hotel on Rue Louise in Bruges, and he obtained a room there. He took a short rest to orient his mind, and then brushed up and made himself more presentable after his dreary night on the road. After another glance through his cryptic notes he went downstairs to the lobby.

The doorman became obsequious at his approach.

"Could you lend me a Michelin Guide?" Bart asked him in a matter-of-fact manner.

The doorman looked around the lobby as though he expected to be arrested. He studied Bart for half a minute. "You are unfamiliar here," he said in a whisper.

"I am Swiss, and yes, I am new to Bruges," Bart explained in his halting German, "but I have an appointment with Colonel von Teuchtmann of the artillery repair depot at Eecloo. I am not sure where Eecloo lies."

The doorman looked relieved. "In that case"—his manner became friendly—"I can lend you mine, but take it up to your room. Don't be seen studying it down here. The Boche ask too many questions."

"You have many Germans here in the hotel?"

"A few. Not the front-line kind. The ones who ask a lot of questions. They interrogate people. Make a lot of trouble for everyone. They'd put you through it if they saw you with a Michelin Guide, my friend. That, and the way you speak."

Crispin could scarcely believe his ears. Obviously here, of all places, the Waterloo Hotel, he had stumbled on a German Intelligence bureau. But he reasoned to himself there probably were such bureaus in most hotels in Bruges and Ostend. Why not?

"These Germans, the ones who make the trouble. Where are they located? What rooms? I mean . . . I'm in 307. I'm not anywhere near them, am I?"

"You're 307? Oh no. They're in 204, a floor below you. You may be on legitimate business but you'd be wise to avoid any contact with them. They ask too many questions."

"A very good idea," Bart said, and tucked the Guide under his arm and headed for the stairway. Upstairs he pored over it for a half hour or so, tracing out the details of the area, and then tossed it on his bed. He took out the sealing-waxed envelope, left his room and walked down one flight of stairs, and in a few minutes was knocking on the door of Room 204. While he waited he selected the half crown from a collection of coins in his pocket.

The door was opened and a young Oberfeldwebel stood

ramrod stiff with his heels together. He raised his eyebrows in inquiry.

Bart flipped the British coin carelessly, and allowed it to fall flat in his palm. It was a commonplace gesture, but the NCO raised his eyebrows even higher with the air of a man expecting an offensive odor. He glanced down at the coin and his face took on an expression of surprise, but he recovered quickly, stood to one side, and bowed Bart in.

The door closed with military precision, and the visitor was guided around a large folding screen behind which a slim-shouldered man in mufti and a black eye-patch sat at a military field desk in a pose of vitriolic contempt. He had pitted, muscular cheeks, a narrow frontal bone, a long thin nose with extended nostrils, and straight blue lips. His salt-and-pepper hair was cropped in true Prussian style. It was the first time Bart had seen one of these Hun caricatures.

"*Ja?*" the figure barked.

The Oberfeldwebel leaned over and whispered magical words of explanation.

"*Gut!*" the man with the eye-patch said. He stood up, snapped to attention, and held out his hand. Bart dropped the half crown into his palm.

"*Guten Tag. . . . Na, wie schaut's?*"

A chair was slid behind the visitor, and he sat down. "Can you get this to the proper authorities, quickly?" He tossed the sealed envelope onto the desk.

The slim-shouldered man weighed the package in his crooked fingers, read and reread the cryptic writing under the "Wilton Road, London," address. He looked like a man enjoying a magic spell.

"You bring this . . . from London? You have been in England?"

"I crossed over from Hartlepool on a Dutch freighter. We docked at Ostend."

"But how did you get it—come in possession?"

"A man named Mackensen."

The Cyclopean eye focused intently. "But Mackensen is in France . . . Royal Flying Corps."

Bart assumed an attitude of a man who was utterly bored. "British airmen go on leave too, you know. I must advise you this material is direct from Haig's headquarters."

"I still don't understand . . ."

"There is much I don't understand. I'm not in this business. I'm a Swiss. I have been in England trying to sell a new type of artillery nose cap. They were not interested, so I decided to offer our product to Germany. I am now on my way to talk to Colonel von Teuchtmann at Eecloo. I agreed to deliver this package to the first German Intelligence bureau . . . for the opportunity to see Colonel von Teuchtmann. That is how we have to do business."

This more than satisfied the man in the eye-patch. He called in the Oberfeldwebel, handed the package to him, and ordered him to take it immediately to Bureau A-6 in Brussels. He pointed at Crispin. "You must have lunch with me. We must have a long talk."

"*Ja*," Crispin replied noncommittally.

While he waited for the man in mufti to complete his instructions to the NCO, Bart vividly realized that so far this in no way resembled the classics of espionage or intrigue as penned by Edgar Allan Poe, Wilkie Collins, and more recently John Buchan and E. Phillips Oppenheim. In those tales everything was preordained and artfully plotted; the stories written so as to draw the reader on page after page, denying him the solution until the close of the book. In real life in an actual war, the intrigue and situations afforded no time to lay down a set of greased guides to confuse an operator. Real life was not that complex or involved, but the situations were real, the dangers were real, the guns and bullets were real. Nothing was imagined or contrived.

So far there had been no decoding of ciphers, no secret inks, none of the tricks or standard routines of the spy trade. This had been a cold, businesslike affair in which all the factors were known. One simply used his wits to over-come the obstacles. It was as routine as that. One needed only a jog or two of unbelievable luck to win—or go down under a torrent of gunfire.

The lunch was highly rewarding. Once Bart had presented his watch-movement gambit, told of some highly fictitious conditions in England, and had commented on the utter idiocy of British artillery experts, he allowed his host to take over the conversation. In his anxiety to make this Swiss clearly understand, the man in the eye-patch completely unraveled his mind, leaving the loose skein to be studied at leisure. Thus the lunch was doubly rewarding.

Bart returned to his room and the Michelin Guide to plan the rest of his operation. For one thing he discovered that Everghem was seemingly located on a private railway that ran between Bruges and Ghent over an area that had once been a marshy wasteland. To get there he would have to get a train out of the Station Centrale on the western side of the town. This would take him through Eecloo, Waerschoot, Sleydinge, and into Everghem. Studying the map, and re-membering much he had been told by the man in mufti, Bart could see why Everghem had been selected for his attention. It was situated directly on the junction of several barge canals that fed the whole of the East Flanders com-plex of waterways.

It was a wobbly-wheeled car with a folding top that had seen its best days. The hood had been scorched at one time, and no longer fitted where the fasteners were supposed to be. Still, the engine hummed contentedly as it was turned into the road that led down to the Everghem barge wharves. The man at the wheel wore a hat at least one size too small that sat on his head dead center. He held the wheel gingerly, sitting painfully upright and peering ahead, seem-ingly ignoring the great piles of supplies that were covered with greenish tarpaulins. Then, without changing his pose, he caught the flutter of a smallish red flag that was nailed to a length of scantling. He eased up to the curb and carefully slipped out from behind the wheel.

He walked to the inner, rear wheel, kicked the tire angrily, and stood wiping a fingertip across his lip. Then, in the manner of a man who has come to an unpleasant decision, he reached inside the rear of the tonneau and brought out a spiral jack and a small socket wrench. Within minutes he had lifted the wheel clear, had taken off the valve cap and, with its slotted tip, pressed down the stem of the valve. The hissing soon stopped, and he worked to remove the nuts that held the demountable rim to the wheel.

A German soldier sauntered up, his Mauser rifle slung from his shoulder in the manner of a veteran Feldwebel sentry.

"Hello!"

"*Guten Tag.*"

"You have trouble?"

"It's nothing. Just a punctured tire."

"You have a vulcanizing set?"

"No. I do not think so. It is a car I borrowed from the Intelligence officer in Ghent. I am on my way to see the commander of the Eecloo artillery repair base."

The sentry raised his eyebrows. "You know such people, eh?"

"In a business way."

"Well, I'm afraid you will have to walk back a kilometer or so to find a motor garage, maybe two kilometers."

The man in the stained raincoat shrugged his shoulders. "One has to face up to such situations these days."

"Ah, well. Good luck."

The German sentry plodded away, leaving the motorist to remove the rest of the lugs from the wheel.

The rim and tire came free after a struggle. The man put the wrench back into the tonneau and took out an ancient leather attaché case. When the sentry had passed out of sight in a curve of the road, he stood the tire against the body of the car, hurried between two great piles of supplies, each wearing a red flag, and disappeared for a minute or so. In that time he removed a heavy tubular instrument from his case, twisted a figured dial at one end, and secreted the instrument under the folds of a tarpaulin. When he returned to the motorcar he was fumbling with the buttons of his fly.

He then tucked the attaché case under his raincoat, hauled the tire from its leaning position, and began to roll it down the road. The German soldier was standing at ease near a sentry box a few hundred yards away. He gave the civilian a friendly salute, smiled, and said, "I'll keep an eye on your motorcar until you get back."

"Thanks," the man in the stained raincoat replied, continuing to roll the tire ahead of him.

CHAPTER TWENTY-ONE

At British Headquarters in Bailleul less than a dozen men in various uniforms sat around a refectory table that had been removed from a nearby abbey. At the head was a massive man who thundered and grumbled through a bristling black mustache. His piercing dark eyes were eaved by eyebrows to match, and his complexion was tanned from years of campaigning in Africa and India. Beside him sat a smaller edition who wore the same pugnacious mien but glared from a more luxuriant facial foliage. There also were two officers of field rank from Hesdin, two colonels from the R.F.C. Wing at St. Omer, a Bristol Fighter squadron commander, and a smallish man who wore civilian clothes and seemed completely out of place. However, he was often consulted, and he made more final decisions than the large man at the head of the table.

An infantry officer whose sleeve insignia had been worn away months before was saying, "It's the only way at this time. From any point between Verdun and the Swiss frontier the ground is unsuitable for a grand offensive. If Ludendorff is coming through, he has about three hundred miles of front from which to select his battleground. Two areas of possibility are the British lines in Flanders or the old French charnel at Verdun. Haig's Passchendaele show has taken the bulk of our forces and left them in the narrow space between Ypres and the coast. If the Hun comes through the vital railway junction of Hazebrouck with his left flank on the La Bassée Canal, Haig will be taken in flank and rear with no room to maneuver. It is a very serious situation, gentlemen."

"We can't rely on the French. They're still staggering from Neville's debacle."

"If Ludendorff has any luck with this move based from Bruges, and takes the three Channel ports, both the British and Belgian armies will be bottled up."

"No question about it. We'll have to withdraw to a line running north from Paris to somewhere in the vicinity of Boulogne, but possibly down to the mouth of the Somme."

"If I can get night-flying defense for my bombers . . ." the large man at the head of the table began.

"I can see where we'll have Abbeville smack on the front line. All British troops and supplies would have to be brought into the field through the port of Le Havre—possibly Cherbourg or Brest."

"In fact, any success against the Channel ports will give the enemy an excellent chance to try an actual invasion of Britain," someone said. The prospect restrained conversation for nearly a minute.

"If I can attack the Bruges target from fields in Britain," the man at the head of the table said, "and if I can get some night-flying defense . . ."

"You'd send your bombers in from Britain? Why?"

"Because they bloody well won't expect me to. If we cross from aerodromes in Kent or Essex we'd be over this place, Blankenberghe, in no time, and all my pilots would have to do would be to follow the rails from Blankenberghe to Bruges. It would be like having a course laid out with silver ribbons for a guide. After that, we can return to the British lines somewhere above Dixmude. There is plenty of space there to accommodate them for a few hours."

The exchange of nods, winks, and expressions of elation indicated full consent, but the little man in civilian clothes was first consulted.

"What do you think, Cosgrove?"

"That supply base must be destroyed," he said, and hunched his shoulders. He lighted a cigarette. "There is everything there to supply a major attack. Dunkirk, Calais, and possibly Boulogne would be gobbled up before you could say 'Bob's your uncle.' If they ever get moving, I don't know what any of you have that will stop them. There already are dozens of Class A divisions coming in from the Eastern Front, and Ludendorff will have enough manpower and inertia to make a second thrust toward Paris. After that, we're all down the pan."

"If I can move my bombers in from the coast, instead of having to rendezvous over Dixmude, I'll blow the bloody lot all the way back to Antwerp," the big man grumbled again. The man beside him agreed.

Major Horne, who had been packing his pipe and ramming a cleaner up and down the stem, rose to his feet.

"Well, Horne, what do you think?"

"As you know, we have started one move. We have a man over there who hopes to take care of the situation at Everghem."

"Any news of him?"

The man in the civilian suit said, "He's in there. He has the wherewithal to take care of the situation. If you time your raid properly . . . two nights from now, we'll have a rather valuable blowup to start the innings."

"You have a man in Everghem?" the giant at the head of the table asked in some disbelief.

"Yes, sir. I took him over myself," Major Horne explained. "We made a good touch-down, and I presume he got into the clear."

"He did," the civilian said without looking up. "He's at Everghem now, just waiting to plant his box of tricks."

The man at the head of the table looked bewildered. Familiarity with matters of this stripe was beyond his ken. He was learning that his military bellow in no way compared to the whisper of a man who knew his way around.

Major Horne continued, "We can provide a fairish amount of night-flying defense, sir, but not enough to hold off the full complement Jerry—er, the Germans can put up if they know where the bombers will be. That's our main problem."

"I can send them off from England to go in from the sea," the bomber man said, and frowned.

"We will stage a diversionary raid at Watteren, which, as you know, is well south of Ghent. That, we hope, will draw the enemy air defense well out of the Bruges area. If you can come in from the sea, our defense job will be made less problematical."

"You mean if I send the bombers in from the sea instead of from the land you will be able to get them to the target. After that, the aerial gunners will have to get them back," the big man said hopefully.

"If we can split the night-flying defense, that will be something," Horne reflected. "Our night-flying Camels ought to put up a bloody good show."

The big man nodded thoughtfully.

The civilian stared at his cigarette butt. "If we could feed the Hun the story that we shall go in from Dixmude," he said, as though talking to himself, and then shrugged out of that, adding, "No, too many tricks can become quite involved. We've already given him the problem of stopping a British push in front of Arras where one hasn't been thought of. I rather liked that idea, what?"

Once more the big man looked bewildered, but his handlebarred partner explained from behind a cupped hand.

"Well, then," Major Horne concluded, "may we agree that the attack on Bruges will come in from the sea; that Number 86-SS Squadron will plan the night defense, and that . . . that is all. I presume the typed orders will be available in the morning."

"I'll send my bombers in from the sea," the big man agreed, and got to his feet.

The following night Major Horne made plans for picking

up Bart Crispin from the Thourout strip. He had every reason to believe Bart would show up, for the hunched civilian, Cosgrove, had told him that Crispin was moving about with rare speed and precision. How he knew all this he did not explain, and Horne refrained from asking. By now he had learned that every man has his forte and it was a waste of time to wheedle it out of him. He would have resented anyone picking his mind on how to make a successful pickup on the other side of the line.

Macintosh was on hand to see him off. He had been haunting Horne for the past few hours, particularly after he had motored down to Bailleul for a conference. What that was all about he had no conception, but Horne had put him off with some claptrap about the squadron being equipped with a new type of Bristol Fighter—an all-metal job that would be more suited to low-level trench strafing. Macintosh bought that, and made up a pretentious message for transmission across the lines. His outlet was now carried from a church tower that stood between Ypres and Boesinghe, and in turn linked with another at Moorslede. Again, they relied on a controlled-beam heliograph that could only be seen within a certain angle and range. The two towers were positioned perfectly for this type of signal.

Horne took off into a clear, starry night, relieved to be off the ground away from the jangle of planning, consultation, decisions, and responsibility. He wondered how Crispin had fared, and pondered on the many pitfalls one would have to avoid. There were spaces in his reflections when he wished he could have gone to Bruges too. He remembered the ancient city with faint nostalgia, for he had made his first trip to the Continent some years before and had stayed at the old Hotel de Flandre on the Rue Nord du Sablon. After he finished at Cambridge, his father had given him a holiday. He remembered the old Gothic railway station, the Cathedral of St. Sauveur, the museum that contained the picture gallery of the Academy. Then there were those delightful summer evenings along the Grand Place. He hoped this bloody dump at Bruges was well outside the city. It didn't seem to be on Cosgrove's little map. Damned shame if any of those pictures were destroyed.

He cruised about beyond Hoogelede to put off the defense. He made a move toward Thielt, and then, after checking with his watch, made an abrupt turn to the northwest and headed for the patchy panorama of Thourout. Memory from a Baedeker handbook returned as he circled the old town that had grown up around a grove that once had been consecrated to the worship of the Germanic god Thor. Today the area contained a seminary for teachers and a handsome church. Carrying out his seemingly aimless devices, he banked over hard, cut his engine, and went into a glide. Toward Bruges a display of searchlights stacked a series of beams to support the sky. A narrow triangular field lay below. He raced along its broad base and saw alternate red and white flashes triggered from a hedge. He moved away, took his position, and glided down for a landing. The whistle of his propeller seemed to add a background of ghostly hissing to the unreal, nocturnal scene.

He touched down with only a moderate bump, and by the time his run was beginning to slow a figure appeared below a wing tip, reached up and grabbed the base of an interplane strut, and dug in its heels. The Bristol Fighter spun on the turf for the take-off.

"Well, good evening, Herr von Moos. How's the clock-mending business?" Major Horne quipped, raising an imaginary fedora.

"Rather well, for a beginner," Crispin explained, and vaulted into the rear cockpit.

"Have any real luck?"

"What time is it?"

"Exactly eleven forty-five, as arranged. Why?"

"Get away, and circle a bit to the east. I would like a confirmation."

The Bristol sped away, bumping over the uneven sward.

Horne hoiked her over a low hedge, leveled off, and then made a wild climbing turn. Crispin spent the next few minutes binding his scarf over his hat and ears, and buttoning up his raincoat.

"Now watch well toward the area just north of Ghent," he said into Horne's ear flap. "We'll see how that timed device works."

"What time was . . . ?"

There was a low roar, a thunderous flash of scarlet and yellow flame, and a monstrous volcanic belch went skyward. It had erupted just north of Ghent.

"I'll be damned!" Horne gasped.

"It worked!"

"You actually planted it?"

"Right! You set the dial, and the darn thing goes off on schedule."

"You actually got there and planted it?" Horne asked again. "I know that's what you went over to do, but damn it all, how did you do it?"

"It's a long story, Major. It'll keep."

Major Horne turned west and headed for the strip at Furnes.

The following night the winged forces assembled to save the Channel ports. Four squadrons of DHs were loaded with 500-pounders and assembled at as many aerodromes in Kent and Essex. Three squadrons of night-flying Camels— all that were available and capable of intercepting enemy fighters—were dispersed over R.F.C. and R.N.A.S. fields between Dunkirk and Dixmude. Number 86-SS Squadron moved up to Cassel where Major Horne and the Air Staff from Hesdin could handle the ground command. All squadron commanders were advised of the general plan, but none knew the key move—that the bombers were to attack from the sea. They were to be in the air in the Bruges area simply to hold off any German night hawks that might move in to intercept the bombers.

Again, Ralph Macintosh was selected to lead the Bristol Fighters on the premise that he had one such experience, and it was hoped he would use that position in his formation to make use of his Very signals.

A short time before take-off Major Horne briefed him. "Now look here, Macintosh. I hope you appreciate the trust we're putting in you tonight. By rights, Captain Ken Masters should have the two streamers, but he hasn't done too much night work."

"You can rely on me, Major," Ralph said, and dug his toe into the frozen mud in front of the hangar.

"I'm going to. You can get your captaincy out of this. Now, listen carefully. You and Masters will take off with sealed orders. You will not open them until you have reached five thousand feet. This is a direct order. It's more than a routine precaution. There is one factor in this raid that all of us have to keep secret until the last minute."

"It's just routine," Macintosh said, because his mind was in a whirl.

"Think of it that way. After you carry out the first requirement, you will then follow the rest of the instructions. You will go where you are ordered, and pick up the Camels that will be escorting three Handley Pages to the main target. From that point you are completely on your own and in full charge of the air defense. You know the signals for the Camels, and you know the signals between your own flights if, for any reason, you have to turn the squadron over to Masters. There isn't any question about that, is there?"

"None, sir. I'll do my best."

"That's all any of us can ask."

"But could I have some idea where the rest of the bombers will be? I mean to say . . . the problem of finding them."

"No! You know all you are to know until you are at five thousand feet. That's final."

Macintosh wondered whether to get lost immediately and head for Paris, or go down inside the German lines and sit it out until the end of the war. After that, he could pick up his wad—and feel well paid for his effort.

The night was inky black with a few stars studded into the dome when the Bristols of Number 86-SS began to roll away. In a few minutes the jeweled heaven was streaked by pennons of exhaust flame, linking up into a majestic circle that encompassed the field. The Fighters climbed, flight by flight, into the cope, each machine clawing to get its position in the formation. Marty Killane in the back seat of Macintosh's Bristol stood up and tried to count the rest as they moved in, one by one, from the sable blackness beyond.

"Just two more to come," he said, and glanced over his pilot's shoulder. Macintosh nodded, and held the stick between his knees as he fumbled to rip open the buff-colored envelope entrusted to him. He turned and glared at Marty, and said, "Keep your eyes open. I'll attend to this."

"Yes, sir. Only one more to come."

Macintosh held the sheet of paper open across the knee of his Sidcot suit. He read:

> Bomb Wetteren dump, southeast of Ghent. Turn back
> to Nieuport and await formation of DH-4s and 9s that
> will approach from the sea. Bombers will cross at
> Blankenberghe and will follow railroad to Bruges.

Macintosh swore under his breath but knew there was little he could do about it. He had promised to advise his masters exactly where the bombers would be expected. They knew that a raid was planned for this night, but that was all they did know.

The renegade led his formation across the line at a point opposite Roulers and then set out for Wetteren. As they roared across the convolutions of the Lys River he searched his mind for some means of warning his opposite number, who was huddled in the church tower at Moorslede. He could think of nothing.

Then as the Bristols, heavily laden with Cooper bombs, turned more directly east, an enemy searchlight blazed up from somewhere near Ingelmunster and caught his flight in its beam. The silver blade slashed back and forth, giving the airmen the shivers. There is something foul about the movement of a searchlight. It has the dominion of striking terror for periods of several seconds. It will throw haunting shadows or rectangles of glare that make men suck in their breaths. Parts of wings seem to disappear. Struts no longer support the airfoils. Traffic is entangled, and all details of the formation seem to be stirred into turmoil by the great spatula. The sense of sight is wiped out by its fiendish light.

Less than a minute later a ragged formation of Pfalz single-seater scouts appeared as though thrown on the night screen by a giant projector. Tracers linked the aircraft, and then the Bristol Fighter gunners went to work. The single-seaters were as confused by the searchlight blade as were the Britishers, and could not find room to maneuver to get their noses on the two-seaters. Within three minutes the aerial gunners had dispersed the D-IIIs, sending one down in a jerky nose dive.

Marty Killane rammed his gun into its prong and slapped his pilot on the shoulder.

"I've stopped one in the arm, sir."

"How bad?"

"Not too bad, as far as I can make out."

Macintosh was swept with a rare wave of compassion. "Take it easy. I'll get you back to an advanced dressing station."

"I might be able to pad it up myself, if I can get my coat off," Marty said, unbuttoning his leather jacket.

"It's too risky. Can't tell what may have been hit. Sit down. I'll delegate Ken Masters to take over," and with that Macintosh fired three green Very lights.

"You . . . you gave the wrong signal, sir. You should have fired whites," Marty yelled.

Macintosh lost his concern for his gunner. "Mind your own Goddamned business. I know what I'm doing."

"But how will Captain Masters . . . ?"

"He'll see me duck out, and he'll take over, signals or no signals."

The lead Bristol heeled over, dived away, and headed for Moorslede. Unable to understand his pilot's actions or apply a logical reason for the Very display, Marty sat supporting one elbow in a gloved hand. Macintosh went down dangerously low as he approached Roulers, and the aerial gunner wondered why it was necessary to skim over the roadside rooftops. He spotted intermittent bursts of machine-gun fire from below and would have replied, but by now his arm was beginning to stiffen, and the glove on that hand was filling with blood.

Then, to his consternation, Macintosh fired three more green lights, but before he could make an inquiry he was delighted to see a Sopwith Camel, a single-seater bearing a silver coin insignia, weaving back and forth behind them. The pilot waved at Marty and then, to the aerial gunner's amazement, he fired three red Very signals.

Macintosh finally caught what was going on, and turned to watch the Camel roar away to follow the twisted silver of the Lys. He bellowed at Marty. "Why didn't you give him a long burst?"

"What for? He's one of ours, ain't he? He probably thought we were in trouble, and made sure we could get across the line safely."

Macintosh stared at the diminishing exhaust plume. "I don't know who the hell he is, but . . ."

"You're afraid of that bloke, ain't you, Mr. Macintosh?" Marty Killane muttered over the pain of his arm.

While Macintosh searched for an emergency strip and finally decided on the one outside Furnes, Bart Crispin returned to the Bristol Fighter formation and sat above, watching them bomb a minor dump at Wetteren. A few more

303

Pfalz barged in, fired a few bursts, and then cleared off when the British aerial gunners sent two more down in flames. Bart stayed with the formation as it turned and headed for the rendezvous with the bombers that were coming in from the British fields.

At the same time a very bewildered German advanced-post observer crouching in the Moorslede church tower had watched three green signal flares arch into the sky, indicating to him that a big bomber attack was to come in from the sea. This was the standard signal, for nighttime operations. But before he could relay the message over his telephone, three red signal flares blazed up from the same area. In his signal book, three reds meant that a raid was to come in direct from front-line fields.

Land or sea? From where was this mysterious attack to come?

There was nothing to do but advise his superiors that an attack might come from two directions and that it would be wise to split the night-flying defense into two parts and hope they could intercept both groups. In this frantic decision, he had confirmed Major Horne's faint hope that the enemy defense could be reduced by half.

Crispin glanced at his watch and realized he had little fuel left, for he had been out long before the air-defense planes took off, so he turned back to his own lines and headed toward Furnes. As he curled around for his glide in, he had to turn away when a Bristol Fighter taxied out for a take-off from the faintly lighted emergency field. Presuming it was one of 86-SS Squadron's planes that had dropped in for some emergency, he stood off and allowed it to get back into the air. The two-seater climbed fast, banked, and then headed for the front line. He was somewhat puzzled to note that the gunner in the back seat stood and waved to him.

Once the strip was clear, he moved in again, landed along the tree-shielded field, and wondered why Husbands was not on hand to douse the flame markers. He rumbled up to the hangar, where he was greeted by Sergeant Crosby.

"Glad to see you back, sir. How's it going?"

"So far, so good. Who was that taking off in that Bristol Fighter?"

"A Lieutenant Macintosh of Number 86-SS Squadron, sir."

"Macintosh?"

"That's right. His aerial gunner, a chap named Killane, had stopped one in the arm."

"That must be Marty Killane. Is he all right?"

"He's inside, sir, getting patched up by an infantry M.O. It's not too bad. Might be a cushy Blighty."

Crispin was not familiar with the term. He gave Crosby a questioning glance.

"I mean a cushy wound that will get him home for a few weeks . . . Blighty, sir."

"Oh. I'll have a look at him. Get Husbands to check my guns, will you? I may be low on ammunition."

"Husbands? He's not here, sir. He went off with Mr. Macintosh . . . as his aerial gunner. I think he rather talked himself into that. Mr. Macintosh said he needed someone who could handle the Lewis, and . . . well, you know Husbands. He's in his element. I'll see to your machine, sir."

Bart swallowed his dismay. Macintosh had no right to take a man like that, a man with no in-air experience, but that was the swine all over. He went into the hangar and found Killane sitting under a naphtha light as an infantry officer applied a thick gauze pad to two clean-looking perforations in his left arm.

"Marty!" Bart cried in greeting. He remembered the Irish lad from his short stay with the Bristol Fighter squadron. "Marty Killane!"

The wounded man jerked as the M.O. started to bandage his arm. "For Christ's sake!" he gasped. "Ain't you . . . wasn't you Bart Crispin? You're supposed to be dead! Mr. Macintosh said you'd been . . ."

305

"Do you mind?" the M.O. interrupted. "I'm trying to patch you up for shipment."

"How is it?" Bart inquired, and put his hand on Killane's head.

The M.O. lifted the sterile pad. "Look for yourself. It's a perfect Blighty. These Flying Corps blokes have all the luck."

"I can't believe my eyes," Marty mumbled, staring up at the pilot.

"Never mind that now. Where's your flying kit . . . goggles and helmet?"

"One of your mechanics took it all. Something about taking my place. Acted bloody balmy."

"You were flying with Macintosh tonight?"

"Right. We were leading the Bristol Fighter lot. I got this packet when some Pfalz scouts came in on us," Marty explained slowly. "You know, old Macintosh would drop dead if he could see you standing there."

"Listen to me, Marty. Was it Macintosh who fired those first three green signals?"

"Right! I tried to tell him he should have fired whites. I mean to say—Captain Masters was supposed to take over if we had to pull out."

"Is Masters a captain now?"

"A bloody good 'un, too."

"I see. Had Macintosh read his sealed orders before he fired that group of green signals? This is important."

"Yes. I remember him opening the envelope right after I reported the formation complete . . . well, almost complete. I know he had *read* the orders, and then I realized we were hardly up to three thousand feet."

"You're sure of that?"

"Abso-bloody-lutely! What I can't make out is why he fired that second lot of greens."

"He was playing it safe; tipping off someone on the ground that the bomber attack was to come in from the sea."

306

The infantry M.O. halted his ministrations to consider this exchange. He felt completely earthborn, a mere mortal.

Bart grinned. "I was flying a Camel, and I decided I might cross up that same someone by firing three signals of another color."

"You were flying the Camel with the big silver insignia?"

Bart nodded, and watched the M.O. finish bandaging. "I suppose I'd better call Major Horne."

Killane assumed a Celtic grin. "He'll go off his napper when he hears your voice, and finds you're alive, and flying Camels," he predicted.

"No. We've been working together for weeks. It's a long story, Marty. I'll tell it in full one of these days. Perhaps I'll come and see you in the hospital. In the meantime . . ." Bart went to the telephone, called Horne, and reported all that had happened.

"Well, you did the best you could. At least you may have split the air defense in half, but here's a monkey for you. The Huns have been making a Gotha raid on London. They'll probably be returning to their sheds in Gontrode just when our blokes are banging at Bruges. You'd better get into the air and see what you can do."

"Holy smoke! What a night!" Bart gasped, and sprinted out to his Camel.

CONCLUSION

Crispin was soon in the air again, anxious, excited, and charged with renewed determination to counter Macintosh's next move. But what could he do while Harry Husbands occupied the rear cockpit? That move—whether Husbands had begged for the chance, or Ralph had induced him to take over Killane's flying kit—was an unfortunate stroke. It would be impossible to engage Macintosh in the air while Husbands was a passenger, but the Bristol Fighter pilot could take opportune shots at the Camel without Husbands being aware of what was going on. On this, his first flight, he'd be as blind as the proverbial bat.

Bart first gave his attention to the Camel formation that had escorted the big Handley Pages from the British lines toward their chief assignment over Bruges. He picked up one squadron over Oudenburg and throttled back to follow them up toward the Belgian coast. As they approached the Blankenberghe–Bruges road he spotted the first flame pennons of the De Havillands coming on in an indistinct formation from the sea. There was little anti-aircraft fire at first, but soon he noticed the exhausts of several German two-seaters. He decided they could be Halberstadt CL-IIs, low-level contour fighters, recruited for this high-level assignment.

"They will have a tough time against Camels or Bristols," he ruminated, "but they can contribute some gunnery."

He wondered about the Bristol Fighters that had been putting on the diversionary show at Wetteren and hoped they would get up here in time to be of some use. He half recalled

Ken Masters, who was now leading the two-seater fighters, but had no idea what kind of a leader he might be tonight; so much of their original planning had gone down the drain.

The Sopwiths circled the oncoming bombers, and Ken Masters fired two white lights to let them know they were in the right hands. The night was spattered with anti-aircraft bursts, streaks of exhaust flame, and the faint glare that came up from the waterways below. A lone searchlight waved back and forth from Dudzele. Bart went over in that direction to investigate and to fire a warning of any defense planes coming up from the fields in the Westkapelle area.

There was nothing but searchlights up there, so he headed back toward Blankenberghe to check on the major's report that German Gothas might be returning from a raid on London. He had hardly sifted out that possibility when he spotted the raven outlines of a swarm of fighters approaching the Belgian coast. He climbed as fast as the Camel would respond, and then moved in closer.

"Good God!" he cried. "They're Pfalz—scouts with those fixed struts—bringing a formation of twin-engined planes back from England. They must have been following the De Havillands without realizing it. What an aerial tangle this will set up!"

He glanced down at the smear that marked Bruges, hoping to see the first eruptions of British bombs, but the landscape there was dull and calm. The bombers had not yet reached the target. The Camels and Bristols would have to be advised of this unexpected opposition from the sea.

Bart took a chance on a coffin-nosed Pfalz and caught the pilot half asleep. The Vickers fire torched the Jerry tank, and the single-seater blew up in mid-air. It writhed about in structural agony, blazing wildly, and then started to fall, dragging a long, gilded plume of flame and smoke. Bart hoped that eerie signal would warn the British bombers there was danger of some kind behind them; that the signal would alert the gunners and remind the pilots not to return home over the sea route.

His mind awhirl with a dozen possibilities, he nosed down for speed and went after the De Havilland formation. As he approached, his Clerget roaring like a banshee, he saw the first probing bombs bore in at a point near the juncture of the Bruges–Ostend Canal and the Bassin de Commerce. "They're in the right area," he decided to himself. "The magazine is just a bit south of the basin, near the railroad tracks."

By now there was plenty of action above Bruges where the Camels had come upon a few Halberstadts. There were geometric tracer designs everywhere, and once Bart spotted a fuselage screwing down with flame spurting from its tail assembly. It was as fanciful as the blast from a falling blow-torch.

The searchlights joined in the fray, their silver blades hacking at small formations, splashing bomber elements with their blinding glare, or bedazzling the fliers by setting up crisscrossing designs that erected a horizon of latticed torment. At times great gobbets of anti-aircraft fire slammed against the searchlight tracery, making the pilots swerve in frantic banks. This mad display played havoc with the run-in approach for the bombers, who hunched over their toggles and birdcage sights. The spatter of blinding glare and slabs of inky blackness presented a futuristic impression that held some men spellbound; others ducked their heads into the shelter of the instrument panels and bore on blindly.

Crispin went down to sit close to the DH-9s, chiefly to make sure they found the all-important dump.

"Come on! Come on!" he screeched over the edge of his cockpit. "You have plenty of time to take aim. Don't miss this chance. We've bottled them up at the Everghem canal junction. They'll be months opening that up. Don't muff this chance to finish the job," he pleaded.

But the twisting bombs only sent up gouts of flame and debris. There was no mighty, titanic explosion or volcanic eruption. None of it was worth the fuel it had taken to get the bombers there, but the searchlights still made their cuts and parries and slashed at these man-made midges. Bart glanced about and spotted the Camels, still in precise formations, circling the area and holding off the brave efforts of the ungainly Halberstadts.

The De Havilland commander was sending in his second squadron to spatter the eruption-pocked area below. If the saturation could be continued, surely one 500-pounder would find the main dump. But the minutes clicked by and the huge stacks of explosives remained untouched.

"What the devil are they aiming at? We gave them a real pinpointed target. How can they miss with all this glare and illumination?" Bart argued with himself.

He saw a De Havilland-9 twist out of formation, shudder into a sideslip, and discard a wing. The nose went down, and it bored into the port's railroad station. He circled again and then saw that the air above was cluttered with planes of all types. The Gotha bombers, with their Pfalz escort, which had picked them up a few miles off Zee-brugge, had either blundered into the Bruges raid or in some manner had been ordered to support the defense.

"Boy, oh, boy!" Bart muttered to himself. "I've heard of dogfights, but this takes the potted palm. In a few minutes we'll have bombers fighting bombers over a Jerry target!"

Over the next ten minutes the sky above Bruges presented a fantastic display of pyrotechnics, the like of which hitherto had not been seen in the war. Gotha bombers were engaging Camels, and Halberstadts were crashing into DH-9s. Krupp and Kynoch ammunition laced aircraft to-gether, weaving a surrealistic carpet of scarlet and gold. Now and then a plane exploded, adding a fiery festoon to the design. Great ribbons of smoke were threaded in and out of the pattern, while an imagery of heroics, tragedy, and blind fury was shuttled into the border designs. Below, bombs fell and footlighted the mad extravaganza. Burning aircraft crashed on the docks and threw great torches of symbolism in all directions.

"Where are the Bristols?" Bart cried, after pouring a long burst into a Pfalz. "Where is Masters?"

He banked over hard and went at a twin-engine Gotha. He shot its tail away with one short burst. He banked again in the opposite direction and drove a Halberstadt from a De Havilland that was starting its run against the Bruges magazine. He climbed away and twisted through a tangle of burning debris, and dodged past a biplane wing panel that was fluttering aimlessly across the sky. He took a long deflection shot at a Pfalz that bore a gaudy insignia on its engine cowling, but the spray only made the German pilot bank, and dart into a smoke trail.

As soon as Macintosh had cleared the Furnes field and was heading back for Bruges he turned in his seat. Husbands was sitting like a muffled gargoyle with one hand on the drum of the Lewis gun.

"You know how to handle a Lewis?" he said over the roar of the Rolls-Royce.

"Yes, sir. I'm Mr. Crispin's armorer."

Macintosh gave the horizon another glance and then yelled back, "Whose armorer?"

"Mr. . . . Lieutenant Crispin's. The man who flies the Camel out of our field."

"That's Lieutenant *Bartley* Crispin?" demanded the pilot.

"Yes, sir. That's 'is name."

"He flies out of Furnes with a Camel . . . a Camel with a silver shilling on its side?"

"Right. I don't quite know what 'e does, but 'e seems to do a lot of it . . . mostly at night, sir."

"Was that Crispin who just landed there . . . after we took off?"

"I should think so, sir. 'E's the only one using our aero-drome. Oh, now and then we get someone who wants some ammo or a bomb or two . . . emergency stops, like you did, tonight."

Macintosh turned back to his front and pondered on this revealing situation. So Crispin had been in this area for weeks. But what was he doing and why was he doing it aboard a Sop Camel marked with a silver shilling? Mac's mind flicked and raced like the cogs of a totalizator, flashing scenes and incidents of the past few weeks. He put the Bristol into a wide circuit while he gained height over the two front lines. It was clear now that Bart was assigned to tracking him down, bringing him to heel, using that damned silly shilling symbol to prey on his conscience. What else could all that shilling business mean? But who was posting them from all over the map? How many others were involved in this damnable scheme, and what were they planning?

"That stinking little punk!" Macintosh snarled. "This is all his idea. Only a swot like him could think of such a trick."

He stared over the side and searched for the Furnes field. "I just hope he'll take off and get into the air again. I won't miss him next time. He'll wish to hell he'd never put that shilling on his bus. What a target! I'll blast him to hell-and-gone. Then . . . the rest will be easy. They'll never get me on Allied soil again while this bloody mess is on."

Husbands wondered when his pilot was going to produce some action. They'd been circling about up here for nearly ten minutes. Why didn't he go lookin' for some of them 'Uns? He decided to check the Lewis gun, just in case.

The drum on the weapon was empty . . . completely used up. That wounded bloke must have been in a wonderful scrap. He removed the empty pan and replaced it with a full one, and sat back to await something wearing black crosses.

Macintosh widened his circuit but kept his eye on the point of the cone and waited for Crispin's Camel to appear.

313

Off to the northeast he could see the pyrotechnics of the bomber attack, but he made no effort to move up and take his place at the head of the Bristols. He had no intention of becoming involved in the searchlight glare and fluttering debris. He knew what he was going to do, regardless of that jackass in the back seat. He could chuck it all now and find a decent strip well clear of Bruges, but the old hate was seething within him and he wanted to make sure this devil Crispin would never haunt him again.

"Ain't we going to 'ave a go up there where all them searchlights and tracers are flashing about, sir?" Harry Husbands inquired.

"You keep quiet. I know what I'm doing. You just keep any Huns off our tail. That's your job," Macintosh said in a high-pitched voice.

Aerial Gunner Husbands thought this was a bloody funny way to fight a war.

Bart Crispin headed straight for the vortex of the main uproar, searching for a Bristol Fighter that carried two streamers on its tail. He knew he had to head Macintosh off in some manner, but at the moment he had no idea how it could be done. The problem was compounded by Harry Husbands in the gunner's seat. He couldn't shoot the renegade down in cold blood—except in a grim emergency. But what was an emergency?

He was climbing through the starry night for a level that would provide a good view of the bombing attack. He spotted the Bristol Fighter formation, which had finally come up from Wetteren, after having been delayed in making contact with the three Handley Pages. In a few minutes they were in the thick of the fray, performing like S.E. 5s, in that they were fast, maneuverable, and in the varying degrees of light looked like single-seaters. The back-seat men had a rewarding time picking off Pfalz pilots who blindly attempted to get on their tails, only to fly into the deadly cones of Lewis-gun fire. The aerial gunners also exchanged broadsides with their opposite numbers aboard the Gothas.

The bomb attack had reached the zenith of its frenzy, and the 500-pounders must have blotted out every square yard of the narrow triangle formed by the canal and the basin docks. Still, nothing had pierced the great tarpaulins that covered the piles of ammunition and war supplies. It seemed to Bart Crispin that any one of the falling aircraft ought to smash into the huge mound.

He was circling well south of the area, fuming with frustration, when he suddenly realized that his Camel was coming under fire from somewhere. He banked hard into a right-hand turn and stared about. What he spotted was exactly what he expected. A Bristol Fighter with twin streamers fluttering from its tail was trying to get its nose around for another burst, but Bart turned well inside and set himself to foil this treacherous madman.

"I'd like to know how many rounds he has left in his Vickers box," he muttered, and went into another tight bank. "If he fired any before he went into Furnes, he could have only a couple of hundred rounds left. It might be worth the risk. I just hope he keeps potting away . . . and I am able to . . ."

Macintosh concentrated on putting his Aldis sight dead on that shilling insignia. He pooped off short bursts, but the Camel flipped back and forth, as if the pilot anticipated every trigger pressure. The Bristol man tried from every angle, but Bart was at his absolute best. He kept well within range, but he never gave his enemy a chance to put in a steady burst. He had no idea how many "outers" had pierced his wings or tail surfaces. These were chances that had to be taken.

Macintosh began to fly erratically, misusing his throttle, applying too much bank on the turns and losing accuracy in a series of sideslips. He wondered why Crispin didn't reply, and then remembered that he had the Furnes armorer in the back seat. He wondered if Bart knew of this situation.

Crispin tried to keep track of the bursts. Macintosh must be firing ten or a dozen rounds at a time; in some instances, many more. He tried wild deflection shots, spraying tracers all over the sky. Bart knew he was taking a crazy risk, but he had little choice. One slug might crease him, one could take out a few ignition wires, or even break up the primitive Le Rhône carburetor. One shot in the wrong place could either finish him or put him in some German prison camp. The full import of the latter swept through Crispin as he evaded another series of bursts from Macintosh's single fixed gun.

"Wot are you trying to do, sir?" inquired his very puzzled aerial gunner. "That's Mr. Crispin you keep firing at. That's a Sopwith Camel, sir."

Macintosh turned and screamed, "Shut up! I know what I'm doing. You blast him too, when you get a chance. We've got to finish that bastard off!"

Such language shocked Husbands and he decided that there was something very fishy going on, and he had no intention of having any part of it. To make sure that he wouldn't, Harry, true to his trust, made certain that this Bristol Fighter cove wouldn't even force him into anything that might harm Mr. Crispin.

He fumbled under his flying coat, reached into his trousers pocket, and brought out a distorted .303 cartridge. He removed the full drum, ejected the rounds already guided into the breech, and slipped the distorted shell into the breech end of the barrel. He glanced at the position of the cocking handle and placed the drum back on the peg . . . and winked at some imaginary conspirator.

In the meantime, Crispin realized that his hawk-and-pigeon game couldn't go on much longer. He evaded another burst and went into a short stall, fell off, and began to work into a series of falling-leaf sideslips. He also made a quick adjustment on his engine's air and petrol controls that set up a series of loud pops and intermittent flashes of exhaust flame. To Macintosh, it appeared that his last burst had found a vulnerable area. He was positive Crispin had been hit—that wild zoom and the pitiful falling-leaf descent marked the agony of a badly wounded man. The pops and flashes added further evidence to his triumph.

Bart kept his eyes peeled as he worked out the ruse. He saw the Bristol nose down to put in the coup de grâce. He had no intention of taking any more from the Vickers, so he ruddered out of the falling leaf and went into a steep dive. It had to be high speed, for the heavier Bristol could outdive him unless he used plenty of engine power.

The trick had to be played to the limit. He sensed that Macintosh would be sitting cool and deliberate by now, satisfied with his effort, but still determined to finish him off. Bart knew that bursts fired from a plane in a straight dive could be more accurate and more difficult to evade. There could be no sitting and taking it now.

He watched the air-speed indicator and saw the needle move over the circle of figures . . . 140—150—160—175 . . . Macintosh would be somewhere within 300—200—100 feet of him now. If he had anything left in his ammo box, this could be a hopeless gamble. Bart had both hands on the spade grip and the pressure was ramming him hard into his seat cushion; he wondered whether the wicker seat would take it. He felt every ounce of breath being compressed from his lungs.

He hoped he'd picked a reasonable spot. He knew they had been circling well inside the enemy lines. He tried to remember where, and with one final, frantic glance decided they were over an open area well east of Oudenburg. He looked back, fully expecting to see a final burst splashing at him with its tracers sparking in crazy twists and turns as the phosphorus burned away the bullet envelope.

But there was no further blast from Macintosh's gun. Either he was out of ammunition or he had finally dredged up some latent spark of pity . . . sympathy . . . compassion. Perhaps mercy was in the air. After all, the wings of the Camel had withstood the headlong plunge. The engine had picked up its regular beat. The throttle had calmed it down to a purring, idling speed; just enough power to assure a normal landing. Bart hoped the stretch below was as level as it was inviting.

Macintosh was undecided as to his next move. He was out of ammunition, for hundreds of rounds had been fired before that damned Camel went down. He watched it gradually pull out of the dive, flounder into something resembling a banked turn, and then nose down for a landing. He expected to see it thump in hard, tear off its undercarriage, and stand up on its nose. That was how most Camel crashes wound up. There would be some dust, a belch of smoke, and then she would tilt over on her back and hack the turf with the top of her rudder. With any luck, Crispin's Sop would then burst into flames . . . and the crusade would end in a fiery finish.

But he saw the bulldog biplane level off, skim along the turf, and make two exploratory dabs with her tail skid. The machine touched down, rolled a few dozen yards, and then seemingly went into a controlled ground loop and pulled up facing down the long run of turf. It was beautifully done, as Harry Husbands loudly proclaimed.

"Keep quiet!" Macintosh said, and moved to follow the Camel in. "You be ready to jump out and turn us around."

"You're going to land, sir? You're on the wrong side of the line, you know."

"I know where I am. You make sure that Lewis is loaded and has a full drum on the peg. I'm going to finish off . . ."

The Bristol went in neatly, nipped over a low hedge, and started to feel for the turf. Macintosh allowed her to stretch her glide until he was almost opposite the Camel, which to his concern stood with her engine ticking over. He forced his tail skid down like a brake and the Bristol came to a halt a few yards short of another hedge.

Bart watched the Bristol Fighter coming in through the starlit night . . . and wondered what Macintosh had in mind. It was difficult to decide, for his imagination was running riot after that banshee dive to earth. Why was Mac following him into this enemy-occupied area? What was his intent? Had he some wild idea of making him change places with Husbands, fly him deeper into Germany and turn him over to Berlin Intelligence, and palm him off as an important Allied Intelligence agent? Just what was Macintosh's game?

Instinctively, he took the Webley pistol from its canvas sheath, unbuckled his belt, and climbed over the cockpit. He realized that the Webley was a puny weapon to pit against another Lewis gun, for certainly Mac would make the most use of it—as he had on that memorable agent pickup. At the moment he had no idea why he had landed and placed himself at the mercy of this madman.

As he stood there, backed against the insignia on his fuselage, he realized that he had not wanted to kill Macintosh. He simply wanted to bring him to justice. Bloodletting was out of the question. He had simply hoped he could capture him quietly and turn him over to some legal custodian. After all, he had to protect Harry Husbands. That was it. Husbands was not to become the innocent victim of this feud.

Macintosh had no such compassion. The instant the Bristol stopped rolling, he bellowed to the man behind him, "Now then, out with you. Let's get her nosed around . . ."

Husbands carried out his part of the operation and then stood by the wing tip, watching the pilot unclamp the Lewis gun from the Scarff mounting bow and cradle it in his arms. He left the engine ticking over and dropped down to the ground.

"What do you want with the gun, sir?" inquired Husbands. "I mean . . ."

"None of your blasted business. If you have any sense you'll start moving off . . . on your own. I'm not going back. Not after tonight."

"You can't . . . can't leave me 'ere. I shall 'ave to report wot you've been up to . . . shootin' at your own aircraft . . ."

"See what I mean? If you're here when I come back from taking care of Crispin, I'll take care of you too. So if you're smart, you'll vamoose . . . fast."

With that warning Macintosh, still cradling the Lewis gun in his arms, started walking toward the Camel. In the half-light he could see a figure standing a few feet aft of the trailing edge of the lower wing. That had to be Crispin, wounded or not.

He approached the shadowy aeroplane but slowed his stride.

"That you, Crispin?" he asked, and felt his throat constrict.

"It's me."

"Caught you neatly, eh?"

"Looks like it."

"I didn't think you'd get down. That was a fake stall and dive, eh? I just had to make sure. I'm sorry but this is how it has to be. I'll get it over quickly."

Crispin stood watching Mac take his stance. He held the barrel casing of the gun in the bend of his left elbow. His right hand took the pistol grip.

"I hope you know what you're doing," Crispin said, without knowing why.

"Goddamn right I know," Mac growled, and fumbled for the trigger. He aimed the muzzle cup straight at the Camel pilot. "You'll never bother me or anyone else again."

He pulled the trigger.

Nothing happened. The Le Rhône engine patiently ticking over made the only sound in the tableau.

Macintosh gargled a bewildered curse, twisted the weapon, and stared at the cocking handle on the side of the breech casing. Its unusual position meant nothing to him. He aimed and pulled the trigger again. The weapon remained silent.

Bart took what seemed a heaven-sent opportunity. "Put it down, Mac. I warn you. . . . Put it down!"

In a frantic rage, Macintosh struggled with the cocking handle again and poked his finger into the trigger guard. "I told you to put it down," Crispin said. He had no other choice. He raised the Webley pistol, took aim, and fired one shot. Ralph Macintosh sprawled flat on his face, the Lewis gun beneath him.

Crispin darted forward, turned Mac over on his back, and saw a wide stream of blood seeping down from beneath the forehead panel of his helmet. His bullet had cut a deep gash along the crown of Macintosh's head. "I'm sorry, but you left me no choice, Mac," he said, and yanked the Lewis gun clear.

He stared around and saw the shielded headlights of a motorcar approaching along the road that bordered the field. He took the Lewis gun and cradled it as Mac had done.

"I'm very glad you stopped 'im, sir," Harry Husbands said, moving into the scene.

"What happened . . . with the gun?" Bart asked, staring at the weapon like a man in a trance.

"Nothink, sir. Nothink could 'appen. I fixed up a Number Three stoppage, and the gun couldn't fire. 'E didn't know anythink about Lewis guns, 'im not being an aerial gunner, like. So 'e didn't see that the cocking 'andle was in the Number Three position. I made sure of that, sir . . . after I saw what 'e was up to."

"He just knew how to pull the trigger . . . that's all," added Crispin. "Well, I'm still here, but Mac . . . he seems to have been grazed badly."

"Well, that'll keep 'im quiet for a while," Husbands

321

said, inspecting the wound by loosening Mac's chin strap.

"Long enough, I hope, for us to fly him back to Furnes."

"All three of us, sir?"

Crispin saw the lights of the car switch off as the sound of the engine died with a series of pops. "Quiet! There's an automobile out there on the road. It has just pulled up."

"I 'ope we ain't being nabbed," Husbands said.

"Here. Clear that gun stoppage. We may have to fight our way out." Bart handed the gun over.

Husbands fumbled with the pan, yanked the cocking handle back twice, and removed the distorted cartridge case. He rammed the drum back on and carried out the normal loading sequence.

"There you are, sir. You 'ave about ninety rounds of the best."

"Good. Keep an eye on Macintosh. There's someone working his way through the hedge."

"Right. Only one, sir."

Bart cradled the Lewis and strode toward the hedge. He spoke low but clearly. "All right. Keep walking toward me. I've got you covered."

There was a low chuckle, just as Bart was ready to press the trigger.

"*Per ardua ad astral*" a voice responded.

Husbands came up flourishing the Webley pistol. "Ain't that wot we 'ave on our cap badges, sir?" he whispered.

Crispin nodded and spoke again. "Come closer. Let's have a look at you." He handed the gun over to Husbands.

An indistinct figure moved closer with its hands in its trousers pockets. "Judas! I never expected to find you messing about out here," Bryce Melville said cheerily, and came close enough to be recognized. "What the hell are you doing? Setting up an aircraft park?"

Crispin was on him in one wide-armed jump. He grabbed Bryce by both elbows and looked him over. He was dressed in a pair of army slacks, a gray flannel shirt, and a peaked cap of indeterminate origin. He also wore a pair of German field boots.

"Well I'll be damned!" Bart gasped. "This must be a family reunion. We have Ralph Macintosh spread-eagled over here. We were just planning to truss him up in that Bristol Fighter."

"What's going on?"

In a few words Bart explained the situation, introduced Husbands, and was completing the plan for the getaway. Just at that minute a tremendous roar went up from the Bruges area. A great bellow shook the earth, and the sky was domed in gold for miles around.

"Cool Wot was that?" Husbands gasped.

"That's what we set out to do," Crispin said with a broad grin. "That's the Bruges dump going up. Thank God for that."

Melville was as startled as Husbands, but he finally jerked out of his surprise and said, "By golly, they got my tip after all, eh?"

Neither Bart nor Husbands had any idea what he was talking about.

"What tip?" inquired Bart, and then added, "by the way, where the devil did you come from?"

"Oh, we broke out . . . a tunnel job, a few days ago, and I started for the line. That mess the bombers started up at Wetteren gave me a chance to swipe a Mercedes, but the damn thing ran out of petrol . . . gasoline, just over there. I was getting ready to lie low for the night, and then spotted these two planes quietly ticking over. I couldn't believe my eyes, or ears. I used the line any R.F.C. guy would recognize, but fully expected to have my legs shot from under me."

"You came at the right time. Think you can still fly a Camel?"

"I haven't been locked up long enough to have forgotten that much."

"Fine! We'll plop Macintosh in the back seat of the

Bristol and have Husbands sit on him. He has a nasty head wound—that couldn't be helped, but I do want to get him back where he's wanted."

They tied Mac up, although he was clearly unconscious. Husbands had ripped out his own first field dressing and had applied the gauze pad, hoping to stop the bleeding. He was then hauled up and made fairly comfortable in the back seat, and Husbands straddled him as best he could.

"You fly the Camel, and sit over my tail," Bart explained to Bryce. "Let's stick together at least while we're on this side of the line. Once we both get into the clear, you follow us back to Furnes, just southwest of Nieuport. We'll head there first. After we put Macintosh in safekeeping, we'll buzz down to Bailleul where we can tell it to the people who matter. Got it?"

"I'm your man," Bryce responded, and scurried over to the Camel.

The Bristol Fighter got away first, and Bart had trouble getting his load off the ground to clear an indistinct hedge. He had been accustomed to the sprightly manner of the Camel and was ill at ease until he finally managed to hoik over the comparatively low barrier. The Camel was up and alongside him before he felt really comfortable, but once he had hauled the two-seater to a reasonable altitude he was pleased to see Bryce nearby, and occasionally waving in high glee.

They had no opposition all the way in. Now and then they saw the flame pennons of a returning bomber or Camel, but they were all heading toward the Poperinghe area where there was plenty of room for all concerned. Bart wondered how many bombers got away from the carnage at Bruges. He took the lead as they approached Furnes, and then guided Bryce down to the emergency strip. The oil-waste flares gleamed upward, and he could see Sergeant Crosby in the low glow of the Camel's hangar. The infantry M.O. was nearby smoking a cigarette, evidently standing by for further emergencies.

"I wondered what had happened to you, sir," Crosby greeted Bart when he saw it was Crispin in the Bristol Fighter. "You've been cutting it very fine . . . on fuel." He spotted Husbands sitting scotched up on the Scarff ring. "And where the hell have you been?"

"It's all right, Sergeant. We were all down for a few minutes, making an exchange of . . . er, seating arrangements. Then we managed to pick up Mr. Melville. He'd just cleared out from a Jerry prison camp. I know it sounds crazy, but there you are."

Sergeant Crosby had brought out his notebook, but looked very bewildered. "Now let me get this straight. I shall have to make some sort of a report, sir."

"I'm still a bit bewildered, Sergeant," Bryce said.

"It goes something like this," Bart began again. "Husbands decided he wanted to be an aerial gunner, which was lucky for all concerned. Actually, he's a better armament man than an engine mechanic, for he pulled a trick . . . well, it will take all night to explain, and then you won't believe me."

"Well I'll be blowed!" Sergeant Crosby said. "I hardly know what to do about Husbands. I mean, he *was* absent from duty."

Crispin cogitated a minute. "Let's say he was temporarily assigned to other tasks and let it go at that."

Sergeant Crosby wagged his head, folded his notebook, and decided to help haul Macintosh from the gunner's pit. The renegade was snuffling and groaning. When he had been laid out on a workbench the M.O. gave him a quick examination. He frowned professionally. "He's taken a very close one, I'd say. A deep grazer that may have resulted in a severe skull fracture. He won't be flying again for a long time." He made that decision and then wound on a new sterile bandage, shaking his head ominously. "That was a bloody deep grazer."

"What do you suggest we do with him? We want him kept under strict guard. I'll explain later," Crispin said.

"We'd better get him up to Furnes, bloody quick. There's a field hospital there, and the Provost Marshal can arrange for whatever guard you think is necessary."

Husbands volunteered to make the run into Furnes. "I'll take a Pyrene wiv me too," he said, cocking his head toward the recumbent airman. "One move from 'im, and 'e'll get another . . . plonk!"

"Do you think you could go along?" Crispin asked the M.O.

"I suppose I'd better. There's nothing much more I can do here."

"Fine. Now I'd better call Major Horne at Cassel."

Bryce agreed. "You do that, and I'll help them get Mac settled in the Crossley."

Major Horne was totally bewildered by all the news telephoned by Bart. "You brought Macintosh and a Lieutenant Melville back to Furnes, you say?"

"Yes, sir."

"Aboard a Camel?"

"No, sir. We also used Macintosh's Bristol Fighter."

"Let me talk to Macintosh."

"He's . . . well, he's unconscious and is being taken to a field hospital in Furnes."

"Look," Major Horne pleaded, "we've had a rough night here. I can't make sense out of anything you're saying. Why don't we all get some sleep, and then you bring your report on to Bailleul in the morning. Perhaps we can straighten it out then. What say?"

"Suits me fine, sir. We'll see you at Bailleul just before lunch. But we did copper the Bruges dump, didn't we?"

"No question about it. See you in the morning."

Bart and Bryce lay stretched out on the bed in Crispin's billet, talking the hours away, but the chief figure in their conversation was Ralph Macintosh.

"What makes a man turn on his friends and his country in that manner?" Bart queried for the third or fourth time.

Bryce was staring at the ceiling. "I think I can tell you. I wasn't in prison camp very long, but I learned a lot about men, and what makes them act as they do. Cooped up like that, you get to know people, and you find out things about the war you never considered before you were captured. It's an entirely different world, and I'm glad, in a way, I was nabbed for a time."

"I would have gone crazy."

"Not you. You would've had a couple of bad days, but then you would have started to think. Remember, I knew something was wrong about Macintosh, and I was determined to break out and track him down."

"Well, you played your part. We couldn't have brought him in if we hadn't had you on hand."

"I just hope they can get the rest of his team."

"Don't worry. Every one has been spotted. It's just a matter of picking them up as they are wanted. Macintosh left a pretty clear trail to all of them, particularly in the last few weeks."

"He turned out to be a real stinker, didn't he?"

"A real stinker, but Mac had no real hate for Britain."

"Yes, he did, in his cockeyed way. My father knew Mac's old man back home in the early days. He was a clever locomotive designer, but he was always at odds with someone—from the Baldwin Locomotive Company on down. By the way, his name is not Macintosh. It's Mackensen. The family is related to the present German General von Mackensen."

"Oh yes. I've heard that too."

"It's true. Mac always resented his German background, and stayed away from his home and his family as much as possible. I don't know whether the family changed its name, or if that was Mac's protest. But he changed it sometime before hostilities broke out in 1914. Don't blame the war."

"So that's why he never brought any of his relatives to Princeton. We couldn't understand that."

327

"But there's more to it then a national background. You won't understand this because you've never had too much in the way of a family . . . or money. Though Mac hated his parents and his name, like all rich kids—I've done it myself all my life—he always sponged on them. But prison camp has taken a lot of that out of me."

"Oh, come on, Bryce. You're one of the few unspoiled rich guys I've ever met."

"Thanks, but like Macintosh, I never had to make a moral decision. I had never known real responsibility. I realize now I have never really earned all the advantages I have enjoyed."

"Just what are you getting at?"

"I could have gone off the rails like Mac. He had no real aim in life. He had no need of one, but what he saw and encountered at Princeton must have made him realize that fellows who had a goal, an ambition, an ideal, were lucky. But he had to make up one. I take it he wasn't a real mixer so he decided to do the opposite of what everyone else was aiming for. The war, and America's sympathy for the British-French cause, gave him his opening. He felt some satisfaction in playing a role no one could recognize. It paid him well and gave him a chance to move around in some mysterious circle."

"You're drawing an interesting picture, Bryce."

"I suppose for a time it was quiet fun and not too hazardous, but when he made that move to get into the Royal Flying Corps he signed his warrant. He soon discovered that he could go only so far, and realized that he would eventually be caught. He also must have realized he was making blunders and betraying everyone in his spy network, but he didn't know what to do about it. He lost his head and left his trail everywhere. That shilling business must have driven him dotty. He should have cleared out the first time he flew a patrol on the front. It would have been easy, but I don't suppose he would have fooled his German bosses."

"He certainly wove a tangled web for himself," Bart agreed, "but I still feel sorry for him . . . in a way. He has no future—anywhere. The Germans will renounce him, and I don't suppose he'll ever be able to return to the United States. That will be his stiffest penalty."

Early the next morning Bart and Bryce took over Number 86-SS Squadron's Bristol Fighter, which overnight had been refueled and had its battle damage patched up. With Bryce in the back seat, they flew down to Bailleul. After a refreshing sleep and hot baths both were physically tip-top, but Bryce still looked more like an itinerant peddler than a commissioned officer of the Royal Flying Corps. However, he was happy, enjoying his freedom, and quietly pleased he had done what was expected of him. He had been captured but had escaped. Whether he would be allowed or expected to fly again on the Western Front never entered his head. He was hopeful that he would spend the rest of the war with Bart Crispin, and what was assigned him did not matter.

The conference room in the British Headquarters was arranged in much the same way it had been a few days previously. Most of the same people were present, including the little civilian who chain-smoked cigarettes. Well-soaped orderlies distributed typed sheets, maps, and copies of glossy photographs that were still wet and sticky.

An infantry brigadier general took the head of the table and after looking over his audience announced, "Well, gentlemen, it looks like we've saved the Channel ports, eh? You'll notice the photographs that were taken early this morning, and processed immediately. It would seem that we need fear no thrust from that direction."

"My bloody bombers did it," the burly giant growled while staring at the wet prints.

"It was a tremendous job."

"All the Handley Pages returned safely, which shows you what two engines will do," the boomer added. "The De

Havillands didn't fare so well. We lost seven of them, but we wiped off that bloody dump . . . as these photographs show."

"Yes. I think we must all agree to that," the brigadier general said, and looked toward the door. "I had expected Colonel Southgate, the Fourth Wing commander, to be here by now. However, I think we can hear a report from the Intelligence side of the table. Mr. Cosgrove?"

The civilian rubbed out his cigarette, sat a trifle straighter, and pointed at Bart Crispin. "There's the gentleman who made the whole show possible. He not only accounted for the Everghem dump and blocked the juncture of two canals, tying up traffic there for weeks, but he also provided the pinpoint location of the Bruges dump, which enabled the R.F.C. bombers to score so effectively."

"It was my Handley Pages," the bewhiskered giant broke in again. "If I can have ten or fifteen squadrons of them, we'll stop any possible spring offensive Ludendorff may start."

"Not only that," Cosgrove went on, ignoring the bomber chief's rumbling, "but Lieutenant Crispin has successfully planted a false plan concerning a 'new British offensive' in the Arras sector. I think we'll soon notice some interesting activity between Valenciennes and Lille; all intended to stop this fictitious push. That should keep the enemy busy until he can get more divisions from the Eastern Front."

"I do wish Wing Commander Southgate were here," the brigadier said, and shuffled his sheaf of papers. "I expect he'll be able to give us complete returns on all aircraft squadrons that took part in the raid. He was to come in from Hesdin. In the meantime, perhaps Lieutenant Crispin will give us some details of his experiences on the other side of the line. It is something all of us should know in order to plan any such future raids."

Over the next fifteen minutes Bart outlined his movements on the other side of the line from the time Major Horne had dropped him at Thourout. He told it with rare simplicity and modesty, explaining that the idea of his playing the role of a Swiss watch-movement salesman had proved to be perfect; how he had used the nose-cap ploy to move from place to place and gain the confidence of the men he wished to impress. Then he related how he planted the time bomb in the center of the supply dump at Everghem and made his getaway simply by rolling an automobile tire past a German sentry who had promised to watch his motorcar.

"I should add," Bart said with a smile, "I was very glad my R.F.C. training had included learning to drive a motorcar. It was something that previously I had not had a chance to learn. The trick of repairing a punctured tire could not have been tried, and I wouldn't have been allowed to get into the dump and plant the time bomb."

"That poor bloody sentry," Major Horne muttered absently. "I suppose he went up with the rest of the stuff."

"No," Bart said. "I think he would have been off duty by the time the dump went up. I hope so, at any rate. He seemed like a nice old codger."

"You know," the brigadier said reflectively, "this war is becoming interesting, but it does seem to me that the R.F.C. is having most of the fun. Ah, here's Southgate now. Good morning, Bill."

The R.F.C. colonel, a tall, broad-shouldered man with two rows of ribbons under his wings, thumped in, wiped a trickle of sweat from his cap band, and looked around the table.

"Where's that man Crispin? And do we have Lieutenant Melville here?"

"Here, sir," Bart replied, and stood up. "This is Melville . . . just as he turned up last night."

"Good Lord! the masquerades you prisoners of war get into. I sometimes think Jerry lets some of you go to get rid of you. However, you're both here, and now . . . outside! There's someone in the front seat of my car who wants to talk to you."

Bart and Bryce exchanged puzzled glances, pushed their chairs back, and walked around the table toward the door. They hesitated, but Wing Commander Southgate waved an imperious hand. "Get a move on!"

They hurried out into the corridor, went down the steps of the formal staircase two at a time, and slid across the portico. There was a Crossley touring car standing with its radiator against a boxwood hedge. They sauntered up to it and glanced under the touring top.

Dianne Melville sat at the wheel reading a copy of the Paris *Daily Mail.*

There was an instant of breathless indecision, then both airmen yelled, "Di!" and put on a rugby scrum to reach her first.

The girl was spellbound. The newspaper slipped from her fingers, and her hands dropped to her sides.

Bryce yanked the door open and shoved her from behind the wheel. He grabbed her in his arms while Bart moved in from the other side.

"What the devil are you doing out here in France?" Bryce demanded after he had kissed his sister tenderly.

"Yes, what are you doing here in Bailleul?" Bart added, and took his turn. "I knew you were to come out, but . . ."

Dianne stared at her brother.

"What are you doing out of prison camp? Nobody told me about that."

The embraces continued between idiotic questions. Finally they all sat back to get a more rational viewpoint.

"There's so much to tell, but what a wonderful reunion," Bart said, and sat worshiping the girl.

"Well, let's get our breaths and tell it slowly. Colonel Southgate will be in there for hours."

"I escaped several days ago, out of the camp, that is," Bryce began.

"And I picked him up in a field, quite by accident, on the other side of the line," Bart continued.

332

"I must say there's more flexibility with aeroplanes than with Crossley cars," Dianne got in.

"We had to get Macintosh back and into a field hospital. He's badly banged up, Di."

"You'll probably explain that, later on," Dianne interposed, and straightened her jacket.

"Then we had to come here and report what had happened, and in the middle of it you turn up, driving some bloomin' wing commander."

"Look," Bart said, grabbing Di's hand. "We can talk about all this later on. Do you think you can get some leave? We could all go back together, if you can."

"Leave? I haven't been over here long enough. It's out of the question."

"Nothing is out of the question. We'll soft-soap old Southgate to let you go. After all, he was late for the conference today. Who would want a driver like that? A mere girl, too!"

"It's ridiculous," Bryce agreed. "There's so much to talk about, and Christmas just round the corner."

Dianne nodded in agreement. "Yes, I think I'd better. You'll need someone to take care of you. Your American girl friend, Cynthia Pollard, isn't around London any more."

"*My* girl friend? She was Ralph Macintosh's sweetheart —I think. But what about her, not being in London?"

"She's also working for British Intelligence, and this is very secret, remember. She was sent into Germany on some important job. We had dinner together before I left for over here. She showed me her new papers. She's operating under a new name. One she selected herself."

"What is it?" Bart asked, wondering what Cynthia Pollard was doing for British Intelligence.

"Belle Goddard. All her papers bear that name."

"Queer," Bart said. "I wonder why."

POSTSCRIPT

This story is pure fiction, inspired by Paul Bewsher's epic poem, *The Bombing of Bruges*. The characters and most events are imaginary but are reflections of people and experiences I encountered during my years of active service in World War I.

While a resident of the United States, I volunteered in 1914 to serve with the British forces and, after a long spell with a mounted-infantry (Yeomanry) regiment, transferred to the Royal Flying Corps. After flying as an NCO for eleven months, to gain my "wing" as an aerial gunner, I was awarded a commission and trained to fly Sopwith Camels. Those thrilling months provided the basis of the chapters devoted to flying on the Western Front. I trust the experience suffices and justifies my effort to set the story against an authentic backdrop.

The delivery and retrieving of Intelligence agents was carried out from early in 1916 to the close of the war. Some were dropped by parachute and some were sent over in the baskets of small spherical balloons, which were valved at a certain time to land in a planned area. Most were taken over in two-seater aircraft and landed in remote fields well behind the enemy lines. The aircraft mentioned were all capable of the tasks I have assigned them, and the aerodromes from which they were carried out were actual service fields at the time. I must admit to some modest license in the timing of the bombing raid on the Bruges supply dump.

I have in no instance included myself in the cast of characters. I was an infantry-trained machine gunner who volunteered to fly with the Royal Flying Corps, and I served with F.E. 2b and Bristol Fighter squadrons, but I took no training at Farnborough. My Sopwith Camel time was put in with a Home Defense squadron located in England.

Uppermost in my mind was the intent to portray active-service flying as it was carried out in World War I, how patrols were planned and flown aboard the planes of the 1917 period; and how we lived between our various periods of duty; not as Hollywood has presented our history on their silver screens. This is how the pilots and observers of the Royal Flying Corps acted, how they talked, how they looked on the right or wrong of the war, and how they lived and died. I am proud to have been one of that glorious company.

As to my academic background: I have never attended Princeton or any other university. I was involved in a global conflict when I might have been in some ivy-walled classroom, but my close friends, George H. Vaughan, Jr., and Jack Morgan, have told me much of the history of the old Princeton Flying Club. Mr. William C. Stryker, director of Sports Information, filled me in on the details of the early Palmer Stadium competitions, and the history of the university's Rhodes scholars of 1915–16. Mr. Sam Stewart, general manager of the Princeton Inn, has provided pertinent information on the popular taverns of the time.

A squadron mate, Mr. Bert B. Perry of Toronto, very kindly provided me with a self-drawn map of that city, as it was when the first R.F.C. training courses were being set up in Canada, a favor that turned out to be enlightening and most valuable.

Per Ardua ad Astra!

Arch Whitehouse
Montvale, New Jersey
March 9, 1968